HER PASSION MATCHED HIS OWN

Wordlessly, Temple rose from the divan and moved toward him as if he had ordered her to come.

She inhaled deeply of his unique masculine scent as her lips traveled eagerly, caressingly, over his smooth, hot flesh. Shuddering as Temple put out the tip of her tongue and licked the hollow of his throat, Sharif put both hands into her hair, pulled her head up, and looked at her beautiful face.

"If I so much as touch you, I will not stop until you are naked beneath me."

Breathlessly, she replied, "I was about to say the same thing to you."

Books by Nan Ryan

You Belong to My Heart
Burning Love

Published by HarperPaperbacks

Harper
Monogram

Burning Love

⊱ NAN RYAN ⊰

HarperPaperbacks
A Division of HarperCollinsPublishers

🏭 HarperPaperbacks

A Division of HarperCollins*Publishers*

10 East 53rd Street, New York, N.Y. 10022-5299

This is a work of fiction. The characters, incidents, and
dialogues are products of the author's imagination and are not to
be construed as real. Any resemblance to actual events or
persons, living or dead, is entirely coincidental.

ISBN 0-06-108417-4

HarperCollins®, 🏭 ®, HarperPaperbacks™, and
HarperMonogram® are trademarks of HarperCollins*Publishers* Inc.

Cover illustration of burnt oval by Danilo Ducak
Stepback illustration by Doreen Minuto

First printing: September 1996

Printed in the United States of America

Visit HarperPaperbacks on the World Wide Web at
http://www.harpercollins.com/paperbacks

❖ 10 9 8 7 6 5 4 3 2 1

For
The Daughters of the Desert
Robyn Carr
Carolyn Connolly
Rosemary Dowe
Christine Flynn
Mary Ann Jones
Jane Kidder
Eileen Nauman
Susie Van Orden
Zelma Orr
Katonna Smothermon
and
Pat Warren

1

A London Cabaret

A Balmy Spring Night in 1898

A ruby was caught in the cabaret's muted light. Tiny spangles inside the red stone reflected the six-rayed glow that gave the gem its name.

Starfire.

This Starfire had come from the fabled mines of Mogok, Burma, home of the world's finest rubies. The ruby was one of those prized gemstones so intensely red in color, it merited the descriptive term "pigeon blood."

The ancient Greeks had described such a ruby's rare color as "anthracite." A deep flaming red, like burning coal. In the Hindu religion the ruby was ranked above all other precious stones. Magical properties were attributed to the ruby, a coveted gemstone believed to bring peace and well-being to its owner.

It was said that the ruby held magical and talismanic significance to its wearer. And legend had it that the rare pigeon blood ruby could warn its owner of imminent peril by turning dark or black . . . and not returning to its normal color until the danger had passed.

All rubies were valuable. But rubies of the dark pigeon blood hue were among the rarest of all the world's finest gemstones. Especially those in excess of three carats. This Starfire ruby now captured in the London cabaret's mellow light was in excess of six carats.

The enormous ruby had once adorned a Burmese Buddha seated high on a Mogok hilltop overlooking the valley from which the stone came. It was now the solitary gem set intact in a simple wide gold ring. The ring encircled the long tapered third finger of a lean, masculine hand. A large, well-tended hand with short, clean, neatly clipped nails. A hand that was strikingly dark against the stark whiteness of the cloth upon which it rested. A hand that lay unmoving on a table.

The wearer of the magnificent six-carat ruby ring was as still as his hand. Seated alone at a tiny table for one set apart on the cabaret's open-balconied mezzanine, he didn't shift or fidget or twist about on his chair. He didn't wave to patrons or call out to acquaintances or signal for a waiter. He didn't so much as turn his head to the left or the right. He sat entirely motionless on his chair yet miraculously managed to look completely comfortable and relaxed.

A man of staggeringly handsome dark good looks, he was graceful, sophisticated, and totally sure of himself. Possessed of a body that was as splendid as his face, the tall, broad-shouldered man had smooth, deeply tanned skin and thick lustrous hair that was so raven black it produced dancing blue highlights.

His attire was impeccable. He wore a smartly tailored suit of crisp white linen, the well-cut jacket now open casually and pushed back. A custom-made powder blue shirt of fine Egyptian cotton lay softly against the hard flat muscles of his chest, the shirt's stiffly starched collar snug around his smooth dark throat. His perfectly knotted cravat was of shimmering maroon silk, and a matching silk handkerchief was tucked into his suit jacket's right breast pocket.

Unaware and uncaring of the covetous female glances boldly cast his way, the handsome, immaculately groomed man continued to sit alone at his table. The small, white-draped table was situated directly beside the wrought-iron railing encircling the mezzanine, overlooking the main floor of the smoky, noisy, dimly lit cabaret.

His dark, half-hooded eyes were focused on the dance floor directly below. The floor was crowded with dancers. Couples swayed and spun about in an ever-changing kaleidoscope of color made up of bright summer ball gowns and gleaming, carefully coiffured tresses and flashing jewels. Skirts of vivid hues flared and swirled as smiling gentlemen turned their radiant partners about.

But the man on the mezzanine saw only one color.

Only one dancer.

Dressed all in red, a young, slender woman was the object of his undivided attention. He watched her unblinkingly, his penetrating dark eyes riveted to her. Had been watching her from the moment she'd arrived with a group of laughing, well-dressed revelers. Now she turned about in the arms of a tall, prosperous-looking partner who was quite clearly captivated by her charms.

Although not dazzled like her enchanted escort, the dark man had quickly determined from his vantage point above that the woman in red was a natural beauty. Silky blond hair spilled around pale bare shoulders and framed a flawless face of classic delicate features. He couldn't ascertain the exact color of her eyes, but he could see that they were large and flashing and ringed with long, dark lashes. Her nose was small and slightly tilted at the tip, and her soft mouth—which never seemed to be closed—was full lipped, perfectly shaped, and as blood red as the ruby adorning his finger.

She was, he discerned, tall, willowy, and attractively long waisted, with the soft, supple curves of a nubile young girl. Hers was a regal, lithe, long-limbed body, the kind of perfect symmetrical frame on which expensive, beautiful clothes were worn so well. And, he surmised calmly, the kind of exquisite female form on which nothing at all was worn even better.

The young woman was stunning in her red chiffon dress, the bodice cut so low that it exposed the creamy white tops of her high, full breasts. Appealingly tight around her trim midriff and narrow waist, the gauzy crimson fabric flared out over the sculpted arch of her hips and fell in graceful swaying folds to the floor.

She was beautiful. And she was vivacious. Too vivacious. She was constantly laughing and talking and louder than the women to whom he was accustomed.

A tiny white scar at the left side of his full lips twitched spasmodically as the dark, somber man in the white linen suit watched the woman in red. His handsome face hardened minutely. His night black eyes narrowed ever so slightly. The smooth flesh of his firm jaw ridged as he involuntarily clamped his teeth too tightly together. And continued to stare unblinkingly at the woman in red.

"My dear, I do so wish you would reconsider," said Sir William Perry as he turned his beautiful blond companion about the dance floor. "Such a journey is not only

totally unnecessary, it's foolhardy and most dangerous."
His handsome, pale patrician face wore a frown of disapproval and worry.

"Ah, Bill, don't. Let's please not speak of it again."
Temple Longworth laughed away his concern. "I shall be perfectly safe, I assure you. Why, men travel into the deserts all the time and no one thinks a thing about it."

"Men, Temple, yes," said Sir William. "Not ladies. Especially not beautiful blond young ladies who—"

"I'm going and that's final," she said, cutting him off. "I've been planning this journey for months, and nothing can stop me."

Sir William sighed with exasperation but said no more, knowing that once the strong-willed Temple Longworth had made up her mind, no one could change it. Certainly not him. Desperate to keep her safe and yearning to have her for his own, he drew her closer into his embrace. He pressed his cheek to hers and closed his eyes, wishing he could persuade her to marry him at once and give up her foolish notions of dangerous journeys to foreign, uncivilized lands.

Temple Longworth allowed Sir William Perry to hold her close for only a few seconds. She sensed what was going through his mind and had no intention of encouraging him. She certainly had no intention of marrying him.

And she had no intention of allowing Sir William or anyone else to put a damper on her high spirits. She wanted to continue to dance and laugh and have a merry time on this, her last night in London.

It was, after all, a celebration.

The twenty-five-year-old American heiress was out for the evening with a lively group of her favorite European friends to celebrate her much anticipated, long-planned trip into the vast Arabian deserts. Couples both young and old had accompanied Temple out for a final gala evening of fun and merrymaking, although many felt as apprehensive as Sir William about her proposed adventure.

It was, they felt certain, more than a little dangerous for a beautiful young woman to go into the vast Arabian deserts with only her middle-aged, dutiful distant cousin, the widowed Rupert Longworth, for protection.

"Cousin Rupert won't be my only escort," Temple argued. "I've engaged a number of dependable Arab scouts to guide us on the entire journey. So you see, there's absolutely nothing to worry about."

And since they were of the privileged elite, unused to worrying a great deal about anything, the revelers in Temple's party put aside their doubts and enjoyed themselves.

No one more so than the bold, thrill-seeking American socialite Temple Longworth, who would leave London at dawn to begin her long journey.

Tonight the mood was gay. The dancing was spirited. And Temple, breathtakingly gorgeous in her elegant long gown of scarlet chiffon, was the center of attention.

As usual.

Blithely ignoring the warnings of her handsome escort, Sir William Perry, as well as the others in her party, the free-spirited Temple was enjoying herself. Excited about her imminent adventure, the slightly tipsy Temple whirled about on the dance floor, a dazzling smile on her flushed face, her slender arms raised above her head, the swaying skirts of her scarlet evening gown lifting to reveal fleeting glimpses of slim ankles and well-shaped legs.

On the landing above, the unsmiling gentleman withdrew a slim gold case from inside his white linen suit jacket. Dark, intense eyes never leaving the woman whirling giddily about below, he lighted one of his favored French Cartier cigarettes. After drawing the smoke deep into his lungs, he took the cigarette from his lips and exhaled slowly, releasing the smoke to spiral upward. He lowered his hand to the table and glanced at the ruby.

His dark eyes widened slightly.

The ruby's blood red color had darkened to near black. But he was not a superstitious man. His full lips stretched into a cynical half smile, and he dismissed the ruby's dramatic change of color as an aberration caused by the cabaret's transforming light.

Languidly he smoked his French cigarette and continued to observe the movements of the beautiful blond American.

All at once Temple felt a hint of a chill skip up her spine. Quite suddenly she was aware of an unsettling presence, felt the disturbing pressure of probing eyes upon her.

Regarding her. Examining her. Touching her.

Temple lifted her head from Sir William's shoulder and looked about. She saw no one but her circle of friends. The lower floor of the opulent club was nearly deserted, as the hour had grown late and the regulars had departed.

She glanced up at the mezzanine and immediately spotted a dark man in a white suit seated alone and apart at a tiny table beside the wrought-iron railing.

She caught only a fleeting glimpse of a dark head before he leaned back into the deep shadow and his face was completely hidden from her view. Curious, half intrigued, Temple was acutely aware that the mysterious man was watching her.

And only her.

Unconsciously she played to him. She caught herself laughing a bit too loudly and dancing a bit too wildly. And pretending to have even more fun than she was actually having. All for his benefit.

Inexplicably, she was bent on holding the dark stranger's attention. She was showing off and couldn't stop herself. She wanted him to continue staring at her. Was determined to hold his interest. She felt strangely hot and cold at the same time, experiencing a definite thrill from feeling the enigmatic stranger's eyes scrutinizing her.

She spun about dizzily, keenly aware that her shiny blond hair was dancing around her bare shoulders and that her scarlet skirts were rising higher and higher above her stockinged ankles.

Temple abruptly threw back her head and looked up challengingly.

And was mildly disappointed to see only an empty table.

The dark stranger was gone.

Temple DuPlessis Longworth felt oddly let down.

2

Midnight had come and gone when the gleaming black coach bearing the Perry heraldic crest neared London's Savoy Hotel. Sir William and Temple were alone in the coach's roomy interior. Temple's indulgent cousin, Rupert Longworth, had joined in the evening's festivities but had tired early. He had made his apologies and returned to the hotel shortly after ten o'clock.

A creature of habit, Rupert Longworth, the fifty-eight-year-old widower and one of Temple's most favorite relatives, never stayed up past eleven, no matter where he was or with whom. Rupert Longworth would gladly tell anyone who would listen that he insisted on being undressed and in his monogrammed silk pajamas each night at precisely ten-thirty, at which time he enjoyed, without fail, exactly two snifters of cognac and at least one chapter of a good book before falling asleep.

As the black brougham rolled to a stop before the Savoy's canopied main entrance, Temple Longworth turned to Sir William and offered her cheek for his good-night kiss, saying, "It's very late, Bill. Let's say good night here."

"Certainly not." Sir William Perry shook his head vigorously. "My dear, do you really suppose I'd allow you to roam the hotel corridors alone at this hour?"

Before Temple could reply, Sir William had stepped across her and was out of the carriage. He turned to offer her his hand. Temple sighed inwardly but placed her slender fingers atop his gloved palm and allowed him to help her down to the curb.

Inside the spacious hotel lobby Temple paused beneath a huge chandelier and tried once more. "It was a lovely evening, Bill, truly lovely. I can't thank you enough."

"The pleasure was all mine," said he, as he took her upper arm and ushered her toward the lift.

"You needn't come up," she said gently. "I'm entirely safe now, and—"

"I shall see you directly to your door," Sir William insisted. "No gentleman would do less." And he handed her inside the lift's barred cage.

The lift began its rise the moment they were inside, and Sir William Perry, turning his back on the uniformed operator, drew Temple close and said in a low voice, "You are beautiful. So incredibly beautiful. All evening I've been wanting—"

"Bill, please, not here. . . ." Temple pulled away and made a face. Her green eyes snapping with annoyance, she inclined her head toward the little uniformed man operating the lift.

"You're right, of course," said Sir William, and gave her a knowing smile that made Temple cringe inwardly.

Her eager escort was undoubtedly counting on being invited in for a nightcap. Well, that wasn't going to happen. She was exhausted from the long evening, and she had a slight headache from the champagne. And she'd had quite enough of him and his company. She hoped he wouldn't make a scene.

The elevator came to a jolting stop. Temple and Sir William stepped out into the silent corridor. Temple began making excuses before they reached the door of her sixth-floor suite.

"I'll have to be extra quiet," she whispered, giving Sir William a small smile. "I wouldn't want to wake Cousin Rupert."

"No, *we* wouldn't," William replied, smiling back at her.

At the door, Temple withdrew a key from her small evening bag. Key in hand, she turned to face Sir William. Swiftly he reached for the key, saying, "Invite me in for a nightcap?"

"I wish I could, Bill, but as I mentioned, Cousin Rupert is—"

"Sound asleep and not likely to wake up anytime soon," he finished for her. His smile and tone mildly accusing, he added, "You've forgotten, Temple. I played cards with your cousin on Tuesday afternoon. I distinctly recall his having his own suite across the corridor."

Caught, Temple smiled and said, "You have me, Bill."

"No. No, I haven't," he said, "But I want you, and—"

"Don't. Don't do this."

"I must. Allow me to come inside, dearest. Just for a moment. Let me say all the things I've been wanting to say since we first—"

"Bill, we've been over this before," Temple cut in anxiously. "I'm sorry if you—"

"Darling, darling," he interrupted, "you know how I feel about you. I love you, Temple," he said, impatiently putting his arms around her and drawing her to him. He bent his head and murmured raggedly against her left ear, "Please don't go. Stay here in London. Marry me, darling. Marry me now, tonight! I'll give you everything you want. I'll take good care of you and—"

"I take good care of myself, thank you very much," Temple cut in, struggling to free herself from his smothering embrace. Reluctantly he released her and looked at her with baleful blue eyes when she stated flatly, "I've told you repeatedly how much I value my independence. You know, as does everyone, exactly what kind of woman I am. I neither need nor want to be married, Bill. You knew that. You swore to me you understood perfectly. You said you admired me for being frank and that you respected my position since you yourself felt much the same way. Remember?"

Half sheepishly he admitted that he did. "But that was long ago, old girl. Since then I've come to—"

"It was less than ten days ago. We met only two weeks ago."

"Two weeks, two years, what does it matter? Our families go back forever," said he. "I could make you happy if only you'd give me the opportunity. Let me come in now and—"

"No. No, I'm sorry," she said, finality in her tone. "My key, please." She held out her hand, palm up.

Beaten, Sir William nodded sadly, unlocked the door, and handed her the key. But before she could slip inside, he said again, "I love you, Temple," and his usually well-modulated voice lifted and there was a hint of a whine to his tone. "I love you madly. I can't live without you. How can you be so cruel? How can you do this to me?"

"Shhh," she scolded, anger replacing any sympathy she might have felt toward him. "Do want to wake the entire hotel?"

"I don't care if I do," he pressed on. "I only care about you. About the two of us. Give me a chance to show you how much I love you. Is that asking too much? Won't you at least—"

He was literally begging now, and Temple was repelled. She had so hoped it wouldn't come to this, had counted on his breeding to make him behave better. Had supposed he would maintain his dignity.

Well, she had been wrong.

"Stop it, Bill!" she interrupted none too sweetly. "Get hold of yourself, for heaven sake! I never led you to believe there was anything between us because there wasn't. I like my life exactly as it is and have no intention of changing it. I've made no secret of that fact. Have I?"

A long moment passed.

"No," he finally admitted, dejected. "No, you haven't."

Her expression softened. She smiled and put out her hand. He took it in both of his, crushing the slim fingers as if he would never let her go.

She said, "Thank you for making my stay in London a pleasant one."

"A good-bye kiss?" Sir William implored hopefully.

And didn't wait for a reply. Gripping her hand, he eagerly leaned down and kissed her fully on the lips. When the kiss ended, he was half dazed. Temple was not.

Seizing the opportunity of his temporary stupor, she mumbled one last quick "Good night," slipped inside, and closed the door.

She was glad to be rid of him. Glad she was leaving London with the dawn. Glad she wouldn't be seeing him again.

Sir William Perry had turned out to be most tiresome. In two short weeks he had fallen in love with her, had begged for her hand in marriage. How disappointing. He had been such an urbane, entertaining companion that first evening they'd met.

As soon as she and Cousin Rupert had arrived in London they had been invited to the country estate of Rupert's dear old friend Lord Hempbill. It was a dinner party for some fifty guests, most of whom—like Cousin Rupert—were getting on in years.

After the lengthy meal Temple had grown restless and had wandered out onto the stone terrace. Sir William Perry was there, smoking alone in the moonlight.

On seeing him, she'd nodded and smiled, then laughed out loud when he'd said bluntly, "Are you as bloody bored as I?"

She had been and she'd thought she'd found a kindred soul in the tall, blond, sophisticated thirty-five-year-old British gentleman. For the next few days—and evenings—she had enjoyed Sir William's company immensely. He was intelligent and charming and totally uncaring of what people thought or said about him.

But the fun didn't last.

Too soon he was looking at her with undisguised longing in his blue eyes and addressing her with an unmistakable sugary tenderness in his tone. Before the week was out he had confessed that he was falling in love with her.

Temple sighed deeply now as she pushed away from the door. She kicked off her dancing slippers as she crossed the suite's opulent sitting room. She extinguished the last of the sitting room's many lamps and moved listlessly toward the bedroom.

Only one light burned there: a small porcelain lamp with a pleated white shade shed a circle of pale illumination on the polished mahogany bedside table. The bed had been turned down for the night. Across its foot lay a fresh nightgown and matching robe.

Wearily Temple began to undress, still bothered by the final unpleasantness with Sir William. It was always the same. Just a different man, a different face. A pleasant, enjoyable relationship with an unfettered, self-confident adult male in the very beginning. Then the inevitable change. The hated transformation into a foolish, lovesick boy. Before her eyes the dreaded metamorphosis into a drooling, addled would-be lover who couldn't think straight for wanting to own her body and soul.

Temple wondered sometimes if perhaps she was the perverse one. Maybe it wasn't they. Maybe there was something terribly wrong with her. Maybe she should be pleased that she could inspire such passion. And maybe she would have been if not for the fact that when a man surrendered to his burning desire he was immediately eager to become putty in her hands. Which repelled her. And why not? Men abhorred women who were clinging vines, and she understood perfectly. She felt the same way. So she quite naturally rebelled against the chafing chains of suffocating devotion from a bewitched beau.

Once, years ago, she had thought for a short while she had found the right man. It had been his intellect, not his looks, that had attracted her. A university professor and a poet, he'd been twenty-eight, she twenty-one. He was slender, bearded, and highly intelligent. He had seemed to be so completely unattainable that it made him incredibly attractive. And he had treated her as an equal, as if she were as bright and brilliant as he. Their highly stimulating conversations might have taken place between two astute, forward-thinking men who respected each other's keen intellects.

It had been wonderful.

Bored with the trivial talk of clothes and food and babies of which her female friends never seemed to tire, she'd been inspired and excited by the sparkling conversation of her scholarly companion. A true academic who wrote beautiful poetry, he was also an excellent listener who encouraged her to think for herself and speak what was on her mind.

It was all perfect until a chilly November afternoon when he persuaded her to visit his remote stone cottage not far from the university.

A blazing fire, a bottle of chilled wine, and a book of his own poetry. No sooner were they inside than he took her in his arms and began kissing her passionately in the entranceway, the weak autumn sunlight spilling through the tall windows.

Their beautiful relationship was forever altered. Overnight the brilliant university professor whose superior intelligence had so attracted her became a besotted admirer who could no longer think straight and wanted immediately to make her his wife.

Temple shook her head now as if to clear it. Where, she wondered miserably, was the man who was as strong and independent as she? The man who wouldn't swoon at her feet the first time she kissed him? The man who would think as she thought? The man who no more wanted the constraints of marriage and home than she did.

Sighing deeply, Temple glanced at the porcelain clock beneath the bedside lamp: two o'clock. She should have been in bed and asleep hours ago. She was to meet Cousin Rupert downstairs in the dining room at dawn for a hasty breakfast before departing for the docks, where they would board the vessel to take them across the Channel on the first leg of their long journey.

Temple began stripping off her clothes. When she was completely bare, she picked up the gossamer night-gown from the foot of the bed and pulled it over her head. She didn't don the matching robe. Nor did she immediately get into bed.

Temple Longworth was, as usual, still restless. Edgy. Unfulfilled. Longing for something. Something . . . she didn't know what. Something that in her twenty-five years she had never found. Something that likely did not exist.

All the light-hearted gaiety of the evening had evaporated, and Temple felt unusually melancholy. A sad, sweet yearning plagued her. Again.

3

The ruby, suffused with an incandescent red glow, produced that unique six-starred prism for which it was famous as its bearer's dark fingers fitted the key into the lock.

He opened the door and stepped quietly into the dimly lit foyer of the luxurious corner suite. Noiselessly he placed the key in a flat silver bowl on a marble-topped table and walked unhurriedly into the hotel suite's high-ceilinged drawing room.

He was unbuttoning his white suit jacket when a beautiful woman wearing only a revealing nightgown of sheer black lace came rushing out of the bedroom. She was Lady Barrow, a blood relative to Queen Victoria, a gorgeous but rather petulant thirty-three-year-old auburn-haired, milky-skinned divorcée and his mistress for the past six months.

An affair that, for him, had become increasingly tiresome. *She* had become increasingly tiresome. She had fallen in love with him and had grown suffocatingly jealous and bad tempered because she so wanted to possess him.

No woman had ever or would ever possess him.

Lady Barrow hurried anxiously toward him now, scolding as she came.

"Christian, you can't treat me this way!" she cried shrewishly. "I will not tolerate it! It's after one in the morning and you said you'd be gone no longer than an hour. Where the hell have you been? And with whom? I want to know her name. Tell me!"

The jealous Lady Barrow continued to rage as the unresponsive Christian Telford calmly shrugged out of his suit jacket, tossed it over a chair back, and crossed to the liquor cabinet to pour himself a brandy.

". . . and I simply will not allow it! Are you listening to me, Christian? I will not be ignored, nor made a fool of! You cannot expect me to . . ." On and on she went, relentlessly rebuking him.

Clasping the crystal snifter lightly in the palm of his tanned hand, Christian swirled the dark amber liquid about, the large ruby ring on his finger shimmering and showering red sparks with his movements. He lifted the glass to his lips and drained it slowly. He swallowed the smooth, warmed brandy and exhaled heavily.

Finally he glanced at the angry, red-faced woman, raised his dark hand, and said in a low but commanding voice, "That's enough, Beatrice."

Lady Barrow broke off in midsentence. She knew he meant it and was immediately contrite. She was sorry she'd said anything. She was frightened because she knew she was losing him, had perhaps already lost him. Their affair, which had been so heated in the beginning, had begun to cool in the past few weeks, and frequently he ignored her completely. She could see it his eyes, hear it in his tone when he spoke that the end was near. His interest had waned, and she was desperate to reclaim it.

"Oh, my love, forgive me," Lady Barrow murmured, and anxiously set about to make him do just that.

"It's all right," he said, and poured himself another brandy.

He sat down on a long beige sofa, yanked impatiently at the creases in his trouser legs, and lighted a Cartier cigarette.

"No, it isn't all right," she said, now thoroughly chastened. "I know how you hate being interrogated, and I shouldn't have said anything." She swept her unbound hair back over her bare shoulders and moved seductively toward the sofa. Smiling sweetly now, she said, "I'm just glad you're back. I missed you terribly."

Christian took a long, deep pull on his cigarette and slowly released the smoke. His night black eyes flicked over—then dismissed—the scantily clad auburn-haired beauty moving toward him.

He said, "I didn't expect you to be here, Beatrice."

She laughed nervously, sat down on the sofa beside him, and said, "Not be here? Why, darling, what a foolish statement. Of course I'm here. Where else would I be?"

He turned his dark head, looked directly at her. His gaze a mixture of annoyance and compassion, he said, "It was settled, was it not? Didn't I made myself clear. We agreed it was over, that we'd—"

"Oh, don't, Christian," she choked, "don't say that. It isn't over, it isn't. I won't let it be over, I can't let you go."

"This is my last night in London," he said flatly. "I've no idea when I'll return. It could be years. You are beautiful, wealthy, titled. You'll find someone else."

"Christian, my love," she said, rising from the sofa and turning about to face him. "I don't want anyone else. I want only you. And you want me, I know you do. You're tired and tense, that's it." She smiled then, catlike, lifted the black lace nightgown high up her milky thighs, and slid swiftly down astride his trousered knees.

"It won't work, Beatrice," he said as she settled herself on him. "It's over. I'm sorry."

"If you wish," she murmured even as she tugged at the knot in his silk cravat. "If it's over, I'll accept it. But does that mean we can't enjoy this final night together?"

Her fingers were nimble on the buttons going down his shirtfront. He made no move either to stop her or to aid her. He sat there sipping his brandy and smoking his French cigarette while she worked furiously to excite him. In seconds the powder blue shirt was completely open down his dark chest.

Eagerly she pushed the shirt apart and ran her nails through the crisp black hair covering his broad chest. She caught and held his gaze as she popped a forefinger into her mouth and sucked on it briefly. She felt his lean, hard body tense slightly when she lowered her finger, placed the tip on a flat brown nipple, and teasingly drew a wet circle around and around it.

"Get down now," he said, the faintest hint of desire creeping into his low voice. "Go on to bed."

"In a while," she said. She moved her tormenting finger, bent her head, and began licking the erect nipple.

Christian exhaled heavily, finally put aside his brandy snifter and snuffed out his smoked-down cigarette. He put both hands in her flowing auburn hair, gripped the lustrous locks in his long fingers, and drew her head up off his chest.

"This will change nothing," he said, and meant it.

"Nothing? How can you say that when already you're hard and throbbing beneath me?"

He released her hair, laid his hands lightly on her thighs. She placed her own hands atop his and guided them carefully to push the black lace nightgown higher up her bare belly. She trembled with delicious pleasure when he settled her more fully upon his straining groin.

She felt a rush of sweet triumph and quick desire ripple her.

Maybe *he* no longer wanted her, but his body still responded. She'd make him want her again. She'd drive him mad with desire until he was ready to admit he still wanted her, had to have her, would never leave her!

Lady Barrow hastily pushed the wispy straps of her black nightgown off her shoulders. Anxiously she shrugged until her pale, full breasts sprang free of the flimsy lace, the large nipples already peaking in anticipation of her lover's heated kisses.

When he didn't immediately lean forward to press his dark face to her bared breasts, Lady Barrow put her hands into the thick dark hair at the sides of his head and kissed him. Her lips moving eagerly on his, she rubbed her naked breasts against his chest, letting him feel the taut nipples brush and graze the crisp dark hair and hard, hot muscle beneath.

During the prolonged, passionate kiss she felt his hands move impatiently under the twisted black lace to the twin cheeks of her bare bottom, and her heart pounded with joy. Her lips still fused with his, she clung to his dark hair with one hand and lowered the other between them. Her nervous fingers fumbled with his belt buckle, managed to get it undone, then deftly flipped open the buttons of his fly.

She gasped excitedly into his mouth when his hard, heavy flesh sprang free of his tight trousers. She immediately took her hand away so that she could settle her own moist, throbbing flesh more fully against that fierce, fully formed erection.

Lady Barrow finally tore her burning lips from Christian's, lifted her head, and looked at him. His dark, hooded eyes were glazed with passion, and his chest was rising and falling rapidly. She was jubilant.

It had taken her longer than usual, but finally the sexually experienced Lady Barrow had managed to arouse her less-than-ardent lover. You won't leave me now, she thought victoriously as she rocked rhythmically against him. Sliding slowly, erotically up and down the impressive length of him, she could hardly wait to have all the pulsating male power inside her.

Christian clasped her waist with his firm fingers and lifted her. Lady Barrow licked her fingers anxiously, took him in her hand, and ran her wet fingertips over the jerking head, then guided the glistening tip into her wet, waiting warmth. Her fingers released him and she put her hands atop his broad shoulders. Both watched as he eased her all the way down on his thrusting masculinity.

Half dressed, they made love there on the sofa, she with her black lace nightgown bunched up and tangled around her waist, he with his shirt and trousers open and his shoes still on. When her climax came, Lady Barrow cried out in her ecstasy, then collapsed against his naked, sweat-dampened chest.

Breathless, sated, she whispered, "Carry me to bed, my love, and hold me in your arms all through the night."

His chest heaving, heart racing, Christian made no reply. He carried her to the bed. She sighed and stretched happily as he stripped and got in beside her. Placing a proprietary hand on the now flaccid flesh that had just given her such incredible pleasure, Lady Barrow began tenderly to toy with him, intending for them to make love again.

But her hand soon stilled and her breathing deepened, and she was almost immediately asleep.

He was not.

Christian Telford lay awake in the darkness. Restless. Irritable. Edgy.

He slipped from the bed and wandered into the

adjoining room. He took a cigarette from his slim gold case and went out onto the darkened hotel balcony.

Standing naked in the cool night air, he put the cigarette between his lips and was starting to light it when a woman stepped out onto the balcony directly next to his.

She wore only a flimsy gossamer nightgown. Her feet were bare, and her heavy blond hair was flowing loose down her pale, bare back. She hurried to the balcony's stone railing, gripped it tightly, threw back her head, and took a long, deep breath.

The cigarette dangling unlit from his mouth, Christian watched her, his dark eyes narrowing. A half-cruel smile touched his lips.

The beautiful blond American he had watched dance at the cabaret.

Temple stood there on the balcony, enjoying the nighttime solitude, the cooling breeze. Locks of her unbound hair lifted and blew around her face. The filmy skirts of her nightgown swirled gently around her long legs and bare feet. The city below was asleep at this late hour. It was wonderfully peaceful, and Temple felt some of her melancholy lifting. It was as if she were all alone in a tranquil world.

Then suddenly she was shaken with the same kind of chill she had experienced earlier at the cabaret. That feeling that she was being watched. Her heartbeat quickening, she whipped her head about.

But the quick, catlike Christian Telford had sunk back into the shadows and disappeared.

Temple saw no one. Nothing. Squinting in the darkness, she peered for a long time at the deserted balcony next to hers.

Finally she shook her head, shrugged, and went back inside.

4

Temple's optimism and excitement returned with the dawn. She'd had only a few hours' sleep, but she felt fresh and rested and eager to begin the long, exciting journey that would take her to far-off Arabia.

The trip had been carefully planned, each detail dealt with, everything that might possibly go wrong hopefully foreseen. It had taken months to map out the complete itinerary and see to all the necessary arrangements. Ship's cabins had been booked, hotel suites reserved, suitable clothing tailored, and experienced desert guides hired through trusted family contacts in Algiers.

The painstaking planning had been easy compared to the difficulty convincing her overprotective family that the desert tour would be perfectly safe, that she would be perfectly safe. More than a trifle doubtful, her mother and father and the childless maternal uncle who looked on her as if she were his own daughter had made every attempt to dissuade her.

All three had warned that the journey was fraught with danger and totally unnecessary. It was, all agreed, out of the question for a beautiful young woman to go alone into the uncivilized deserts of Arabia.

The forward-thinking Temple had been ready for that argument.

"Why, I wouldn't consider going into Arabia alone," she'd told them. "Cousin Rupert is going along as my protector and chaperon."

In unison all three had said incredulously, "Cousin Rupert has agreed to go to Arabia?"

The fussy, set-in-his-ways Rupert Longworth was not known as a man with a taste for adventure. And his idea of hardship was to sleep on sheets that were not made of silk. They couldn't imagine him agreeing to ride into the burning deserts atop a smelly camel.

"Absolutely! He's looking forward to it!" Temple had exclaimed, omitting the fact that she'd not yet told Cousin Rupert he'd be going with her. She could persuade him, she knew she could. She'd always been able to get her way with Cousin Rupert. She could cajole or bully him into saying yes to just about anything. Hurrying on, she'd said excitedly, "The two of us will be gone for five, perhaps six months."

"That long?" her mother had said, her delicate brow wrinkling with concern.

"We'll sail to England, where we'll spend two weeks in London," Temple had stated confidently, focusing first on her father, then on her uncle James DuPlessis. "You know how Cousin Rupert loves London. A couple of weeks there, then we'll cross the channel to Calais, where we'll board a train to take us across France. Once we reach Toulon, we'll sail the Mediterranean all the way to Bur Sa'id. We'll go down through the Suez Canal and across the Red Sea to Al Muway. In Al Muway we'll meet up with our caravan guides and head out into the deserts!"

"And how long will you be in the desert?" her father had asked, still worried.

"Two months," she'd replied. "Two months after leaving Al Muway, we should arrive in Baghdad, where I promise to send you a wire so you'll know we're safe and sound."

The skeptical trio had continued their attempts to dissuade her but finally had given up. They'd realized it was futile. Temple was no longer a willful child. She was a headstrong, twenty-five-year-old woman with complete financial independence from a generous family trust. She had no need of monetary aid; therefore to her way of thinking she had no need of permission to do as she pleased.

"Once we've rested in Baghdad for a few days, we'll begin the journey home," Temple had told them, her emerald eyes dancing with delight. Impulsively taking her father's arm in hers, she'd given it an affectionate squeeze and said, "I ask you, what could possibly go wrong?"

"What indeed?" her father had muttered.

As Temple and Cousin Rupert reached the docks, the dark, cloudy London morning had given way to rain and a chill wind was blowing. But the nasty weather didn't dampen Temple's high spirits.

Looking youthful and lovely in a bright yellow rain cape, its hood raised to cover her blond hair, and carrying a matching parasol raised above her head, Temple laughed happily as she climbed the ship's slippery gangway.

His mood not nearly as jovial as hers, Rupert Longworth gripped the collars of his suit coat, which were turned up around his scowling face. A black rain cloak was draped around his shoulders. Hatless, he was sharing Temple's raised parasol and grumbling about having lost his own large, serviceable black umbrella, the third one he'd misplaced since arriving in London.

As soon as they stepped on deck, Rupert suggested they go below and enjoy a hot cup of coffee or perhaps even something a little stronger. Temple declined. She wasn't bothered by the rain or wind. She preferred to stay topside.

"Suit yourself, child," said the finicky, silver-haired gentleman, frowning and blinking away the rain.

"Here, take this." Temple thrust her yellow parasol at him. "I don't need it."

"Of course you need it if you're staying up here." He eyed the dark clouds overhead. She shook her head and pressed it on him. "Well, all right, but don't you go catching a cold. Be a shame if you got sick and couldn't go to Arabia." He hurried away.

Temple smiled as she turned back to the railing. She knew Cousin Rupert would like nothing better than for her to come down with a cold severe enough to force her to cancel their journey. He had agreed, under duress, to go with her to the desert, but he didn't really want to go. If he'd had his way, they would both have stayed in London.

Well, he could forget it. She wasn't about to get sick.

The idling vessel finally threw off its moorings and began to move away from the busy docks. Temple laughed gaily as the falling rain and salty sea spray dampened her cheeks and tendrils of blond hair that had escaped the hood of her rain cape.

Out in the Channel the murky waters were unusually turbulent and choppy. The winds were growing higher, beginning to blow so hard that it seemed they were reaching gale force. The ship's bow slapped against the high-tossing waves, and the vessel pitched up and down wildly. Frightened passengers scurried inside, but Temple stayed put.

She found the wild ride exhilarating. She felt gloriously alive. Courting danger appealed to her sense of adventure, which was one of the reasons for this planned foray into the desert. It would be incredibly exciting and different from anything she'd ever experienced. And, yes, there was a degree of risk involved. Which made the undertaking all the more thrilling.

She was grateful for her safe, privileged life, of course, glad that she was fortunate enough to have been born into a prominent family whose wealth and power were unmeasured. Certainly she wouldn't have traded places with anyone on earth.

But there were times when she felt smothered by her orderly, secure, sheltered existence. Every luxury the civilized world had to offer had been hers from the moment she had opened her eyes. She was the only child born of a union that had been advantageous to both partners.

Her distinguished father, the brilliant Walter Wilson Longworth, a man of modest means, had come from a fine old family of scholars, university presidents, and members of presidential cabinets.

Her mother, the beautiful Anna DuPlessis Longworth, had come from a family possessing great wealth. Anna, along with her older brother, Temple's uncle, James Douglas DuPlessis, were the major heirs to the vast DuPlessis fortune. A fortune amassed through the years from a large, highly profitable munitions business. A family fortune from which she herself had been awarded a generous trust upon reaching twenty-one.

Temple was not foolish enough to wish that she were not wealthy. But there were times when she did wish that her illustrious family name were not quite so well known.

And where she was going, it wasn't.

Temple was pleased with the thought. Perhaps the one place on earth where the DuPlessis name was unknown was where she was headed. The nomadic bedouin caravans roaming the vast Arabian deserts had surely never heard of a DuPlessis.

For two glorious months she would be like those bedouins: a totally free, nameless, faceless soul roaming about at will atop a camel, camping at the desert wells, and sleeping in a tent.

Such marvelous fun!

"Miss, you'd best get inside."

Temple looked up into the rain-streaked face of a slickered crewman. Not waiting for her reply, the big, brawny seaman took her arm and guided her across the wet, rolling decks.

Once inside the ship's warm, lighted shelter, Temple threw off her rain hood and began searching the sea of frightened faces for Cousin Rupert.

She didn't see him.

A mild tremor of alarm rippled through her as she waded into the crowd and began asking if anyone had seen a middle-aged, silver-haired man wearing a dark rain cloak and carrying a lady's yellow parasol.

Several people pointed toward the aft exit door.

Temple looked in that direction and momentarily caught sight her cousin staggering toward her. His rain cloak was missing and so was his suit coat. His cravat was askew, his shirt collar open. His silver hair was badly ruffled, and he looked as if he'd been perspiring profusely. His usually alert gray eyes were dulled and filled with misery.

One glance and Temple knew it was a wretched case of mal de mer.

"Oh, Rupert, dear Cousin Rupert," she exclaimed, hurrying toward him, her heart going out to him.

She was almost to him when Rupert's eyes widened, his hand flew up to cover his mouth, and, shaking his head violently, he turned and rushed back toward the exit. A few short steps from the door he slipped on the rain-wet floor.

Temple screamed in horror as Rupert's feet flew out

from under him. Arms flailing wildly, helpless to prevent
it, he took a bad fall, striking his head on the corner of a
table as he went down.

He was flat on his back and unconscious when
Temple fell to her knees beside him.

"Ah, no, no. Do not look so troubled, *mademoiselle*,"
said the white-coated, bearded physician whose English
was limited.

"Are you sure he's going to be all right, Dr. Ledet?"

A worried Temple faced the doctor in the narrow hallway of a small hospital in Calais. They stood just outside
the room where Rupert Longworth lay in a clean white
bed, a hovering nurse constantly checking his vital signs.

When the seasick Rupert had fallen and hit his head,
he'd been knocked out cold. Terrified her cousin was
dead, Temple had screamed for help. Unfortunately there
had been no physicians among the passengers. But a crewman had quickly responded to her cries for help, felt for a
pulse, lifted Rupert's eyelids to check his eyes, and
assured Temple there was a strong, steady heartbeat.

It was decided, since the ship was almost to France's
shores, that Rupert would be taken to a Calais clinic.

Now, a few short hours after reaching the hospital,
Temple listened as the French doctor explained that
Cousin Rupert had a slight concussion. It was not life-
threatening. He would most assuredly survive, and in
time he would be his old self again.

"In time?" Temple's finely arched eyebrows lifted.
"How much time?"

The doctor's narrow, white-coated shoulders lifted in
a shrug. "This depends," he said, scratching his bearded
face. "On how well he responds to total rest and relaxation. If he is very quiet and behaves himself, he should

be ready to leave us in . . . mmmm . . . a week. Perhaps two."

"Two weeks! That long?" Temple couldn't keep the dismay from her tone. Then immediately she felt guilty. She was thinking mainly of herself, disappointed at having to cancel her long-planned trip. She should be ashamed of herself, and she was. Poor Cousin Rupert, lying helpless in a French hospital bed with a concussion.

"When I release him," the doctor continued, lifting a bony finger to shake it in her face, "he is to do nothing strenuous or stressful for several weeks."

Temple nodded. "He won't," she said, "I promise."

"Bon. Bon," murmured the doctor. "Now, I have other patients. I'll be back to check on *Monsieur* Longworth in an hour, *oui?"* He clicked his heels together and hurried off down the corridor.

"Oui."

Exhaling loudly, Temple shook her head and frowned. Then she drew a deep breath, put a smile on her face, and went inside.

Cousin Rupert, fully awake now, looked up as she entered, smiled sheepishly, and said, "Child, I'm so sorry. I've spoiled everything, haven't I?'

"Don't talk nonsense, Cousin. You haven't spoiled anything."

"But the trip . . . your desert tour."

"Will have to be canceled for now." She took hold of his hand, tried to smile, failed.

"No, no," he said, "we can still go. I shouldn't be here but a few days, and then we could—"

"Dr. Ledet says you're not to . . . to . . ." Her words trailed away, and a flash of hope appeared in Temple's green eyes.

"What?" He gave her a puzzled look. "What is it?"

She squeezed his hand. "You've always loved spending the summer season in London, haven't you, Cousin Rupert?"

"You know I have, but I—"

"How would you like to spend *this* summer season in London?"

Rupert's gray eyes lighted the way hers just had. "Are you saying what I think you're saying? That when I'm released the two of us will go directly back to London and stay the summer?"

"No, I'm saying when you're released, *you'll* go back to London and stay the summer." An infectious smile was spreading over her face as the wheels turned in her nimble brain.

Puzzled, Rupert's bushy silver eyebrows lifted questioningly. "And where will you be?"

"In Arabia."

"Alone? God forbid!"

"No, God doesn't forbid," she said, merriment flashing from her eyes. "Nor will you. It can be our secret. No one need ever know, and we both get to do what we want. What do you say?" She could tell by the glow in his eyes he was seriously entertaining the idea.

Yet he reasoned, "It won't work, child. It's too risky."

"There is nothing risky about it. You go back to the Savoy and enjoy yourself. I go to the desert and enjoy myself. I'll meet you in London in the fall and we'll sail home together."

A long pause.

Rupert pondering, wondering, weighing the possibilities. "It does sound reasonable," he said finally, starting to grin impishly. "You'd be careful. Promise me you'd be very careful?"

"Extremely careful, Cousin dear."

5

Five Weeks Later

Al Muway, Arabia

Temple DuPlessis Longworth raised eyebrows when she walked into the inn's crowded outdoor restaurant on that early June morning. Patrons stopped eating their breakfast to stare, and a buzz of whispered outrage followed her. Ignoring the stir she caused, Temple strode confidently toward the small table on the shaded stone terrace, where Sarhan, her head guide, awaited.

Dressed for the forbidding terrain she was about to enter, she wore snug-fitting riding breeches of durable dark twill, a long-sleeved white shirt, and brown knee-high boots of smooth Italian leather. She carried a pair of brown kid gloves, and in the crook of her bent arm rested a sturdy sun helmet with a white silk head scarf tucked neatly inside.

Temple was well aware of the disapproving foreign eyes following her, but she was not bothered by the scrutiny. She'd often been stared at. She had learned long ago that when one was the DuPlessis heiress, one's every move was monitored, commented on, talked about.

Temple realized these people were not staring because she was a DuPlessis. They stared and whispered because they didn't approve of her attire. She understood that. But what they didn't understand was that she was about to ride into the pitiless desert, and she had no intention of starting out on such a journey wearing long skirts and heavy petticoats.

Sarhan, her guide, rose when she reached the table. A black-bearded giant with a patch over his right eye, he wore a dark *thobe*, the traditional long robe favored by all Arabs. His *guttrah*, or headdress, was held in place by strands of black woolen headrope. His one good eye flickered with momentary censure before he smiled politely, greeted her with respect, and came around to pull out the chair for her.

"The baggage caravan has gone on ahead," he informed her. "We will meet up with them at the oasis where we're to spend the first night."

Nodding, Temple picked up the small white cup placed before her, took a drink of the bitter black coffee, and involuntarily made a face. Then she smiled. The coffee tasted wretched, but what did it matter? She was about to embark on a thrilling escapade filled with all sorts of excitements and dangers. How fortunate she was! What a lucky woman to lead such a glorious life.

As Sarhan talked of the preparations and of what to expect on the first day out, Temple thought of Cousin Rupert back in London. She thanked the fates that he wasn't with her now. She was glad that when she looked across the table she saw Sarhan's stern, swarthy countenance, not Cousin Rupert's ruddy, cherubic face. Cousin Rupert would hate every minute of the grand adventure, and that would spoil the fun for her.

She was happy she was going alone. Eager and unafraid, Temple was delighted with the knowledge that for the next two months no one she knew could reach her, write to her, cable her, or intrude on her pleasure in any form or fashion. This very special trip was hers and hers alone, and she meant to enjoy and savor every precious moment of it.

Impatient to be off, Temple squirmed on her chair as Sarhan lingered over his fourth cup of coffee. When finally he lifted his white napkin and wiped his bearded mouth, Temple said hopefully, "We're ready to leave now?"

Sarhan carefully placed the napkin on the table, smiled, and said, "Not quite."

"No? Why not?"

"First we must go shopping," said the big Arab, pushing back from the table and rising to his feet.

Temple stood up. "Shopping? I don't want to go shopping. I have everything I need."

Again he said, "Not quite."

Annoyed, Temple found herself ushered off the shaded hotel terrace and down into the narrow, crowded street. His huge hand gripping her elbow, the Arab guided her past market stalls where flowers and fruits and vegetables were heaped in colorful masses. Merchants called out to them as they passed, holding up samples of their wares. Sarhan stopped abruptly at a tiny stall where a stooped, badly wrinkled old man sat dozing on a stool. The old man's eyes opened immediately, and he leapt up from his stool and started making his sales pitch in rapid-fire Arabic.

"What is he saying?" Temple looked up at Sarhan.

"He's telling you he makes the finest camel sticks to be found in all Arabia."

"Camel sticks? Do I need one?"

"Most assuredly. Anyone who rides a camel must use a stick to prod the animal and to direct him." He inclined his turbaned head to the array of sticks lined up behind the old man. "See the beautiful sticks? He makes them from the *abal* root he brings out of the desert. He heats them and bends the ends into intricately designed handles."

"I see," Temple mused aloud, studying the various camel sticks displayed in the small booth. Then: "That one," she said, pointing, and laughed with him when the ancient camel stick maker chuckled and clapped his hands, his watery eyes flashing. "Why is he so happy?" she asked Sarhan.

"Because you have chosen his most expensive one."

As the sun climbed over the turreted roofs and spires of the tiny coastal city, Temple stood beside Sarhan, laughing. The tall Arab guide held firmly to the reins of a saddled camel, speaking to the big ugly beast.

"*Zizz,*" he said, and waited. Nothing happened. More firmly then, "*Zizz.*"

Temple jumped back as the camel went down on its knees. Sarhan explained that *zizz* meant get down and *zist* meant get up.

"It's as simple as that?" she said, stepping up to the kneeling camel.

The Arab grinned. "The command generally needs to be reinforced by a stick laid not too roughly on the camel's neck."

Her newly purchased camel stick in hand, Temple mounted the gurgling camel, then obeyed Sarhan's immediate instructions to "lean back" to assist the animal in heaving from a kneeling position to hind legs extended. Temple let out a yelp of surprised glee when the creature lurched up onto all four legs.

The ground seemed a long way down.

Sarhan mounted his own camel, and immediately they got under way. With Sarhan riding beside her and the others following at a short distance, they left the coastal city behind. In no time at all Temple adjusted to her camel's easy pace. She rocked in the saddle, noting the way the Arabs rode as effortlessly as if they were sitting on rocking chairs.

Just when she thought she'd mastered it, Sarhan picked up the pace.

Temple attempted to adapt to the heavier, faster gait, but much as she tried to change the sequence of movements, when the camel stepped she rubbed forward in the saddle, then rubbed back again, her spine performing what felt to her like a figure eight. She'd be sore come night, no doubt about it.

Still, the ride was exhilarating, and Temple forgot her discomfort. Her gloved hand gripping the reins and her new camel stick, her long, heavy hair tucked up under her sun helmet, and a small Mauser pistol holstered at her waist, she swayed contentedly atop the big ugly beast she affectionately called Haj. Seduced by the beauty and grandeur of the vast golden deserts stretching before her, Temple was assailed with a wonderful feeling of well-being. The blood seemed to sing through her veins and her heart beat with a firm, steady cadence. When at noon the caravan stopped at a palm-fringed oasis, Temple ate with a hunger and relish that matched that of the men.

Back in the saddle that afternoon, she noted the bedouins rode with legs crossed nonchalantly at the ankles on their camels' necks. Temple laughed and imitated them. And happily discovered that such a position offered a degree of comfort. Watching her, they nodded and grinned. One lifted his hands and applauded.

She was pleased and surprised by how quickly she seemed to have gained the respect of her knowledgeable guides. She sighed with satisfaction, feeling that her journey promised to be a richly rewarding one.

6

On the third day out, the small caravan was resting the animals at a desert well and enjoying a leisurely noontime meal of rice cakes and braised lamb. Full and half sleepy, Temple felt her eyelids growing increasingly heavy. She glanced at Sarhan, bent over the small smoking brazier. He was cooking more lamb for the hungry men.

Temple sighed softly with the simple pleasure of being alive and content. She stretched out on the ground with her arms folded beneath her head, her booted feet crossed at the ankles.

A hint of a desert breeze fanned the palm fronds over her head and cooled her hot cheeks. The chattering of the men in their native tongue was somehow soothing to the ear. Their voices soon softened to a low hum and then fell silent.

All was quiet and peaceful.

Her head turned, and resting on her bent arm, Temple was on the verge of falling asleep. Her drowsy eyes opened and closed slowly like a dozing cat's.

Then all at once they widened as a great cloud of dust appeared on the eastern horizon.

Temple levered herself up into a sitting position, her eyes now squinting at the rapidly growing cloud of dust in the east. She was afraid it was a *schmaal*, one of those fast-moving Arabian sandstorms she'd read about.

Suddenly, with an explosive roar, a gang of black-robed desert warriors atop swift Arabian horses descended from out of the thick cloud of dust, riding at full gallop. Swords flashed and sand rose. Rifles raised, voices lifted and shouting commands in Arabic, the turbaned tribesmen raced across the desert.

Directly toward camp.

In an flash of understanding it registered on Temple. Her small caravan was being attacked by an outlaw band of thieving Barbary pirates.

Without taking her eyes off the swarming black-robed bandits, Temple reached for her pistol. Only to find it missing. Disbelieving, she looked down. The smooth leather holster lay on the ground where she had left it, but the Mauser was gone.

"What the . . . ?" She leapt to her feet and shouted for Sarhan and the others to fire on the intruders. "What are you waiting for?" she called above the deafening din. "Fire on them! Shoot over their heads! Scare them off!"

Her guides did not obey.

Baffled, Temple glanced anxiously at Sarhan. The giant Arab hadn't so much as picked up his rifle. He stood there by the smoking brazier, empty-handed, watching calmly as the fast-riding robbers closed in.

"Damn you, Sarhan!" she shouted angrily, fists clenched. "What do you think I hired you for? Don't just stand there and let them steal everything we have!"

No reply.

The bearded one-eyed guide acted as if he hadn't heard her. He never turned to look at her.

Confused and angry, Temple lifted her clenched fist

and shrieked oaths at the armed trespassers as they swooped down upon the camp like a great flock of black-winged carrion.

"You'll get nothing here!" she screamed at the destructive trespassers. "Do you hear me? We've nothing for you to steal! Nothing!"

Fearful yet furious, she stood her ground as the mounted men thundered toward her. They crashed through the camp, their horses snorting and kicking, sharp hooves wrecking everything in their path. A slashing sword sliced through the square tarpaulin raised for shade, while a horse's lathered fetlock knocked down one of the tarpaulin's supporting poles.

In the midst of shouting threats at the barbarous horsemen, Temple wailed in shock and outrage when a turbaned, bearded bandit leaned down, grabbed her, and hauled her up onto the saddle before him. Squirming furiously in his muscular arms, she kicked and screamed like a madwoman until her captor pulled her back against his chest with such force that she momentarily lost her breath.

Gasping, eyes rolling, she fought for oxygen as her callous abductor wheeled the dark stallion about so swiftly, she would have fallen if not for his arm clamped firmly around her waist. Shouting commands to his tribesmen, he put his horse into a fast gallop and headed east.

Although she'd regained her breath, Temple's eyes were watering and her heart was slamming against her ribs. She twisted about and saw, over the Arab bandit's broad shoulder, the camp being left behind. The guides all stood there calmly, not moving a muscle to help as she was carried away by these dark demons of the desert.

Enraged, Temple watched as the camp and the cowardly guides became smaller and smaller. And finally disappeared completely as the snorting mount on which she was atop galloped over a high dune and down the other side.

Swallowing convulsively, Temple continued to stare over the Arab's shoulder—watching, waiting, hoping that by some miracle Sarhan and the others would come to their senses and rescue her.

Long minutes passed with no sign of salvation.

Temple was forced to face the terrible truth. They weren't coming. No one was coming. She was on her own. She would have to save herself from these swarthy Barbary corsairs.

Slowly she turned back around, looked at the bearded, hawk face of her captor. She swallowed hard, then shouted to be heard, "What do you want with me? Where are you taking me?"

And promptly realized that she might as well have been talking to the wind.

For the next terrifying twenty-four hours Temple was taken farther and farther into the desert by her captors. She had no idea where they were taking her or what they intended to do with her. She could get nothing out of them. When they spoke it was only in Arabic, and she couldn't understand a word.

They rode steadily toward the southeast throughout the long, hot afternoon. The moon was high in the desert sky when finally they stopped for the night. A terrible dread overcame Temple as the robed men went about making camp. They built a fire for cooking and rolled out rugs for sleeping.

She refused to eat. She refused to lie down on the rug meant for her. She stubbornly sat before the fire, staring into the flames, her arms wrapped around her knees. She fully intended to sit there all night, unless the opportunity presented itself for her to get away.

She experienced a measure of relief when she was not made to lie down and sleep beside one of the bandits. For that she was extremely grateful. But she quickly learned there would be no chance to get away. A lone guard stood watch all night, a rifle resting across his robed knees, his dark eyes watching her across the fire.

Deep in the dead of night, Temple could no longer hold her eyes open. Frightened though she was, she was bone tired and so sleepy that she couldn't stay awake. Glancing at the armed sentinel, she slowly scooted away from the fire, lay down on her side with her knees raised, and folded her arms beneath her cheek.

She was instantly asleep.

When morning came and Temple realized she hadn't been harmed by any of the desert pirates, she felt a glimmer of hope. But it evaporated as once again she was thrust upon a horse and carried deeper into the desert.

She imagined the worst.

And then found out that the worst was even worse than she'd imagined.

At straight up noon with the burning desert sun at its zenith, her burly, bearded captor abruptly pulled up on his stallion, bringing the big snorting beast to a sand-flinging stop. Without a word he put his hands to Temple's waist and lowered her from the saddle. The minute her booted feet touched the sandy soil, he wheeled his big mount about and rode away. The others followed, leaving Temple standing there alone on the desert floor.

Confounded, frightened, Temple stood there for only a second, then foolishly began running after them.

"Please," she called out to them, "come back! Don't leave me here! Come back! Come back!"

She ran until her breathing was labored and she had a painful stitch in her left side. She was still running after them when they disappeared among the dunes. And still she ran, holding her side and gasping for breath.

At last she slowed and stopped.

Wind tears stung her eyes as she bent over from the waist, holding her side with both hands and trembling with exertion. Her head bowed, her long perspiration-dampened hair falling around her flushed face, she licked her dry, chapped lips and tried to swallow. After several attempts she was successful.

Temple straightened and pushed her hair out of her eyes. She tried to think. More confused and frightened than ever, she knew she wouldn't last long in the searing desert heat. She had no water. No food.

She would die in this desolate place and never know the reason.

Swallowing the fear that threatened to choke her, she told herself she had to keep her wits about her. She turned round and round in a circle, trying to decide in which direction to head. Biting her bottom lip and shading her eyes with a raised hand, she tried to determine where the nearest village would be. The closest desert well? A cooling oasis with shade trees? People? Friendly Arabs who would help her?

She sighed heavily with frustration. She had no idea which way to go and no map to guide her. But she had to do something. To go somewhere. She couldn't simply stay here and perish. She had to at least try to save herself.

Wishing she had her sun helmet, but thankful at least that she was wearing breeches and boots and a long-sleeved shirt, Temple set out in a northerly direction. Her chin lifted in determination, she walked directly toward a line of distant mountains, their thrusting peaks barely visible on the northern horizon.

She had no idea where she was or how far away from the sea, but she hoped that the Mediterranean might lie on the other side of those faraway mountains.

The pitiless sun beat down with a vengeance, reflecting off the burning sands she trod. The shimmering mountains in the distance began to look like a beautiful golden city of promise and pleasure that she would never reach.

More than once Temple blinked and squinted when she spotted a sparkling pool of water ahead, the ripples on its surface winking in the sun like thousands of priceless diamonds. But each time she neared the pond of cool, clear water, it evaporated before her burning, bloodshot eyes.

The mirages continued to torment her cruelly as a tired, thirsty Temple struggled across the scorching desert. Her face red and flushed with heat, her lips painfully sunburned, her white blouse soaked with perspiration and sticking to her prickled skin, she staggered forward on weak, trembling legs. She stumbled and fell, rose and labored on again, her throat so dry it hurt, her head throbbing with pain.

She kept going when she felt as if she could no longer put one foot before the other. She kept going when she thought she might faint from the horrible heat. She kept going when she became so weak and dizzy that her vision blurred and she was half disoriented. The endless sands swam before her eyes, rising and falling like waves on an ocean.

Refusing to be beaten, she reeled drunkenly on, wondering how many miles she had gone. How many more she had yet to go.

Temple fell, got up, and pressed on several times before, choking with thirst and burning up from the relentless heat, she finally could go no farther. She had to rest. She fell to her knees, fighting the tears of defeat and despair filling her stinging eyes. Dashing away the unwanted tears with the back of her hand, she sank back on her booted heels and looked around at mile upon mile of nothing.

Nothing.

Nothing but sand and sun and heat and . . . death.

Half dazed, Temple continued to stare out upon the great sea of sand surrounding her. Not a sound in the silence. Not a breath of wind stirring the tiny grains of sand.

Transfixed, she knelt there in the middle of that golden sea of sand and spotted, far out on the eastern horizon, behind a high dune, a faint plume of sand rising from the desert floor.

She blinked to clear her tear-blurred vision, raised a hand to shade her smarting eyes, and watched entranced as suddenly the sand exploded from the dune and a horseman vaulted into view.

For a second the snow white horse was suspended gloriously against the clear blue sky, the rider's ivory robes billowing out like giant snowy wings.

Temple's lips fell open in a mixture wonder and horror. Automatically she rose to her knees as the lone horseman rapidly approached.

Too weak and too transfixed to rise, Temple knelt in the sand as the rider bore steadily down upon her. The great galloping stallion halted abruptly only a few short feet away from her. The white-robed rider leaned down and extended a lean, tanned hand.

On the third finger of that hand was an enormous blood red ruby.

7

Temple didn't hesitate.

Barely managing to stifle a sob of relief and gratitude, she laid her trembling fingers on the palm of this white-robed horseman she looked on as her savior. He drew her to her feet, leaned down, and put strong hands around her waist. Easily he lifted her and placed her astride the saddle in front of him. Immediately he spurred the white stallion into motion.

Exhausted, relieved, Temple thanked him with her eyes. She didn't try to speak. Wasn't sure she could. She simply sighed and sagged gratefully back against the rider's broad chest. After a moment she turned her head slightly, and raised her stinging eyes to his face.

She could see almost nothing.

A white turban completely covered his head and was wound around the lower half of his face, concealing his nose and his mouth. Only his eyes were visible. Temple stared at the dark, luminous eyes that were focused straight ahead. Gazing at those long-lashed, night black eyes, she was struck by the insane thought that they were the most mysterious, the most beautiful eyes she had ever seen.

Without glancing at her or slowing the stallion's rapid pace, the Arab reached inside his white robes and withdrew a shiny silver flask. He held it out to her. Not knowing or caring what was in the flask, Temple seized it.

Fingers shaking, she unscrewed the lid and tipped the flask up to her badly chapped lips. Overjoyed to find it contained cool, clear water, she drank greedily. Wrapping both hands around the silver flask and leaning her head back, she tilted the flask almost straight up. She swilled the water down so rapidly, she couldn't quite swallow fast enough. Water spilled from the sides of her mouth and trickled down her chin.

She never noticed.

She frowned and groaned in protest when the Arab took the flask from her after she'd drunk only half the contents. He paid her no mind. She tried to talk, to tell him she was still thirsty, but she had difficulty speaking. Her throat was sore and scratchy, her voice hoarse.

He shook his head to silence her. Nodding, she obeyed. But she continued to eye the half-full flask, hoping he'd allow her another drink soon.

He held the silver flask in his right hand, resting it lightly atop the saddle's pommel, his long, tanned fingers wrapped loosely around it. Eyes focused there, Temple noticed the enormous ruby ring on his finger just as the magnificent stone caught the sun, reflecting a six-rayed star. Automatically she shut her eyes against the ruby's blinding radiance.

So her eyes were closed when the Arab lifted the flask directly above her head, turned it upside-down, and emptied it.

"Ooooooh!" Temple gasped in shocked surprise, her eyes flying open as the cool water saturated her limp blond hair and trickled down over her face. "Ahhh, yes!" She lifted her hands to smear the cool water over her feverish cheeks, her dusty throat, the sticky back of her neck. "Mmmmmm," she sighed as her soaked white blouse stuck to her flushed skin, cooling her.

She whipped her head around so quickly to smile her thanks, she unintentionally hit the Arab in the eye with a dampened lock of her tangled hair.

"Sorry," she said, horrified, and automatically raised her hand to his face. But his grasp was too quick, too strong. His fingers encircled her wrist, staying her hand. She looked at his eyes. "I was only going to—" Her words were choked off in her raw throat as she stared at those mysterious black eyes. Diamond drops of water clung to the long thick lashes, and a hint of red showed in the left eye from the whiplash sting of her flailing hair.

He didn't blink away the moisture from his lashes or close his irritated left eye, although she knew it surely hurt. He continued to stare straight ahead, urging his mount steadily eastward.

His single-minded determination was strangely comforting.

Confident he knew exactly where they were and how far it was to the next village, Temple exhaled heavily and lowered her eyes from his turban-covered face. She turned slowly to look straight ahead, as he was doing.

She clung to the saddle horn with both hands to keep from leaning heavily against him, lest he resent it. But it was all she could do to stay upright. In no time her poor back felt as if it might break from holding it rigid.

The burning sun overhead beat down with a vengeance from a cloudless sky, and a shimmering haze of heat rose from the desert floor ahead. The harsh, unforgiving landscape began to blur before Temple's eyes. Her lids grew so heavy, she could hardly hold them open.

The only sounds were those of the stallion's hooves

regularly striking the ground and the moan of the desert winds blowing against her face. Both were oddly sooth- ing, as was the sight of those tanned, well-tended hands loosely holding the reins in front of her. Firmly in com- mand of the galloping horse.

And of her.

Without warning the Arab dropped the reins, con- trolling the racing stallion with the pressure of his knees, and encircled her with strong arms to draw her back against his hard, supporting chest. Exhausted, relieved she'd been found by this calm, authoritative man, Temple put up no fight; sighing, she allowed herself to relax against him. A reward of gold beyond this Arab's dreams would soon be his. She'd see to it personally.

Almost immediately the pain of her aching back began to ease, and the slackening of tensed muscles was pure heaven. She smiled with pleasure and turned her face inward a little.

Her hot cheek resting against the flat muscles of his robed chest, she gazed again at those incredible ebony eyes. Surprisingly, the desert Arab was immaculate. His white robes were spotless, and his masculine scent was of clean, sun-warmed flesh.

She allowed her heavy eyelids to close completely over her bloodshot eyes. How fortunate she was. She could have perished alone in the heat and desolation of the desert. Or she could have been found by another tribe of lawless raiders like the savages who had heart- lessly dumped her to die.

Instead this kind, compassionate Arab had come along just in time. He was probably a simple, good- hearted bedouin who roamed the endless stretches of this harsh land eking out a meager living for him and his family. Chances were he knew—without the aid of a map—where every desert well and wadi and oasis and village in Arabia was located.

He would, she felt sure, take good care of her. It was her last thought before sleep overtook her.

It seemed she'd been asleep for only a few minutes when Temple was jolted awake as the lathered white stallion came to an abrupt, plunging halt.

She looked up to see those dark, heavily lashed eyes flick to her face as the Arab's arm tightened around her. It was then she realized she was no longer seated astride the stallion in front of him. She was lying across the saddle in his arms.

Temple jerked to total consciousness with a start as the Arab threw the reins to a waiting groom and gathered her more closely in his arms. Holding her against his chest, he threw a leg over the stallion's back and dropped agilely to the ground.

He lowered Temple to her feet and she immediately asked, "Where are we?" She looked around at the palm-shaded oasis. "Is this your village? Are we far from a city? Can you take me to a city so that I can send a cable to my family?"

Robed men swarmed around them, speaking rapidly, excitedly. Temple couldn't understand a word. She was beginning to grow uneasy again. What if none of them spoke English? How could she make them understand that she couldn't stay here? She had to get out of the desert. To get to a city. A real city.

"I can't stay here," she said to the tall Arab who had saved her. "I'm very grateful to you, but I must get to a larger village. Do you understand? I must go someplace where I can send a cable. My family will be worried."

The Arab gave no reply, merely took her upper arm

and propelled her forward. Temple reluctantly allowed
him to usher her through the crowd. Throngs of curious,
chattering men moved swiftly, respectfully out of their
way as she walked along beside the tall, silent Arab, hurrying to keep up with his long, fluid strides.

"Where are we going?" she asked. "Where are you
taking me?"

He said nothing, but inclined his turbaned head, indi-
cating a tent several yards ahead. The large white tent
was set apart from the other smaller ones at the edge of a
palm-shaded pool of clear sparkling water.

As they walked toward the tent, Temple looked
around curiously at the men lining their path—and soon
spotted, to her surprise and confusion, a number of the
same barbarian brutes who had captured her yesterday,
then left her in the desert to die. And there, towering
above the crowd, stood her hired head guide, the big
one-eyed giant, Sarhan.

Horribly, instantly, it dawned.

She hadn't been saved at all! This tall, white-robed
Arab propelling her toward the isolated tent was her kid-
nappers' chieftain!

"No!" The word tore from her aching throat. Her eyes
wild, she suddenly screamed at the top of her lungs,
balking, refusing to go another step, clawing at his hand
to free herself from his grip.

"Hush. Behave yourself," he warned in flawless
English, speaking in a voice so soft and deadly cold, it
chilled the blood in her veins.

The scream immediately died in her throat, and he
thrust her forward. In seconds they had reached the enormous white tent. Roughly he handed her into the spacious,
well-appointed desert dwelling and followed her inside,
pulling the flap closed behind them.

Turning to face him, Temple was almost paralyzed

with fear. Attempting to understand what this abduction was all about—fearing she knew—she looked questioningly at the tall Arab standing before her.

He pulled the white turban from his face, then flung it off his head. His hair was as black as the darkest desert night, and his was the handsomest, cruelest face she had ever seen. Tall and broad shouldered, he stood there in his flowing white robes, his ruby-adorned right hand resting on the jeweled hilt of a curved Saracen scimitar stuck in the sash at his waist. His black eyes narrowed as if in distaste.

Unable to tear her frightened gaze from his, Temple asked finally, "Who are you?"

"I am *El Siif*, Sheik Sharif Aziz Hamid," he said, casting aside his heavy white robes. "Get undressed."

8

At his shocking command, Temple's anger and pride shot to the surface. Shedding the last traces of debilitating fear and lethargy, she put her hands on her hips, narrowed her green eyes, and took a half step toward him, shouting, "No! I most certainly will not! Not now! Not ever!" Her voice rose as she added loudly, "I will *never* undress for you!"

She lifted her chin defiantly as she shouted, but her slender body was trembling.

Unperturbed by her outburst, the Sheik stood there waiting for her to calm down. His heavy robes cast aside, he wore a white shirt, dark riding breeches, and shiny black boots. The curved dagger, removed from his robe's sash, now rested in a smooth black leather scabbard at his waist.

"Never, never, never!" Temple continued to shriek, her wild eyes fixed on him.

The Sheik came toward her, his own eyes half-hooded, a light beginning to burn in their dark depths.

"Stay away from me," she ordered him, lifting her hands defensively. "I'm warning you!"

He continued to advance. She attempted to step around him, but he was too quick for her. He caught her in his arms and drew her to him. Certain she knew his vile intention, Temple shuddered with dread and disgust. She struggled in his powerful arms but couldn't free herself. She tried desperately to pull away as he bent his dark head and pressed his searing lips against her own.

His hot mouth on hers, she was crushed against the hard length of his warm body and she knew, sickeningly, that she was no match for his superior strength. She couldn't free her lips from his, couldn't throw off the strong arms enfolding her.

In her furious attempts to extricate herself from his fierce embrace, she pummeled his muscular shoulders and back, beating on him with all her strength. As her fists rained rapid but impotent blows on him, her right hand slipped on the slick silk fabric of his shirt, fell to his trim waist, and brushed against smooth leather.

And then Temple remembered.

The scimitar! The Sheik was wearing it. It was sheathed just inside the smooth leather her hand touched. In the blink of an eye Temple's fingers found and closed around the dagger's jeweled hilt as the Sheik's heated lips continued to move persuasively on hers.

With lightning speed she drew the razor-sharp dagger, pulled back her arm, and thrust the gleaming blade's tip into his ribs.

The Sheik's reaction was swift beyond belief. His mouth still fused hers, his strong fingers gripped her wrist to stay the blade just as it ripped through his shirt and pricked his flesh.

Slowly his lips released hers. He raised his head and looked at her, his dark, penetrating eyes unreadable.

Temple was instantly terrified. She had tried to kill him and failed. Would he kill her now? Would he take the dagger from her and drive it into her racing heart?

His fingers were firmly encircling her wrist, applying increasing pressure. Temple opened her hand and let the dagger fall to the thick Persian carpets at their feet. He released her at once. She stepped back fearfully and watched as he calmly began to unbutton his shirt.

He removed the shirt, and Temple's eyes, like his own, lowered to the blossom of bright red blood that had already begun to spread and trickle down his corded ribs. "Come here," he said, dabbing at the blood with his discarded silk shirt. Cringing, Temple shook her head, stayed where she was. His dark eyes lifted, touched her coldly. "I said come here."

She swallowed hard but didn't move. Hands balled into fists at her sides, she said unapologetically, "You aren't badly hurt." Hoping that it was true, she added, "It's only a scratch."

The words were hardly out of her mouth when she gasped, stunned, as his hand shot out like a striking serpent. He grabbed her arm, drew her to him.

His voice continuing to maintain a low, level tone, he said, "Since you seem so eager to taste my blood, I insist you do so. Go ahead."

"What . . . what are you saying?" Temple was baffled by his words. "That you'll give me another chance to kill you?"

"I'll give you another chance. Many chances. But first . . . "

He took her hand, guided it to the blood oozing down his side. Temple winced when her fingers touched the fresh, warm blood. She tried to pull her hand away, but he wouldn't let her. He forced her to leave it there until her fingertips were wet and red with his blood. Only then did he lift her bloodstained fingers up before her face.

"Taste it," he coolly ordered.

"I will not!" she hotly refused.

"It's your first and last chance," he said in low, level tones, shrugging bare shoulders negligently. And to her relieved surprise he released her hand, adding casually, "I assure you you will *never* get another opportunity to taste my blood."

Rubbing her fingers clean on her dusty riding breeches, Temple hissed, "Damn you, you are totally insane. A mad savage! A dirty, demented Arab beast!"

As if she hadn't spoken, he carefully blotted the residue of blood from his ribs with his shirt, bent, and picked up the dagger. Tossing aside the soiled shirt, he held out the jeweled hilt of the dagger to her.

Temple stared at the dagger, not understanding his meaning.

He prompted, "Go ahead, take it. Try again. Maybe you won't fail this time."

Her jaw hardening, her eyes snapping with anger and frustration, Temple reached out and took it. She gripped the handle tightly in her hand and looked up at him. Their gazes locked for a long tense moment. Her eyes were hot green fire. His icy black stone.

Big and bare chested, he stood there unmoving, his arms at his sides, his booted feet slightly apart. Silently daring her to try it.

Temple watched him closely, like a predator with dangerous prey. Was this a trick? Did he have another weapon hidden somewhere on his person?

"It's no trick," he said softly, as if he'd read her mind. "I'm unarmed." He lifted his leanly muscled arms and raised his palms. He turned about in a complete circle so that she could examine him.

When he was again facing her, he lowered his arms to his sides and asked, "What are you waiting for?"

She gave no reply, stared at him unblinkingly, wondering if she had the nerve. Could she actually bury the blade in his abdomen and twist until his lifeblood flowed from him? Could she kill this dark, dangerous Arab who very likely meant to rape and kill her?

Acting on the survival instinct so strong in all living beings, Temple abruptly lunged at the Sheik, intent on killing him before he could kill her. She brought the dagger's flashing curved blade up in a swift, underhand arc that would rip open his stomach if she succeeded in hitting her target.

She was quick.

But the Sheik was quicker.

His reaction was so incredibly swift, Temple never knew exactly what happened. She knew only that one second she had the dagger in her hand and was lunging at him and the next she was in his forced embrace, her arm twisted behind her back, the dagger now in his hand, its tip stuck beneath a pearl button at the center front of her soiled white blouse.

Poised, his dark eyes holding hers, he made her wait and wonder.

Temple's breath came in strangled gasps, and her heart throbbed painfully.

One quick flick of his wrist and the button flew off, the blouse parted over her breasts. She tensed and held her breath, bracing for what was to come.

But it never came.

A hint of a cruel smile touched his lips as he lowered the dagger and said, "You jump to conclusions, Temple. When I want you, you will know it." He set her back from him and added, "And when I want you, I'll take you without a struggle. You will gladly give yourself to me."

* * *

A long, perplexing stay in the lush desert oasis of Sheik Sharif Aziz Hamid had begun for a frightened and totally baffled Temple Longworth.

After his utterly arrogant pronouncement, the Sheik had turned his back on her and walked away. At the far side of the room he had stepped through some curtains and disappeared.

In seconds he'd returned to the main room, shoving his long, bronzed arms into the sleeves of a clean white shirt. He'd never looked at her. He hadn't said a word. Unhurriedly he'd buttoned the shirt, shoved the long tails inside his trousers, crossed the spacious tent to the entrance, bent his head, and ducked outside, leaving her alone.

For a long time after he'd gone, Temple continued to stand there, in limbo. Confused and frightened and angry. She had felt sure, when he had kissed her, that he'd meant to take her against her will. Had he stopped only because she'd tried to stab him with his dagger? Would he try again later?

She shuddered.

Why had he brought her to his oasis? How long would he keep her? And why did a wandering desert Sheik speak fluent, flawless English? And why did he . . . did he . . . Temple suddenly remembered.

He had called her by her name! He had called her Temple. She hadn't told him her name. He hadn't asked.

He already knew.

But how?

9

Temple forced herself to take several slow, deep breaths. She had to be clear-headed. She had to think. To figure a way out of this terrible predicament.

She looked appraisingly around the spacious room. A tall center pole supported the tent's high ceiling. The floor was covered with rich Persian carpets. A long divan and colorful hassocks were arranged around a low ebony lacquered table. On the table was an ebony-and-silver chess board with carved ivory pieces. Leather-bound books filled a tall ebony bookcase.

It was a well-appointed room, but the furnishings were not what commanded Temple's attention. Only the tent's walls interested her. She moved along them quickly, looking for an opening other than the main entrance. Her hands glided along, searching for a break in the creamy white fabric, but she soon ground her teeth in frustration.

There was no other entrance.

She glanced at the curtains through which the Sheik had gone for a clean shirt. She hurried across the tent, slapped at the heavy hangings until she found the separation, yanked them apart, rushed inside—

And stopped short.

The Sheik's bedroom.

It was like the man himself, she thought, shivering inwardly. Dark and exotic and intimidating. An over-size bed dominated the aggressively masculine room. Neatly made, it was covered with an inky black counterpane. A profusion of pillows—half of them black, half white—rested against the massive bed's tall ebony headboard. To the left of the bed was a tall, heavy wardrobe, beside it a many-drawered bureau. A discarded white shirt, stained with blood, was tossed atop the chest. To the right of the bed and not three feet from it was a long, comfortable-looking black divan with many cushions and a high back.

A lone globed lamp rested on an ebony night table by the enormous bed, the room's only light. Her eyes made a slow, assessing sweep of the Sheik's shadowy bedroom. Temple saw no entrance. No way to get outside without going through the tent's main room.

She hurried back through the curtains and into the large room. It had been several minutes since the Sheik had left the tent. Maybe, she thought hopefully, he had ridden away and left her here alone. Perhaps he had to tend to business at some other desert location and would be gone for hours. If so, she could slip out and get away before he returned.

A glimmer of hope putting a new spring into her step, Temple hurried to the tent's canopied entrance, lifted the flap, turned it back, and peered out cautiously.

And her heart sank.

"Damn him!" she muttered, her face falling like that of a thwarted child.

His back to her, the Sheik stood not twenty yards away, towering over a group of robed brigands gathered around him. His was the only uncovered head, and his black hair glittered in the strong sunlight as he leaned down to listen to a short little man standing directly next to him. The fabric of his fresh white shirt pulled taut across his back as he laid a long arm affectionately around his comrade's narrow, robed shoulders.

It was more than apparent that the Sheik was the camp's revered chieftain, the able leader they greatly respected, the beloved master they all gladly served.

Temple gritted her teeth and let the tent flap fall back in place.

Well, *they* could worship him for all she cared! But he was not *her* chieftain or leader or master. And she was not his liege or follower or slave. She wasn't about to bow down to him or to serve him in any way whatsoever.

Pacing, hugging herself with her arms, Temple soon passed from anger and frustration to a growing anxiety as she contemplated what might be in store for her. Although ignorant of most of their customs, she had heard that if an Arab Sheik saw a woman he wanted, he simply bought her or stole her and added her to his harem.

Dear God, was that to be her fate? It seemed likely that it was what the Sheik had in mind. Why else would he capture a white woman and bring her to this remote oasis? What use could the Sheik possibly have for her except . . .

A tiny gurgle of panic escaped her lips as Temple considered the horror of becoming the unwilling slave of this dark prince of the desert.

It was approaching sundown when the tent flap suddenly opened. Temple, seated on the long divan, sprang defensively to her feet.

The Sheik stepped inside. He was followed by a short, wiry little Arab man with a deeply lined face and a ready grin, and an Arab woman of medium height and stocky build who appeared ill at ease.

Gently taking the woman's arm, the Sheik said, "Temple, this is Rhikia. She will tend you while you are inside the tent." The woman bobbed her head. Her dark eyes met Temple's for only an instant, before she lowered them shyly. "Rhikia speaks no English," the Sheik continued, "but she is well trained and highly proficient at taking care of a lady's needs."

He waited for Temple to speak. She said nothing, just glared at him. He ignored her rudeness.

"And this," he said, pulling the short little man in front of him, "is my dearest and oldest friend, Tariz."

"*Ahlan.* Welcome!" Tariz said warmly, his white teeth flashing in a wide smile. "Rhikia and I will do everything in our power to make your stay a pleasant one." He salaamed to her then, his fingers touching first his forehead, then his chest.

He was so friendly, so eager to please, it was hard for Temple to keep from smiling back at him. But she managed.

Over Tariz's head, the Sheik said, "Outside the tent, Tariz will be at your side anytime I am not." He then looked down at the woman, Rhikia, and said something to her in Arabic. She nodded, and both she and Tariz promptly left.

As soon as they were alone Temple said, "So I'm to stay here in your tent?"

"You are."

"Oh? And where will you stay?"

That cruel smile, then: "Here, of course," he said, turned, and was gone.

Sunset in the Arabian desert.

Sheik Sharif Aziz Hamid stood alone on the crest of a great dune overlooking his sprawling camp below. His desert-bred stallion, Bandit, was at his side, nudging his master's shoulder with a velvet muzzle.

The dying sun had turned the golden sand to varying shades of pink and purple, and already guttered torches were flickering with light down in camp. A cooling breeze stirred locks of Sharif's black hair, billowed his shirt out in back, and blew orange sparks from the cigarette in his hand.

This desert was his favorite place on the entire earth.

And sunset was his favorite time of day in this desert.

The Sheik didn't fall to his knees and face Mecca as his Muslim followers did. But he experienced a great measure of inner peace whenever he was in his beloved desert at sundown.

A peace no other time or place afforded.

It was not so tonight.

He found no serenity in the desert sunset. No tranquillity in his hour of sacred solitude.

The Sheik lowered his gaze to the large white tent in the distance. He pictured the blond American inside who was his source of unrest. He flicked away his smoked-down cigarette and reached into his trouser pocket. He withdrew the shiny brass shell casing he carried with him always. Rolling the small metal casing back and forth in his fingers, he lifted it, focused on it with cold dark eyes.

In the fading light he could barely make out the unique manufacturer's stamp on the casing's flat bottom. But he knew it was there. He ran his thumb over the imprint that had been rubbed so many times over the years, it was almost worn smooth.

But not quite.

Sharif could still trace the damning telltale stamp, still feel it as he had on that long-ago day when the wise old Sheik he'd called Father had first given it to him.

Du-P

Sharif's firm jaw clenched reflexively and his eyes narrowed with the hatred that never left him. His hand closed so tightly around the brass shell casing, it cut into his palm.

In the Sheik's lamplit tent, a rebellious Temple stalked back and forth as day turned to night. A meal, served on a tray by the shy, dutiful Rhikia, sat untouched on the low lacquered table before the divan. A warm bath, provided by the smiling little Tariz and a muscular helper, was cooling and unused in the bedroom.

Temple had hotly refused to strip and get into the tub. Neither Tariz nor Rhikia knew what to do about it, so they'd left her alone.

Now, as the hour approached midnight, Temple walked back and forth, back and forth, before the tent's entrance. She felt hungry, dirty, and uneasy. She wondered miserably if the Sheik had actually meant what he'd said when he'd told her he would be staying in the tent with her. Afraid that he had, she didn't dare go to bed, tired though she was. She wasn't about to undress and lie down and drift off to sleep when he could walk in any minute.

Muttering to herself, working up her courage for when he did return, Temple felt ready to face him. Or so she thought.

A few minutes past midnight she heard his low, distinctive voice just outside. She stopped her pacing, hurried to the tent flap, and peeked out. The Sheik stood gripping one of the poles supporting the shade canopy, speaking in low tones to the burly Arab guard.

He radiated an unquestionable power and presence, and with the flickering torchlight casting shadows beneath his high, slanted cheekbones, he looked sinister, dangerous.

He moved and Temple jumped back. She commanded her heart to slow its fierce beating and rehearsed, one last time, exactly what she was going to say to him.

Her resolve slipped slightly when he came inside. He glanced at her, and he looked even meaner than when he'd stood outdoors in the torchlight. It was as if the sight of her evoked some powerful hatred or passion.

Approaching her, he said, "Why aren't you asleep?"

"I have a better question." She squared her shoulders, determined to stick to her guns and not shrink before him. "Why am I here? Answer me that!"

"In time you will know."

"That's no answer! How do you know my name? We've never met, and I didn't tell you. What's this all about? I demand to know why you brought me here and what you plan to do with me! Answer me, damn you!" she shouted in rising frustration, and stomped her booted foot.

"Be quiet," he said, and his tone, though low and soft, was masterful.

"I won't be quiet, and I won't stay here," she announced haughtily. "You can't keep me here. I'll get away from you. I'll escape. So help me, I'll escape you. You'll see! I'll run away, I will, I swear I will!"

Glaring at him, her green eyes snapping with scorn, Temple experienced a fleeting moment of triumph. She'd said what she had to say. Stood up to him. Hadn't flinched or backed away. Hadn't recoiled or lowered her eyes from his. Had met his intimidating gaze.

But she wished to high heaven she'd kept her mouth shut when the Sheik, now coolly impersonal again, said, "You force me to implement methods to keep that from happening."

He turned away and started toward the tent's entrance. Nervously she called after him, "Wh . . . what methods?"

He left without answering. He returned five minutes later with the sleepy Rhikia at his side. Temple looked from him to the servant, her perfectly arched eyebrows lifted questioningly.

He said, pointing with a long forefinger, "You will go into the bedroom with Rhikia. She will make up a nice bed for you on the divan. While she is doing that, you will undress. You will hand all your clothes—including your underthings—to Rhikia. You will get into the bed she's fixed for you, and there you will sleep." He paused for a couple of heartbeats. "Naked."

Temple wanted to shout at him that she wouldn't do it, he couldn't make her.

But she didn't dare.

There was about him—as he calmly issued orders—an aura of barely leashed brutality. A quiet but impressive display of raw, absolute power and total disregard for her dignity or even her life. He was a cold, savagely beautiful madman, and the threat of impending violence clung to him like the tightly tailored trousers he wore.

Meek as a child, Temple followed Rhikia into the tent's shadowy bedroom. Hands trembling, she unbuttoned her soiled blouse, shaking her head no when Rhikia reached out in an offer to help. The polite servant nodded, turned away, and began spreading clean white sheets on the long divan.

By the time Temple had stripped to the skin, her divan bed was ready. Face flaming, she hurriedly slipped between the sheets and watched as Rhikia carried away all her clothes, including her underwear and boots. As soon as the Arab woman had gone, Temple tossed off the covering sheet, leapt up, and blew out the lamp beside the bed.

She heard the Sheik speaking softly to Rhikia in Arabic. Then she heard nothing at all. Back in bed, the sheet pulled up to her chin, Temple waited in the darkness. Tense, trembling with shame and fear, she was sure that at any moment the Sheik would walk in, rip off the covering sheet, snatch her up, toss her into his bed, and force her to submit in the hot darkness of the night.

Long minutes passed.

Her teeth clamped together so tightly that her jaws ached, Temple lay rigid as a poker beneath the cool silky sheet, her arms crossed protectively over her bare breasts, her long slender legs pressed tightly together, bare feet crossed at the ankles.

Her eyes beginning to adjust to the room's darkness, she saw the curtains part and trembled involuntarily. The Sheik walked noiselessly into the room. Biting back the moan of terror threatening to erupt from her aching throat, Temple watched as he crossed the room.

Her racing heart stopped beating entirely when, unbuttoning his shirt, he came directly toward the long divan where she lay, naked and defenseless. She couldn't stand to look. She closed her eyes, squeezed them shut and waited—not daring to breathe—expecting to feel his hot breath on her face, his cruel hands on her flesh.

Seconds passed.

The rustle of clothing.

Her held breath escaped in a rush. Her heart started beating again. Temple cracked one eye open. Then two.

The Sheik stood between the divan and the bed—so close she could have reached out and touched him—undressing casually. His shirt was already off. In the shadowy light he stood there leisurely unbuttoning his dark riding breeches.

When the breeches were open down his naked belly, he paused and raised both arms above his head. Temple watched the pull and play of muscles in his smooth olive back as he ran his hands through his midnight hair. He yawned sleepily then and lowered his hands, hooking his thumbs into the waistband of his opened trousers. With one swift shove he sent the pants to the carpeted floor and stepped out of them.

Temple quickly closed her eyes again, but not before she'd caught a fleeting glance of him naked in the shadows. He looked big and sleek and dangerous. Temple waited in agony, knowing she was totally defenseless against him.

She breathed a shallow sigh of relief when she heard him getting into his large bed. Not daring to move a muscle, she peeked at him through lowered lashes.

He lay in the bed, the sheet riding his waist. Stretched out on his back, his arms folded beneath his head. Even in the unlighted, shadowy room, the darkness of the Sheik's bare shoulders and chest contrasted starkly with the whiteness of the sheets.

He exhaled heavily.

Temple remained as quiet as possible, hoping he'd think she was fast asleep.

When several minutes passed in silence, she supposed he was asleep and relaxed a little.

Then out of the darkness came that low, calm voice. "Now you cannot escape." His head turned slowly on the pillow. He looked directly at her, his eyes flashing in the darkness. "Surely even in America a lady can go nowhere naked."

"You'll pay for this, you barbaric bastard," she threatened with a strangled sob.

"Good night," said he, unfazed by the threat. "Sleep well, Temple DuPlessis Longworth."

10

The Sheik rose before the desert sun.

In the gray murky light of early dawn, he slipped silently from his bed. His glance immediately went to the pale blond woman on the divan.

She was asleep. Finally. He was glad. He wasn't sure, but he thought he had heard her weeping softly in the night. He hated hearing a woman weep.

His dark gaze riveted to Temple's sleeping face, Sharif stood naked above her, studying her carefully. She lay on her side, facing him, her knees drawn up in a fetal position. Tangled golden hair spilled across the pillow, and one long silky strand swirled appealingly across her cheek, its wispy end curled around her slender throat. The covering sheet had slipped minutely as she slept, revealing a bare shoulder and a portion of her ivory back.

Sharif's lean body tensed when she abruptly moaned, squirmed, and turned over onto her back, flinging a slender arm up above her head.

She didn't awaken.

She sighed softly and slept on, the long dusky lashes remaining closed over those extraordinary emerald eyes.

Her lips, having lost their habitual tightness in slumber, were soft and full and perfectly shaped. She might have been a child, she looked so young and innocent. Like a sweet, beautiful little girl.

Sharif's dark gaze lowered from her sleeping face to the swell of her breasts exposed by the sliding sheet.

This was no child. She was a woman. All woman. A beautiful, golden-haired temptress with more spirit than was good for a woman. Which made her nothing but trouble for a man. The muscles in his lower abdomen tightened, and his dark eyes narrowed.

One flick of his wrist and the covering sheet could be swept away. Then she would be stretched out naked and vulnerable before him, a lovely sacrifice on the altar of his innate lust.

Sharif turned away, a muscle spasming in his tanned cheek. He moved to the other side of the room and dressed quickly in the gray dawn light. In minutes he left the room, never so much as glancing at the sleeping Temple again.

In the tent's main room, he lifted the fragile cup of steaming hot, thick black coffee that was waiting for him. He lighted one of his favored French cigarettes and exited the tent. Just outside he saw the burly Arab sentinel who was supposed to be standing guard. He was not even standing, much less guarding the tent. Seated cross-legged on the canopied carpet, his rifle across his knees, he was dozing.

Sharif's face instantly darkened with anger. But he didn't awaken the sleeping sentinel. The harsh reprimand could wait. It was growing light now. The danger of attack from enemy tribes had passed with the night. The woman asleep in his tent was safe.

For now.

Sharif drained the last of his hot black coffee and set

the cup on a nearby table. He walked away from the lance-propped awning and the dozing guard. Moving quickly beneath the huge palms through the lush tropical growth that partially concealed his tent from the rest of the camp, he went to keep an early morning appointment.

In a designated grove of date palms just north of the sleeping encampment, Naguib awaited his master. One of the Sheik's most trusted lieutenants, Naguib was a fearless, loyal friend who could be unfailingly counted on to complete any duty assigned to him, no matter how difficult or dangerous.

For that reason, the sheik had chosen Naguib to ride alone across the desert all the way to the city of Baghdad. He was to leave today at sunup. Naguib did not yet know what his master wanted with him. It mattered not. He would obey without question.

Sharif reached the grove of date palms as the first pink rays of the rising sun colored the eastern horizon. The two men greeted each other, made small talk briefly, then Sharif reached into his shirt pocket.

He withdrew a small sealed envelope containing a message written both in English and in Arabic. He handed the envelope to Naguib. Naguib took it without question and carefully concealed the envelope inside his flowing robes, patting the spot just under his heart to show the Sheik it was well hidden and safe.

Sharif put a hand on the shorter man's shoulder and said in their native tongue, "You're to ride to Baghdad. As soon as you reach the city, you will send a cable to the address on the envelope." Naguib nodded his turbaned head in understanding. The Sheik continued, "Once you have sent the telegram—when you are absolutely positive that the message you carry has gone to the addressee—you stay on in Baghdad, cultivate

sources, make friends, glean what you can from
Mustafa's minions." He smiled then and added, "Try
not to enjoy yourself too much."

Naguib was smiling, too, his thoughts leaping ahead
to the many delights to be found in the sinful, seductive
city. Eager to be on his way, he assured the Sheik that
his trust had not been misplaced. He, Naguib, would see
to it the cable was sent.

He then salaamed to his respected leader and started
to step around Sharif.

The Sheik stopped him. "Be very careful, Naguib,"
he said softly. "Mustafa's raiders have been roaming
the desert again, terrorizing some of our neighboring
tribes."

The other man nodded. He knew. He had heard the
sickening story of how the hated Turks, heavily armed
and showing no mercy, had only last week surprised a
small family caravan resting at a desert well. The robed
horsemen had swooped down on a couple of young children who'd wandered away from their mother. When
the poor mother had screamed and run after them, the
Turks had shot her squarely between the eyes, then carried the children away.

It was no mystery what had happened to the helpless
little children.

All Arabia and North Africa knew about the ruthless
old Turk, Sultan Agha Hussain, and his fat son, Mustafa
Ibn Agha Hussain. Sharif's hereditary enemies, the
despised pair were unspeakably evil.

Especially the son.

Those whom Mustafa's men killed were said to be the
fortunate ones. To be captured and taken to the sultan's
seaside palace was a fate far worse than death. It was
whispered that Mustafa's sexual hungers were voracious
and depraved and that no young boy or beautiful woman

was safe once the poor unfortunate had caught his jaundiced eye.

"Do not worry, master," said Naguib, "I will take great care. No fat Turk's lawless horde can catch the elusive Naguib."

The Sheik smiled and nodded as Naguib again salaamed.

Sharif raised his hand. His fingers lightly touched his forehead, then his chest. *"Salaam aleikum,"* he said softly, "Peace be with you."

Temple opened her eyes slowly, saw the shimmering white tented ceiling above her, and was momentarily confused. Still half asleep, she didn't know where she was. What was this strange place? And what was she doing here? And why in the world was she naked?

Then it all came back in a rush.

Her eyes widening with remembrance and alarm, she grabbed the sheet more closely to her breasts, sat up, and looked at the Sheik's bed. On seeing that it was empty, she exhaled with relief.

Keeping the sheet wrapped securely around her, Temple rose from the divan. Pushing her sleep-tangled hair from her eyes, she looked across the room at the tall ebony wardrobe. It was, she assumed, filled with the Sheik's clothes. She had to have something to wear, and she had no qualms about taking one of his shirts and a pair of trousers. If his plan was to hold her prisoner here by keeping her naked, he had the wrong girl! He might be used to timid, spineless women who would never consider wearing men's clothing, but it didn't bother her one bit to dress like a man.

Temple started toward the wardrobe, but before she had gone just a few steps, the curtains parted and

Rhikia, bowing and averting her eyes, entered the bedroom. In her hand was a pair of embroidered blue velvet slippers, and over her arm was a pale yellow garment and lace trimmed underthings.

"What's all this?" Temple asked, startled by the servant's silent entrance and therefore irritated. Rhikia smiled shyly and held out the yellow dress to Temple. Temple refused to take it. "Whose dress is it? I don't want it. I won't take it." Rhikia shook her head in puzzlement and moved closer. Her dark eyes held an almost pleading look when she again attempted to press the garment on Temple.

"No, Rhikia," Temple said, supposing the dress belonged to one of the Sheik's lovers. "Take it away. I don't want another woman's dress! I won't wear it! Get out of here and leave me alone."

Stung by the reprimand that Temple's tone clearly conveyed, Rhikia bowed her head, nodded meekly, and began to back away.

From the corner of her eye Temple saw the curtains part again, saw the Sheik step inside. Tightening the hold on her sheet, she looked at him, lifted her chin, and said, "Tell her to take these things away. I refuse to wear them. Give them back to the harem slave they belong to!"

The Sheik approached, his bearing imperial, his dark eyes cold and emotionless. Temple felt her confidence waning, as it did whenever he was in sight. He placed a gentle hand on Rhikia's shoulder and said something to her in a kind voice. She quickly handed him the yellow dress, the lacy underclothes, and the blue velvet slippers. Then she disappeared through the curtains.

For a moment Sharif said nothing. Did nothing. He waited until he was sure Rhikia had left the tent entirely. Then the Sheik approached with a lithe quickness, his coal black hair and coppery complexion creating a menacing presence. His night black eyes and the small white dueling scar above his lip only heightened this aura.

When he stood directly before her, Temple had to tip her head back to look up at him. He was well over six feet tall and splendidly built, with broad shoulders, a trim waist, and long muscular legs. All that power, all that strength, all that forceful masculinity, made her feel small and weak and inferior.

That uncomfortable feeling, that terrible imbalance of power, was intensified by the fact that he was fully dressed while she was naked beneath the sheet. She swallowed with difficulty.

He spoke finally and Temple flinched.

"Never," he said in that same low, infuriatingly calm voice he always used, "treat Rhikia like that again."

It was the last thing she had expected him to say. Her eyebrows shot up. "I have no idea what you're—"

"Never," he interrupted, and although his tone didn't change, a warning light blazed in the depths of his dark eyes. "Rhikia is more than a servant, she's a friend. She does not understand the rudeness of a spoiled, ill-tempered American. I will not tolerate you hurting her feelings." Temple opened her mouth, started to speak, but the expression in his eyes stopped her.

He moved disturbingly closer. Temple started to step back but wasn't quite quick enough. His hand flashed out and his fingers curled around the sheet's top edge where it was pulled taut across her breasts.

"Let go!" she said, incredulous, her own hand clutching the sheet.

As if she hadn't spoken, he drew her to him by tightening his grip on the sheet and reeling her in. He pulled her up onto her bare toes and said, "Let your hands fall to your sides."

"Never," she said, wishing there was more command in her tone, wishing she could make herself look away from those scary, mesmerizing dark eyes.

"Now," he said, the chilling inflection of his voice mirrored by the icy authority in his eyes.

Hating him, hating herself for being afraid of him, Temple reluctantly released her hold on the sheet, allowed her weak arms to fall to her sides. Her heart tried to beat its way out of her chest as he eased her down off her tiptoes.

If he released his hold on the sheet, it would fall to the carpet and she would be left standing there naked before him.

Continuing to grip the sheet firmly, the Sheik held the yellow dress, underwear, and velvet slippers before her face. "These things are new, they were purchased especially for you," he said. "No other has ever worn them. They are yours."

Temple said nothing, just stared at him, afraid to trust to her voice to speak. Afraid he would release the sheet.

"The choice is yours, Temple," he said, tossing the clothing onto his bed. "Either you wear the things I bought for you or you will go naked. It makes no difference to me." His hand began to relax its hold on the sheet as he said, "Which is it to be?"

Temple's hands flew up automatically to grab his. "I'll wear the clothes!"

"A wise decision," he said, released the sheet to her clutching hands, turned, and walked away. At the entrance to the main room he turned back and said, "Cleanliness is *not* a matter of choice here. You will bathe or"—he paused and allowed his dark gaze to move slowly down her body—"I will give you a bath myself."

11

Noontime approached.

Temple was more at a loss than ever.

The elegant yellow dress, the satin-and-lace underwear, the gold-embroidered blue velvet slippers. Not only were they quite obviously brand new, all were a perfect fit. As if they had been commissioned especially for her by someone who knew her exact measurements.

How could that possibly be? In the first place, how could a desert sheik know anything about women's fashionable European clothes? And how could he possibly know what size she wore?

Then again, how was it that this enigmatic Arab chieftain spoke fluent, flawless English? Where had he learned it? From his personal servant, Tariz, perhaps? But if that were the case, where had Tariz learned English?

Frowning, trying to sort it out and discover the missing pieces of this bewildering puzzle, Temple smoothed her hands over the fine fabric of the dress. Whoever had chosen it had excellent, expensive taste. Save for the comfortable velvet slippers, she might have been ready to make an afternoon call on one of New York City's wealthy Fifth

Avenue hostesses with her mother. Or to go for a ride in London's Hyde Park with a titled gentleman.

Admittedly feeling better—physically, at least—after the morning's long, soaking bath, Temple, wearing the scoop-necked, short-sleeved summer dress, ventured out into the tent's main room.

No one was there.

Thank heaven.

Wondering where the Sheik had gone, wishing he would *never* return, Temple hoped he might at least stay away until bedtime. If there was one thing she didn't need in her agitated state, it was to be trapped inside this luxurious prison with him all day. Temple shuddered involuntarily as she relived those tense, terrible moments of the morning when the Sheik's hand had gripped the sheet covering her nakedness. She felt again—as if they were touching her now—those lean, tanned fingers thrusting intimately between the tightly pulled fabric and her bare, tingling breasts.

At the vivid recollection, a curious mixture of fear and heat rushed through her slender body, and Temple felt her face flush with disturbing warmth. Telling herself the harsh desert heat was responsible for the sudden rise in her body temperature, she took a bit of comfort in the Sheik's probable discomfort.

Imagining him bareheaded under the white hot sun of noon brought the beginnings of a smile to her compressed lips.

But that hinted-at smile died before it could be fully realized.

As if her errant thoughts had summoned him to the tent, the Sheik abruptly appeared. Just as she'd imagined, he was bareheaded. And he looked uncomfortably hot. His dark face shiny with sweat, his black hair glistening with diamond drop beads of perspiration. The white cotton shirt was damp and sticking to his skin. His sculpted bronzed shoulders and the thick dark hair of his chest showed through the sodden fabric.

The Sheik looked directly at her, but it was impossible to read the expression in his eyes. His manner, his face, his pantherlike grace, everything about him bred uneasy feelings in Temple. Those feelings were intensified when, nodding almost imperceptibly to her, he moved across the room and began unbuttoning his sweat-soaked shirt. When all but a couple of buttons were undone, he pulled the tails of the shirt free of his tan riding breeches, then drew the shirt up over his head and off in one fluid masculine movement.

Temple finally found her tongue. "What are you doing?"

"Preparing to take a bath," the Sheik said matter-of-factly, and stood holding the soiled shirt in his right hand.

"Here?" she asked, horrified.

"Where else?" he said, shrugging gleaming brown shoulders.

Temple purposely made a face to let him know she found him offensive. But she stared helplessly, unable to take her eyes off him. She couldn't help but marvel at the smooth olive skin, the hard muscle, the curves and flat planes of his magnificent body.

Her attention was immediately drawn to the rivulets of sweat trickling down his tanned throat into the dense growth of black hair that grew in an appealing fanlike pattern on his naked torso. He raised the soiled shirt to blot away drops of moisture from the crisp chest hair, and Temple felt her cheeks burn.

And she hated him for it.

She forced herself to meet his eyes. She looked at the Sheik contemptuously, wrinkled her nose, then turned away.

"If you're to clean up here," she said, trying for a degree of calm in her voice she didn't feel, "then I shall go outside until you have finished."

She waited, holding her breath, hoping he would allow it. He might, since numerous men were wandering about just outside the tent and she'd have no chance to escape.

"You'll go nowhere," he said in a flat, low voice. She sensed that he had quietly moved closer, was now standing directly behind her.

The scent of his sun-warmed flesh assailed her senses, as did the fierce heat emanating from his lean, perspiration-drenched body. She felt suddenly weak, half dizzy. She swayed slightly on her feet, fighting to keep her equilibrium. If she turned about, she'd bump into him. If he moved one step closer, she'd be touching him.

"Should you try to leave," he continued softly, "you will be brought back inside and made to sit quietly beside the tub while I bathe."

At the arrogant threat, Temple's innate pride reasserted itself. Angered by his proposal of such an indecent alternative and momentarily forgetting that he stood so close, she whirled about. And slammed into his naked chest. A sharp shriek of pain and surprise escaped her lips. In danger of losing her balance, she grabbed at him automatically. Quickly his hands lifted, clasped her upper arms to steady her.

"Damn you!" she said, one of her hands caught between them and splayed on his bare torso, the spread fingers threaded through damp curly chest hair. "Now see what you've done!"

"I've done nothing," he said, and calmly set her back, his hands remaining on her upper arms.

"You have," she argued, badly flustered and therefore furious. Her fingertips wet with his perspiration, her heart pounding, she said witlessly, "You . . . you've gotten my

dress dirty!" Frowning, she ran her moist fingertips over
the tight-fitting bodice where telltale stains of dirt and perspiration had been left from the brief but close contact
with his body. "Now what shall I do? What shall I wear?"

His hands dropping away from her, he said, "You will
simply put on another dress."

"Another dress?" Her voice had risen with her ire. "I
have no other dresses!"

"Yes," he said, "you have."

He turned away, crossed to the tent's entrance, called
for Tariz. In minutes Tariz came inside, followed by a
pair of muscular Arab men toting a huge, heavy steamer
trunk. The trunk was lowered to the carpeted floor, and
the bearers departed. Tariz, smiling and bowing, was the
last to leave.

"Just what is this?" Temple asked, eyeing the chest
suspiciously.

Sharif opened the lid. "Clothes," he said. "Dresses
and things for you."

When she made no move to see for herself, Sharif
rubbed his hands clean on his trousers, reached inside
the opened trunk, withdrew a shimmering white silk
evening gown, and draped it over the chest's open lid.
He reached for another, an afternoon dress of crisp lilac
cotton trimmed with delicate Irish lace. He tossed it atop
the white silk and reached into chest again. And lifted a
gorgeous gown of lush emerald chiffon, held it up for
her brief appraisal, then released it. The frothy green
garment fluttered back down to the chest.

"They're all yours," he said, taking out a large velvet-
lined tray filled with jewels.

Necklaces and bracelets and ear screws of diamonds
and rubies and emeralds were heaped in a glittering colorful mound in the velvet-lined tray. The Sheik placed
the gem-filled tray on the low table before the divan.

He turned back to the trunk, dipped both hands inside, and brought forth an array of lace-trimmed negligees and nightgowns and chemises and underwear and silken hose.

"I believe," he said, tossing the wispy underthings back into the trunk, "you'll find everything you need."

He waited for her to speak.

Temple said nothing.

She barely looked at the lacy underwear or the beautiful dresses or even the tray of sparkling priceless jewels.

Instead she stared at the tall, shirtless Sheik.

He had made her spend the long, frightening night totally naked, and she had cursed him for his cruelty. Had seethed at such inhumane treatment, hating the strange dark-skinned savage with all the passion of her being.

Now here he was offering her beautiful clothes and expensive jewels as if she were his adored mistress. And she hated him all the more. His intent, his plan for her, was becoming increasingly clear. While his command of the English language and his fastidious cleanliness made him seem a bit more civilized than his counterparts, he was, after all, only an amoral Arab.

"You arrogant Arab fool," she murmured, the affront and its meaning giving her courage. "You offer me a few showy dresses and a couple of gaudy baubles and expect me to do anything and everything you want?" Her eyes flashed with green fire that matched the exquisite emeralds in the velvet-lined tray.

"No. I expect you to do anything and everything I want, with or without the clothes and jewels." His sensual lips curled into a cruel smile. "And so you will."

Then without another word he turned, like a masterful matador turning his back on a raging bull, and walked away.

"The devil I will!" Temple said at last.

But she wisely waited until the Sheik had stepped outside to call for his manservant and could not hear her.

12

Naguib was pleased.

Four days and nights had passed since he had left Sheik Sharif Aziz Hamid's desert city. Naguib had encountered only a couple of small friendly caravans snaking across the endless sands.

His mount was one of the Sheik's desert-bred, blooded Arabians, a big, fast, well-trained stallion with stamina to match his incredible speed.

Loping across the endless dunes, Naguib patted his robed chest, as he had done dozens of times on this long, solitary ride. He smiled, satisfied. The sealed envelope entrusted to him by his revered leader rested safely next to his heart.

Before another twenty-four hours had passed, he would reach bustling Baghdad, go straight to the establishment where he could send a cable to the addressee on the envelope.

When it was confirmed that the wire had indeed been sent—and that it contained the exact words of the message personally written by the Sheik—he, Naguib, would go back outdoors, slip into one of the many dark, narrow alleys of the city, and burn the envelope and message.

When both were nothing more than ash, he would return to the sun-filled streets and begin a weeks-long quest for any scrap of pertinent information on the evil empire whose high-handed rule reached all the way to Baghdad. He would learn all that he could of the spreading migration of the greedy, hated Turks.

Duty first, then diversion.

Naguib began to smile. He was looking forward to a bit of selfish, satisfying pleasure that was to be his just reward for a job well done.

Envisioning a pleasing scene filled with beautiful dark-eyed women and exotic foods and cool hotel rooms, Naguib smiled broadly as the day drew to a close. He loped over yet another towering sand dune as the blood red sun disappeared completely, leaving only a bright orange gloaming of light above the horizon.

He topped the sandy rise and saw them.

An armed brigade of black-robed men was riding straight toward him. He hoped they were a friendly tribe. He didn't think they were. Soon enough he would know.

Nervously touching the envelope hidden inside his robes, Naguib pulled up on the stallion, then raised a hand in friendly salute. When it was not returned, he knew his thirty-eight years on this earth were about to come to an end. He looked wistfully at the dying summer sun and understood instinctively that he would never see it rise.

Naguib wheeled the big stallion about in a tight semicircle, then urged the tired, foam-flecked beast into a fast gallop back across the burning sands. Behind him he could hear the thunder of horses' hooves, the shouts of the bloodthirsty bandits, as they pursued him.

Naguib called on Allah for help. Not to spare his life; that was not important. But to keep hidden from these desert pirates the secret message he carried for his master. Racing headlong across the pinkened dunes, Naguib anxiously stuck a hand inside his robes. His intent: to retrieve the important envelope, put it into his mouth, and chew it up before he could be caught by his pursuers.

It never happened.

The lathered stallion gave it all he had, but the black-robed band caught up with Naguib, pulled him off his horse, and wrenched the envelope from his fist before he could dispose of it.

He lost all hope when, laughing and brandishing their rifles, they spoke to each other in Turkish. He understood only a few words of their language, but he recognized the name they bandied about to frighten him.

The hated old Turkish sultan's son, the evil Mustafa Ibn Agha Hussain.

"Daheelek," Naguib murmured as they threw him roughly to the sand and aimed their rifles at his turbaned head. *For the mercy of God.*

A measure of mercy was granted by his God.

Naguib died instantly from a half dozen shots to the head.

Within seconds the Turks had stripped him bare and left him there, where his bones would soon be bleached by the fierce desert sun.

Empty brass shell casings were scattered around his body.

The spent casings carried a distinctive manufacturer's stamp:

Du-P

Temple attempted, again and again, to find out why the Sheik was holding her. Was it for the ransom? Her family was extremely wealthy, they would gladly pay his price. Just name a sum and it was his.

But the Sheik showed no interest in money.

The first few days and nights of her captivity were particularly terrifying. She never knew what to expect. She didn't know what the uncommunicative Sheik meant to do with her. To her.

When he was inside the tent she was constantly on edge, unnerved by his cold, unsmiling aloofness, wondering what was going through his mind. Often she would look up to find him staring at her, cold and emotionless. She would meet his gaze and purposely glare at him with eyes in which stormy resentment burned bright.

He was unbothered. His expression never changed.

Even more unsettling was when he glanced at her and the curve of his mouth was brutal and his dark eyes appeared angry.

As if he hated her.

When he was outside the tent, she still couldn't relax. She never knew when he might return. She couldn't enjoy her morning bath for fear he would walk in on her. She couldn't take a nap knowing he might slip quietly into the shadowy bedroom and catch her unawares.

She spent most of the time pacing the carpeted floor, glancing anxiously every few minutes at the tent's entrance, expecting to see his dark head duck inside.

The long hot nights were even worse than the dreadful days.

Much worse.

Lying quietly in the pitch black darkness with the Sheik only a few feet from her was an agony of a kind she'd never imagined. His nearness was a very real and growing danger that robbed her of sleep and rest. Listening anxiously for the slightest sound, watching blindly for any movement that might signal his approach, Temple was so tense that her slender body ached from the stress.

Hour after miserable hour she lay there, wet with perspiration from the oppressive desert heat, her nerves raw, fearful of what her dark abductor might do to her in the still of the night.

Never for a moment could she forget that she was naked and he was naked and they were alone in this secluded tent. The knowledge excited her even as it terrified her.

And that really terrified her.

But she couldn't get out of bed and flee from his disturbing presence. He had seen to that. She had nothing to wear. The beautiful nightgowns and negligees and underthings he'd shown her from the large trunk had been promptly taken away. She was not allowed to wear them.

Just as on the very first night, she was forced to hand over her clothes to Rhikia each evening at bedtime. The servant took everything away and left Temple with no clothing of any kind. Nothing. Until Rhikia returned the next morning with a new ensemble for the day.

So she lay awake in the darkness, listening for the sound of the Sheik's slow, heavy breathing, which would signal he was asleep.

And even then, when her eyes grew adjusted to the darkness, Temple warily watched him as he slept.

Even in sleep he appeared dangerous. She stared at him and felt her stomach muscles contract, involuntary chills skipping up her spine. He looked for all the world like a sleek, untamed animal who was only catnapping. As if, even in sleep, all that masculine power was still tightly coiled and he might instantly spring up and pounce on his prey in the blink of an eye.

Temple kept cautious vigil for as long as she could hold her eyes open. And as she watched him, she confronted her worst nightmare. Her deepest fear was that she was to be kept here at this remote desert outpost forever.

Her abduction, she realized with numbing despair, had been carefully planned. Every detail had been worked out well in advance.

The Sheik seemed to know everything about her. He knew what kinds of clothes she liked to wear. He knew the shades and styles she most preferred. He knew her exact measurements. The beautiful gowns and dresses, perfectly sized, were unquestionably made especially for her. He even knew her shoe size and her underwear sizes. He knew which perfume she presently favored: an expensive Lalique flagon of Coty's new scent, La Rose Jacqueminot, was among the many personal items intended for her.

The glittering jewels had clearly been chosen to adorn her throat and wrists. The leather-bound books—all in English—were meant to be read by her. The sedate, pampering servant, Rhikia, who seemed to anticipate her every need. The sunny, brown-faced Tariz, who happily catered to her. All had been in readiness, awaiting her arrival.

In the deep lonely silence of the night, Temple was forced to face the frightening facts.

If Sheik Sharif Aziz Hamid wanted to keep her here, he could. For months or years, if he chose to do so. When she failed to show up in Baghdad on the appointed date, no one would know what had happened to her.

Search teams would be sent out immediately. But they would not find her. She would never be found. The Arabian deserts were vast and merciless. Thousands of square miles of harsh, hot emptiness. In time all hope would be lost and the search would cease.

She would be given up for dead.

13

But Temple had plans.

Come morning, Rhikia awakened her very early. The quiet servant had laid out her own clothes instead of one of the many new dresses. Her well-worn riding breeches and white blouse were now spotlessly clean and meticulously pressed. Her boots were polished to a high gleam.

Temple dressed in the familiar things, feeling somehow safer and more like herself wearing her own comfortable clothes. A degree of her natural confidence returning, she sauntered out into the main room—and immediately noticed that the tent flap was open wide. Drawn to it, hoping it meant she was to be allowed outdoors for a breath of fresh air, she crossed the tent eagerly.

But she jumped when she heard the Sheik's low voice—just beyond the tent's billowing white walls—order her outside. Tempted to neither answer nor obey, but so tired of being cooped up that she thought she'd go mad if she didn't get out for a while, Temple waited a couple of heartbeats, then regally exited the tent.

The Sheik—with little Tariz close on his heels—had brought around a beautiful stallion whose shimmering coat was a pale saffron hue. Temple's emerald eyes lighted with pleasure when she saw the big, exotic, incredibly handsome creature. Pointedly ignoring the big, exotic, incredibly handsome man holding the horse, she reached up to touch the stallion's velvet muzzle. "He's absolutely exquisite. What is he called?"

"His name is Toz," said Sharif, looking not at the stallion, but at the pale, slender woman whose loose golden hair was afire in the rising sun.

"Toz," Temple repeated, affectionately running a hand over the stallion's gleaming neck. "A strange name for a horse. What does it mean?"

The Sheik made no comment.

"The stallion's unique color gave him his name," Tariz spoke up eagerly. "*Toz* is Arabic for that rusty mist that shrouds everything when the desert wind whips up the powdery sands."

Temple smiled and said, "Then his name suits him well." She reached up and clasped a handful of saffron-colored mane and murmured to the stallion, "Will you allow me to ride you, Toz? Will you, boy?"

The horse danced excitedly in place, neighed loudly, and began shaking his great head up and down. Temple laughed delightedly.

"Toz is yours to ride," said the Sheik. "He is as gentle or as spirited as you wish him to be. I trained him myself. He will run swiftly, when asked gently."

Temple nodded. "May I ride him now? Take him out—"

"Tariz will ride with you," Sharif interrupted, stepped closer, lifted her from the ground, and sat her astride the heavily embellished Moorish saddle.

"That was totally unnecessary," Temple promptly informed him. "I have been riding all my life, and I'm quite capable of mounting a horse without assistance."

In a split second the Sheik had plucked her out of the saddle and planted her on her feet. His hands on her waist, his jet eyes holding hers, he said, "My apologies. I forgot for a moment that you are not a lady." He seemed to savor the words. His dark eyes narrowed then, and he added, "If you ever lay a whip to Toz, that same whip will be laid to you." He released her, turned, and walked away.

"The master loves his horses very much," said Tariz by way of explanation and apology.

Bristling, Temple replied, "It's nice to know he loves something, even if it's only an animal."

With that she looped the long leather reins over her mount's neck, grabbed the saddle horn, and swung up astride the big saffron-colored stallion. She wheeled him about, dug her booted heels into his sleek flanks, and guided him directly toward the retreating Sheik's back.

If Sharif was aware of the snorting stallion bearing swiftly down on him, he never let on. He didn't stop and turn. He didn't so much as look over his shoulder. He continued to walk away at a graceful, leisurely pace.

At the last possible minute his long arm shot out, and he caught the speeding stallion's reins and jerked his great head down. The horse stopped so abruptly, the unsuspecting Temple was thrown. She landed on her stomach, her hands stretched out before her, her eyes wide with shock.

Gasping for breath, she was yanked to her feet by a pair of strong brown hands.

"Are you all right?" asked the Sheik, his dark face

bent close to hers, his ebony eyes registering a surprising degree of worry.

"Y-yes . . . I . . ." She nodded, sucking in air eagerly. "I . . . I think I am."

His eyes changed immediately. Coldness replaced concern. Anger supplanted alarm. His hands gripping her upper arms, his dark head bent, he leaned close and said through thinned lips, "Do not forget who I am again. I am Sheik Sharif Aziz Hamid, the only son of Sheik Aziz Ibrahim Hamid, leader of the most powerful tribe in northern Arabia." He drew her closer, so close that her legs brushed his hard thighs and her stomach was pressed against his rock-hard belly. "Every man, woman, and beast here are under my command, in my control. All answer to me. All do as I wish or they reap the consequences. That includes you. You will obey me. If you do not learn to do so on your own"—his tone was level, but his words held a dark promise that unnerved Temple—"I will teach you." Flustered by his nearness, Temple found herself nodding her assent. "Now," he said, "assure me that you will give Tariz no trouble, and I will allow you to go on your ride."

For a second Temple didn't speak. But the look in his eyes told her that if she didn't agree to behave, she would be taken back to the tent at once and never be allowed to go riding.

"I will give Tariz no trouble," she said grudgingly.

The Sheik released her immediately. That cruel smile she'd come to dread lifted the corners of his full lips as he told her, "You couldn't have actually run me down. Toz is far too well trained to kill his own master." The smile broadened, grew more sinister. "You'll have to find some other weapon."

Wishing she could smack his smug, handsome face, Temple said, "And so I will. You may count on it!" She

spun around on her boot heel, lithely mounted the waiting
Toz, and rode away, her unbound hair flying about her
head.

Tariz, on his iron gray stallion, smiled down at Sharif
and said, "The American is a spirited young woman, is
she not, master?"

"Don't let her out of your sight," said the Sheik, snapping his long fingers. The dutiful Tariz went racing after
her.

"The Rub al Khali," said Tariz, pointing, "the Empty
Quarter. The world's largest sand desert. Thousands of
square miles of emptiness."

"Do people live there?" Temple asked, shading her
eyes.

Tariz grinned impishly and said, "Not for long." Then
he chuckled merrily at his own little joke, and Temple
laughed companionably with him.

The two of them were now miles away from camp.
Both were enjoying the long ride, especially Temple. It
was the first time she'd been outside the Sheik's tent
since her arrival. Having no idea how long it might be
before she was allowed out again, she was bent on glean-
ing all the information she could as to the chances of
surviving alone in the merciless deserts.

"So to ride into the Empty Quarter would mean certain death?"

Tariz bobbed his turbaned head. "Only the most
skilled of desert dwellers would stand a chance of making it through the Rub al Khali."

"Why?" she asked, staring at the desolate, sandy plain
stretching before them. "Is the Empty Quarter so different from the rest of the desert?"

"Ah, yes, yes, it is very different," Tariz said, spreading his short arms to encompass the miles and miles of emptiness he went on to describe. "We are right now on the beginning fringe of Arabia's dead southern waste, and this is like a cool, verdant oasis compared to what lies beyond."

"Extremely hostile land?"

"The normal midday temperatures in the summer months are one hundred twenty-five, one hundred thirty degrees Fahrenheit. It is so hot the skin tightens painfully, and the eyes ache at the pressure." He squinched his own eyes shut for emphasis. Then he opened them and said, "The only hope of making it across is after the rains of December and January, and then only if one has a great mastery of the desert." He stared at the endless dunes stretching before them like waves on a mighty ocean and said, "Over the years scores of bedouins have vanished from the world by attempting to cross the merciless Empty Quarter. Many of the wells have dried up, and unless a rider knows the exact location of the remaining wells, he will die of thirst before he finds one. And with the lack of water, the only food to be found is an occasional *dihab* or *jerboa.*"

"Oh? Some kind of hearty desert plants?"

"No. Lizards and rats." Temple made a face. Tariz turned in the saddle to look at her. "It is said that the bleached bones of many an ill-fated caravan litter the old trade trails."

"Mmm," Temple mused, then asked conversationally, "So if riding into the Empty Quarter is suicide, which way would you ride if you decided to go on a journey and hoped to arrive at your destination?"

Tariz laughed. "The only journey I ever make is from our village north up to the . . . the . . ." Abruptly he stopped speaking, looked slightly troubled, as if he'd almost revealed more than he should.

Although curious as to what he'd meant to say, Temple did not prompt him. He obviously was not supposed to tell her where he went when he traveled to the north. So instead of pressing him, she lifted a hand, pointed, and asked, "Is that due north?"

He chuckled merrily. "No, no, that is west." And he helpfully went about explaining how to divine directions without benefit of a compass. "Look down at the desert floor," he said. "You see the ridges of sand? They tend to run north from south. The moist morning breeze tends to come from the Gulf. The east." He pointed toward the east, and Temple nodded her understanding. He continued, "The wise desert traveler makes his best time between midnight and ten A.M.—resting the horse and himself in the P.M."

"I see," she said, showing a casual interest while taking great care not to alert him to her reasons for asking. "And he would need to know the location of the desert wells?"

"He would be a fool to set out otherwise."

Proud of his knowledge, Tariz was more than willing to share it. Temple paid close attention as he spoke of the landmarks designating those life-giving wells that contained sweet, pure water. "Mind you, a man must be extremely careful," he warned, shaking a finger at her. "Some of the wells have gone dry, while others have been poisoned by the vengeful Turks."

"Why on earth would the Turks do a thing like that?" she asked, brows knitted.

His dark little face darkened even more. "Because they are evil incarnate." Then, almost at once he brightened, smiled again, and said, "The sun is climbing. We must start back before the heat of the day sets in."

*   *   *

The early morning rides continued, and Temple found the aging little Arab to be the perfect companion. He was also endlessly resourceful. From him she learned more and more about her harsh surroundings and carefully stored all the pertinent information in her brain, to be written down when she returned to camp and had a moment to herself.

Tariz was consistently cheerful and talkative, unlike his maddeningly taciturn master. Hoping to learn more about the mysterious, unreachable Sheik and his purpose for holding her, Temple had wisely not yet questioned Tariz about her strange abduction. She knew that she first had to make a friend of him. She had gradually to gain his trust, to make him like her enough to tell her what she most wanted to know. Maybe in time he could even be persuaded to help her escape.

So, as they rode together, Temple laughed and joked with Tariz, taking care to ask the kinds of questions she knew the lively little Arab would be only too happy to answer. He never tired of telling her about the desert, his home.

The two of them quickly became friends. Temple genuinely liked the good-natured little man of indeterminate age. If she so much as smiled at him, he got excited and salaamed and grinned and chattered like a magpie. His dark eyes were constantly atwinkle and his manner unfailingly warm and friendly.

Unlike the dark, aloof man he served.

Clearly the cheerful Tariz loved the laconic Sheik. At Temple's gentle prodding, he revealed how proud he was to have been Sharif's personal body servant and faithful companion for all the years of the young Sheik's life.

That he would gladly lay down his life for Sheik Sharif Aziz Hamid was more than evident. That he would guard the Sheik's secrets soon became just as apparent when Temple cautiously attempted to learn more about the Sheik from his smiling little manservant.

Completely loyal to his chieftain, Tariz would tell her little, other than the fact that Sheik Sharif Aziz Hamid was a man among men, a scholar, a leader, and a mighty warrior.

"A scholar?" Temple arched her eyebrows. "You're teasing me, Tariz."

Excited, literally beaming with pride, he threw back his narrow shoulders and announced, "Young Sharif was educated in England. He is an Oxford scholar."

"No!"

"By Allah, it is true." He bobbed his turbaned head in emphasis. "When he went away to the university, his father and I were afraid he might never want to come back to the desert. I will never forget the day Sharif left us. The old Sheik and I watched with sad eyes as he rode away and we . . . we . . ." Abruptly Tariz stopped speaking and his expression changed. Contrite, he said, "Sometimes Tariz talks too much."

"No, no, you don't. Please, go on," Temple encouraged him. "Tell me about Sharif's father. And about his mother. Where are they? Why have I not seen either of them in camp? And why did his father send Sharif to England to be educated if he was afraid his son might not return?"

"It is time we start back," Tariz said, pulling up on his mount.

"Yes, all right," Temple drew Toz closer to Tariz. "Sharif's parents?"

"They are dead," said Tariz.

"I'm sorry," Temple replied. "Was it recently, or . . . "

Tariz shook his head. "The old Sheik has been dead for five years."

"And Sharif's mother?"

"A long, long time ago." Tariz kicked his gray into motion.

Temple quickly caught up to him and prompted, "The Oxford education?"

But Tariz had clammed up, refused to say anything more. "We must hurry back to camp. The master will be worried."

14

Naked Nereids in gay abandon.

The youngest and the fairest of Sultan Agha Hussain's large harem played in the enormous blue-tiled bathing pool while bright sunlight spilled in through the high latticed windows. The aged sultan's son, the indolent, obese, thirty-five-year-old Mustafa Ibn Agha Hussain, watched the young women from his perch at pool's edge.

Lolling lazily on a many-pillowed divan, Mustafa greedily devoured candied dates from a silver tray as the most beautiful of his father's many young female slaves splashed about and squealed.

Wiping his plump fingers on his white robes, Mustafa smiled with pleasure when a phalanx of beautifully built black eunuchs appeared. He licked his lips lustily when the tall, lithe Nubians disrobed in preparation of the daily bathing rituals.

The women did not bathe themselves. They were not allowed. They could frolic together in the water, they could giggle and tease each other and indulge in mock fights, but only this team of handpicked Nubian eunuchs bathed them.

And while the eunuchs sensuously scrubbed the lovely young nymphets, Mustafa paid close attention, carefully appraising, studying, and finally singling out from the bevy of bare beauties not one, but three. Two of those chosen would accompany him directly to his private chambers for a morning sexual romp. The third would be sent to his eighty-one-year-old father.

A greedy, selfish man, Mustafa purposely chose for the ailing Agha Hussain a woman he wouldn't particularly want for himself. The old sultan's eyesight had been failing for years; he never knew the difference. When the conniving son swore to his father that only the fairest of the harem were sent to his bed, the sultan believed him and warmly welcomed the woman.

Popping another candied date into his loose-lipped mouth, then sucking on his short, bejeweled fingers, Mustafa made the morning's choice. He picked for himself a pair of tall, slender, dark-eyed beauties with full, high breasts and long, shapely legs. For his father he chose a short, full-figured girl who, though fair, did not appeal to him.

His choices made, he struggled to get up from the divan. Far too jealous to allow his muscular bodyguards inside the bathing chamber, he puffed and labored and finally managed to lift his heavy body off the couch.

Looking forward to a full morning of delightful libidinous diversion, he exited the blue-tiled bathing room. Then, flanked by his two able bodyguards, he headed directly for his spacious suite, which lay just beyond the bathing room.

The choice location and the suite's unique design had been commissioned by Agha Hussain and had originally been the old sultan's own personal suite. Behind weighted, gold-threaded brocade curtains that ran the length of the room, a latticed wall separated the blue-tiled bathing room from the plush chamber.

The curtains could be drawn so that the suite's occupant or occupants could—if choosing not to go to the bathing chamber—nonetheless observe the bathers. From the first time he'd slipped into his father's suite at age fourteen to spy on the unsuspecting women, Mustafa had vowed to make the chamber his own. He had carried out the plan a decade ago when he turned twenty-five.

His father had been moved to a lesser suite within the palace, and Mustafa had threatened the servants with their lives if they failed to convince the half-blind sultan that he was merely confused, that he had not been moved at all but was in the same chamber where he'd always been.

Now, as the rotund young ruler lumbered down the hallway toward the master suite, he was well pleased with himself and his lot in life. His father, he mused joyfully, could not live much longer. With Agha Hussain's death, Mustafa would be a very powerful man. He would finally hold the exalted position he relished.

Ah, life was good indeed.

The Ottoman empire controlled much of the Middle East. His powerful Turkish dynasty not only ruled Palestine and all her neighboring lands, it dominated the eastern and western coastlines of Arabia. He foresaw more expansion in the future, and why not? The British, having no wish to involve themselves in ancient rivalries, hadn't raised a hand to interfere. So why not expand the growing base until nothing was left for the hated Arabs but the worthless Rub al Khali?

Mustafa chuckled at the notion.

Waddling into his cool, sea-fronting suite, he gleefully envisioned all the troublesome Arabs being banished to the waterless wastelands of the useless Empty Quarter until they were brought to heel and would bow down before him.

Particularly pleasing was the idea of the damnable, imperious Arab sheik he'd hated since boyhood kneeling before him, begging for mercy, swearing allegiance. There was no one on earth he'd rather break than the despised Sheik Sharif Aziz Hamid.

"Excellency." The soft feminine voice snapped him out of his pleasant reverie.

Mustafa turned to see the two tall female slaves, dressed now in seductive clothing. Harem pants of gauzy transparent silk revealed long legs and flaring hips. Short colorful vests, provocatively open, revealed teasing glimpses of their full, high breasts. Bracelets of gleaming gold decorated their slender arms, and tiny gold bells encircling their shapely ankles tinkled as they walked toward him.

"Ah, yes," Mustafa said in his native tongue, holding his arms open wide in invitation, "come. Pleasure me, my pretty pomegranates."

The beautiful slaves promptly obeyed.

If either of the young women found the portly sultan with his soiled robes and smelly, unwashed body repugnant, they knew better than to show it. Every slave in the evil emir's empire knew of his penchant for cruelty. As distasteful as it was to make love with a soft, overweight man who, after watching the others bathe, always forgot to wash himself, they never complained lest they be tortured and beaten.

"My master has chosen well this morning," said the woman garbed in sky blue as she took his hand and led him to the satin-covered couch that had been specially built for the purpose of copulating.

"This is true, Excellency," said the girl swathed in

pale pink. "We are so honored that you picked us. We wish to make you happy."

"You had better make me happy," said Mustafa, and standing beside the unique divan, he ordered them to undress him.

When he was naked, the slave girls—one on either side holding his arms—helped ease him down upon the divan that was really an upholstered slant board. The board had come about when his father had heard stories of a fat maharajah who had had great difficulty in having sexual intercourse until, employing the method used to aid elephants mate, he'd had such a board built for himself. After that, it was said, the maharajah had been able to perform admirably.

Agha Hussain had immediately commissioned such a divan/board built for his seventeen-year-old son. With the aid of the board and the help of a beautiful slave twice his age, young Mustafa had—for the first time in his life—been able to achieve the sex act and attain satisfaction.

He had used the board ever since.

Everything was now ready. He was stripped and resting comfortably on his cushioned slant board. A golden goblet filled with his favorite liqueur awaited him. Chocolate bon-bons from Belgium rested on a golden tray at his elbow. Exotic oils were heating in tiny vials over a brazier's small flame. A lute played softly just beyond the tall front windows that were thrown open to catch the sea breezes.

His white belly shaking with laughter as one of the girls teasingly tickled him under his double chins, Mustafa folded his fleshy arms beneath his head.

"First you will dance for me," he said, and it was an order.

The words had hardly passed his slack lips before the two women were swaying seductively to the haunting melody from the hidden lute. Their tall, near naked bodies moving slowly, sensuously, as if in invitation and yearning, they willingly performed, just as they would soon willingly do any and all of the outrageous things this depraved man might require.

Licking his slack lips, Mustafa lowered a hand, ran his fingers through the damp, wispy hair at the middle of his chest, and was about to call one or both of the girls to him when a loud rap on the chamber door made him cut his beady dark eyes to the closed portal.

"Enter," he called out, not bothering to cover himself.

The girls continued to dance. The door opened and Mustafa's loyal manservant, Alwan, entered, carrying a small silver tray upon which lay a crumpled envelope.

"Forgive me, Excellency," he said. "I was told you would want to see this immediately."

Frowning, Mustafa motioned the servant forward. "What is it? What have you brought me?"

"See for yourself, master." The servant handed over the envelope.

Mustafa's scowl deepened when he took the message out of the envelope and looked at it. "You know I read neither Arabic nor English," he said irritably. "Get Jamal in here!"

"Right here, Excellency," said the bowing interpreter, stepping inside. Jamal, who had been waiting just beyond the open door, hurried across the richly carpeted room to where his leader lay naked and frowning on his pillowed playground.

"What does this say?" Mustafa asked, thrusting the message at Jamal.

Interpreting, Jamal read it aloud, and Mustafa's annoyance vanished. He began to smile, and his beady black eyes lighted with pleasure. "Where did you get this, Alwan?"

"Your men took it from a lone Arab rider in the northern deserts three days ago."

His smile growing broader, Mustafa fell to pleasantly pondering what he might do with this newly gleaned knowledge. Forgetting the others were present, he stopped smiling and his round face took on an almost somber look as he considered and discarded several options before hitting on an idea that pleased him.

Several tense moments passed for those in dutiful attendance before finally Mustafa's beady eyes began to shine anew and he gave a great shout of laughter that caused his bare belly to shake and roll like the waves on the sea below his cliffside kingdom. All immediately laughed with their merry master.

When the laughter died down a bit, Mustafa tried but failed to snap his short, beringed fingers. Pointing, he commanded, "Summon my top lieutenants! I have an important assignment for them."

And fell once more into fits of gleeful laughter.

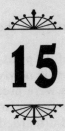

15

Days.

A week. Two.

Three weeks went by and Temple was, admittedly, treated well in the lush desert oasis of Sheik Sharif Aziz Hamid. She wanted for nothing in the way of creature comforts. She was pampered and cared for by Rhikia and watched over solicitously by Tariz.

Early each morning she was allowed to take a long ride on the saffron-colored stallion, Toz. The rides were exhilarating and enjoyable, but more important, they afforded her the perfect opportunity to better acquaint herself with the dangerous deserts that she planned to soon cross alone.

If the friendly little Tariz did not escort her on the daily morning rides, his handsome, hard-faced master rode with her on one of his two favorite Arabian mounts. Bandit, the magnificent milk white stallion on which she'd first seen him, was alternated with Prince, a fleet-footed black whose shimmering coat was the exact hue of the Sheik's luxuriant locks.

Those early morning rides were as different as the men who accompanied her.

If Tariz was with her, she questioned him, in a casual manner, about the many trade routes crisscrossing these inhospitable lands he knew like the back of his hand. Pretending nonchalance, she listened closely and hung on to every word he said. Then, fearing she might arouse his suspicions, she would abruptly change the subject.

The two of them laughed and chattered like children, and Temple was amazed at how much he knew of the civilized world. He swore he'd never been farther away than Cairo but told her proudly that he had read all the leather-bound books in the Sheik's tent not once, but twice.

"You know, Tariz," she said early one morning when they had dashed across the sand dunes and then pulled up on their stallions to rest, "you are highly intelligent and better educated than many Europeans and Americans. You could be much more than a servant. You could hold an important, responsible position in the business world. You would be a great asset to an international company. You could travel extensively, meet many interesting people, and command respect. Best of all, you could make a great deal of money."

"A heart free from care is better than a full purse," was his quick reply, followed by an ear-to-ear grin.

Tariz was, Temple realized, a happy, content man.

She had no idea if the enigmatic master he served was happy or content. Furthermore, she didn't care.

When the Sheik rode with her, he said little, never laughed, revealed nothing of his mood or his feelings. The only real communication she had with him on those rides was the camaraderie that existed between two people who had a great passion for fast, beautiful horses.

Riding knee to knee on spirited, equally powerful mounts generated—if only for a few fleeting moments at a time—a curious unspoken bond. When their steeds raced stride for stride and she felt the warm desert wind on her face and the mighty stallion's heart beating between her trousered legs, Temple would turn her head quickly. And she'd catch an unguarded expression on the Sheik's dark face that told her he shared the same nameless joy she experienced.

Those rare moments were the only times she was remotely at ease with him. Otherwise she was constantly on guard, anxious and distrustful of this strange man who could be brutal and insensitive. When she stole covert glances at his face, she saw the potency there, the cold intensity. It was frightening.

All that savage vitality and dark sexuality were a constant threat to Temple. And she hated him for it. She despised him for possessing the power to make her feel uncomfortable and awkward and afraid.

No man had ever had the upper hand with her. She had never allowed it. Now this debonair savage dominated her with nothing more than his intimidating presence and cold good looks.

Temple caught herself vacillating constantly, which was totally unlike her.

One moment she'd decide her best strategy was to keep as quiet as a mouse, to stay out of his way as much as possible, to avoid attracting undue attention to herself. She would, she resolved, make herself so still and insignificant, he would take no notice of her. Then he would leave her alone.

The very next minute she would change her mind completely and vow to fight back. She would bring him down a peg, let him know he couldn't bully her. No man could. She would show this dark devil of the desert that she had no fear of him.

When she was in such a reckless mood, Temple attempted—time and time again—to goad him, to effectively defuse that silent but ever-present sexual threat. She insulted him. She ridiculed him. She derided him.

Her innate temperament governing her rash actions, Temple purposely broke the uncomfortable silence between them one morning as they rode. She abruptly pulled up on her lathered mount. The Sheik swiftly halted his black stallion, rode back to her.

She looked at him angrily and said, "Who are you, really?"

"I have told you many times."

"Tell me again."

"I am Sheik Sharif Aziz Hamid. *El Siif.* The Sword. Lord of the desert, defender of the faithful."

"Is this your custom, then? To kidnap helpless women and hold them against their will?"

"You are the first," he said calmly, resting a tanned hand on the saddle horn, sparks of red fire leaping from the enormous ruby on his finger.

"I don't believe you!"

"That is your prerogative."

"Yes, it certainly is, and don't you forget it." Her emerald eyes narrowed when she added, "Now hear this, O great lord of the desert, I don't know who you really are or what you want with me, but you've picked the wrong woman. I am no coward! I am not afraid of you!"

"You have pointed this out many times." A faint, derisive smile lifted the corners of his full lips as he asked, "What is it, Temple? Can't you convince yourself?"

"Don't you dare make fun of me!" she yelled at him. "I warn you, if you ever try to lay a hand on me, I'll kill you. I will, so help me. I'll kill you if it's the last thing I do on this earth!"

"Stop shouting, please," he said softly. "It's most unladylike."

"I'll shout as often and as loudly as I please!" she screamed at him. "It's not like you're some fine gentlemen! You're not. You're an animal. That's what you are, that's *all* you are." She made a sour face and her eyes blazed. "No dirty, backward, illiterate Arab can tell me—"

In an arrow-swift movement his hand shot out and grabbed her startled stallion's reins. He dismounted and hauled her out of the saddle. Fierce as a hawk pouncing, he was on her, pressing her back against her horse with his tall, lean body.

His eyes as black and as cold as chips of basalt, he said, "Be careful you do not overstep your bounds and anger me. I am not one of your adoring British fools, that you may speak to me any way you choose. Your beauty has no power here, Miss Longworth. None. *I* am the only force. *I* am the one who gives the orders, not you." He moved aggressively closer, so close she could feel the saddle's stirrup cutting into her back, and she winced. Yet far more disturbing was the fierce heat and hardness of the lean, muscular body crushed suffocatingly close to hers. "*Never* forget that it is I who holds your fate in my hands. You are impotent against me; I can and will do with you as I choose. Do you understand me?"

Trapped, trying desperately not to tremble against him, Temple remained mute. Her jaw locked, she refused to reply. He lifted his hands, cupped her cheeks roughly, turned her face up to his, and said again, "Do you understand me?"

"Y-yes," she finally muttered grudgingly, hating herself for knuckling under to him.

"Say it. Say you understand me."

"I understand you," she replied, frantic for him to release her.

His hands stayed on her face, his icy hot gaze lowered

lazily to her lips. For a few anxious heartbeats she thought he was going to kiss her. She was certain of his intent when his dark head lowered slowly and his cruel mouth opened slightly to reveal his perfect gleaming white teeth.

His lips hovering a scant inch above her own, the Sheik said, "Do not test me too often. One day even I might run out of patience."

Abruptly he lifted his head, his hands dropped from her face, and he stepped away so fast that Temple blinked and sagged back against her horse.

The Sheik remounted and rode away without a backward glance. Temple swallowed hard. She had no idea where they were or how to get back to camp. She suspected the Sheik had planned it that way. She had no choice but to climb into the saddle and follow him. He didn't look at her or say a word for the remainder of the ride.

Temple was more than a little relieved when finally they reached the relative safety of the busy camp.

The long hot afternoons belonged to Temple. The Sheik was otherwise engaged. Mildly curious, she had asked Tariz what kept the Sheik occupied in the afternoons. Half expecting to hear that the inherently sensual Arab leader whiled away the hottest hours of the day in the arms of some adoring, dark-eyed female, she was oddly relieved to learn that he spent the time schooling his magnificent horses, training his hunting falcons, and presiding over tribal meetings.

And who knew what else.

All she knew was that the afternoons were hers and she was able to relax somewhat. She read and rested, grateful to be alone and confident that the dark man she feared and hated would stay away from the tent until sunset.

Evenings she donned one of the elegant new gowns Rhikia laid out for her to choose from. Then, after selecting the appropriate jewelry to complement the gown's cut and color, she would clasp a necklace of emeralds or diamonds around her neck or slip a sapphire-and-diamond bracelet on her wrist along with matching ear screws.

Thus dressed appropriately for dinner, she dined with the silent, immaculately groomed Sheik.

After learning of his Oxford education, Temple, seated across a candlelighted table from him in the tent's main room, broke the silence one evening by saying impulsively, "I've found you out, Sharif."

For a split second his dark eyes flickered as if she had said something startling. But his voice maintained that low, even tone when he replied, "Have you? And just what have you learned about me?"

"That you were educated at Oxford. That's why you speak fluent English."

He shrugged and wrapped his long tanned fingers around a silver goblet. The ruby on his hand caught the candle's glow. She noticed that a perfect six-faceted star appeared in the stone's face.

"Many people are educated at Oxford," he said, picked up the goblet, and drank.

"Not piratical savages."

He swallowed slowly, set the goblet down on the white cloth. "Piratical savages, yes—and a noble heritage it is, too," he said, but his dark eyes narrowed minutely and the tiny white scar above his lip seemed to stiffen as he added, "While your Anglo ancestors were painting their faces blue and worshiping at tree roots, these piratical savages had charted the stars and timed the tides."

"Painted their faces blue . . . that's utterly absurd!"

"Then tell that to Walter Scott and your Mark Twain." He leaned forward and declared softly, "*We* are the lineal heirs of a very ancient civilization."

"I've no doubt you are," she said, leaning forward as he had done. "But why would an Arab Sheik's only son choose to be educated in England?"

"Why would an American aristocrat's only daughter choose to cross the Arabian deserts?" was his reply.

Temple was taken aback. Her brows knitted together. "How do you know I'm an American aristocrat's only daughter?"

The Sheik laid his white napkin on the table, pushed back his chair, and rose. "If you'll excuse me, I believe I'll have a walk before bedtime."

And he was gone, leaving her to worry and wonder how he knew so much about her while she knew so little about him. She still had not learned the reason for her strange abduction. Obviously it had to do with her being an American heiress, yet money didn't seem to be the object.

It was a mystery.

He was a mystery. He had revealed nothing of himself in all the time they had been together. She knew him no better after three weeks than she'd known him that first hour of her captivity.

She lived in his tent. She wore his clothes. She ate at his table. She slept in his bedroom. But she did not know the man.

The Sheik was a paradox beyond comprehension. As was her questionable reaction—and growing attraction—to him. It troubled Temple that her hot hatred for him was already beginning to cool. She didn't understand him. She had never known anyone like him. He was the coldest, cruelest man she'd ever seen one minute, then uncommonly kind, almost tender, the next.

He frustrated her. He frightened her. He fascinated her.

She was not herself anymore. She didn't feel like Temple DuPlessis Longworth.

The Sheik was not the only one she didn't know. She no longer knew herself.

16

The warmth and beauty of the seductive desert nights and the constant nearness of the coldly handsome Sheik had begun to take their toll on Temple. When he was with her, she wished he would go away. But when he was away, she lay awake, tense and restless on her pillowed divan, dreading—at the same time awaiting—his return.

On those occasions when midnight came and went and still he had not returned to the tent, Temple couldn't help but wonder where he was. And what he was doing. She had caught glimpses of other women—Arab women—in camp. Was he with one of them? Was he lover to some exotic dark-eyed, dark-haired beauty? While she lay naked and alone in the hot darkness, was he lying naked in the arms of a favored lover?

When finally, in the deep of the night, he returned to the tent, Temple lay silent and tense in the darkness, listening to the brush of fabric as he stripped. And when he stretched out on his bed and was so close she could almost reach out and touch him, she was sometimes tempted to do just that.

She never did.

And she was horrified that she was even imagining touching him. But she was. The Sheik was an arrogant and dangerous savage, but a beautiful one. His presence was overwhelming. He was a menacing, masterful, magnificent specimen of manhood.

Dark, intense, and erotically handsome. That strong masculine face. Those cold yet compelling jet black eyes. His flawless olive complexion. And the lean, muscular body.

The mere sight of him had the power to stir her shamefully. Quick, scary surges of primal passion—to the degree that long after he had gone to sleep, she continued to lie awake.

There had been nights when, blinking to see better in the inky darkness, she had gazed helplessly at the splendid bare body of the mysterious man she no longer hated as violently as she should. Mesmerized, she watched the gentle rhythm of his breathing and the rise and fall of his rib cage beneath his smooth, tanned skin. And it seemed as if the walls of the tent pulsed and throbbed, moving in slowly around her, smothering her, the potent sexual milieu sucking the very air out of her lungs.

It was then, as she lay breathless and tense, watching the slumbering Sheik, that crazy thoughts ran through her mind—like getting into bed with him while he slept peacefully on, unaware of her presence. Lying close beside him in the stifling sensual darkness. Pressing her bare taut body intimately against the heat and hardness of his. Sweeping her hand familiarly over the muscled contours of his naked chest. Raking her nails through the thick growth of crisp raven chest hair. Experiencing the tingling sensation of feeling the steady cadence of his heart beating through her sensitive fingertips.

Temple was distressed and ashamed of having such

indecent thoughts, but she couldn't keep them from recurring.

In the harsh light of day she was far less vulnerable to the dark, mysterious man whose nightly nearness disturbed her rest. Seeing the Sheik in the hot desert sun in his native dress made it easier to remember exactly who he was.

He was an Arab, a lawless Arab chieftain who had taken her against her will. She was revolted by the heinous act of this uncivilized Barbary pirate. He knew no shame or remorse. Had less regard for her than his blooded horses stabled just beyond the village or his hunting falcons perched atop their blocks.

She was just grateful that the dark devil hadn't harmed her. Yet.

Still she sensed, instinctively, fearfully, that if she didn't get away from Sharif Aziz Hamid very soon, his egotistical prediction made on her first day in camp would come true.

And if I want you, I'll take you without a struggle. You will give yourself to me gladly.

She could wait no longer to escape!

Temple's carefully made plans to get away were almost complete. Not trusting her memory to recall all that Tariz had told her of the land and the wells and routes leading out of the desert, she had requested a pad and a pencil, explaining that she enjoyed sketching. She had drawn a crude map and then concealed it beneath the cushions of her divan.

A canteen of water and some dates and nuts and other edibles soon joined the hidden map. All she lacked was something to wear on her ride across the desert. That would be the tricky part.

But she managed to hide a dress.

Each day toward dusk Rhikia brought several elegant gowns to the Sheik's tent, and it was always from among these that Temple was to choose one for the evening. This time Temple acted as if she couldn't make up her mind which one she wanted to wear. All were so lovely, she would need a few moments to decide. Pondering, making faces, she held up one dress, then another. Understanding, Rhikia smiled, turned away, and busied herself with laying out lacy underwear and checking the temperature of Temple's bath water.

By the time the unsuspecting Rhikia turned back, Temple had hidden—beneath the pillows of her sleeping divan with the rest of her stash—a white silk dress.

"This one," Temple said, smiling, holding up an ice blue evening gown of shimmering silk shantung. "I'll wear this blue one tonight."

Rhikia nodded and took an exquisite necklace from the velvet-lined case. A huge square-cut sapphire, surrounded by diamonds, was suspended from a delicate platinum chain. She held the exquisite sapphire against the blue gown and raised her eyebrows questioningly to Temple.

"Yes," said Temple, taking the necklace, "perfect. Just perfect."

Pleased, Rhikia began gathering up the garments that were not to be worn. Soon she began to frown and Temple tensed and held her breath. She knew what was going through Rhikia's mind. Did I bring five or six dresses with me? Rhikia looked all about, puzzled, unsure.

Temple remained outwardly composed. Ignoring the bewildered expression on Rhikia's face, she began to strip for her bath. Naked she eased down into the steaming water and watched from beneath lowered lashes as

Rhikia continued her search. Finally the servant gave up, decided she had miscounted, shrugged, and gathered up the clothes.

When Rhikia left, Temple exhaled heavily with relief. She started to smile as she lifted the soapy washcloth to her left shoulder.

Concealed safely beneath the pillows on her sleeping divan was the dress she would wear to make her escape. A more serviceable garment would have been preferable, but the wispy white silk gown had been the easiest to snatch away and hide.

Temple was so nervous at dinner, her hand shook when she picked up the heavy silver cutlery. She tried in vain to slow her anxious breathing, the furious beating of her heart. She flushed when the Sheik, seated across the candle-lighted table, brazenly lowered his inky dark gaze to her exposed bosom.

Had she realized the blue shantung's bodice was so daring, she would have chosen another gown. And had she known that the chain of the stunning sapphire necklace was too long, she wouldn't have worn it, either.

She felt naked and vulnerable and miserable. Her shoulders, back, and arms were completely bare. Worse, the gown's bodice was so uncomfortably tight and dipped so embarrassingly low, her pushed-up breasts came dangerously close to spilling from the plunging décolletage with each rapid rise and fall of her diaphragm.

The huge, heavy sapphire was wedged painfully in her cleavage, and she longed to lift it free but didn't dare. Not with his dark eyes fixed on her, watching her every move.

Maybe it was the way the candlelight played on the

planes and hollows of his dark, brooding features or the fact that she was so nervous over her planned escape, but it seemed to her he looked even more menacing than usual this evening. Maybe it was the way he was dressed.

The Sheik wore a black evening suit of European cut. But instead of the requisite white dress shirt, he wore one of fine black silk. No cravat or tie. No studs or cuff links. The black shirt's collar was open at the throat and unbuttoned midway down his dark chest.

Black hair, black eyes, black suit, black shirt. The provocative Prince of Darkness. That's what he looked like. He might have been Satan himself come to steal her soul and spirit her down to hell. Never had he seemed more frightening or more fascinating.

The meal was an exercise in strained silence. Temple, far too nervous to actually be hungry, knew the Sheik was watching her closely. She would have known even if she had never looked up. She could feel the hot pressure of his eyes on her, causing her skin to grow warm, her heart to misbehave.

She raised her head anxiously, looked at him. The flame from the candlelight reflected in the depths of his black eyes, he stared at her unblinkingly, saying nothing. It made her more nervous than ever. She felt as if she would surely choke on every mouthful of food she raised to her lips. She wondered if she could possibly make it through the entire evening without falling apart.

After what seemed an eternity, the tension-filled meal ended and Temple could hardly keep from leaping out of her chair. She didn't. She stayed where she was as the Sheik rose languidly to his feet, pushed back his chair, and came around the table.

He pulled out her chair and politely offered his hand. Temple took it, hoping her fingers wouldn't tremble too much in his firm grasp. She allowed him to draw her to her feet. As soon as he released her hand she turned to move away, but he caught her elbow, drew her back.

"What?" she asked, overwrought. "What is it?"

"Just this," he said, and Temple stared at him, her lips pressed together, as he raised his hand and wrapped his fingers around the delicate platinum chain supporting the heavy diamond-rimmed sapphire.

Slowly he lifted the weighty blue stone up out of her low-cut gown from where it was lodged.

"Just what are you doing?" she asked, appalled by the shiver of excitement that raced up her spine at the brush of his hand on her flesh.

"I'll have the chain shortened," he said, "so that the necklace will no longer hurt your—"

"I have no idea what you're talking about," she interrupted, flustered, her cheeks aflame. "Take the necklace if you like, but take your hands off me."

"The stone wasn't hurting you?"

"No, of course not."

"My mistake, then," he said, and his black eyes told her he knew he had made no mistake.

His lean fingers continuing to grip the platinum chain, he smiled satanically and, boldly pulling the low-cut bodice of her dress lower still, inserted the immense sapphire back in its warm resting place between her full breasts. He released it, turned, and walked away.

Her hands balled into fists at her sides, Temple watched as he leaned over and took a cigarette from the silver box on the table. To her dismay, he did not leave the tent as she had hoped. He did not go for his usual walk after dinner.

He sat down on the divan, lighted his cigarette, and stretched his long legs out before him.

17

"Check . . ." *Temple* delicately advanced the carved ivory knight. "And mate." She looked up and gave him a self-satisfied smile.

"Give me another chance?" Sharif asked, reaching for a cigarette.

Temple nodded, barely able to conceal her irritation. Her teeth clamped tightly together, she set up the black and white ivory pieces for another game of chess. Sharif put the cigarette between his lips, struck a match, cupped his hands around the tiny flame, and puffed the smoke to life. He inhaled deeply, blew a perfect blue smoke ring that hung in the still air.

Temple was silently seething. Obviously he intended to spend the entire evening with her. She might have known! It was just like him to do the unexpected. He had stayed away from the tent almost every evening until way into the night since she'd been in camp, but not tonight. Oh, no. He was going to stay right here and watch her every move like a cat with a mouse. Damn him. Damn him to eternal hell!

"Your first move," she said as calmly as she could.

For another agonizingly long hour they played chess, he sitting on the long divan with his knees wide apart, leaning over the low ebony table, she on the opposite side of the table, seated on the lush Persian rug.

He had won the first two games. She the next five. She had the advantage.

The Sheik couldn't keep his mind on the board. Not with this beautiful woman facing him. She was breathtaking with her shimmering blue skirts spread out around her and her pale, full breasts swelling against her low-cut bodice and her glorious blond hair pulled up atop her head to expose the graceful curve of her neck.

He was an expert chess player, but he'd never been pitted against a feminine foe whose radiance had clouded his brain. He had never sat across from a player whose fragile beauty made him want to sweep all the men off the board and declare her the winner.

Let her win.

All he really wanted was to take her in his arms, yank down the low-cut bodice, and press his lips to the spot where the heavy sapphire stone rested.

"Check and mate!" Temple again announced as she won her eighth straight game.

"I'm outclassed," said Sharif, his hand toying with one of the carved ivory pieces.

"And I'm exhausted," said Temple, raising a hand to her mouth and yawning dramatically.

"I don't get at least one more chance?"

"Not tonight," she said, rising to her knees.

He was up and around the table to her before she could stand. He took her hand in his but didn't immediately draw her to her feet. He left her there on her knees. Puzzled, Temple threw back her head and looked up at him.

He enclosed her hand in both of his, drew it up slowly, pressed it against his hard abdomen, and pinned her with his penetrating stare. His black gleaming eyes so bewitched her, Temple made no move to rise. She couldn't. She allowed him to keep her there, kneeling before him, unable to move or to look away.

His hypnotic gaze rendering her totally defenseless, she knelt willingly before him as if she were one of his obedient slaves. She didn't flinch or make a sound when he lowered a hand, cupped her upper arm. But her breath grew short when his fingertips stole possessively up over her bare shoulder, caressed the side of her throat, touched the pulse that was throbbing wildly there, and finally settled under her jaw.

The rough pad of his thumb skimming back and forth over her chin, he said, "To suppose you can outwit or deceive me is a mistake, Temple."

"I've made no attempt to deceive you," she said, a chill of fear racing up her spine, her heart thundering against her ribs.

In the flick of an eyelash, he yanked her to her feet, drew her close against him. His feet apart, a steely muscled arm around her waist, he held her so close that she could feel the granite hardness of his body crushed intimately to hers. Temple's arms remained at her sides. She made no effort to pull away. She was powerless against him and knew it. The Sheik put a hand in her hair, tipped her head back, and lowered his dark face until his lips were almost touching hers.

"You cannot win against me," he said, his eyes holding hers. "You will not go until I set you free, Temple."

"I . . . I . . . know."

"Remember it," he said, then swiftly released her.

He reached for another cigarette, crossed the tent, and called for Rhikia. Rhikia appeared almost instantly, and Temple followed her into the bedroom without saying another word to Sharif.

Inside the bedroom Temple stripped dutifully. She was hoping against hope that she might somehow manage to hang on to an article of underwear, but she failed. Rhikia took everything. Naked, Temple crawled into bed while Rhikia carried the clothes away. Moments later—to Temple's astonishment—Sharif came through the curtains.

She closed her eyes tightly and waited. He blew out the lamp. Her eyes opened and she watched through lowered lashes as he undressed. Tense, unnerved by his strange behavior, Temple wondered if he had somehow learned of her plan to escape. Was that why he had stayed in all evening? Had he come to bed early to keep a watchful eye on her? What if he didn't go to sleep? What if he stayed awake all night so that she wouldn't have a chance to slip away?

In agony, Temple lay there in the darkness, filled with doubt. But soon, to her surprise and relief, Sharif fell asleep.

Temple's heart began to pound with hope and anticipation. She waited an hour. Two. And longer. Finally, shortly before three o'clock in the morning, she threw back the sheet and rose. She glanced at the face of the sleeping Sheik, then took the crudely drawn map, the canteen, the food, and the folded white silk dress from underneath the sofa pillows.

After glancing cautiously at Sharif once again, she slipped out into the tent's main room. There she hurriedly pulled the silk dress over her head, wishing she had some underwear and a pair of shoes. She reminded herself she was lucky to have the dress.

Certain the lone sentry guarding the tent would be dozing by now, Temple moved toward the closed flap, planning how she would circle behind the tent, slip quietly down to where her stallion, Toz, was stabled. Toz would recognize her, and she could quickly quiet him. She would grab a bridle from the wall, lead Toz outside, and when they were a few yards away from camp, she'd mount him and ride to freedom!

Pausing directly before the tent's entrance, clutching the map, canteen, and the precious food tied up neatly in a silk scarf, Temple glanced one final time at the curtains separating the main room from the bedroom. All was silent. The Sheik slept on. Freedom was within reach.

Temple lifted the tent flap and stepped outside.

And screamed in terror, dropping everything, when a jewel-collared cheetah, its golden eyes gleaming, growled menacingly and lunged at her. The big black-and-gold cat, flicking its tail and making low, guttural sounds in its throat, padded back and forth before her. Pinning her where she stood, threatening to pounce.

Frozen with fear and unable to move, Temple whimpered with relief when she felt a pair of strong arms come around her.

The Sheik swung Temple off her feet and into his arms as he spoke to the snarling cheetah in a low, calm voice. At once the cheetah fell silent and stretched back out on the ground beneath the shade canopy to take up his vigil.

Sharif carried the badly shaken Temple back inside as the dozing sentry, awakened and apologetic, begged for his chieftain's forgiveness.

"You little fool," the Sheik said when he got Temple inside. "Do you really suppose you can escape me?"

He lowered her to her feet in the tent's main room but continued to hold her, his hands gripping her upper arms.

"Did you plan to ride across the desert in a silk dress?" He shook his dark head, and his black eyes blazed with fury. "Hear me, Temple. I told you earlier that until I am ready to let you go, you will not go."

Angered, he released her so abruptly, she lost her balance, had to reach out and grab his biceps to keep from falling. Just as abruptly, Sharif drew her roughly to him. A strong arm encircled her waist.

It was then that Temple realized he was still naked. Instant heat flooded her from the incredible warmth of his hard flesh pressed against her, from the feel of his hand cradling her head against his bare chest. Temple's face burned hot as she involuntarily lowered inquiring eyes. She was unable to see anything. The fabric of her dress covered the part of his anatomy about which she was so curious.

She was mortified to realize he had read her guilty thoughts when he said above her head, "Shall I release you so that you can see everything?"

Anger flaring, Temple jerked her head up and looked into his half-mean, half-smiling eyes. Longing to hurt him, she said, "Let me assure you, Sheik Sharif Aziz Hamid, that the last thing I want to see is the unclothed body of an uncivilized desert pirate, a dirty, despicable savage!"

She tried to pull away.

He held her fast.

"You, Miss High-and-Mighty Temple DuPlessis Longworth, not only wish to look, you are wondering what it might be like to share the bed of this particular dirty, despicable savage." That cruel smile twisted his full lips as he asked, "Shall I show you?"

Her eyes shooting green fire, Temple pulled free of his embrace, whirled about angrily, dashed into the bedroom, and dove beneath the covers of her sleeping couch.

The Sheik followed calmly.

Seeing his large frame loom closer in the deep shadows, Temple shrank away from him as he came toward her. He reached the divan, stood beside it, tall and naked and sinister. He yanked the covers away, took hold of her arm, and forcefully drew her up onto her knees atop the pillows.

"Please . . . please, don't," she begged, badly frightened now.

Holding her by one arm, the Sheik curled lean fingers down into the dress's low neckline. The ruby on his third finger cut into her sensitive flesh. She sobbed, "No . . . no," when she heard the delicate fabric of her dress rip.

Shaking with a mixture of icy fear and blazing attraction, Temple was held there on her knees while an angered Sharif tore the white silk dress from her bare, shaking body and tossed the ruined garment to the rug below.

She was now as naked as he.

His piercing eyes snaring hers in the shadowy bedchamber, the Sheik put a knee on the mattress and drew the trembling Temple into his close embrace.

Spellbound by the unreadable expression in his gleaming black eyes and tingling from the feel of his hard, bare body pressed to hers, Temple didn't fight him when he bent his head and kissed her hotly.

His plundering mouth stayed locked on hers until she was rendered powerless against the wild, unwanted passion he aroused. If he meant to take her now—and she was certain that he did—she couldn't save herself. Couldn't stop him. Wasn't sure she wanted to stop him.

Despite all efforts to resist, Temple felt herself melting against him as his masterful mouth did wonderful things to hers and his hands, so strong yet so gentle, spread incredible fire with their skilled touch.

Ever an enigma, the Sheik abruptly ended the searing kiss, roughly lowered the stunned Temple to the divan, and said softly, "Try escaping again and I will not be as merciful."

18

An early summer dawn streaked the desert's eastern horizon with tinges of pale pink. A gathering of eager men and high-strung horses waited impatiently for the appearance of their leader. All eyes were fixed on the large tent set apart from the others on the far side of the palm-lined pool.

Cheers rose from the group when the black-clad Sheik stepped from the white tent and out into the aurora of a new day.

There was no mistaking the tall, powerful figure in black striding purposely toward them. Tariz, standing beside his saddled iron gray, caught sight of Sharif and immediately began to beam. Pride swelled in his breast as he watched the Sheik approach. His imposing looks matched his exalted position. The strong features, the powerful black eyes, the imperial bearing. Lord of the land, unquestionably.

The Sheik reached the waiting assembly. A young groom stepped forward hastily and handed him the reins to the saddled black mount, Prince. Sharif swung up astride the big dancing stallion, turned, smiled down at Tariz, and asked, "Are you ready, my friend?"

Tariz mounted quickly and nodded, his smile wide and radiant. Indeed he was ready. He had hardly slept and couldn't wait to be off. He was as excited as a child. That excitement grew when Sharif extended a leather-gloved arm to receive his hooded falcon.

Tariz loved the sport of falconry, as did the young master. Falconing was in their blood, and riding out into the deserts with the winged hunters never failed to bring great joy and peace of mind.

The Sheik kicked the black into motion, and the camping party departed for the rolling, dawn-lit deserts where game was plentiful. Unlike the forays of the old days, when they relied on falcons to hunt food for their nightly campfires, this hunt was more for sport and for pleasure.

Tariz recalled those long-ago times when the hunting parties sometimes lasted for weeks. Now they would stay gone no more than a couple of days, if that long. So he knew he must savor every precious moment of the brief adventure.

Tariz looked at Sharif riding several lengths ahead now, the hooded falcon perched atop his gloved right hand. The amazing bird had always inspired great awe in Tariz. Passive on the master's arm, but a terror in the sky, the falcon could dive on prey at speeds of up to two hundred miles an hour.

Yet a single broken feather could impede performance.

As the party rode directly southward, Tariz recalled fondly how the old Sheik had loved the hunt. Many was the time they had ridden into the deserts with their trained falcons and returned with enough game to feed the entire camp.

Tariz smiled, remembering the feasts that followed

those hunts, the joy and laughter and dancing. And then the towering Sheik Aziz Ibrahim Hamid rising to stand before the shooting flames of the campfire with his long arms extended as he'd said in that deep, commanding voice, "Eat freely that which you have taught the birds and beasts of prey to catch, training them as Allah has taught you."

Tariz's smile broadened at the recollection of the day he and the aging sheik had taught a seven-year-old Sharif how to handle the dangerous hunting falcons. He could still see the pained expression on Sharif's boyish face when the old sheik had ordered him to hold out his short brown arm. Sharif had obeyed instantly, but his head had turned and his dark eyes had closed when the old sheik placed the big peregrine falcon on his small gloved hand.

"Open your eyes, my son," the old sheik had ordered, stern faced. Sharif had complied, nodding obediently at the tall, robed man, who said, "Do not shame your father before his men. You must be afraid of nothing, as I am afraid of nothing. I am a powerful man, and you are my son." He had laid a gentle hand atop Sharif's dark head then, ruffled his dark hair affectionately, and said softly, "My son. My beloved son."

Those words came back to Tariz later in the day when the air had cooled and the desert glare had softened. The Sheik, leading the hunting party, took his falcon to the northern rim of the Rub al Khali, that vast sea of sand that extended into the heart of Arabia.

There, repeating the traditional words of the falconer, he said, "In the name of Allah," and released his bird to hunt.

The falcon took wing. Sharif removed his leather glove. The ruby on his right hand caught the strong rays of the desert sun. In a flash the blinding red reflection brought back to Tariz the first time he had seen both the ruby and its wearer.

His eyes closed. The years fell away, and Tariz was a strong healthy man of thirty-nine, the old sheik a vigorous fifty-one.

It was a day much like this one, very hot and very still. Their week-long falcon hunt had been successful. He and the old sheik had left the party early.

The two of them were returning to camp. They said little as they rode across the endless dunes. The heat and the monotony making them sleepy, they dozed sporadically in the saddle, trusting their well-trained mounts to carry them safely home.

The sudden nervous whinnying of Tariz's chestnut stallion jolted him abruptly to full consciousness. He touched his weapon automatically, his dark eyes scanning the horizons.

He heard the old sheik say, "I don't see anything."

"Nor I, but the horses smell danger." Tariz twisted about in the saddle, searching the silent dunes for signs of approaching horsemen.

He saw none.

"Listen," said the old sheik, and pulled up on his mount.

Tariz halted immediately, turned his head, and listened.

A faint sound shattered the stillness.

"The wail of an animal?" Tariz asked, expecting no answer.

"Look," said the old sheik, pointing at a huge black buzzard circling low in the cloudless sky less than a hundred yards ahead.

The two men exchanged worried looks. Simultaneously

they drew their weapons and kneed their stallions into a fast gallop. They topped a long slanting dune and saw what the hungry carrion were circling.

Shouting loudly to frighten away the vultures, Tariz and the old sheik thundered down the dune to the desert floor. Tariz was the first one out of the saddle. His wide dark eyes took in the horrible scene in one quick, disbelieving minute.

A blond young man lay on his back, his clothes soaked in blood, his sightless eyes open and staring in horror. Mercifully, he was dead.

A few yards away a young, dark-haired woman lay on her side. She was naked save for a torn riding skirt twisted and bunched up around her bruised, bloodied thighs. A slim, blood-streaked arm was curled protectively around a wailing, red-faced baby, who was seated in the sand beside her, patting her face with short, chubby fingers.

The old sheik swiftly shrugged out of his flowing white robes and covered the woman. He shaded her face while Tariz felt her throat for a pulse. At his gentle touch her tear-swollen eyelids lifted slightly. She saw the two brown-skinned men leaning over her, and terror filled her pain-dulled dark eyes.

"We will not harm you," said the old sheik in his native tongue as Tariz reached for his goatskin to dribble cooling water across the woman's badly chapped lips.

Tears of relief sprang to her eyes, and she whispered in accented Arabic, "You are Arabs?"

"We are," said Sheik Aziz Hamid, and reached for the crying baby.

"My son," she rasped, starting to cry softly now. "Please . . . you must take my son with you."

"We will take you both," said the old sheik, and

stroked the tangled, blood-caked hair back off her fore-head. "You are safe now."

Cradling the crying baby close to his massive chest, he held out his hand for Tariz to pour water into his palm. He brought the water to the baby's lips, and miraculously the infant stopped crying and drank thirstily from the old sheik's cupped palm.

"We will take you to our camp," Tariz told the suffering woman. "And when you are better, we will—"

"No," she murmured. "No. I will not live to reach your camp." The old sheik and Tariz knew that it was true. "You must listen to me," she said, a pleading expression in her tear-filled eyes. "There is so much I must tell you, and so little time."

Nodding, comforting her as best they could, the two friends listened as the dying woman revealed, in horrifying detail, what had happened.

They learned that she and her husband were English geologists, in the Arabian deserts for their latest dig. They loved their baby son so much, they couldn't bear leaving him behind, so they had brought him with them.

Only this morning they and their native guides and bearers had left their caravan and set out on their own across northern Arabia. Not an hour later they had met up with a horde of black-robed horsemen carrying European rifles and wearing crossed bandoliers of ammunition. There had been nowhere to run. No place to hide.

The bandits had quickly surrounded them. The guides and bearers bolted and were swiftly slaughtered. In desperation, her husband had attempted to reason with the bandits. They would not listen; they shot him in the chest. But he didn't die. Badly wounded, he lay helpless and in pain a few feet away while the bloodthirsty bar-

barians raped and tortured her. When finally, after long, agonizing hours, the depraved animals tired of their evil sport, they shot her husband in the head and left her and her son to die in the desert.

As she spoke the old sheik took from the baby's clenched fist a spent brass shell casing. He turned it up and saw the telltale munitions stamp.

Du-P

Tears of compassion mingling with hatred in his dark eyes, the old sheik stated simply, "The Turks."

"Yes," she confirmed. "I heard them speak of their leader, Sultan Agha Hussain."

The old sheik's broad hand closed around the brass shell casing and he said softly, "Allah is waiting for you in Paradise, my child. Never will you suffer again."

"You will take my son?" she asked, the light fading in her dark eyes as she slipped toward that other world.

"And raise him as my own," said the childless old sheik.

She nodded feebly, relieved, then said, "When he's of an age, he must learn who he is. Who his parents were."

"He will," promised Sheik Aziz Ibrahim Hamid.

The dying young mother told them that the baby, born nine months ago in London, was Christian Telford. She, Maureen O'Neil Telford, black Irish born, was his mother. His father, the fair-haired man lying dead in the sand, was Albert Telford, Lord DunRaven, son and heir to a sizable fortune.

Suddenly she struggled to reach something hidden deep in the pocket of her torn riding skirt. She produced a dazzling rope of Starfire Burma rubies. Tariz and the old sheik blinked as the magnificent rubies caught the sunlight. Her weak arm lifting, she pressed the rope of rubies into the sheik's large hand and said, "These rubies were my wedding present." Tears slipped down her cheeks. "Give them to my son and promise me you will educate him in England."

"It will be done," swore Sheik Aziz Ibrahim Hamid.

"Christian," she sobbed the name softly, her lifeblood ebbing away.

The old sheik lowered the squirming baby, gently laid him on his mother's breast, and wrapped her tired, weak arms around him.

She turned sad, grateful eyes on the old sheik, kissed her son's downy head, and cooed to the baby, "My son. My beloved son."

19

Sharif's falcon soared off and turned in its first slow circle. It wheeled leisurely above a thorny acacia tree, then rose majestically and swooped at breakneck speed toward its prey.

Before it made the kill, the Sheik was distracted by the ruby on his hand. It had lost some of its brilliant fire.

The stone had mysteriously darkened.

The Sheik's heart slammed against his ribs. Without a word he turned away and headed for his horse.

Puzzled, Tariz scurried after him. "What is it?"

"We must return to camp at once," said the stern-faced Sheik.

"Return to . . . But why?" questioned the disappointed Tariz. "The hunt has only just begun."

"Tell the men to collect the birds and follow me," said Sharif. Dumbfounded, Tariz stood there staring at him, unmoving. "Now!" It was a command, a tone of voice Tariz had never heard out of him before.

Sharif leapt up astride his waiting black and raced away.

* * *

Temple was fidgety.

A growing uneasiness afflicted her.

She paced restlessly back and forth in the tent's main room, unnerved, jittery, questioning her very sanity.

A week had passed since her failed attempt to escape. Since that night the Sheik had ignored her completely. He did not talk to her. He did not acknowledge her when she walked into the room. And, perversely, she was bothered by his lack of interest, his utter coldness.

She wondered at herself. In the beginning all she had wanted was for Sharif to leave her alone. Now he was leaving her alone and she was more miserable than ever. As hard as it was to understand, she wanted his attention. She watched him eagerly for some sign of change, a softening toward her. She wished he would laugh and talk with her as he did with his loyal followers.

But he did not.

It was as if she were not there. As if she didn't exist. She was left alone to languish while the distant Sheik occupied himself with his tribal meetings and blooded horses and hunting falcons.

He was gone now on a falcon hunt and was not to return for at least two or three days.

Temple sighed wearily.

All week long Tariz had talked excitedly of the planned falcon hunt. The little Arab had been counting the days, looking forward to the big hunt. No more so than she. As soon as she had determined that Sharif would be leading the hunt, she too began counting the days, eagerly anticipating the hour when the Sheik would leave camp and be gone for two or three whole days.

And nights.

Yet now, as bedtime approached on his first day out,

she found surprisingly little joy in his absence. She almost wished he hadn't gone. Now that he had gone, she half hoped he wouldn't stay away for the entire hunt. God, she was surely losing her mind.

Perplexed, Temple stopped pacing. She shook her head in self-disgust and flung herself down amid the cushions of the long soft sofa. She kicked off her velvet slippers and curled her long slender legs beneath her.

She sat rigid and troubled on the sofa in the flickering lamplight, unable to get Sharif off her mind. Try as she might, she couldn't forget how she had felt when the angered Sheik had torn off her white silk dress.

Temple experienced a quick fluttering in her stomach as she recalled those dangerous, exciting moments when she was naked and he was naked and he held her in his powerful arms and kissed her as she'd never been kissed before.

She lifted a hand to her mouth, touched her lips, and sighed. No man's kiss had ever thrilled her half so much. No man's touch had set her afire as had a single caress of his hand. His burning kiss, his masterful touch, had awakened in her a passion of which she'd never thought herself capable.

How strangely ironic that the only man to stir such emotion was not one of the kind, tender, attentive gentlemen who had courted her, loved her, wanted to marry her. Oh, no. He was a callous, harsh, neglectful bastard who paid her no attention, didn't even like her, much less love her, and was probably already married to several wives.

And what did that say about her?

It made no difference.

While her head told her how she should feel about the Sheik, her heart wouldn't listen. She feared him but was attracted to him. She hated him, but she desired him. She loathed him. She wanted him.

There, she'd admitted it! She was drawn to him with a power and a passion that left little room for logic or reason.

Her heart suddenly pounded with panic as Temple faced these shocking truths about herself. She was, she realized, anxiously awaiting the return of the hard, heartless Arab Sheik who was her callous captor.

She wanted the Sheik to come home!

The tent's flap suddenly opened, and as if brought forth by a rub of Aladdin's lamp, the Sheik ducked inside and straightened to his full, impressive height. Startled, Temple shot to her feet. A hand went to her throat.

She looked at him.

He looked at her.

Their gazes held, and for a moment Temple caught a puzzling expression of relief shining from Sharif's night black eyes.

It was gone at once, replaced by the usual coldness as he approached her, saying crisply, "It's time you were in bed." They were the first words he had spoken to her in a week.

"I was just about to call for Rhikia," she lied, and involuntarily took a step backward from the tall, compelling man who was dressed entirely in black and badly in need of a shave. He looked singularly dangerous and demonic. And incredibly attractive and desirable. "Back so soon? I thought you were to be gone several days."

"I was, but I heard you calling out to me." A cruel smile lifted his full lips, and he added, "You missed me and wanted me to return."

His sarcastic remark struck too close to home for

comfort. Temple felt herself flush and wondered if he could somehow read her innermost thoughts.

She turned her back on him haughtily and said over her shoulder, "If I never saw you again, it would be much too soon." She marched toward the bedchamber, paused at the entrance, and commanded, "Get Rhikia in here. I'm bored and sleepy." She turned about to face him, yawned dramatically, and said, "Your company always seems to have that effect on me."

The sudden eruption of gunfire jolted Temple awake later in the night. Her eyes had barely popped open when the Sheik was upon her, his hand clamped over her mouth so that she couldn't scream or speak. Roughly he dragged her off her divan to the floor and shoved her underneath his big bed.

Outside, the high whine of bullets and the sound of whinnying horses and shouting men shattered the stillness of the night. Temple was terrified, her eyes wide and wild with fear. She didn't know what was happening.

The Sheik knew.

Continuing to cover her mouth with his hand, he put his lips close to Temple's ear and whispered, "Stay down. Do not move and do not make a sound!"

She nodded anxiously.

His hand left her mouth, and he rolled away from her. Her heart drumming double time, Temple clutched at the bedsheet tangled around her trembling body and stared at Sharif's muscular bare legs as he stood beside the bed and hurriedly donned his discarded black trousers. Not bothering with shoes or shirt, he rushed out of the darkened room, and within seconds Temple could hear him outside, issuing orders to his men.

She squeezed her eyes shut and gritted her teeth as the frightening melee just beyond the tent walls became a deafening din of whizzing bullets and screams of men who'd been hit and the hysterical neighing of terrified horses.

Outside, the Sheik stepped over the body of the fallen night sentinel and swiftly rallied his forces against the mounted intruders, whom he recognized instantly.

The hated Turks.

The main thrust of the attack was clearly centered on his tent, and the thought immediately flashed through his mind that Mustafa had somehow learned of Temple's presence.

Dodging bullets and shouting commands, Sharif fearlessly charged into the thick of the battle, enraged that the evil Turkish emir dared attack his peaceful sovereign desert city.

Wrath sending great rushes of adrenaline coursing through his body, Sharif rushed forward to meet the charging mounted raiders. Possessed of superior strength produced by fury and fear, he ripped rifles from the hands of his enemies as they took aim to fire. He dragged shouting black-robed men off their horses. He slashed throats with one clean slice of his Saracen scimitar and raised his muscular arm high to drive the long curved blade directly into beating hearts.

Blood flew.

Men screamed.

Dying Turks gurgled their last strangled breaths at his feet.

A bullet struck the Sheik's left shoulder, ripping away flesh, drawing blood. Another stung his right cheek. He never flinched. He hardly noticed. Black eyes ablaze with hatred and rage, he fought as if possessed by demons, determined to vanquish the hated Turks before they got the opportunity to harm one golden hair on the head of the woman inside his tent.

Less than fifteen minutes after it had begun, the bloody battle had ended. Half a dozen of the Sheik's men lay dead in the shadowy moonlight. Of the thirty Turkish bandits who had viciously sprung the surprise nighttime attack, only one remained alive.

The Sheik had spared him purposely.

While the smoke from the gunfire still hung heavy in the night air, Sharif, splattered with the blood of his conquered enemy, stood directly before the quaking Turkish wretch.

"I am," said the Sheik, calmly, slowly, his hand still gripping the jeweled hilt of his bloodstained scimitar, "sparing your life for a reason."

Eyes round with fright, the grateful Turk fell to his knees before the Sheik, his hands raised in supplication, murmuring hysterically, *"Al handu illah.* Allah be praised. *Al handu—"*

"Be quiet!" said the Sheik, his black eyes narrowed. Then: "Stand up." Bobbing his head, the sobbing Turk rose before the tall, coldly furious Sheik.

Sharif questioned the trembling Turk. Anxiously the terrified man confirmed that his master, Mustafa Ibn Agha Hussain, had sent him and the others on this nighttime raid, but he honestly didn't know the raid's purpose. He had not been told. Only the top lieutenants were taken into the master's confidence. He himself had been given his orders with no explanation. There was talk that they had been sent here to get something or someone, but what or who he knew not.

Though the Sheik showed absolutely no emotion, he felt his stomach muscles clench. Was the something or someone they'd been sent here to seize Temple DuPlessis Longworth?

He sent the Turk back to Mustafa with a message: Come anywhere near this desert camp again and he, *El Siif*, Sheik Sharif Aziz Hamid, would invade the Turk's seaside stronghold and personally kill him.

"Tell Mustafa his death at my hands will be neither easy nor quick," said the Sheik, his eyes now a fierce burning black. "I will see to it he is tortured in cruelly exotic ways that even he with his sick, twisted mind could never imagine."

20

The deafening sound of gunfire ceased as abruptly as it started and the camp had returned to its relative nighttime quiet, but Temple didn't dare move or make a sound. She stayed where the Sheik had placed her, lying on her back beneath his massive bed. Trembling in the darkness, she was unsure what she should do.

She knew the fighting was over, but she had no idea who had won the fierce battle. Nor was she sure which side she hoped were the victors. The surprise attack might well have been designed to free her from her captors.

Maybe her family had learned of her abduction and hired mercenaries from a rival Arab tribe to ride into the Sheik's village under the cover of darkness and set her free. Maybe this was to be her last night held captive in this remote desert stronghold. Maybe as she lay here hidden in the Sheik's tent, her liberators were anxiously searching the camp for her. Maybe she should get up, rush outside, and immediately make her presence known.

Quick on the heels of all those hopeful maybes came

another maybe, this one so dreadful that Temple felt her throbbing heart almost stop its beating.

Maybe the Sheik had been slaughtered in the attack!

Into her racing mind flashed the horrifying vision of Sharif lying dead in the desert moonlight, his lean brown body riddled with bullets, his black eyes fixed in a sightless stare at the heavens.

Temple blinked away the terrible image and swallowed convulsively when light suddenly poured into the shadowy bedroom. She held her breath. Waited. And winced when a strong hand closed firmly over her upper arm. Her head snapped around, and she squinted to see.

And exhaled with mild disappointment and great relief when she saw the distinctive ruby ring shimmering in the half-light.

But she screamed in shock when, pulled swiftly from under the bed and hauled to her feet, she stood facing a tall, menacing man she hardly recognized as the Sheik. Bare chested, unshaven, and wild-eyed, he was shiny with sweat and splattered with drying blood. His left shoulder was dripping fresh blood down his muscular arm, and directly beneath his right eye an abrasion on his high cheekbone was caked with dirt and blood.

"Are you all right?" he asked, his voice uncommonly rough, his scrutinizing gaze sliding over her. He didn't wait for a reply.

Before she could speak he was turning her about, patting her down with a bloodstained hand, searching for any telltale signs of injury or wounds.

"Will you stop it!" she protested, clutching her covering sheet with one hand and attempting to push him away with the other. "I'm fine! Just fine."

He paid her no mind. His fingers firmly encircling her wrist, he held her to him and examined her carefully, much to Temple's rapidly rising anger and aggravation.

Needing to convince himself she was unharmed, he continued—over her indignant objections—to touch and probe and check, running his hand through her unbound hair, over her throat, along her bare arms, across her back and shoulders, and down her slender, sheet-draped body.

Eyes squinted in concentration, the Sheik momentarily shifted his intense gaze from her to the divan on which she slept each night. His chest constricted when he saw that it was riddled with bullet holes. He turned back, looked at her directly, and Temple caught the strange new softness that had come into his eyes. She saw his hand tremble slightly as he lifted it toward her cheek.

She turned her head to avoid his touch and found her face only inches from his bare left shoulder. Her lips fell open and her eyes widened.

She pulled free of his imprisoning grasp and murmured in surprised concern, "You . . . you've been shot." Her slender fingers rose automatically toward his wounded shoulder.

"It's nothing," Sharif said, catching and staying her hand before she could touch him. "A small flesh wound." He set her back and said, "I'll have hot water sent in so you can clean up." He indicated the bloodstains left by his exploring hands on the white sheet wrapped around her. He turned and walked away, saying over his shoulder, "Take my bed for tonight. I'll sleep on the divan in the main room."

Temple followed him. "But what about your wound? It needs to be washed and dressed and—"

"Tariz will do it."

"I'll help him," she said, relieved to hear that the little man of whom she'd grown quite fond was safe.

"No need."

"I *am* helping," she announced, following right behind him, her green eyes riveted to his bleeding shoulder. "Does it hurt awfully bad?" she asked in a soft voice.

"Not a bit," he lied, so weak and light-headed that he made a misstep and stumbled.

Temple's slender arms were around him in an instant, steadying him, supporting him. Her hands clasped across his hard, sweat-slick abdomen, her cheek pressed against his blood-splattered brown back, she said, "It's all right. I have you."

"No," he said, speaking so softly she didn't hear, "you do not."

But as he said it, the Sheik's dark eyes closed helplessly, and it wasn't from the pain. It was from the relief of knowing this beautiful golden-haired woman was unharmed.

That, and the dizzying pleasure of having her soft, bare arms wrapped tightly around him.

The Sheik sat alone on a dune and gazed across the heat haze into the endless deserts.

A week had passed since Mustafa's men had invaded his camp, and he still worried and wondered if the Turkish emir had somehow learned of Temple's presence. It didn't seem likely. Naguib was a brave and trusted courier who over the years had delivered many a secret message to allies scattered across Arabia. A fearless man who would gladly give up his life before allowing a missive to fall into the wrong hands, Naguib had undoubtedly reached Baghdad and sent the telegram to Temple's family in America.

Nodding his head, Sharif convinced himself that all was well. He was worrying needlessly. Nobody knew he was holding an American heiress captive in his desert village.

Nonetheless he would take every precaution to ensure Temple's safety. It was up to him. She was in his care.

The night of the raid, while she'd assisted Tariz in cleansing and dressing his shoulder wound, he had told her exactly who the invaders were and warned her that if Mustafa's men ever got their hands on her, she would pray for death.

"Never leave the village alone," he'd concluded with as much authority as possible.

Temple, standing above him, preoccupied with cleaning the dirt and dried blood from his wound, had given no reply.

His jaw hardening, he had clutched her arm, made her stop what she was doing.

"Look at me, Temple." His tone of voice had made both Temple and Tariz jump. Temple had looked into his eyes and he'd asked, "Did you hear me?"

"Yes," she'd said, exasperated. "You said look at you."

"I *said* you are never to leave the village alone. *Never!* Promise me you won't."

She'd hesitated, finally said, "I promise."

But now, as he sat here alone worrying, he wondered if she'd actually paid attention to his warnings. Knowing her, he doubted it. She was foolish and stubborn, a dangerous combination.

Temple Longworth was dangerous in more ways than one.

Sharif felt his lower belly tighten, felt himself stir and surge against the fabric of his snug riding breeches. He cursed himself for his weakness, cursed her for having such power over him.

He muttered oaths and ground his teeth. The mere

sight of her made him long to take her in his arms. Just thinking about her heated the blood in his veins. He'd had only a fleeting glimpse of her beautiful body the night he had angrily torn off her white dress, but the vision was stamped indelibly on his brain. He could call it up whenever he wished. But he couldn't black it out when he wanted to forget.

He would never forget.

If he lived to be a very old man whose eyesight failed, he would still be able to see the naked, pale-skinned Temple kneeling on the bed with her golden hair spilling around her shoulders. By Allah, she was a temptress no mere mortal could resist.

Sharif exhaled heavily.

It was agony to sleep in the same room with her each night, knowing she was only a few feet away, naked and vulnerable. How many times had he been tempted to get into bed with her when she was sleeping? To kiss her into partial wakefulness and touch her before she realized what was happening and take her before she was fully conscious?

Awake or asleep, he dreamed constantly of making love to her. No matter how hard he tried to ignore her, he couldn't. He was acutely aware of her every second of every day. And night.

He should never have brought her here. Should never have captured her. It was all a terrible mistake, and one for which he was destined to pay for eternity.

He thought he'd planned so well. The strategy had been simple. Kidnap Temple and send a wire to her powerful uncle in America, informing him that when he stopped shipping ammunition to the Turks, Temple would be released, unharmed.

The abduction had been a last resort. How many years had he and the old sheik before him attempted, through every diplomatic source available, to persuade

DuPlessis to stop the flow of ammunition from their American factories to the bloodthirsty Turks.

They had never listened.

Sharif reached into his pocket, withdrew the spent brass shell casing he always carried. He opened his hand and stared at it, recalling the story the old sheik had told of finding this very casing in his, Sharif's, tiny hand when he was discovered in the desert with his dead father and dying mother.

Sharif closed his hand.

His tanned jaw clenched and ridged in frustration, then he willed himself to dismiss from his troubled thoughts the worrisome woman and her reason for being in his desert camp. Soon she would be gone.

But not, Sharif knew instinctively, soon enough.

The bullet nick on Sharif's right cheek showed pink against the darkness of his olive skin. And beneath his heavy robes, a bandage still covered the healing bullet wound on his left shoulder.

As he had done several times each day since being hit, Sharif flexed his injured shoulder, lifting and lowering it in a circular, testing motion. He winced at the searing pain and gritted his even white teeth. Perspiration dotted his hairline as he forced himself to continue the punishing, loosening-up exercises. He was determined to work the stiffness out of his shoulder muscles before tomorrow's guests arrived.

The throbbing pain, the agonizing soreness, Sharif kept to himself. Only when he was alone did he groan and grind his teeth and wince with pain. He had learned, by example, that a respected tribal chieftain showed no weakness. Ever. The old sheik never allowed anyone to know of his suffering, either physical or mental. Not even at the end, when he endured intolerable pain before, mercifully, dying.

In those last moments, when Sharif, with unshed tears stinging his eyes, knelt beside the bed, Sheik Aziz Ibrahim Hamid told him, "The Prophet said, 'You must not weep or cry over your dead.'" Sharif knew the man he called father was reminding him he was *never* to cry before anyone. Not even at the loss of a loved one.

How many times, since he was a boy, had the old sheik told him, "A successful leader of men must control and conceal his emotions, lest he be perceived as weak in the eyes of his followers and his enemies."

Sharif knew the truth and importance of that statement. He knew as well that few tribes commanded more respect than his own, and few chieftains had followers as loyal as those who served him and his father before him.

So he sat alone on the sand dune far from the village and worked his stiff shoulder muscles and tight biceps and aching arm, flexing and flinching and making faces. He had always kept himself in perfect physical condition, his steely muscles toughened by years of the strenuous desert life. He would not allow a simple flesh wound to slow him down. He was determined to get in top form for the welcoming festivities planned for tomorrow's visit of Sheik Hishman Zahrah Rahman and his tribe.

Sharif knew that as a part of the celebration he would be required to take part in the ceremonial *Ardah.*

He smiled wryly.

It wouldn't do for a tribal leader known across North Africa as *El Siif*—the Sword—to be unable to perform the ritual Sword Dance.

Temple stood outside in the shade of the lance-supported canopy, watching Sharif through narrowed eyes. She had casually sauntered out when, from inside the cool interior of the tent, she had heard his men calling out to him.

Acting nonchalant, pretending that she had no idea he had returned, Temple stood there under the shade canopy, watching as the Sheik appeared on the horizon, silhouetted against the burning sun. She watched as the white-robed chieftain neck-reined Bandit, his prancing white stallion, down a long slanting dune east of the camp directly toward the maze of tents and palm trees.

Her breath caught when he suddenly kicked Bandit's sleek flanks and sent the stallion racing rapidly into the village. Temple's hand lifted to her tight throat and she felt her entire body tense for what was about to come. She knew exactly what Sharif was going to do. But still it frightened and impressed her.

Riding at a tremendous speed, his white robes billowing out behind him, Sharif abruptly gave the reins a powerful jerk that sent the big white straight up into the air, spinning high on his hind legs. It was a favored trick among these fearless Arab horsemen, and it never failed to quicken Temple's heartbeat.

Especially when it was the Sheik who pulled the dangerous stunt.

Relief flooded through her when the rearing stallion's front feet came back down and again struck the earth. She exhaled heavily as the daredevil Sheik dismounted, tossed the reins to a smiling young groom, and joined a waiting, worshipful gathering of his men, all applauding his bravado and anxious to talk with him.

Sharif, Temple knew, had been out for a long morning ride in the desert alone.

Again.

For two weeks now the Sheik had not ridden with her once. Nor had he ridden with anyone else. Each morning he set out alone, refusing the company of any of his trusted lieutenants or even that of the loyal Tariz. Tariz was hurt, but Temple was simply puzzled.

The man was ever a mystery.

It had been only a week since he'd been wounded in the frightening nighttime raid, but to look at him you'd never know it. His broad shoulders were firmly erect beneath his long flowing robes, and he moved his left arm as if he had never been injured.

He stood now, booted feet apart, hands on his slim hips, looking every inch the formidable, hawk-faced desert Sheik.

Well, good!

She was glad. She hoped he would always look as he did right now. Then she'd never be able to forget just how different were their two worlds, their cultures, their civilizations.

Temple's delicate jaw hardened, and her eyes narrowed as she continued to stare at him. A slight breeze came up out of the north and blew the tasseled ends of his black double headcord about his tanned, handsome face. He raised a lean hand, brushed them away, threw back his head and laughed at something that amused him.

The conversation grew livelier. All the men were laughing now, their voices rising and falling excitedly. Temple heard the name "Hishman" spoken several times and knew they were talking about tomorrow's upcoming visit from one of the tribes allied with the Sheik. Tariz had told her about it. He'd said Sheik Hishman Zahrah Rahman and his tribe would be arriving tomorrow, the honored guests of Sharif. They would stay in the village for at least two or three days.

Obviously everyone was looking forward to the visiting Sheik's arrival. They were probably planning all kinds of primitive festivities. Well, they could count her out. She had no intention of sitting around sweltering before a roaring campfire while they drank that horrid thick black coffee they all loved so much and stuffed greasy strips of half-done mutton into their bearded mouths.

Temple shook her head in scorn.

She could well imagine what passed for entertainment among a bunch of unwashed, uncouth, uncivilized Arab heathens.

21

"I've no intention of joining your 'barbaric little celebration,' Arab."

"Yes, I know."

It was early afternoon.

Temple and Sharif were alone in the tent's main room. She was seated on one end of the long divan, he on the other.

The visiting Sheik Hishman Zahrah Rahman and his large entourage had arrived shortly before noon. Sharif had greeted them personally, and Temple had watched, fascinated, from just inside the tent's entrance as each of the men in Sheik Rahman's entourage had come forward and kissed Sharif's right shoulder in the traditional bedouin sign of respect. After the greetings were concluded, the visitors had been shown to their quarters to rest before the day's activities began and Sharif had returned to his own tent to relax.

If he was relaxed, Temple was anything but.

Her steadily growing attraction to the indifferent Sheik made her want to lash out at him. To hurt him. To make him angry. To prove to him and herself that she could get his attention if she wanted it.

"Did you hear what I said?" she asked, disappointed by his reply.

Thinking she must have misunderstood him—that he surely meant for her to attend, would *insist* she attend—Temple laid aside her book, rose, and repeated herself, making her statement a bit stronger.

"I refuse to take part in a ridiculous celebration with a bunch of pagans who know nothing of manners or morals." She looked at him contemptuously. "You cannot force me to associate with men who believe violence, brutality, and the swaggering display of raw power is acceptable behavior."

"As you wish," said Sharif, rising from the long sofa, stretching, rippling his muscles like a large jungle cat.

He stood facing her, casually loosening the neck of his linen shirt. His strong hands, brown against the whiteness of the shirt, flipped the buttons from their loops, one by one, each one undone exposing a wider portion of his dark, broad chest.

"You concur?" Temple asked, distracted, wishing he would stop unbuttoning his shirt.

He did.

The linen shirt was half open down his chest. Sharif yanked it free of his trousers, peeled it up past his corded ribs, and pulled it over his head and off. Idly blotting away the drops of perspiration dotting the dense black chest hair, he said, "No, I don't mind."

Temple's perfectly arched eyebrows lifted in surprise and confusion.

"You don't?" She forced her captured gaze to lift from a slow-moving trickle of sweat slipping down his tanned throat. "Honestly?"

"Honestly," he said, raised the wadded shirt, and

wiped away the trickle that so fascinated her. Then the curve of his full mouth was brutal when he added, "I forbid you to join in my 'barbaric little celebration.'"

Temple's mouth fell open and she blinked at him. "You forbid me to . . . ?" She was immediately indignant. "But why?"

The Sheik shrugged his bare bronzed shoulders. "What does it matter? You do not wish to attend."

"Well, no. No, but I thought . . . I naturally assumed . . ." Feeling foolish, Temple stopped speaking.

She was annoyed with him, agitated by the sight of his naked chest glistening with sweat, the unbandaged bullet wound on his left shoulder vicious looking. She turned away and strolled across the room to the tall ebony bookcase, where she took a leather-bound book of poetry from the shelf and flipped through the pages impatiently. With her back to him, she said sarcastically, "I do hope your little all-male gathering won't turn into a drunken brawl and keep me awake half the night."

"It isn't an all-male gathering."

Temple whirled around. "It isn't? I thought that's why you . . . you . . . "

"Didn't request your attendance," he finished for her. "That has nothing to do with it. Females will most definitely be present."

Stung, Temple turned back quickly to face the bookcase. She replaced the book of poetry on the shelf and gritted her teeth, and her well-shaped jaw jutted forward an nth of an inch. Sharif tossed his soiled linen shirt to the low ebony table and languidly crossed the room. His booted feet made no sound on the lush Persian carpet, but when he reached her, Temple knew he was there.

Heat emanated from his tall, lean body, assaulting her, enveloping her. And his subtle yet powerful scent—a captivating mixture of sun-warmed flesh and aromatic Cartier cigarettes and supple leather and potent masculinity—told her he was standing directly behind her.

"You arrogant, ignorant Americans," Sharif said coldly. "You know nothing of my people and our customs. Alcoholic drinks are forbidden by the Koran."

"I knew that," said Temple, turning about so quickly that she bumped into his naked chest. She made a face, recoiled, and, her eyes snapping with displeasure, demanded, "Why am I not invited to the festivities?"

He said, "Sheik Rahman has brought his young daughter with him on this visit."

"So?" Frowning, Temple folded her arms and glared at him. "What does this sheik's little girl have to do with my not being invited? I know how to behave around children, for heaven's sake. I like them and they like me. Is she pretty and sweet?"

"Yes," he said, "she is." He turned away. "It's time I get dressed."

"It's only two in the afternoon," Temple said, incredulous.

He crossed to the tent's entrance, threw back the flap, and called for Tariz. In moments a platoon of strong-backed Arabs were carrying great vats of hot water through to the bedchamber for the Sheik's bath.

"The opening ceremonies begin at three," said Sharif.

"Oh?" Temple attempted to sound disinterested. "And how long will they last?"

"Until three in the morning."

Tariz and the servants departed. Sharif crossed to the bedroom, drew aside the curtains. Temple glanced toward the shadowy bedchamber, saw the tub at the foot of the bed. It was brimful of hot, steaming water. Sharif disappeared inside, drawing the curtains behind him.

Then, for what seemed an eternity to her, Temple sat on the divan and attempted to concentrate on her book. It was impossible. She couldn't forget for a moment that Sharif was just on the other side of the curtains, naked in his bath.

The village was well into the afternoon lull, a daily period of inactivity and silence. There was no noise from outside the tent to cover the unsettling cacophony coming from inside the bedroom. The vigorous splashing of water. The gliding of a soapy washcloth over slippery male flesh. The sound of a low, smooth baritone singing a ballad in English.

Temple finally gave up on the book.

With a grimace, she laid it aside, leaned her head against the divan's high back, focused fixedly on the tent's entrance, and put her hands over her ears.

"Temple? Are you ill?"

She jumped, startled. She had no idea how long he'd been standing there. The Sheik, fully dressed, had walked noiselessly into the room.

"An earache?" he asked. "Rhikia will heat a bit of oil and—"

"My ears are perfect, thank you very much," she snapped, lowering her hands and reaching for her book.

But she didn't open it.

She couldn't take her eyes off the tall, striking Arab chieftain. He was dressed all in white, the jeweled dagger at his waist. His bronzed face was smoothly shaven and glowing with good health. A lock of raven hair fell from one side of his snowy white turban. He raised a hand to sweep it aside. The ruby on his finger flashed red fire.

In his jet black eyes was that compelling icy hot expression that had the power to chill and burn her at the same time. Temple was instantly cold, shivering on the inside so that she felt as if she couldn't sit still.

She was also feverish, suddenly so hot and uncomfortable that it was all she could do not to reach up and loosen the collar of her choking dress to let the air cool her scorching skin.

"You look pale," said the Sheik, unsmiling, and advanced on her.

"Do I?" she managed, hardly daring to breathe when he went down on one knee before her and placed a hand on her brow.

"You feel a little warm," he said. He took his hand away but stayed on his knee. His inky eyes holding hers in an unblinking stare, he said, "This desert heat can be hard on you."

"Yes. Yes, that's it. The desert heat," she replied, knowing it was the hotness of his gaze that had undone her. Hoping he didn't know, but knowing that he did by the faint cruel smile on his lips and the flame in his dark eyes.

He rose gracefully to his feet, turned, and crossed the tent. At the entrance he paused and said over his shoulder, "You are not to come outside the tent."

Then he was gone.

Temple stayed where she was as long as she could make herself. Which wasn't very long. Only a few seconds passed before she hurried to the tent's flap, parted it back a couple of inches, peeked out, and watched him walk away.

The Sheik with his sleek saturnine good looks and his immaculate white robes was every inch the imperial Arab chieftain. He stood six feet three inches tall, with glossy coal black hair and a dark, noble face that gave no hint of emotion, that hid everything.

His bearing regal, he moved unhurriedly toward the crowds amassing on the far side of the palm-fringed lagoon. At his side padded the sleek black-and-gold cheetah, as docile as a house tabby.

Temple shuddered involuntarily. If he chose to do so, could the Sheik tame her as easily he had tamed the ferocious cheetah?

She quickly dropped the tent flap back in place and turned away.

Temple forced herself to pay no attention to the bustle of activity going on outside the tent throughout the long summer day. The shouting and the laughter and the noise soon became a constant that she hardly noticed.

Until late in the afternoon, when she heard the muffled throbbing of drums. She was curious. She had to see what was going on. Sharif had told her to stay inside. To hell with him.

She sprang to her feet and hurriedly crossed the tent. At the entrance she hesitated, then took a deep breath, squared her slender shoulders, swept back the flap, stepped out under the shade canopy—and stared.

Directly across the palm-fringed lagoon, thick rugs had been spread in a colorful patchwork, one atop the other, on the grassy banks beneath the tall palms. Throngs of tribesmen from two separate empires, all of them wearing their finest robes, were gathered, sitting about on pillows and hassocks. The evening meal had just ended, and now they were drinking that thick sweet coffee from delicate demitasse cups.

Scanning the sea of dark faces, Temple anxiously sought out the handsome face of the Sheik. He was easy to spot. His were the robes that were snowy white. He sat cross-legged at the center of a low table upon which rested a long-beaked brass coffeepot and silver platters filled with dates, figs, fruits, and sugary cakes.

On his right was a small, bearded man who was grandly robed in varying shades of blue. Temple recognized him as the visiting Sheik Hishman Zahrah Rahman. On Sharif's left was a young dark-haired woman garbed in modest but exquisite robes of pink rose brocade. A transparent pink veil, weighted with sparkling jewels, covered the lower half of her face but did not conceal the fact that she was beautiful. Bracelets of glittering gold adorned both her wrists, and golden rings gilded each slim finger.

Sharif's white teeth flashed in a smile as he turned and whispered something in the young woman's ear.

"No!" Temple murmured as it dawned on her.

Sheik Rahman's daughter was not a little girl at all, but a gorgeous fully grown woman.

As Temple watched, frowning, Sharif bowed his head and leaned close while the dark-eyed young beauty whispered to him. As she spoke the woman laid a small hand on his forearm and Sharif's tanned fingers covered hers.

Temple swallowed hard. Her hand went to her heart. She tried to turn away but couldn't. All kinds of strangely unacceptable thoughts ran through her mind. The real purpose of Sheik Rahman's visit was to deliver his beautiful daughter to Sharif. This feast was actually a prenuptial celebration. Sharif was to marry the woman!

Sharif gracefully rose to his feet. Temple's eyes clung to him as he made his way through the crowd and disappeared into the thickest part of the palm grove. Other tribesmen were rising, following him.

A large circular space was being cleared at the center of the crowd, directly before the low table where the visiting sheik and his daughter sat. The throb of the silver drums grew louder. Men with tambourines began playing their instruments.

A buzz of excitement rippled through the crowd.

All at once a group of men carrying long swords

appeared in the clearing. Singers joined them. They linked arms together and faced each other in two long lines. The singers chanted verses in Arabic as they swayed back and forth. Then the men carrying swords began a slow walk around the circle, keeping in step with the beating of the drums.

A deafening shout and a great round of applause went up from the crowd when a tall, lean swordsman materialized from the dense palm grove.

Sharif stepped into the center of the circle, and every pair of eyes, including Temple's, was instantly riveted to him.

Gone were the flowing white robes, the silver-corded headdress, the handsome, loose-sleeved white blouse.

He wore a only pair of baggy, calf-length white trousers riding low on his flat brown belly and secured by a long silver sash tied atop his hipbone, the ends flowing down his thigh to his knee. He was shirtless. A vest of flaming crimson was open over his dark chest, and wide armbands of gleaming gold adorned his bulging biceps.

He was barefoot and bareheaded, and his naked torso and muscular arms glistened with a gloss of rich oils that had been rubbed into every inch of undraped olive flesh. In his strong right hand he carried a heavy gleaming sharp-edged sword. His bearing, as was to be expected, was haughty.

For a long moment he stood there unmoving as the late afternoon sun struck him fully, adding an ethereal radiance to his magnificent physique and dark head and fine features. He was so arrestingly beautiful that he appeared to be not a man, but a god, not of this world.

Oohs and aahs rose from the large assembly when Sharif began to swing his heavy sword over his head in a slow, fluid motion. Temple, watching with her heart in her throat, was instantly worried about his injured shoulder. The bandages were gone. Oil covered the not-yet-healed purple bullet wound. She was afraid he was not really able to swing the heavy sword. Surely it was dangerous to engage in such a perilous exercise when he wasn't fully recovered.

"Oh, God, no," she murmured when he threw the sword high into the air and caught it as it fell.

The excitement grew as the *Ardah*, the Sword Dance, went on. The low singsong chant and the sensual, slow-motion dance made the ceremony a stunning, unusual sight to behold, and Temple was captivated.

As Sharif continued to perform such heart-stopping feats of derring-do, she wrung her hands with worry even as she watched, entranced. Each time he swung or tossed his sword, she stopped breathing. And when he threw it straight up and spun about in a full circle before reaching out to pluck it from the air, she impulsively cried out his name.

"Sharif!"

His hand firmly gripping the sword's heavy handle, the Sheik froze and his dark head snapped around. Horrified, Temple ducked back inside the tent.

But not before he had spotted her.

22

Temple was barely back inside and stretched out on the long sofa before the tent's flap was yanked open. She sat up quickly, blinking against the sudden infusion of light. She gasped and swung her slippered feet to the floor.

Backlit by the dying sun, Sharif stood in the open portal, the heavy sword still gripped firmly in his right hand. He advanced swiftly, the gold bands encircling his oiled biceps winking in the wide shaft of sunlight as he bore down on her.

Temple flinched instinctively when he reached out, wrapped his lean fingers around her upper arm, and pulled her to her feet. She found herself slammed up against his solid length, his muscular forearm wrapped around her in a viselike grip. The ruby ring bit into her back, and she was acutely aware of the Saracen sword, its long metal blade resting heavily against her buttocks, nudging her closer to him.

Her hands fluttering up to brace against his bare, slippery shoulders, she shuddered against him when he glared into her eyes and said, "I have been patient with you, American, but you continue to try me at every turn." She started to speak, but he stopped her. "You were forbidden to leave the tent."

In a voice at once defiant and defensive, "I did not leave, I—"

"Calling my name while I was performing the *Ardah* could have cost me my life."

Her sliding fingers unable to get a grip on his oiled shoulders, Temple stared right back at him and replied, "Performing a dangerous sword dance with your injured shoulder could have cost you your life."

As if she hadn't spoken, he said, "You will stay inside this tent until I give you permission to leave."

"Oh? Am I required to stay shut up here until your guests leave the village?"

"You are required to obey my wishes."

Temple couldn't stop herself. She asked, "Is the visiting sheik's daughter required to obey your wishes as well?"

"You are a great deal of trouble," was his reply as his arm tightened around her. The heavy sword pressed against her backside, forcing her more fully to him. "The visiting sheik's daughter gives me no trouble."

"What does she give you?"

"Only joy."

Temple felt a quick stab of jealousy pierce her breast. "You told me she was a child."

"No. You assumed she was child."

Temple's emerald eyes narrowed. "You will marry her, then? That is the reason she is here, isn't it?"

"Need you know everything?"

"Everything? You tell me nothing! I've no idea why you're holding me. Or how long you plan to keep me. Or what you mean to do with me." She took a quick, shallow breath and added quickly, questioningly, "Am I to be added to your harem?"

"No." She winced at the cold brutality of his tone when he said, "You could never be properly trained."

"Let me go!" Temple demanded angrily, pushing on his chest, struggling to free herself.

"I will release you, Temple, but you are *not* to go outside this tent until I say you may."

"I'm to live hidden away forever like a prisoner?"

"You're to do as I tell you."

"And if I disobey you?"

"You won't," he said arrogantly, and released her.

She looked down at her dress. It was stained with oil where his arms had held her, spotted where his chest had pressed against her breasts. Plucking at the soiled fabric, pulling it away from her skin, she made a face, wrinkled her nose, and said, "You've ruined my dress! You know very well I have nothing else to wear! Now what shall I do?"

Shrugging out of his soiled crimson vest, he said coldly, "You will stay in the tent where you belong."

Temple stayed in the tent.

Bored, restless, she was all but forgotten by Sharif. She languished alone in the lonely silk-walled prison, overlooked, ignored as if she were a piece of furniture, while Sharif lavishly entertained his guests. She saw him only on those occasions when he returned to the tent to clean up and change clothes for yet another of the many elaborate feasts honoring his exalted visitors, an endless round of celebrations to which she was never invited.

Tariz admitted, under Temple's seemingly casual questioning, that Mumtaz, Sheik Hishman Zahrah Rahman's lovely daughter, had been brought along in the hope that she would find favor with Sharif. Temple had to bite her tongue to keep from asking if Mumtaz had indeed found favor with Sharif.

What did she care?

She didn't, really. It made no difference to her if he had one wife or four. It meant nothing to her. *He* meant nothing to her.

Still, when three days and nights passed and finally Sheik Hishman Zahrah Rahman rode out of the village, taking his clearly disappointed daughter with him, Temple was relieved to see them go. She realized, with a quick stab of guilt, that although it made no sense, she *was* jealous of this young Arabian beauty, had been afraid Sharif would want her, desire her.

After the visitors' departure, life in the desert village returned to normal. Nothing had changed. The Sheik continued to act as if she were not there. He became increasingly aloof. Maddeningly distant. Coldly indifferent.

The Sheik drove his booted heels into Prince's lathered flanks one blistering hot afternoon. He had been away at a three-day tribal meeting with his allies, the Otaybas. He was anxious to get back to camp.

His eyes squinted against the sun's fierce glare, and his head was throbbing from the sleeplessness of the past two nights. He hadn't slept a wink, hadn't rested a minute.

She was on his mind constantly, he could think of nothing else. Of no one else. Just Temple. Only Temple

For days, weeks, he had wrestled with his conscience, fought to cling to his weakening control, battled the growing lust that was tearing him apart.

He wanted her.

He wanted Temple DuPlessis Longworth. He desired

her with all the driving power of the passionate nature he had inherited. He yearned for her with an intensity that was nothing short of torture. He could no longer endure the agony. He was torn apart, rendered helpless by the force of his primeval hunger for the beautiful blond American.

Despising his weakness, Sharif was nonetheless propelled by it. He was racing back to her, his intent evil, his purpose inexcusable. He was going to take her, willing or unwilling, despite honor, despite reason. The maddening temptation had driven him over the edge, and he could stand it no longer.

The decision had been made. There was no turning back. He was racing headlong into hell, and he didn't care.

He had tried everything. He had forced himself to remain withdrawn, detached. He had willed himself to pay her no attention. Had pretended she was not there, that he was actually alone in the tent.

At times he dared not even look at her, so afraid was he of what the sight of her delicate blond loveliness would do to him. And even then, with his eyes tightly closed against her, he saw her all too plainly—the gentle curve of her ivory throat and the golden blond of her hair and the emerald green of her eyes and the soft fullness of her lips.

A hundred times a day he would find himself lost in a daze from which only her image emerged. He could see nothing else. Could hear no one else. Only Temple. Just Temple.

Temple in tight riding pants mounted astride the stallion Toz, racing over the sands. Temple seated across the dinner table in a lush, low-cut gown. Temple curled up on the floor before the chess board. Temple sleeping peacefully beneath the sheet covering her warm nakedness.

Temple. Temple. Temple.

He had to have her to save his sanity. Nothing else would. It was the only hope he had of getting her off his mind and out of his blood.

Through the heat haze, the squinting Sharif finally saw his cool green oasis in the near distance, waiting, beckoning to him. He spotted the large white tent and pictured her there, napping on the divan in the main room, a book resting on her chest, gently rising and falling.

A tightness filled his own chest. The muscles in his arms bunched, and his hands tightened on the leather reins as he envisioned sweeping her into his arms and carrying her to the shadowy privacy of his bedroom. There he would strip her naked, put her into his bed, and keep her there, wallowing in the evil splendor and primitive ecstasy until he was totally sated.

Sharif again spurred the stallion, and the lathered beast responded with a great burst of speed, sensing the depth of his master's desperation.

His black eyes narrowed against the burning sun and stinging wind, his heart drumming with rising anticipation, Sharif raced toward the encampment. When he reached the outskirts of the oasis, he ignored shouted greetings from his men, galloped past them, heading directly to his tent.

There he leapt off the winded stallion, threw the reins to the ground, stepped under the shade canopy, and yanked back the tent flap.

He ducked inside, saw her, and trembled. He wanted her so badly that a vein pulsed on his dark forehead and his groin swelled and ached painfully.

But, he realized angrily, he could not do it.

He could not take her by force. He could not make love to her when she didn't want him, when she hated the sight of him. She was far too beautiful, too fragile.

* * *

Temple stared at the Sheik, whose black eyes were glittering in the dimness of the tent. His usually spotless white robes were covered with sand and grime. A dark stubble of beard covered his handsome face, accentuating the small white scar above his lip and the menacing aura that clung to him. He flung off his turban, and his black hair was dirty and plastered to his noble head. Sweat gleamed on his dark face and ran in rivulets down his dark throat.

He was dirty, unkempt, and mean visaged.

Never had he looked more appealing.

Wordlessly Temple rose from the divan and moved toward him as if he had ordered her to come. She reached him as he shrugged out of his soiled white robe and tossed it aside. His imposing height never more in evidence, the Sheik towered over her. Her face was on the level of his sweat-soaked chest.

"Sharif," she murmured, and laid her hands on his soiled shirtfront.

He shook his dark head and said, "I am not clean."

"I know," she said softly. "I don't care."

And as if in a dream, she leaned forward and pressed her lips to his gleaming brown throat. The taste of his salty flesh on her tongue made her instantly weak in the knees.

The Sheik's labored breath caught, and he lifted his right hand and cradled her golden head as she opened his shirt and began sprinkling kisses over the broad expanse of his chest. His dark eyes closed with tortured pleasure.

Temple inhaled deeply of his unique masculine scent as her lips traveled eagerly, caressingly, over his smooth, hot flesh. She felt herself swaying against him, felt the strength of his tall, hard body thrumming through hers, felt her knees buckling.

Shuddering as Temple put out the tip of her tongue and licked the hollow of his throat, Sharif put both hands into her hair, pulled her head up, and looked at her beautiful face. He saw in her expressive emerald eyes a passion that matched his own, and he knew that the power of their physical attraction could no longer be denied.

Still, he warned her, "If I so much as touch you, I will not stop until you are naked beneath me."

Breathlessly she replied, "I was about to say the same thing to you."

23

The Sheik put his hand behind the back of Temple's neck and began to draw her to him. His sultry black gaze focused on her parted lips, he pressed her back into the curve of his supporting arm, bent his dark head, and—just before he kissed her—murmured softly, *"Naksedil."*

Temple was given no opportunity to ask what the Arabic word meant. Sharif's mouth closed over hers in a stunning, breath-stealing kiss that began softly, gently, his smooth warm lips tasting and teasing hers, leisurely exploring.

The surprisingly sweet beginning of that devastating kiss would be the last slow part of their lovemaking. What started as a tender, closed-mouth caress swiftly graduated in intensity to an open-lipped, stroking-tongued kiss of such blazing passion, the pair were immediately set afire.

By the time the highly erotic kiss ended, they were like two wild animals finally freed from their cages. Unleashed passion made sexual savages of them both, as practiced control disintegrated in the raging, enveloping heat.

His mouth melded hotly with hers, Sharif grasped the front of Temple's bodice. A firm, forceful yank and the delicate fabric tore.

Temple was just as rash, just as aggressive. Her mouth open wide to his thrusting tongue, she gripped his half-opened shirt and tugged hard. Buttons flew. Linen ripped. The shirt hung open. She pushed it over his left shoulder, pulled it down his arm and off. She couldn't get to his other arm. It was wrapped around her, supporting her head as he pressed her against it. Her hand went to his back, and she spread her fingers wide to touch as much of him as possible.

Temple trembled.

It was as if under the smooth hot skin she could feel the sinew of steel, reminding her just how strong he was. But his superior strength no longer frightened her. It excited her. Enraptured, she ran her hand up and down the deep cleft in his long, beautifully configured back. And she promised herself that when the opportunity presented itself, she would press her lips to each and every one of the vertebrae.

Continuing to kiss her hungrily, Sharif swept apart Temple's torn dress and yanked at a delicate lacy strap of her chemise, breaking it. He impatiently pushed down the gauzy undergarment, freeing a soft, full breast. Both moaned in rising arousal when that freed breast with its taut, throbbing nipple was pressed against his partially bared chest.

Gasping, Temple finally tore her lips from Sharif's. Trembling with anticipation, she looked into his fiery black eyes as he deftly lowered her ruined dress to her waist. His gaze holding hers, he slipped the tip of his little finger under the other strap of her chemise. He slid it over her shoulder and down her upper arm, then released it. But the lace-trimmed satin stayed in place, snagged on her full breast. Temple lifted her shoulder and drew in her breath. The chemise whispered to her waist.

They hurriedly changed positions so that Temple could get Sharif's remaining shirt sleeve down his arm. Anxiously she tugged and yanked while he extended his arm to aid her, his lips traveling eagerly over her face, her throat. Temple exhaled with delight when the shirt fell to the floor.

Both were now naked to the waist. They kissed again, clinging to each other, relishing the stirring touch of flesh on flesh. Their hearts thundering in their naked breasts, their heated, perspiring bodies pressed closely together, they kissed greedily and sighed loudly and finally sagged weakly to their knees.

Her arms wrapped around his neck, Temple arched her back and thrust her bare breasts into the crisp hair covering the flat hard muscles of Sharif's broad chest. The tickling, tantalizing texture teased at her sensitive nipples, sending tingles of sensation through her swelling breasts and fluttering stomach and pulsing groin.

Their lips finally separated. His breath was labored, his chest heaving. A vein throbbed on his dark forehead. In his hot black eyes was a dangerous wildness that thrilled and pleased Temple. Missing was his armor of calmness and self-possession. Gone was the impassive, unreachable man who took no notice of her. In his place was an anxious, fiery lover who wanted her as much as she wanted him.

His teeth clenched as if in pain, Sharif began tearing off her remaining clothes, intent on stripping her bare. He could not wait another minute to get her undressed.

Temple was just as eager, just as ardent, as the Sheik. While he yanked at her skirts, her hands went to his belt buckle. Feverishly she worked, her nervous fingers managing to unbuckle the belt and move on to the buttons of his snug riding breeches.

All restraint was gone.

They literally tore the clothes off one another, frantic to get at each other. Sharif was surer, swifter than Temple. In seconds he had stripped her of everything and she was naked in his arms. Holding her, kissing her, he managed—with her frenzied assistance—to shed the rest of his own clothes.

When both were wonderfully bare at last, they fell over onto the thick Persian rug, panting from exertion and excitement. Their hot bodies slippery with perspiration, they lay on their sides, facing each other—but only for a second. Quickly Sharif urged Temple onto her back and rose above her, making a place for himself between her slender legs.

Temple trembled when she felt his hard heavy flesh pulse against her burning groin. His weight supported on an elbow, his hand gripping her hair at the crown, Sharif laid his fingers to her lips. Instinctively Temple knew what to do: she put out her tongue and licked the tips of his fingers until they were wet.

She watched, enthralled, as he lowered his hand between their bodies and hastily rubbed the rocket-shaped tip of his throbbing tumescence until it glistened wetly. Then he moved his hand to her. He touched her gently, his licked-wet fingers stroking coaxingly, inquiringly.

At the sudden look of pleased surprise on his face, Temple felt herself flush with embarrassment. She knew exactly what he was thinking: that there'd been no need to moisten his fingers because she was already wet and ready for him.

And it was true.

She was so hot for him that she could feel the silky wetness flowing freely from herself.

Sharif waited not one second more.

He positioned himself perfectly, thrust into her quickly, and Temple, looking into his night black eyes, winced only softly at his deep penetration. The pain was so minimal, it was quickly overridden by the pleasure. New infusions of heat engulfing her, Temple instinctively tilted up her pelvis to receive him as Sharif drove into her deeply, forcefully, stretching and filling her with his awesome pulsating power.

Logic and reason no longer existed in their special world.

The two of them were pagans, naked in a hot desert paradise, determined to taste all the delicious forbidden pleasures of their carnal universe. Their heated, hurried mating there on the tent's plush Persian rugs was totally wild and uninhibited. With an animal passion and brute sensuality, they made such love as few mortals ever experienced.

Surrendering to the outrageous urges of burning desire, they gladly gave themselves up to each other. Moaning and panting, Temple bucked and thrust against Sharif, giving as good as she got, urging him on, daring him to go even farther, matching him movement for movement in his almost brutal lovemaking.

She loved every savage second of their ruthless mating.

The dry oppressive heat of the still Arabian afternoon only intensified the pleasure of the frenzied naked pair who were on fire for each other. The heat rising from the desert floor mingled delightfully with the heat rising from their joined, surging bodies. Both kinds of heat felt good. Good, right, wonderful, as their perspiration-soaked bodies slipped and slid oh so sensuously together.

Every bit as aroused as he, Temple did not whimper

or stiffen when Sharif drove into her repeatedly. She did not demur or try to pull away when he impaled her. She made no attempt to evade him when, buried deeply inside her, he put his hands on her knees and urged her legs to fall wider apart so that he might sink even farther into her.

If he seemed intent on claiming and conquering her completely, Temple was equally eager to capture and keep him there. She pushed her pelvis up as she allowed her open legs to fall more widely apart. Outside herself, fever-hot with passion, she felt as if she wanted to pry herself more fully open to him, for him. To happily offer it all for his taking. To make of her body a hot receptive sacrifice to his potently aggressive masculinity.

She would hold nothing back, she would give everything to him.

And she would take everything from him as well, refusing to let him go until all that he had was hers.

Writhing in her building ecstasy, Temple clutched Sharif's sweat-slick biceps and looked into his hot black eyes as he pounded into her, the force and feel of him thrusting and throbbing inside her filling her with an indescribable excitement.

Temple was so aroused and lost in him, she no longer cared what he was or who he was. She had never known this kind of passion existed. Had never dreamed she could feel like this with a man.

It didn't matter that the lover responsible for such exquisite pleasure was a pirate sheik who had abducted her. She didn't care. It made no difference that this dark-skinned god of love was heartless. Wicked. Disreputable. Lawless. Nothing mattered but the burning touch of his caressing brown hands on her tingling skin, the taste of his searing kisses on her lips, and the feel of his hard, hot flesh pulsing strongly inside her.

All she wanted, now or ever, was to lie here beneath this naked chieftain while he made primitive, passionate love to her. She realized, without the slightest degree of shame, that whatever he wanted her to do, she would do gladly, eagerly. Wherever he wanted to take her, she would go. Whatever he wanted her to be, she would be.

Surrendering totally to her masterful lover, Temple soon found herself on the edge of orgasm. Almost afraid of the frightening ecstasy to come, she wrapped her arms around Sharif's neck and drew his mouth down to hers. Frantically she kissed him as though only his kiss could save her.

Sensing her climax was at hand and feeling as though he couldn't hold his back much longer, Sharif dipped both hands beneath Temple as he kissed her.

He spread his fingers, cupped the twin cheeks of her bottom, lifted her to him, and speeded his movements. Clenching and unclenching his lean hard buttocks, he plunged aggressively into her in a rhythmic rocking motion not unlike the force of waves pounding into a beach.

Her orgasm began almost immediately.

Temple tore her burning lips from Sharif's. Her eyes wide with fright and wonder, she flung her head from side to side and began to whimper. The whimper became a moan, and finally a loud piercing scream of shocked rapture tore from her throat.

Sharif pressed her face against his slick shoulder. She bit him viciously.

He didn't feel it.

Groaning out his own shuddering release, he closed his eyes and bowed his neck backward, the tendons standing out in bold relief. Temple's teeth released his punished flesh, her head dropped back to the rug, and she looked up at his dark, sweat-streaked face, contorted in ecstasy.

Then all at once an incredibly peaceful expression came over his handsome features, and for an instant he looked almost like an innocent young boy. The long dark lashes slowly lifted over his black eyes and he looked at her.

And there was not that cold, indifferent beauty about him, no hint of his impassive nature.

His lips curved into an endearing half smile that was the opposite of the cruel sneer she'd come to dread. Without a word he laid his dark head on her breasts and collapsed atop her.

Sighing with satisfaction, Temple wrapped her weak arms around his slick brown shoulders and pressed her lips to the luxuriant black locks falling appealingly over his forehead.

24

Sharif immediately fell into a deep, dreamless sleep.

Moments later, Temple too was dozing.

The naked pair slept there on the floor as the long somnolent summer afternoon passed. When the burning desert sun finally sank toward the western horizon and the still air began to cool, Sharif awakened.

His lashes fluttered restlessly, then lifted lazily.

Above him was the shimmering white of his tent's roof and beneath him the luxurious softness of the Persian rugs. He was, he realized foggily, Adam naked and flat of his back on the floor in the tent's main room.

Yawning sleepily, he wondered why.

Then a rush of remembering. It all came back, and Sharif felt his bare belly contract reflexively.

Slowly, cautiously, he turned his head.

And saw her.

Temple, as naked as he and more beautiful than a sinless angel, was sleeping beside him amid their torn, scattered clothing. She, too, lay on her back, with one shapely leg stretched out fully, the other bent at the knee, raised slightly and cocked to one side. One of her small hands lay draped over her bare midriff; the other was flung up above her head.

Her tousled blond hair was in tangled disarray. A portion of the wild golden mane partially hid her beautiful face. One long wayward lock was curled around her throat, its wispy ends fanned out on her bare right breast.

Silently Sharif turned onto his side, levered himself onto an elbow, and stared at the sleeping blond beauty. His dark gaze slid admiringly down her pale body. She was more slender than she appeared to be when clothed. Each fragile rib showed beneath the flawless ivory skin, and because she was lying on her back, her flat stomach was concave. Delicate hipbones rose prominently, leaving a taut, shadowed plane between.

Her slender legs were long and perfectly formed, the knees dimpled, the slim ankles shapely. Even her feet were pretty, the toes as precious as a child's.

Sharif's assessing gaze climbed slowly back up her nude white body.

Her chest rose and fell gently as she slumbered. The soft breasts were flattened a little in her reclining position but stood up alluringly enough, their large, soft, rose pink centers sleeping just as she was.

How long, Sharif wondered idly, would it take to awaken those nipples—and her—if he were to bend his head and begin gently kissing them? He was tempted to find out.

Those bare creamy breasts were not all he wanted to kiss.

His dark gaze slid lower, touched her narrow waist briefly, then followed the line of pale wispy hair in its descent from the small indentation of her navel to the dense growth of golden curls between her pale thighs.

His heart began to thud against the wall of his chest. He stared at the tempting triangle of crisp blond coils, totally tantalized. His fingers itched to touch, to stroke, to tunnel through the pale springy curlicues.

He swallowed with difficulty.

He was tempted to reach out, spread his hand, and possessively cup that enticing mound of warm femininity.

And claim it for his own.

To push her legs apart and gently sweep aside the pale angel curls and kiss her there, where that tiny bud of sensation was asleep as she was asleep. One stroke of his tongue and it would awaken as she would awaken. After the initial shock, she would sigh and moan and squirm while he licked it to throbbing life.

Sharif exhaled heavily and ground his even white teeth.

Already he wanted her again. Had to have her. Couldn't rest until he'd made love to her. Was aroused just from looking at her. Sexual sweat beaded his hairline and upper lip, and a fully formed erection bobbed and surged on his bare brown belly.

His hot black eyes suddenly went cold, and he scowled at her. His weakness angered him, and that anger was directed at her. She looked so sweet, so innocent in slumber, but she was dangerous and deadly in her desirability.

He shuddered.

She held a mysterious power over him no woman ever had. The startling knowledge rankled him. Made him want to show her right here, right now, that *he* was the master, *she* nothing more than an available plaything. *He* exercised all the power. *She* had no control over him. None.

His eyes flashing with a mixture of fury and desire, he stared at her, grinding his teeth.

There she lay, stretched out naked and defenseless, his to do with as he pleased. Over the years more than one jaded lover had been awakened to his less-than-tender lovemaking.

This one was no different from the others. He felt no need to act the sensitive suitor. No obligation to kiss and coax her before taking her. She thought him an animal, a heathen, a dark, dirty savage. Why not prove her right? Why not force her to endure the sexual whims of a base barbarian?

At that moment Temple awakened.

The first thing she saw was a naked, angry-looking Sharif looming menacingly over her. Fear immediately filled her emerald eyes, and she tried to lunge up.

"No, it's all right," he murmured soothingly, her fright instantly undermining his wrath. "*Naksedil*," he whispered, the intent to roughly take her forgotten. "Be still now."

Gently he urged her back down onto the soft rug. He was, oddly, overcome with the need to put her completely at her ease, to be tender and caring so that she would *want* to give herself to him.

Looking into his jet black eyes, full consciousness returning, Temple was immediately filled with shame and regret. Her face flamed as she recalled with appalling clarity their frenzied bout of animalistic love-making a few short hours before. Dear God, what had she done? How had it happened? How could she have possibly allowed this heartless Arab pirate chieftain to . . . to . . .

Temple's eyes closed as Sharif lowered his face to hers, brushed his smooth, warm mouth against her lips. No pressure. No force. Simply a gentle, nonthreatening caress, his full lips pressing tenderly against her own.

No. No. It had all been a terrible mistake and one she

wouldn't repeat. Temple turned her head away in an attempt to evade his kiss.

"No," she said. "Don't . . . please."

"I won't," he murmured even as his lips followed and found hers again.

He kissed her and kept on kissing her. The soft, sweet kisses continued as Sharif, supporting his weight on an elbow, leaned over her face but did not lay a hand on her. He touched only her lips with his lips.

Temple ordered herself to push him away, to leap up from the lush Persian carpet and flee. But it was as if she couldn't find the strength to move, couldn't make herself roll away from him and rise. Still, she wouldn't, she promised herself, allow him to make love to her again.

Not now.

Not ever.

His tender, disarming kisses continued, and try as she might not to, Temple slowly began to respond to the brushing, teasing feel of his persuasive lips on hers. Her pulse quickened. Her will weakened.

How strangely seductive it was to lie here naked while the equally bare Sharif kissed but did not touch her. Her lips began to respond to his, to cling to his. She began to lift her head in an effort to keep his lips on hers longer.

Sharif took his time kissing her. Savoring the warmth and softness of her mouth, he continued to press gentle, unhurried kisses to her lips until they were opening to him, inviting him to stay longer, to take more.

Still he waited.

It was several long minutes before his kisses changed, became seeking and demanding. His tongue finally delved into her mouth to explore and probe its inner sweetness.

Sighing, welcoming the intrusion of his sleek fiery tongue, Temple felt her resolve slipping away. Desire was starting to build and with it a kind of pleasure that was like a powerful drug. The more of it she tasted, the more she wanted, the more she had to have. It was impossible to forget the ecstasy that awaited if only she would stay right here on the floor with the amorous Sheik.

Surrendering to his stirring kisses, Temple felt as if the masterful mouth moving so expertly on her trembling lips were searing them and burning all the way down into her body. Nobody kissed like the Sheik. His kisses were an irresistible blend of fierceness and tenderness, oddly soft and at the same time violently demanding.

Thrilling beyond belief.

Quivering from the probing of his tongue, Temple felt her fingertips tingle with the need to stroke his smooth back, his hair-covered chest, his flat belly. But still she hesitated. He hadn't yet touched her. Why, she didn't know. But she decided she would wait until he could no longer stand not having his arms around her, his hands on her flesh. Let him be the one to weaken first. Make him touch her.

Then she would respond in kind.

Her arms lay at her sides, her hands flattened on the thick Persian rug, fingers clutching the lush nap. It was all she could do to keep them there. Surely any second he would reach for her.

He didn't.

While his kisses grew increasingly hotter and prolonged, Sharif kept his hands to himself, as if he had read her thoughts. When his heated lips left hers Temple was sure he would raise his head and reach for her. But his head never lifted, his hands didn't stir.

His mouth moved across her flushed face, pressing kisses to her hot cheeks, the tip of her nose, her closing eyes. She trembled when his lips traveled along her high cheekbone and moved to her ear, to kiss the sensitive spot just below it. His silky black hair tickling her face, he slid his open lips along the cord going down the side of her throat, and Temple shivered.

Her head bowed backward and she drew in her breath when his mouth sank into the hollow of her throat and his tongue gently stroked. Involuntarily she squirmed about, her bare bottom wiggling, her shoulder blades digging into the cushioning softness of the Persian rug.

She wanted so badly to touch him. She wanted so badly for him to touch her. To feel his hands on her. To have her hands on him.

It had become an erotic game of torment, and both were playing to win. As the game progressed, both became more and more aroused. While she writhed and wiggled, his roving lips drove her half crazy with desire until the blood in her veins became liquid fire.

She would never be able to figure out just how Sharif managed to continue his invasive exploration of her body with just his mouth. But he did. And it was both maddening and thrilling.

Nuzzling and nibbling a wet, hot path down from her throat, Sharif moved his lips to her left breast, pressed kisses to the rising swell before opening over the taut nipple. A strangled cry caught in her throat. Her hands automatically lifted a couple of inches off the floor. She caught herself, placed them back palms down beside her.

A little wince of joy escaped her when Sharif raked his sharp teeth across her tingling nipple. She sighed when he flicked his tongue back and forth over the pebble-hard crest, circled it with quick swirling motions, licked it as though it were a sweet candy, then opened his mouth wide and sucked forcefully, sending her into deep shudders of ecstasy.

Oh, God, how she wanted to put her hands into his thick raven hair and press his hot face even closer to her swelling breast.

The game continued.

One of his hands supporting his weight, the other wrapped almost protectively around his jerking, bobbing tumescence, Sharif kissed her breasts until they were pink and throbbing. He kissed her pale shoulders. He kissed her warm underarms. He kissed her delicate ribs. He kissed her flat stomach. He kissed her prominent hip-bones. He kissed her navel.

All without the use of his hands.

Finally, when he began to kiss the wispy line of blond hair going down her jerking belly, Temple lost the hard-fought game.

She was dazed with uncontrollable desire. Seized by a hot longing so novel and foreign to her that she was no longer herself. Her hands frantically went to the sides of Sharif's dark head and she pulled up his handsome face.

"Sharif, Sharif," she gasped, her fingers clutching the thick hair at his temples.

"*Chérie,*" he murmured, the pulse in his throat throbbing.

Then his hands were all over her and hers were all over him. She didn't flinch or try to pull away when he drew her hand to his throbbing, blood-filled erection and whispered, "Touch me, hold me."

Sharif swallowed hard and his hand fell away. He watched through smoldering eyes as she began to toy with him, letting her slender white fingers glide up to the jerking tip, then move slowly all the way back down to cup and gently squeeze. "Like this?" she asked, and slid her caressing fingers back up his impressive length.

"Exactly like that," he said, his eyes closing, his chest heaving.

After only a minute he jerked her hand away, stretched out on his back, and lifted her astride his hips. All the breath left his body when she settled comfortably atop him, her parted thighs warmly cradling his erection.

Temple extended her arm, laid her fingers on his lips. He put out his tongue and licked her fingertips until they were wet.

When she then hesitated, uncertain, he said, his tone a low caress, "Do it, *chérie.*"

Then he watched, transfixed, as she rose to her knees, took him gently in her hand, and ran her dampened fingertips over the velvet smooth head until it glistened. Again she looked at him.

"Take me now," he encouraged gently.

Obeying, Temple carefully guided just the glistening tip up inside herself.

"Settle down on me," he coaxed. "Slowly. Easy."

Nodding, feeling incredibly hot and bold and sexy, Temple took her hands away.

She raised her arms, put them behind her head, and, watching him watch her, slowly, seductively sank down on him until she was completely impaled. Only then did her hands come down from behind her head. She gripped his ribs, leaned down so that her bare breasts rubbed against his chest, and brushed her mouth to his.

Before he could capture her lips in a kiss, she whispered, "What do you want from me?"

His hands came up, swept the heavy blond hair back from her face, and he said, "Everything. All of you. Withhold nothing from me. Give it to me, *Naksedil.*"

25

Her terrified screams pierced the dawn silence.

Tears streaming down her cheeks, she pleaded for mercy. It did no good. He was merciless.

He raised his hand and hit her again, his open palm striking her with such force that blood gushed from her nose and her split bottom lip began to bleed anew.

Her left eye was blackened and swollen almost shut. Her right arm was badly sprained from being twisted cruelly behind her back. Blue-and-purple bruises covered her naked body from his vicious slaps and brutal punches. Her bare buttocks were crisscrossed with raw red welts left by the braided leather riding crop with which he had enthusiastically flogged her. Teeth marks decorated the tender insides of her firm thighs.

And both earlobes—not yet fully healed—had been viciously clipped away with a pair of pinking shears at a similar session a few nights ago.

Sobbing uncontrollably, she continued to kneel beside the bed, within his reach. Even if she had not been afraid to try to get away from him, she was too weak and battered even to attempt it. She could hardly move. There was not a single square inch of her flesh that had not been severely punished by him. Not one thing about her that didn't bleed, sting, throb, or ache.

After an agonizingly long night of his perversion and brutality, she had absolutely no strength left. She couldn't leave if he ordered her to do so. She was utterly under his power, at his mercy. All she could hope for was that he, too, was growing tired and would soon finally fall asleep.

"Stand up!" he ordered in his native tongue.

"Master, I cannot," she whimpered.

Her response displeased the sultan.

Mustafa Ibn Agha Hussain, lounging indolently among the satin pillows on his solid gold bed encrusted with diamonds and emeralds, made a sour face.

He was out of sorts.

The entire night had been wasted, not to mention the generous sum of money he had paid for Leyla, this beautiful but disappointing creature, kneeling cowed and tyrannized beside the bed. Leyla was Circassian, as were most of the ladies of his harem. The Circassian girls were heralded for their beauty and were therefore very expensive. Leyla was extraordinarily beautiful and had therefore been extraordinarily expensive. But he had paid the price willingly, eager to own such an exquisite jewel.

Now he found Leyla disgusting. At this moment he hated the sight of her. She was not at all what she had seemed, what he had paid so dearly for, and he was sadly disillusioned. He'd heard of Leyla's fire and beauty well before he ever saw her. And when finally she was brought to him, a tall, lithe gem with golden brown skin and blazing dark eyes, she appeared to be haughty and spirited. He was sure he had himself a spitfire, a wildcat, a she-devil he would spend many a long, lust-filled evening taming.

How wrong he was.

Leyla was a sniveling coward and a bore. She was like all the rest. No spirit. No passion. He'd had her for less than a week and already he was tired of her. Sick to death of her meekness and her whining. He wanted a woman who would challenge him. Defy him. Amuse him. In the name of Allah, he would gladly give up his entire harem for just one such woman!

Sighing with self-pitying despair, Mustafa reached out a fat, bejeweled hand to a golden tray resting on the bed. He dipped his short fingers into a stemmed crystal bowl of sherbet, scooped up a big blob, and plopped it into his mouth. Then he reached for a golden goblet that was filled with a special, sticky sweet liqueur. He drank thirstily, slammed the goblet back down on the tray, and glared at the woman's bent head. Melting sherbet dripped down his sausage fingers and spotted his already soiled robes of gold-trimmed scarlet.

He hardly noticed.

His wet tongue coming out of his fleshy lips, he licked his chin and continued to glare at the weeping woman.

"You have disappointed me, slave," he said, unable at the moment to recall the young woman's name.

"I am sorry, Excellency," Leyla sobbed.

With a great groan of effort, the heavy Turkish sultan turned over onto his rounded belly, raised his massive arms, crossed them, and leaned his double chins atop them.

"Get out of my sight," he said coldly. "Go away."

"Yes, Excellency."

The pain-racked young woman attempted to rise to her feet but failed. Her weak legs wouldn't support her. She fell against the edge of the golden bed. Her long unbound hair swished against the reclining ruler's fleshy face.

It angered him.

Mustafa grabbed her dark flowing locks and pulled violently, causing the woman to cry out once more in pain. A generous portion of her hair clutched in his fat fist, he began bellowing loudly for his manservant, Alwan.

Alwan was just outside the door.

He immediately leapt up from the chair where he sat dozing sporadically and drew a deep breath to stiffen his spine. It had been a very long night, one of many very long nights of late. The master had been more impossible than usual since the failed attack on the desert village of Sheik Sharif Aziz Hamid.

Alwan had so hoped this beautiful young Circassian for whom the sultan had paid an astronomical sum might sweeten his disposition. She hadn't. Leyla had been at the seaside palace for a week and there had been no change in Mustafa's disposition. Alwan knew the reason.

The master wanted Sheik Hamid's American woman. He would not rest until he had her.

Alwan hurried inside the vast bedchamber as the rising summer sun painted the room in varying shades of pink. He saw the red-robed Mustafa sprawled on his stomach, the mammoth cheeks of his buttocks rising in the air like twin red domes. His hand was gripping something dark, which, Alwan learned as he proceeded into the opulent chamber, was the flowing dark hair of the beautiful slave whose screams he had heard throughout the night.

"Yes, Excellency," said Alwan. "How may I be of service?"

"Get *this* out of my sight." He nodded to the weeping woman. "It is ugly and it offends me."

"Yes, Excellency. Right away."

Alwan hurried to the bed. He anxiously set about to

untangle the sultan's fat fingers from the sobbing Leyla's long hair, but his master stopped him.

"Don't waste time with that," said Mustafa, annoyed. "Cut it."

"Cut it, master?" Alwan looked questioningly at him.

"Her hair!" snapped a petulant Mustafa. "Cut it off so I may free my fingers."

"Yes, Excellency."

Alwan scurried across the room, found a pair of sharp barber's scissors, returned to the bed, and snipped away a large portion of the woman's hair an inch from her scalp. The lazy sultan then straightened his stubby fingers and the shorn locks fell onto the mattress.

Again Mustafa made a face.

Alwan quickly brushed the severed hair off the bed. It fluttered to the richly carpeted floor, landing beside the kneeling woman. Crying heartbrokenly, Leyla picked up the discarded hair as if hoping she could reattach it to her head.

Alwan knelt beside her, put an arm around her slender waist, and helped her to stand. Clutching the severed hair to her bare, trembling bosom, she wept and leaned on him as he slowly walked her from the room.

Before they could reach the door, the sultan shouted, "Get rid of her and come back. And bring Mahdi with you. And bring Jamal, too! Hurry!"

"Yes, Excellency."

Minutes later Alwan returned with Mahdi and Jamal. Mahdi was the lone survivor of the nighttime raid on *El Siif*'s desert stronghold. To him had fallen the unpleasant task of returning alone and empty-handed from the failed invasion to relay the Sheik's message to Mustafa.

Enraged, the sultan had had Mahdi beaten, as if it had all been the messenger's fault. Mustafa had been furious with him ever since, and each time he was summoned, Mahdi was fearful.

Jamal was the sultan's interpreter. He, too, was afraid of the sadistic ruler, but he was clever. He regularly reminded Mustafa that he could speak six languages: Turkish, English, French, Italian, German, and most important of all, Arabic. No other interpreter could keep the sultan as well informed as he, Jamal.

Both men, roused from their beds at this early hour, hurried down the long marble-floored corridor toward the royal bedchamber. They knew what the sultan wanted. It was not the first time they had been summoned to his bedchamber in the past few weeks.

Mustafa had turned onto his back atop the gem-encrusted golden bed. He had turned, the soiled scarlet robe had not. Open down the front, it lay twisted beneath his massive girth, leaving his portly lower body and flabby legs exposed. Making no effort to cover himself, he lay propped up amid the satin pillows, one hand idly scratching his itching groin, the other stuffing figs into his mouth.

"Come closer," he commanded, motioning the three men to the bed, chewing with his mouth open.

The trio approached. When they stood directly beside the bed, lined up, their hands clasped before them, the sultan said, "Jamal, did you bring it?"

"Yes, Excellency."

"Let me see it. Give it to me."

Nodding, the slender interpreter withdrew from the folds of his robe a well-thumbed newspaper clipping along with a crumpled message written on heavy vellum. He unfolded the clipping carefully and handed it to the reclining ruler. Mustafa wiped his sticky fingers on the bed linens and reached for it.

He stared at the article.

And he began to lick his thick lips as he studied the rotogravure of an attractive, light-haired woman smiling into the camera. A string of drool began to slide from the corner of his mouth, and his beady dark eyes gleamed demonically.

"Here, read it to me," he ordered, thrusting the clipping back at his interpreter.

As he had done at least fifty times, Jamal read aloud the article, which had been cut from a copy of the London *Times.*

LONDON TIMES

MAY 7, 1898. MISS TEMPLE DUPLESSIS LONGWORTH OF WILMINGTON, DELAWARE, ARRIVED IN LONDON LAST EVENING. THE BEAUTIFUL, BLOND AMERICAN MUNITIONS HEIRESS WAS ACCOMPANIED BY HER COUSIN, RUPERT LONGWORTH, A GENTLEMAN OF LEISURE WELL KNOWN IN MAYFAIR'S SOCIAL CIRCLES. THE PAIR'S STAY AT THE SAVOY WILL BE A BRIEF ONE. AFTER TWO SHORT WEEKS, THE LONGWORTHS ARE TO LEAVE ON AN EXTENDED TOUR OF THE ARABIAN DESERTS. . . .

Jamal continued, reading the entire article aloud while the sultan's lips moved along with him on the parts he had memorized. The reading of the newspaper article completed, Jamal then read the communication that Mustafa's men had taken from the Sheik's slain courier. The message was to have been cabled to the American heiress's family.

Mustafa knew every word of the missive. And when the interpreter concluded, the sultan, looking furious now, grabbed the message back and motioned Mahdi forward. Cringing inwardly, Mahdi stepped closer to the gem-encrusted golden bed and the spoiled, half-naked despot who lay upon it.

"You didn't see the blond American on that night?" Mustafa asked Mahdi.

"No, Excellency," said Mahdi. "I did not."

"Fool!" Mustafa thundered. "Fools, all of you!" He waved the crumpled piece of paper and said, "This clearly states that the woman is being held by the Sheik!"

"Yes, Excellency."

"Fools and cowards, the lot of you. I should kill you!" He reached for the riding crop he'd used on the girl, slapped it cruelly across Mahdi's startled face. "I send you to get her and you come back alone, spouting idle threats from that arrogant desert bastard." His beady dark eyes narrowed to slits in his dark fleshy face, and he added, "You think I fear that son of a camel? I fear no man, least of all the impostor who calls himself Sheik Sharif Aziz Hamid."

"No, Excellency."

Exhaustion finally defanging the raging sultan, he began to yawn and his eyelids grew heavy. He reached for one of the satin-cased pillows, groaned, and turned over onto his left side. "Leave me," he said softly.

But his voice boomed and reverberated throughout the vast bedchamber when he lifted his head and shouted, "That blond woman will be mine or heads will roll!"

26

Temple awakened slowly from a delightfully pleasant dream.

Only half conscious, her eyes remaining closed, she lay still on the soft, silk-sheeted bed, suspended trance-like in that foggy state between deep slumber and full wakefulness. Not wanting to wake up, willing herself to drift back off so that the beautiful dream would continue, Temple lay there contentedly reliving every thrilling second of the wonderfully erotic dream.

Warm, masterful hands moved over her bare tingling body, touching, caressing, exploring. Burning lips followed closely in their wake, spreading fire and pleasure to all the sensitive areas of her flesh.

Sighing, squirming, Temple slowly opened her emerald eyes, and a foolish little smile tugged at her kiss-swollen lips. Happily she realized the dream had been real.

She turned her head slowly, expecting to see the dark, handsome head of the Sheik lying on the pillow beside her. He was not there. She sighed in mild disappointment and turned onto her side, sweeping a hand over the cool silken sheets where he had so recently lain. She recalled with a rush of excitement how incredibly dark his long, lean body had looked against the snowy whiteness of the bed.

Her cheeks reddened as she remembered how they had both been so aroused that when—sometime around midnight—they'd finally come into the bedroom, they hadn't bothered turning out the lamp. Its mellow light had washed over them as they'd made wild, uninhibited love.

A delicious little tremble raced through Temple's slender body at the vivid recollection of Sharif's dark face looming above her own, the lamplight striking the high planes of his cheekbones and reflecting in the fathomless depths of those burning black eyes.

Again she could hear him murmuring in Arabic, and although she understood not a word, his tone made every utterance sound like a caress. And when her eyes had slipped closed in pleasure, he had switched to English, saying softly, commandingly, "Do not close your eyes, *chérie*. Look at me while I love you."

Temple sat up in the bed. Allowing the sheet to fall forgotten to her waist, she yawned and stretched lazily like a contented feline. Looking languidly around the luxurious room, she was delighted to see that a tub of hot steaming water awaited. She was further pleased to see that her riding clothes had been laid out.

A shiver of anticipation shot up her spine.

She had forgotten. She was to ride with the Sheik this morning! He was probably waiting for her right now, eager to be off, their horses saddled and whinnying restlessly just outside the tent.

Temple threw back the sheet and leapt out of bed. She climbed into the tub and groaned softly from the welcome comfort of its soothing heat, but she did not

linger to enjoy it. Ignoring the soreness between her legs
and the slight aching of her limbs from being stretched
and pressed into unusual positions, Temple bathed
speedily.

Out of the tub after only a few short minutes, she
dressed in a fresh pair of tan gabardine riding breeches,
a pale blue cotton blouse, and knee-high boots of
smooth oxblood leather. She pulled a brush through her
tangled hair, wound the loose locks into a thick rope,
and pinned them atop her head.

Her heart was beating erratically when, clutching a
cork sun helmet in nervous fingers, she paused before
the curtains separating the two rooms.

How would the Sheik behave this morning? Would
he be as anxious to see her as she was to see him? Would
he smile and open his arms to her? Would he eagerly
kiss her and hold her close as he had done throughout
the night?

Temple inhaled deeply, fighting the dizziness of
excitement. She swept through the curtains with a glowing smile on her face.

The room was empty.

Her smile fading only a little, she hurried to the tent's
entrance and stepped into the bright morning sunlight.
The saddled salmon-hued stallion, Toz, was waiting for
her.

The Sheik was not.

Smiling broadly, little Tariz stepped forward to greet
her. "Ah, you are feeling well this morning, Temple?"

"I . . . yes, yes, I feel . . . fine." She looked about, then
blurted out, "Where is Sharif?"

"The master is not here at the moment," said Tariz.

"Oh? We are to ride together this morning. Will he be
back soon or . . . "

"I think not," said the servant, noticing the quick flash

of disappointment that came into her expressive green eyes. "I am to ride with you this morning, mistress."

Temple longed to ask why, to make Tariz tell her just where the Sheik was and why he had changed his mind about their morning ride. She wanted to shout at the grinning little man that last night the Sheik had told her—as she'd lain naked in his arms—that the two of them would ride out of camp early this morning. He knew of a secret uninhabited oasis. They would spend the day there together, bathing in the cool clear waters, making love on the grassy banks.

But she remained outwardly composed.

Her smile back in place, she said, "Good. I'd much rather ride with you."

Alone at that secret desert oasis, miles away from camp, Sharif swam in the cool, cleansing waters of the palm-shaded pool. Slicing through the water with long, fluid strokes, he swam gracefully, determinedly. His muscular arms, moving in perfect precision, effortlessly pulled him along while his kicking feet propelled him forward.

His dark face ducking beneath, then emerging from the water's smooth surface, he found little pleasure or relaxation in the strenuous exercise. He swam as swiftly as could, as if he were in a life-or-death race that he was desperate to win.

And in a way, he was.

Sharif had awakened at dawn to find Temple naked in his bed. His first impulse had been to draw her into his arms and make love to her.

His second had been to get as far away from her as possible.

He had risen quickly, taking care not to disturb her.

Dressing hurriedly in the dim half-light, he'd forced himself to keep his eyes and his thoughts off the beautiful woman asleep in his bed. His back to her, he drew a pair of soft suede riding breeches up over his hips and buttoned them swiftly with sure, deft fingers. He sank onto the divan, pulled on a pair of supple leather boots, and immediately shot back to his feet. In his haste to be gone, he thrust his long arms into a freshly laundered linen shirt but did not button it up his dark chest.

Not daring to look back, he swept through the heavy curtains. Emerging into the tent's main room, he exhaled, feeling as if he had successfully escaped a dungeon—an irresistibly erotic dungeon wherein lay a seductive golden-haired dragon far more dangerous than any fire-breathing monster.

Stuffing the long tails of his shirt into the waistband of his suede trousers, Sharif paused only long enough to take a cigarette from the silver Tiffany box on the table. He stuck it between his lips, unlighted, and crossed to the tent's entrance, where he yanked back the flap and stepped out into the breaking dawn.

His mouth opened in surprise on seeing Tariz. The unlighted cigarette fell from his lips; he caught it as it hit his chest.

"Is everything all right?" Sharif asked.

"That is what I would like to know," Tariz replied, his usual sunny smile absent.

Sharif shrugged. "Everything is fine."

He put the cigarette back into his mouth and leaned down to the tiny flame of the match Tariz struck. He drew the smoke deep into his lungs, held it there, and said, "Why wouldn't it be?" He slowly released the smoke.

"My stallion and yours are saddled and waiting," Tariz said. "I will ride with you and we will talk."

The cigarette dangling from his lips, smoke drifting up into his narrowed black eyes, Sharif shook his head. "No. I wish to ride alone this morning." He moved toward the waiting stallion, took the cigarette from his mouth, and flicked an ash. "You will ride with Temple when she awakens."

Then, purposely ignoring Tariz's inquisitive fatherly look, he mounted hastily and rode the black stallion, Prince, at breakneck speed to get to this remote oasis. Both man and horse were hot and winded and sweating profusely by the time they reached the first sparse stand of tall date palms. Sharif jumped to the ground before Prince came to a complete stop. While the lathered stallion blew and whinnied appreciatively, Sharif reached up, unbuckled his jaw strap, and unbited him, tossing the bridle to the grassy ground.

Sharif then impatiently shrugged out of his sweat-soaked white shirt and went directly to the water's edge. He dropped onto his stomach and braced his weight on bent arms. He leaned out, lowered his hot face, and began to drink of the cold, clear water.

The lathered Prince moved down beside his supine master, lowered his velvet muzzle into the pool, and swilled noisily, lifting his regal head between long pulls of the refreshing water to whinny his gratitude and pleasure.

The man lying beside him didn't raise his head. Sharif drank like a cat, lapping at the cold water, pacing himself, drinking slowly until he'd finally quenched his thirst. At last his face came up out of the water, and he levered himself to his knees and rose to his feet.

While Prince continued to swill and blow and carry on, Sharif stripped. He was completely naked by the time Prince finished drinking. The stallion lifted his head and began nudging Sharif's bare shoulder.

"All right," Sharif said, and worked swiftly to unsaddle the stallion.

He hauled the Moorish leather saddle off Prince's back, tossed it to the ground, and told the big beast, "You do what you want, I'm taking a swim."

He gave the stallion an affectionate slap on the withers, then turned and dove into the clear, deep pool. The shimmering black neighed and trembled and plunged in beside him. As soon as they were in the invigorating water, Prince wanted to play. He bumped his master's back in an invitation to frolic.

But Sharif was not in the mood.

He plunged under the surface and shot away, swimming underwater, putting distance between himself and the stallion. So Prince stayed in only long enough to cool off. Then he clopped back up onto the bank, shimmering wet, and began to crop the grass contentedly.

Contentment was not so easily obtained for Prince's troubled master.

Sharif remained in the water for a long time, swimming with vigor and purpose, single-mindedly determined to wash away Temple's lingering scent—and her lingering hold on him.

He continued to swim until the blood in his veins cooled and his head cleared. When finally he was so tired he could hardly move his weak arms and legs and his breath was so rapid and labored that it burned in his chest, Sharif pulled himself up onto the bank. His rubbery knees folding beneath him, he sank to the ground and stretched out on his back atop the soft, cushioning grass.

A gentle breeze blew from out of the south, swaying the tall palm fronds and stroking Sharif's gleaming wet body. Exhausted from the long sleepless night of savage lovemaking and dead tired from the taxing exercise of swimming, Sharif was ready for a nice long nap.

He shifted his shoulders a little to get more comfortable, folded an arm beneath his wet head, closed his eyes, and exhaled. But sleep didn't come.

A vivid vision did.

The indelible vision of a lovely, naked Temple seated astride him, her luminous skin washed in the mellow lamplight, her golden hair dancing about her pale shoulders, and her ivory breasts swaying provocatively as she rode him.

Sharif's dark eyes opened.

He muttered expletives. He cursed his body's immediate and automatic response to the graphic recollection. The blood rushed into his groin, causing an inevitable expansion there, then hammered upward and spread an almost suffocating heat throughout his body so that he could hardly breathe.

His face a mask of torture, Sharif rolled to a sitting position. He clenched his jaw and ground his teeth. He shook his head to clear it. He willed her to disappear, to leave him alone, to let him go.

He forced himself to remember exactly who she was. And he knew well.

He knew all about Miss Temple DuPlessis Longworth. He had studied her.

He knew about the Delaware family estate, Edgewater, with its Greek Revival, eight-columned white mansion and the vast lawn that ended at the river's edge. He knew she had been expelled from Sophie Newcomb in her senior year. Jailed with Susan B. Anthony for leading a suffrage march on the capital—embarrassing her father, Walter Wilson Longworth, then President Cleveland's secretary of the interior and at the same time pleasing her mother's brother, James DuPlessis, chief operator of the powerful engine that generated the family fortune, the DuPlessis munitions empire.

He knew she was intelligent, willful, and sought after by the most eligible bachelors in Europe and America. He knew she collected male hearts without even trying and discarded them as she might discard a gown she'd worn but once. He knew that she tired of a suitor the moment the poor chap fell in love with her.

He even knew about the poet. . . .

Grinding his teeth, Sharif reached for his discarded suede trousers, withdrew from a pocket the spent brass shell casing he always carried. He held it in his hand, stared at the telltale stamp on its end.

Du-P

It did no good.

The beguiling vision of Temple would not fade away.

Sharif's face darkened with the sudden startling realization that it would *never* leave him.

He knew in that instant that now and tonight and tomorrow and for all the rest of his life, he would hold that vision of Temple. And he knew as well that it was not just his groin she tugged at.

It was his heart as well.

The Sheik trembled.

27

Temple and Tariz returned to camp at mid-morning. The fierce desert heat had cut short their ride, and Temple was glad. She was more than a little anxious to get back to the village.

As soon as she pulled up on Toz, hauling him to a stop, she leapt off his back and dashed into the tent, hoping to find Sharif there.

The tent was empty.

Temple made a face, then laughed at herself for being so foolish. Sharif was never in the tent at this hour. He was, after all, the Sheik, the leader of large scattered tribes of men who constantly commanded his time and attention. He was, understandably, busy. She could hardly expect him to drop everything and come rushing back to spend the day in idle pleasure with her.

Still very much aglow with sweet satisfaction, Temple passed the remainder of the morning recalling—with smiles and shivers—the thrillingly passionate night she'd spent with the handsome Sharif. Already looking forward to the magical moment when she would again be in his arms, Temple moved about the tent, touching things that belonged to the Sheik.

A shirt was tossed over the back of a chair in the bedroom. She picked it up, pressed it to her face, and inhaled the faint smell of shaving soap and the French cigarettes he favored. She sighed and rubbed her cheek against the collar. She laid down the shirt, went to the tall ebony chest, and picked up some black pearl studs that were scattered carelessly on its polished top. She closed her palm around the studs and held them in her hand for a time before placing them back where she'd found them.

She was tempted to open one or two of the chest drawers and look inside, but she checked herself. Instead she turned away and strolled over to the massive bed, which was now neatly made. It looked more inviting than ever. Temple smiled, thinking how incredibly sensual it would be to make love atop the shimmering black silk counterpane with all the black and white bolsters and pillows stacked up against the tall headboard.

Noon came and went with no sign of the Sheik.

The rosy blush of bliss had faded from Temple's pale face and her wonderful sense of well-being had begun to dissipate. Mindless euphoria had given way to speculative worry. Conflicting emotions now warred within her. Left alone with too much time to think, she had started to suffer growing pangs of guilt and remorse. Terrible doubts assailed her.

The long, hot afternoon dragged by torturously, and with each passing hour Temple became more upset, more contrite, more angry with herself. Rebelling now against the constant flood of fresh memories that caused her cheeks to burn and her heart to throb, she began to pace and ponder and scold herself for what she had done.

She was appalled.

It had seemed so right at the time. Now she couldn't believe that she had—of her own free will—gone eagerly into the Sheik's arms. And into his bed. She had done absolutely scandalous things with him and had gloried openly in the shocking intimacy they'd shared. She had experienced an ever-changing kaleidoscope of new emotions she'd never known herself capable of. With each penetrating possession of her body, she had become immersed in waves of ever escalating ecstasy that were frightening in their intensity.

Oh, God, what had she done?

Temple's hands rose to her face to press her burning cheeks.

Sharif was an Arab. To him every woman was a slave, including her. He was a lawless barbarian who had abducted her! He was holding her prisoner against her will in this remote desert village, for God's sake. And she had let him make love to her! How could she have been so stupid, so unforgivably weak!

She knew full well what a cold, uncaring man he was. Last night had meant nothing to him. She was merely a convenient diversion, a balm to his boredom. Worse, if he happened to be bored and wanted her right now, this minute, he had only to come to the tent and take her.

But if she wanted him, what could she do about it? Nothing. Not a thing. She couldn't go to him. She couldn't ask him to take her in his arms. She couldn't summon him back to the tent and command him to make love to her.

She was to give him everything and ask for nothing?

"No!" Temple spoke the word aloud. "Oh, no, you don't, *El Siif!* You may be the feared Sword of Arabia, but I'll be damned if you'll hoist *me* on your big bad blade again!"

Her hands clenching into tight fists at her sides, her chin lifting, Temple felt her fiery independence surfacing. She was, in case he had forgotten, Temple DuPlessis Longworth. In twenty-five years no man had ever had the upper hand with her and no man ever would. No pagan sheik could beckon her to his bed as if she were a slave.

Temple's placed her hands on her hips, and her green eyes snapped with renewed defiance.

So she had made a mistake! So what! That's all it had been. She was human, and she had made an incredibly foolish mistake in a moment of weakness. The deed was done, and she couldn't undo it, but she had no intention of paying for it forever.

She would simply forget it. It would not be repeated. She would see to that. She had come to her senses, thought things out, and had reached a decision. And having done so, she began to relax a little and finally even to smile.

She would, she decided wickedly, make the arrogant Arab aware of just exactly who possessed the power.

It was not he.

It was she.

She would prove it. To him and to herself. She would make him want her. She would make him desire her again, then coldly refuse him. She would not, she promised herself, allow Sheik Sharif Aziz Hamid to *ever* touch her again.

The long afternoon finally drew to a close. The sun had begun to set. And still no Sharif.

Darkness fell.

The dinner hour rapidly approached, and Temple, by now on pins and needles again, was dressed for the evening in a stunning gown of alluring black lace. She had chosen it from the half dozen dresses Rhikia had brought for her to pick from. The gown was daring and sexy. The sleeves were long and tight on her arms, coming to delicate points at her wrists, and the bodice was fitted and high throated.

But beneath the black lace, the flesh of her arms and shoulders and back were totally bare. An insert of black moiré taffeta lining the tight bodice covered her bosom, but just barely. The swell of her breasts was clearly visible above the inset, the pale flesh made all the more enticing by the covering of provocative black lace that enhanced but did not conceal.

Her long hair, shimmering with healthy highlights, was dressed elaborately atop her head. Circling the delicate column of her throat—less than an inch above the band of her tight lace collar—was a narrow black velvet ribbon. A large perfect black pearl was suspended from the ribbon, resting in the hollow of her throat.

On her feet were black satin dancing slippers, and underneath the narrow skirt of her black lace gown, sheer black stockings hugged her slender legs. Saucy black lace garters, circling each pale thigh just above her knee, held the stockings in place. She wore no petticoats beneath the slim-skirted gown. No chemise. No corsets. No stays. Nothing but a pair of shockingly skimpy French drawers fashioned from tiny bits of black satin and lace.

She had carefully, calculatingly made herself look as seductive as possible, and she only hoped that the Sheik would find her utterly irresistible. She wanted him to look at her and want so badly that he hurt!

Temple's brittle resolve crumbled considerably well before the Sheik's return. While the agonizingly long minutes of waiting ticked away, she began once more to vacillate. She bounced back and forth between fierce determination to resist him no matter what and unabashed longing to have him hold her in his arms at any cost.

Nervous, unsure just exactly how the evening would unfold, Temple checked her appearance in the mirror one last time, turning her head to the side, lifting her chin, critically examining and appraising. She touched the luminous black pearl at her throat. She swept a nervous hand up the back of her sleekly dressed blond hair. She tugged gently at the snug midriff of her evening gown, urging the paneled bodice to slip lower so that a greater expanse of her breasts was covered only with teasing black lace.

At that moment the Sheik walked in.

Temple turned about quickly, and her breath caught in her throat. He nodded his head almost imperceptibly. His cold glance touched, then dismissed her. If he even noticed her appearance, he didn't show it.

Temple's heart sank and she stood there stiffly as he went directly to the bedroom. She paced nervously while a bath was brought for him and a flurry of activity took place as a white-clothed table for two with heavy silver and fragile china was swiftly set up. Soon the tub was taken away, lamps were turned down, candles on the table were lighted, and silver-domed platters of food were brought in.

As suddenly as they had appeared, the servants disappeared and Temple was left alone in the candlelighted room, waiting. Uncertain. Jittery.

Seconds seemed like hours.

Then the Sheik stepped through the curtains, and at the sight of him a momentary weakness seized her. He too was dressed all in black. He wore a perfectly tailored tuxedo, the fine fabric of the jacket stretching appealingly across his broad shoulders. The shimmering black satin of the jacket's wide lapels was further emphasized by the narrow bands of satin going down the outside of each long leg. The sharp crease of the black trousers broke at exactly the right spot on the instep of his shiny patent-leather shoes. An ebony dress shirt with a pleated front was of the finest Egyptian cotton and was fastened with studs of black pearl, the same black pearl studs she had held in her hand earlier the day. Matching pearl cuff links adorned his wrists, and when he raised his hand, the Burma ruby, caught in the candlelight, flashed brilliant red fire. His night black hair, in need of a cut, was brushed straight back and curling over his shirt collar. His face was smoothly shaven, the tiny curved scar beside his lip starkly white against the darkness of his skin.

Temple stared at the tall, handsome Sheik, and all resolutions were instantly forgotten.

She wanted the Sheik.

She wanted him with a passion that made her blind and deaf to logic and reason. She wasn't the power. He was. And she wanted to be in his arms again, to surrender to that awesome strength, to awaken all that latent desire. She wanted—had—to make love to him tonight no matter the consequences.

The pulse in her throat throbbed. She could hardly draw a breath, and she couldn't think clearly.

The only thing of which she was absolutely certain was that she couldn't wait to have his beautiful bronzed hands on her again, to feel those long tapered fingers touching, caressing her.

All over.

28

A cold mask had dropped over the Sheik's handsome features. His black eyes, looking out from between their thick lashes, were hard and flat and totally unreadable. With an air of bored indifference he walked directly toward the table, and Temple realized, sickly, that he was feeling none of the attraction and excitement and wild desire she felt for him.

Mortified, she flushed hotly and hoped that her taut, aching nipples, pressing against her gown's tight bodice, were not visible. She'd die of shame if he had only to look at her and know exactly what his presence had done.

Sharif reached the table, pulled out a chair, and waited. Temple didn't move. He finally spoke.

"Have you already had dinner?"

"No, I was waiting for . . . No."

She moved toward him unsteadily, seeking his eyes as she sat down on the chair he held for her. But he withheld his gaze. Still, when he pushed her chair up to the table Temple half expected him to place his warm brown hands atop her lace-covered shoulders, lean down, and brush a kiss to her cheek.

He didn't.

Sharif moved lithely around the table, took the chair across from her, draped a damask napkin over his knee, and lifted a domed silver lid from a steaming platter of curried lamb. He held out his hand, and she automatically passed him her plate. After two or three attempts at making conversation, Temple gave up and the meal was consumed in strained silence.

Temple wasn't hungry.

She forced herself to eat a little. It seemed that the longer she chewed each mouthful of food, the larger it became, until she felt as if she couldn't possibly swallow one more bite. She laid her heavy sterling fork on the plate and looked at him from beneath lowered lashes—and was startled to find he was watching her coldly, the cruel lines around his mouth more clearly in evidence than ever.

She was relieved when—after the longest half hour of her life—he finally laid his napkin on the table and rose. He came around, helped to her feet, then turned and walked away. Temple remained standing at the table, busying herself pouring hot black coffee from a long-beaked pot into two fragile demitasse cups.

Not trusting her unsteady hands to carry both at once, she took a steaming cup to the Sheik where he stood just outside the tent's open entrance, smoking a cigarette, gazing out at the moonlit desert.

"Thank you," he said politely, taking the cup but avoiding her eyes.

"You're very welcome," she replied bitingly, and went back inside, at a loss, wondering what she could have done to so displease him.

He was far too complex for her to understand. The mystery of the man into whose hands she had fallen was beyond her solving. She had seen him go from cruelty to tenderness in the blink of an eye. And then back again. She had watched him show infinite patience with Rhikia, genuine affection toward Tariz, and respect to the loyal men who served him.

At the same time he had exhibited no compunction about wielding his jewel-hilted dagger to slit the throats of the raiding Turks. Nor did he hesitate to mete out harsh punishment to one of his tribe if he felt strict discipline was warranted. And while he had never raised a hand to her, he had treated her with a coldness that bordered on cruelty.

She didn't know why his mood was so black this evening but could only suppose that with last night's loving he was satisfied he had conquered her fully, had tamed her as completely as one of his harem girls, so he was now finished with her.

He was, she knew, extremely cunning. He had never made a move to force her. He had never really attempted to seduce her. He had simply made her live in very close quarters with him until she had weakened and walked right into his arms. Now he'd had her and that was that. She was no longer a challenge, and he was no longer interested.

It was a bitter pill to swallow, and Temple had no one to blame but herself. For the first time in her life she was getting a dose of her own medicine. And it hurt. It hurt badly.

Temple went back to the table, lifted the demitasse to her lips, and took a sip of the strong black coffee she'd come to like. She realized with a jolt of astonishment that she had come to like many things about this simple, basic life in the Sheik's desert village.

She finished her coffee and carefully set the empty cup back on the table. Then she turned about and saw the Sheik walk back into the room and shrug out of his tuxedo jacket. He was offhand, cool. Without so much as an inquiring glance in her direction, he went to the long divan and, as if she were not there, lay down.

Temple braced herself against the table as she looked at his tall, lean body stretched out in repose. The steely strength of his long arms and legs was more than conspicuous even in the relaxed attitude in which he was lying. The soft black cotton of his pleated shirt clearly contoured the iron muscles of his chest. And beneath the fine fabric of his tuxedo trousers, the sinews in his long hard thighs bunched and pulled as if rebelling against their restraint.

Her fingertips gripping the table's edge, she watched the way his deep, slow breaths caused his broad chest to expand, his drum-tight belly to contract so that the waistband of his pants fell away, leaving a space between trousers and man. Temple bit her lip.

She was assailed with an almost overwhelming desire to go to him. To fall to her knees beside the divan, lay her hand on his stomach, and slowly slide her fingers down inside his trousers. Imagining her fingertips gliding over the smooth cotton of his shirt and the hot flesh beneath, her gaze guiltily moved lower. His full groin was appealingly cupped by the fabric of his tight trousers, and Temple felt her own groin stir inside the lace-and-satin confines of her French underwear.

She turned her head quickly, clutched the table until her knuckles turned white, and took a couple of quick breaths to compose herself. When she was fairly confident that she was capable of walking—that her weak knees wouldn't fold beneath her—she released her death grip on the table. For a moment longer she stood there working up her nerve, then bravely she crossed the large room to stand before the tall ebony bookcase.

Pretending to deliberate over her choice of reading material, Temple stared unseeing at the dozens of leather-bound volumes before taking one from the shelf. Swallowing with difficulty, she moved to a big comfortable hassock, sat down, carefully crossed her legs, and began to read. Or to act as if she were reading.

The silence in the room was deafening.

Each turn of the page resonated; each breath she drew was amplified. The beating of her heart reverberated like the throbbing of a bass drum.

Temple stood it for as long as she could, which was only a few minutes. She slammed the book shut. It sounded like a pistol shot. She laid it aside, rose to her feet, and said, "If you'll excuse me, I . . ." Her words trailed away.

Sharif didn't look up. He didn't move a muscle. His dark head didn't even turn. He continued to lie there stretched out on the long divan, smoking a cigarette and staring at the billowing white tent ceiling overhead.

"Good night," she said evenly, trying to sound calm, desperate to hide her hurt from him.

"Night," he replied, and his deep, soft voice in the quiet room made her jump.

Temple forced herself to walk across the room at a normal, unhurried pace. It was a dreadfully long walk. Finally she reached the dividing curtains, stepped through sedately, and allowed them to fall back in place behind her.

She expelled a long, painful breath as her eyes filled with burning tears.

Once she had gone, Sharif's dark eyes closed helplessly in misery. He clenched his teeth together so strongly, pain shot up his jaw. His breath was labored, and he felt as if someone had ripped open his chest, reached inside, and viciously squeezed his heart.

His belly contracted.

His groin expanded.

He was in agony.

Purposely he had stayed away from camp all day. He had sought complete solitude in an all-out effort to clear his head of her. He had berated himself for what he had done to her. Had reminded himself exactly who she was and why he had brought here. And he had sworn to himself that he would not touch her again.

Sharif opened his eyes, swung his long legs to the floor, sat up, and reached for a cigarette.

He shook his dark head in despair.

When finally he had returned to the village and stepped into the tent, the sight of her had taken his breath—and his self-control—away. Never had she been more beautiful, more bewitching. It was as if she had deliberately made herself irresistibly seductive in order to undermine his resolve.

Sharif lighted his cigarette, badly needing to calm his raw nerves. He took a long, deep drag on the aromatic cigarette. He closed his eyes, but it did no good. He opened them.

Open or closed, he saw Temple. Temple in the stunning black lace gown standing there with one knee slightly bent, the long dress molded to her tall, slender body. He couldn't forget the way the gown clung like a second skin to the tempting roundness of her buttocks and stretched across her flat stomach and the arch of her hips. He hadn't been able to ignore the fact that her shoulders and back were the same as bare, covered only with alluring black lace.

Sharif reached up and jerked open his shirt collar as

the recurring sight of pale, full breasts swelling beneath black lace made him feel as if he were choking. A muscle jumped in his lean jaw at the recollection of tempting nipples, conspicuously taut, rising in twin points to push provocatively against the gown's tight bodice. His lower belly spasmed as he recalled the fleeting glimpse he'd caught of her rigid right nipple when she'd raised her arm to push a fallen lock of hair back up in place.

Impatiently Sharif snuffed out the smoked-down cigarette and reached for another. But he didn't light it. Teeth grinding again, a vein pulsing on his tanned forehead, he dropped the cigarette back into the silver box. His head swung around and he stared at the curtains behind which was the pale-skinned blond beauty in black lace responsible for his suffering.

Sharif knew he would find no peace. He would not sleep this night. The woman on the other side of the curtains was already in his blood, and he knew there was only one way of getting her out of it.

His dark eyes icy with determination, yet smoldering with heat, the Sheik rose to his feet.

29

Temple blinked back the tears.

She refused to let herself cry. Gritting her teeth, she began dispiritedly to undress. Or attempt to get undressed. Her arms behind her back, her fingers tugging and pulling, she struggled with the tiny hooks of her black lace gown. But her trembling hands were inept, and the hooks were stubborn. After much wasted effort, she managed to get only a few undone.

It was futile.

"Damnation!" she muttered in rising frustration, tears threatening again.

Exasperated, she whirled about and sank onto the edge of the Sheik's large black-silk-covered bed. She sighed heavily, made a terrible face, and shook her head in despair. She had always prided herself on being intelligent and self-reliant and resourceful. She was none of those things! She was a foolish woman at the mercy of an imperious male, and she couldn't even undress herself!

Forced to wait for Rhikia, Temple sat on the bed with her arms crossed, humbled and humiliated by her helplessness.

Emerald eyes snapping with self-reproach, she turned her head quickly when the curtains parted. Expecting Rhikia, she was speechless when she saw the Sheik. Her lips parting in stunned surprise, she rose to her feet and started to speak. But what she saw in his glittering black eyes silenced her before she could utter a word.

In their fathomless depths was a hunger that bordered on savagery.

Temple trembled as he decisively approached, but it was not with fear. It was from her undeniable physical attraction to him.

Sharif reached her, stood towering over her, his wide black-shirted shoulders blocking the light spilling into the bedroom through the open curtains. Wordlessly he held out his hand to her. Hurt pride made her refuse to take it.

"No," she warned, finding her voice at last. "You touch me and you won't live 'til morning."

"A chance," he said, unfazed, "I will have to take."

He reached out and eased her half-open black lace dress off a pale shoulder. She trembled at the touch of his warm, gentle fingers.

"I do not want this," she protested in a shaky, unconvincing whisper, knowing even as she said the words that she couldn't resist his dark power, couldn't combat her unholy attraction to him. She drew a shallow, ragged breath and stared, entranced, at this virile, nonworshiping lover whose passionate embrace, though deadly, was addictive.

Nonetheless she managed to say a bit more firmly, "And I do not want you."

"Then I shall have to make you want me," he replied, wrapping a long arm around her waist, tempting her into complicity with his overpowering maleness. Pressing her up against his tall, hot body so ropy hard with muscle that she winced from the sudden electric contact, he bent his dark head and buried his lips in the curve of her neck and shoulder.

Temple shuddered, but she pushed on his chest, fighting to maintain some semblance of composure. It was a losing battle, and she knew it. There was about this man something intoxicating, something magnetic, something powerfully primitive that made him utterly irresistible. He effortlessly awakened in her a strong desire she was unable to control and afraid to reveal. From the very beginning she had fought her strangely overwhelming attraction to him; had known instinctively that he had the power to make her do things no one else could. It was all that and more. He had, inexplicably, touched something in her no other ever had.

Her eyes closing with a mixture of defeat and desire, Temple murmured his name on a sigh, "Sharif . . . no . . . Sharif."

"*Chérie,*" he replied in a low, gentle whisper, and his words warmed the blood in her veins when he said, "I want you so badly. Please, *chérie*, want me even half as much as I want you."

"Oh, God," she breathed, "I do. I do want you."

He kissed her then, and any traces of lingering doubt or resistance were kissed away by his warm, demanding mouth. Temple's head fell back as her whole body arched into his embrace and her eyelids drifted closed with pleasure. He nudged her trembling lips apart with his tongue. Their teeth touched, then her mouth opened. His tongue ran over her teeth, caressed her lips, teased and taunted her. He sucked her full bottom lip into his mouth, bit it playfully, and breathed hotly into her mouth.

She sighed and trembled against him. Sharif deepened the kiss, and his tongue felt like slick wet fire as it probed the inner recesses of her mouth. Temple stood there, arching eagerly against him, acutely aware of the heat and hardness of him, thrilling to the pressure of every muscle and sinew in his solid length. Her head thrown back, her mouth open wide to his burning kisses, she melted against him.

And when, his passion-hardened lips never leaving hers, Sharif began deftly to flip open the tiny hooks going down the back of her black lace evening gown, she simply sighed her approval.

In seconds he was removing the dress, drawing the long lace sleeves down her slender arms and pushing the bodice to her waist. When the gown snagged on her flared hips, he lost patience. He yanked on the fragile fabric, and the dress slithered over her hips. He pushed it down her thighs and released it, allowing it to fall past her stockinged knees to the thick rug below.

Sharif put his hands to her waist, lifted her free of the lace garment, kicked it aside, and lowered her slowly back to her feet. Then for a long moment he held her at arm's length to look at her, and Temple realized with mild surprise that she was now wearing only the skimpy satin-and-lace black drawers, the sheer black stockings, and high-heeled black satin slippers.

She didn't care.

She stood there, unflinching, rooted to the spot, staring at him staring at her. A fresh infusion of heat brightened his night black eyes, and he slowly drew her back into his arms.

His hands slipping around her, he again held her in his close embrace and kissed her hungrily. Temple sighed, wrapped her arms around his neck, and kissed him back greedily, pressing herself against him, yearning to dissolve into him.

It was strangely thrilling to be nearly naked in Sharif's

long arms while he was fully clothed. The narrow symmetric pleats of his black dress shirt teased and tickled her erect nipples, and the black pearl studs going down the shirt's front bit into her tender flesh. The fabric of his tuxedo trousers was pleasingly rough against her bare thighs and stockinged legs.

Sinuously she rubbed herself against him, catlike, while he kissed her and ran his hands over her bare shoulders and pale back and satin-and-lace covered hips. Momentarily Temple tore her lips from his and pulled back a little. Suddenly dying to feel her bare flesh against his bare flesh, she pulled the black pearl studs from his shirtfront, cast them to the rug as if they were worthless, shoved his shirt apart, and entwined her fingers in the thick, crisp hair covering his broad chest.

While his breath grew ragged and his hands danced along her shoulders, Temple pressed openmouthed kisses to his bronzed throat, scraped her nails down his naked torso, then clasped his ribs and pressed herself to him. Both sighed and shuddered as her soft, warm breasts flattened against his hard chest and her diamond-hard nipples stabbed into him. Shivering from the delicious feel of the crisp hair and muscled strength beneath, Temple shamelessly rubbed herself back and forth, up and down, against him as she lifted her mouth for his searing kiss.

Sharif cradled her head in his hand while she kissed him hotly, starvingly, as he had kissed her a moment ago. Her silky tongue's caress, as it boldly searched his mouth, drove him half mad with desire and need. Her honeyed lips and the unbearably erotic undulating of her half-naked body were arousing him to a height of passion that made him want to love her in ways that she might not allow.

His mouth stayed fused with hers as his hands moved

down to settle on her hips. Assisting, showing her how to undulate even more sensuously against him, he filled his hands with the twin cheeks of her bottom. Then, gently controlling and guiding her movements, he demonstrated with the languid roll and intimate thrust of own trousered pelvis.

Instantly she caught on.

And for a brief enjoyable interlude they stood there, lustfully hunching and sliding and rocking and slithering against each other in an erotic prelude to total lovemaking.

Dizzy with desire, Temple blinked in surprise when Sharif turned her about and gently sat her down on the edge of his bed. He cupped her face in his hands and stood before her, looking down into her eyes.

"I must have you, *Naksedil*," he told her in low, husky voice. "Let me make love to you in every way a man can love a woman." His thumb skimmed back and forth over her parted lips, and he added, "Yield to me, Temple. Let me show you all the myriad pleasures of loving."

Before she could speak he lowered his face to hers and kissed her with heart-stopping tenderness. As he kissed her, Sharif sat down on the bed beside her, put a stiffened arm on the mattress, and slowly lay back across it, bringing Temple with him. He took her slender arms and drew them up around his neck as he turned her onto her back and continued to kiss her.

On fire, her heart racing in her naked breasts, she slanted her lips across his and drew his mouth more fully to hers, eager for him to deepen the kiss. He did. He thrust his tongue into her mouth, and she sucked at it as her passions rose and her inhibitions lowered.

His marvelous mouth conquering hers, Sharif worked with deft, sure fingers to sweep away her satin-and-lace underwear, leaving her naked save for the sheer black stockings and black slippers. Temple squirmed with pleasure and sighed into his mouth. Beneath her bare, yearning body, the black counterpane felt even more wonderful than she had imagined. The stark contrast between hot burning skin and cool slick silk was incredibly sensual.

Sharif's searing mouth finally left hers, moved to her throat. Temple's weak arms fell away from him when his open mouth warmly surrounded the black pearl she had forgotten still hung suspended from a black velvet ribbon circling her neck. When his tongue pressed the pearl into the hollow of her throat, Temple smiled foolishly and swept her open palms over the pleasingly smooth texture of the shimmering black silk bedspread.

Her eyes closed in pleasure, she felt Sharif's tongue sweep aside the pearl and flick across her throat, a touch that was so delicate yet so intense, it made her gasp. Her eyes fluttered open when slowly, surely, he kissed a path downward until his tongue swirled around her breast. She gripped his hair and writhed in wild abandon as his mouth moved over the desire-swollen nipple, his teeth grazing it, nibbling, tormenting her sweetly.

Sharif shifted, sliding slowly toward the edge of the mattress, his mouth never leaving Temple's flesh. Responding totally, helplessly, she gave herself over to the fiery pulse now beating inside her, growing hotter and stronger as his lips skimmed over her fluttering stomach. Her breath came out in a rush of increased excitement when his warm lips drifted to her navel, his tongue probing and flicking with slow, sensuous strokes that she could somehow feel in each aching breast and between her closed legs.

Temple couldn't lie still.

She writhed and wiggled sinuously upon the slippery black silk bedspread, needing its soothing coolness to counterbalance the raging fever of her body. Sharif's mouth was spreading such incredible heat, she felt as if her temperature were rising rapidly to the danger point. And she was torn between the need to push him away and immerse herself in the counterpane's soothing coolness and the even stronger desire to have him continue kissing her until she burst into flame.

Her burning body no longer belonged to her. It was his. *She* was his. And he could continue to feast on her for as long as he wanted. Without a word being spoken, she freely gave herself in sweet surrender to this dark, determined lover, and Sharif took that which was offered.

His lips moving softly down her silken belly, he slid from the bed and went down on his knees beside it. His dark face continuing to brush kisses to her lower belly, he felt the muscles jerking, jumping beneath the pale, flawless skin.

He raised his head, put his hands to Temple's waist, and drew her up into a sitting position. He sank back on the floor before her and pressed a kiss to her stockinged left knee. Her heart beating wildly, she looked into his smoldering black eyes and read the message there as clearly as if he had issued an order. "Sharif," she murmured breathlessly.

"Yes, Temple. Yes."

Her thighs opened to him. He held her gaze as his fingers curled around the back of a stocking-clad knee. He lifted her leg over his head as he smoothly ducked underneath. Then he was directly between her parted legs. Temple shivered and found herself suddenly plagued with a touch of embarrassed modesty. Her hands automatically flew down to cover herself, and she blushed.

Sharif's hand lifted to her flaming face. He touched her cheek and said, "No, *chérie*, do not hide yourself from me." His hand moved down her body, pausing briefly to cup a bare breast, then brushed across her trembling belly and came to rest atop her hands. His lean fingers spreading to cover both her cupping hands, he said, "I want to kiss you here where you love me."

He took his hand away then, leaned down, and kissed her protective fingers. Biting the fragile knuckles with harmless little nips, he said, "Let me taste you. Move your hands, *chérie*. For me."

Shocked, but at the same time almost unbearably thrilled, she whispered, "Yes. For you, Sharif, only for you."

And she took her shaking hands away and placed them on the mattress's edge, leaving herself exposed and vulnerable.

His bronzed hand returned to the tempting golden triangle, his long tapered fingers gently parting the curls and the slick flesh beneath. When her eyes began to close and she started to sag back onto the bed, he said, "No, *chérie*. Watch me while I love you. Watch us together like this."

And he bent his dark head to her, nuzzled his face in the crisp golden curls, and blew his hot breath upon her. A strangled moan broke from her tight throat. Withholding that which would give her instant ecstasy and release, Sharif let his lips travel tormentingly up and down the warm insides of her bare thighs atop her sheer black stockings.

Temple moaned and shuddered and turned her head from side to side. Her hands gripping the mattress's edge, she breathed through her mouth in short little pants, feeling as if she couldn't possibly stand one more second of this exciting torture. Her bare buttocks began to wiggle about on the silken bed as she instinctively thrust her pelvis up and forward.

When finally his lips touched her there, where she most wanted it, she cried out in a little sob of wonder and gratitude. She could not believe his tender touch. He was kissing her in that hottest of all spots, kissing her just as if he were tenderly kissing her mouth. His smooth, warm lips were closed as he pressed the sweetest of kisses to her scorching flesh. And then, at last, his lips opened upon her, enclosing her, caressing her.

It was the most incredible pleasure.

Temple couldn't believe they were really doing this. She couldn't believe what Sharif was doing to her. She couldn't believe what she was letting him to do. She could not believe that she was actually sitting on a fully made bed wearing nothing but the black pearl around her throat and black stockings and shoes, while he, fully dressed in evening clothes, was on the floor between her open legs, hotly kissing her in that most feminine of all places.

All at once it was as if she were outside herself, watching the two of them engage in this highly carnal act. As if she were watching some other couple, she could see herself perched naked on the edge of the black silken bed with her stockinged legs parted. She could see Sharif in his black dress shirt and tuxedo trousers sitting on his heels before her, his dark face buried between her trembling thighs.

It was appallingly shocking.

It was extraordinarily erotic.

It was absolutely wonderful!

Temple was spellbound—she was his slave as his hot face sank in her and his magical, flickering tongue swirled around and around that tiny throbbing bud that was the source of all her passion. Burning up now, feeling as if the entire universe were located between her legs and that his licking tongue was the hot radiant sun in that universe, she arched her back and thrust her pelvis forward as she sagged back helplessly onto her bent elbows.

His loving mouth never leaving her flaming flesh, Sharif put his hands beneath her buttocks, lifted her as he rose slowly to his knees, reached for one of the many black-covered pillows, and slid it under her hips. Her breath coming out in a strangled sigh, Temple fell over onto her back and watched through passion-glazed eyes as his dark face stayed buried between her elevated thighs and his tongue continued to send jolts of unbelievable pleasure through her.

Until finally the pleasure became too intense, the ecstasy too profound. She was splintering into a million pieces, erupting in a volcanic frenzy, over and over. Gasps were tearing out of her throat, her whole body was shuddering, and she was sobbing helplessly with ecstatic joy.

A great wrenching, as if she were coming apart, had her in the throes of sexual orgasm. She was coming, over and over now, in a violent, shattering climax.

Crying out in her wild ecstasy, Temple clutched at the silk counterpane and prayed Sharif would not take his dazzling mouth from her.

He didn't.

He stayed with her throughout the frenzied eruptions, his mouth fused to her, his tongue stroking gently, until all the fierce tremors climaxed into one giant forceful explosion.

Then he moved up to stretch out on the bed beside her. Taking her in his arms, he held her still-jerking body close and kissed her flushed face until all the tiny aftershocks and passed.

30

Murmuring endearments in soft, low-timbred Arabic, Sharif held Temple until she was calm and limp in his arms.

Then he brushed one last kiss to her forehead, released her, and rose from the bed. As he undressed, he gazed down at her lying across his bed.

She was the most beautiful creature he had ever seen. The expression of total serenity on her lovely face made her look young and innocent and trusting. Her fancily dressed hair had come undone and spilled over the black silk counterpane, shimmering like Midas' gold in the amber lamplight.

Her pale, slender body, stretched out in arrestingly insolent repose, was pure perfection. The luminosity of her flawless ivory skin gave the impression of cool priceless marble. She might have been an ice goddess to be worshiped but not touched, or an exquisite ethereal angel—if not for the sheer black stockings, sassy lace garters, and high-heeled slippers that magically transformed her into a naughty and highly desirable courtesan.

She was, as she lay there below him, stretching lazily

and sighing softly, every man's erotic dream. The consummate combination of appealing girlish innocence and irresistible womanly seductiveness.

By the time he had shed his clothes, Sharif's whole body ached with the overwhelming impact of his desire. He leaned down and removed Temple's black slippers. The stockings he purposely left in place, anticipating the provocative feel of their smooth silkiness when her legs were wrapped around him.

He put a knee on the mattress, picked up the limp, sighing Temple, and laid her up among the many black and white pillows and bolsters resting against the tall ebony headboard.

Joining her on the bed, lying down beside her, he held his raging passion in check long enough to kiss and caress her into the beginnings of new arousal.

Temple was shocked at how quickly she awakened to his fiery touch. At first she simply lay there, propped up among the silk-covered pillows, too weak to move, too sated to care, allowing him to gently kiss her lips and stroke her breasts and belly.

But the next thing she knew, she was responding to his kiss, stirring to his touch. In moments she was so faint with desire that when he rose above her, she eagerly allowed him to lift her stockinged legs over his shoulders. She gazed into his hot black eyes as he slowly buried every throbbing inch of his heavy tumescence in her, filling her with himself.

Temple lifted her arms over her head and gripped the ebony headboard as he thrust forcefully into her.

His handsome face shiny with perspiration, his eyes fixed on her face, Sharif drove into her, sliding almost all the way in, then almost all the way out, each thrust penetrating deeper so that Temple could feel herself being stretched to accept him.

Her body rising to meet every powerful plunge of his, she was drowning in the splendid sensations, wanting them to last, to go on and on forever. A master of sexual self-control, Sharif knew how she felt. So he kept her in this suspended state of pleasure, enjoying her joy, able and willing to wait until she became so hot that she begged for release.

Sooner than he'd expected she was murmuring, "Sharif, Sharif . . . please, I . . . I want . . . I . . . "

"Yes, *chérie*," he whispered, and immediately speeded his movements.

Faster, harder, he thrust into her, taking her all the way to paradise, giving her sublime pleasure that built and built until she felt she could endure it no longer, could not stand one more second of the startlingly intense rapture.

And then came her wild, wrenching explosion of ecstasy, which brought on his shuddering, spurting climax.

Afterward Sharif gently lowered Temple's legs to the bed and carefully lay down atop her. They stayed that way for a long, peaceful time, still joined and panting for breath. His black hair ruffling against her chin, Temple sighed and smiled, thinking that making love with Sharif on the black silk counterpane had been even more thrilling than her fantasy. Dreamily she hoped they would do it again sometime.

When Temple's limp arms finally fell away from him, Sharif lifted his dark head, looked at her, and smiled.

She was sound asleep.

He slid out of her, sat up, slowly stripped the sheer black stockings from her long, slender legs, and tossed them to the floor with the rest of their discarded clothing. Then he stretched out beside her, swept a wide portion of the black silk counterpane up over them, put an arm around her, and drew her soft, bare body close to his.

He fell asleep thinking how highly erotic and enjoyable making love with this beautiful blond woman on the slippery black silk bedspread had been.

They would have to do it again.

From that day forward, the passionate Sheik took Temple to the heights of rapture each night in his big, soft bed. Stretched out on the cool silken sheets of snowy white, they found awesome ecstasy. And sometimes—requesting that Rhikia leave the bed neatly made up—they reached carnal nirvana playing naked on the black silk counterpane.

Still, to Temple's bitter disappointment, except for their incredible sexual liaison, their relationship did not change. Sharif still went for hours—even days—at a time hardly noticing her. More than one long hot day passed without his so much as speaking to her.

Yet when night fell and the village grew silent, he came to her where she now slept in his bed, and he took her physically—either with great tenderness and patient care, or almost violently with a passion and fire so wonderfully savage, she cried out again and again.

He was as much a paradox as ever, but one thing she knew about him: he could no more resist making love to her each night than she could refuse him. And deep in her heart, she couldn't help but cling to the slender thread of hope that his total inability to keep from touching her, kissing her, wanting her, meant that he cared for her.

Just a little.

As for how she felt about him, she was uncertain. Reason told her she should hate him, but she didn't. Couldn't. Never would she have admitted it to anyone, but the truth was that the weeks she had spent with the enigmatic Sheik was the first time in years she had lost her constant restlessness. The yearning, the edginess, the wish for something more, something, she didn't know what, had gone.

He was responsible.

The Sheik.

So whatever happened, no matter how it all ended, she would, ironically, look on this time as the desert hostage of Sheik Sharif Aziz Hamid as a warm season in the sun. A secret, precious interlude in which there had been, at long last, fulfillment.

If only physical.

Sharif surprised Temple when, one early morning as the desert dawn was breaking, he awakened her from a deep, dreamless sleep. He touched her cheek and spoke her name softly. When her eyes fluttered open, he leaned over her face and kissed her.

He kept on kissing her until she roused from her drowsiness, stirring against him and sighing softly. Then, wordlessly, he made slow, erotic love to her.

Responding to his skilled, languid lovemaking, Temple wondered at him. This was a first. Never before had he touched her in the morning.

When, afterward, she lay sated and again growing drowsy in his embrace, she learned the reason for the mysterious dawn loving.

Her head on his shoulder, her body curled comfortably against his, she was ready to drift back to sleep when he said, almost apologetically, "I am to have a visitor. An invited guest is arriving today."

31

To Temple's relief, the Sheik's guest turned out to be a man.

"Temple, meet my old friend, Chauncey Wellshanse," Sharif introduced the two at noontime.

"A pleasure to meet you, Mr. Wellshanse," Temple said as she reached out to shake the hand of the tall, blond man beaming down at her.

"Chauncey, Miss Temple Longworth," said Sharif.

His big square hand enclosing hers firmly, Chauncey Wellshanse said, "Miss Longworth, the pleasure is all mine, I assure you. Tell me that you and I are going to be real good friends." He shook her hand vigorously as he spoke.

Her laugh was genuine as she nodded and replied, "I certainly hope so. Your accent gives you away, Mr. Wellshanse. You're American, are you not?"

"Guilty as charged," Chauncey responded with a nod of his head.

"Let me see if I can guess," said Temple. "Mmmm . . . Arkansas. No, Oklahoma. Or perhaps—"

"Why, bite your tongue, Miss Longworth," Chauncey

scolded mockingly. "Honey, I'm a Texan and mighty proud of it."

Again Temple laughed. "My apologies, Mr. Wellshanse. I should have known. You'll forgive me?"

"A woman as pretty as you?" The eyebrows above his sparkling blue eyes lifted. "I'd forgive you just about anything. And I *insist* you call me Chauncey."

Sharif needlessly cleared his throat. Temple and Chauncey turned quickly to look at him. "Lunch is ready," he announced in a flat, low voice. Extending his hand, he directed them from where they now stood beneath the tent's shade canopy down to the water's edge.

"And a good thing, too," said the smiling Chauncey, "I'm starved." Still clinging to Temple's hand, he immediately turned his attention back on her. "How about you, Temple—if I may call you Temple. You have an appetite?"

"I'm famished," she said, and allowed the tall Texan to take her arm and escort her down to the sequestered, palm-shaded spot some fifty yards below the white tent where comfortable hassocks and pillows and a table for dining had been set up on a thick rug directly beside the water.

Sharif followed, frowning.

Temple liked Chauncey instantly. Immensely attractive in a rough-hewn, unpolished kind of way, he was a big, brawny man with pale blond hair, a healthy ruddy complexion, bright blue eyes that flashed with mischief, a nose that looked as if it had been many times broken, and a mouth full of teeth that showed often in a wide smile.

She was delighted to learn that her fellow American planned to stay at the Sheik's desert village for an extended period of time. He was friendly and talkative, fond of laughter, and full of fun.

"You must be wondering," Chauncey said, looking across the table at Temple once they were seated, "how a big ole loudmouthed Texas boy and a taciturn Arabian desert sheik ever came to be friends."

"Yes. Yes, I was," Temple said, smiling, and glanced at Sharif.

Chauncey reached out, clamped a broad, sunburned hand atop Sharif's shoulder, and said, "When old Cold Eyes here showed up at Oxford, he could barely speak English. Am I right, Sharif?" Not waiting for an answer, Chauncey went on, "The two of us were assigned to the same set of rooms in college. I don't know which of us was the unhappiest, him or me."

He laughed loudly then, remembering, and told Temple about how they became friends after he, Chauncey, decided he didn't like Sharif's looks or his attitude and told him so in loud, simple English to make sure he was understood. Sharif, Chauncey recalled, responded calmly—in broken English—that the feeling was indeed mutual. That he, Sharif Aziz Hamid, would rather share his lodgings with a stinking camel than with Chauncey.

"So I said, 'How would you like to get that sneer knocked right off your dark face, Arab?' And Sharif stood up, fixed me with those frigid black eyes, and said—in so many words—'How would you like to try it, Texan?'"

Telling it now, Chauncey slapped his knee and laughed. Amused, but smiling somewhat warily, Temple looked from Chauncey to Sharif and back again. "So? Did the two of you fight?" she asked.

"Honey, we like to killed each other," said Chauncey, still chuckling, tears of laughter filling his sparkling blue eyes. "When that long, bloody fight finally ended, all the furniture in our shared digs was smashed and we were hanging on to each other, each refusing to be the first one to go down. And then all at once the whole thing seemed so ridiculous that it was funny. We started laughing. And once we got started, we couldn't stop. We fell on the floor and rolled around, laughing like a couple of wild hyenas."

Temple glanced at Sharif. He was smiling easily now, as if fondly remembering. While Chauncey laughed heartily, Sharif took up the story.

"We were very nearly expelled from the university," he told Temple. "The horrified porter immediately turned us over to the Head of College. He was ready to kick us both out. The Vice Chancellor intervened or we'd have been sent down."

"We've been good friends ever since, haven't we, Sheik?" Chauncey said proudly, looking at Sharif with genuine affection.

"The best," confirmed Sharif.

Chauncey continued to regale Temple with colorful tales of the days he and Sharif spent together at Oxford. As he spoke she pictured, in her mind's eye, two lost lads at a staid British college, both lonely and out of place, struggling to adjust to a totally different way of life. Learning a new language. A new culture. Missing their respective faraway desert homes.

She could have listened forever.

But as soon as lunch was finished, the Sheik, to her disappointment, promptly excused Temple.

Rising, the two men silently watched her walk away. When she disappeared inside the tent, Chauncey dropped heavily back down onto his chair, shaking his blond head.

When Sharif was again seated, Chauncey looked at him and said, "Lord God almighty, Christian, how in the hell do you do it? Where did you meet her? In London?

Women still can't resist you, can they? She follow you into the desert once you'd made love to her?"

"She followed me nowhere," said Sharif. He looked Chauncey straight in the eye. "I did not meet her in London. I saw her in London. I knew she was coming to Arabia. I waited until she rode into the desert and I took her."

"Took her?" Chauncey frowned, not fully understanding. "What do you mean, 'you took her'?"

"I abducted her," Sharif confessed.

Chauncey's blue eyes widened in horror and shock. "You kidnapped her? Jesus, Christian, don't you know who she is? Temple Longworth, the daredevil daughter of the richest family in America!"

"Her mother was a DuPlessis," Sharif said calmly, reaching for the long-beaked coffeepot.

"Yes, and her father is a Longworth! President McKinley likely has the American fleet steaming off Tripoli even as we speak. What in God's name are you thinking of, my friend?"

Sharif expelled a slow breath, raised his demitasse cup, and drank a large swallow of the thick black coffee. He said, "The abduction was necessary."

"To what end? I don't see how—"

"I have—and you know it is true—exhausted every avenue open to me in a years-long attempt to force the powerful DuPlessis Munitions to *stop* supplying arms and ammunition to the Turks. Nothing has worked." His tone remained level, but his black eyes flashed with hatred when he said, "My people have endured four centuries of cruel subjection by the Turks. That is enough. It must be stopped. And to that end—"

"I know how you feel about the Turks, but to kidnap an innocent young woman . . . the heiress to . . ." Chauncey shook his head again, sincerely worried.

"Christian, you're like a brother to me, but this is wrong and it won't stand—"

Sharif interrupted, "Whatever it takes to force DuPlessis to cease supplying the Agha Hussain and that fat, depraved son of his with arms and ammunition with which to slaughter my people, I will do." His tanned jaw ridged, he added, "Need I remind you of what the Agha Hussain did to my natural parents? Do I have to tell you again of all the vile and corrupt and oppressive things Mustafa has done to my people?"

"No. No, you don't," Chauncey replied, sympathetic, "but this is unconscionable. Temple Longworth is guilty only of being a rich, headstrong young beauty who loves adventure and excitement. She doesn't deserve this, Christian. She's had nothing to do with the shipment of arms or the deaths of your people."

Sharif abruptly pushed back his chair and rose. "Shall we walk out to the stables? I've a number of fine new stallions to show you."

"Sure," said Chauncey, getting to his feet. "Lead the way."

The two friends continued to debate the issue as they walked unhurriedly to the stables, each arguing his point passionately. Chauncey begged Sharif to let Temple go at once. He pointed out that if she were released immediately, unharmed, there was the outside chance she might even keep quiet about the kidnapping, since it would surely be a terrible embarrassment to her and her prominent family.

Sharif refused to consider letting her go. He held his position stubbornly, assuring Chauncey that Temple would be freed just as soon as her uncle James DuPlessis agreed to cease supplying Mustafa's bloodthirsty Turks with guns, cannons, and grenades.

"She will," Sharif said in conclusion, "arrive in Baghdad right on schedule—according to her family's expectations—and go on about her hedonistic search for pleasure as if none of this ever happened."

Unconvinced, Chauncey said, "You'll hang for this, Christian."

"If Allah wills," said the Sheik.

Temple and Chauncey became fast friends. Far more open and talkative than the taciturn Sheik, Chauncey was full of amusing stories about the days the two had spent together at Oxford. And he told of how, when they left the university upon graduation, they promised always to keep in touch.

"We don't see each other as often as we'd like," Chauncey said one afternoon a week after his arrival. Sharif was gone from the village that day, and he and Temple sat alone beneath the shade canopy. "But at least once every two or three years we manage to get together." He smiled then and told her, "Sharif wasn't expecting me for another couple of months, but I changed my mind and sent word I'd be arriving early."

"I see," she replied, thinking back to how Sharif had acted on the morning he'd told her they were to have a visitor. She realized now that Sharif had been displeased that his old friend had chosen this particular time to visit the desert village. Apparently he hadn't wanted Chauncey to know about her—to know what he had done. She decided to say nothing about it . . . for the moment. "Sharif has been to America to visit you?" she asked.

"Sure he has. He'll come to America and spend a few weeks at the Wellshanse ranch in southwest Texas, and the next time I'll come over and visit with him. Either here in the desert or at the Emerald City."

"The Emerald City?" Temple's brows knitted questioningly.

"Sharif hasn't told you about the Emerald City?"

"No. I've never heard him mention such a place."

"Well, he's always been a man of few words," said Chauncey.

"Please, Chauncey. You tell me about it."

"You won't tell him I spilled the beans, will you?" He winked at her.

"Never," she assured him. "I swear it."

Chauncey grinned, nodded, then ran a big hand through his tousled blond hair. "Sharif dwells part of the time at a magnificent white marble palace. Right on the Mediterranean coast."

"You're teasing me."

"No. It's a small coastal village, fully walled and guarded. It's called the Emerald City. It's *his* Emerald City. And Sharif rules supreme from his white palace on the jutting cliffs high above the blue green sea. It's a breathtakingly beautiful place. Perhaps he should have whisked you off to the palace instead of . . . of . . ." His words trailed away and he looked sheepish, knowing he had already said too much.

Temple reached out and touched his arm, fixing him with her wide green eyes. "You know, don't you? You know Sharif has kidnapped me. You must know. I'm sure he has told you." Chauncey said nothing, remained totally silent, though an expression of kindness and concern quickly altered his features. "Why, Chauncey? Why is he holding me here? What does he want of me? When will he . . . he . . ."

Temple looked up, saw the Sheik walking toward them, and whispered anxiously, "He wouldn't like it if he thought I'd been questioning you. You won't say anything to him about this, will you?"

"Not a word."

And to the best of Temple's knowledge, he didn't.

The big blond Texan with his sunny personality and eagerness to laugh and the dark, lean Sheik with his impenetrable demeanor and his icy air of command were as different as two men could possibly be. Yet it was obvious they were genuinely fond of each other. So Temple was puzzled when, as Chauncey's stay in the desert lengthened, Sharif's initial good humor at seeing his old friend left him.

The Sheik became more and more withdrawn.

32

"Well, thunderation, Temple!" Chauncey exclaimed late one evening as she again beat him at chess.

It was nearing midnight.

Chauncey was seated on the long divan, leaning his elbows on his spread knees while he pondered his next play. Temple sat on the floor opposite him, one slender arm propped on the low ebony table before the black-and-ivory chess set. Sharif, smoking another of his Cartier cigarettes, stood alone outside the tent.

But only for a moment.

Since dinner less than two hours before, he had been outside, then back inside, several times. No sooner would he get outdoors than he was impatient to get back indoors. Inside, he would become fitful and edgy and go back outside to gaze at the starry brilliance of the desert sky.

Now inside again, he prowled restlessly for a while, then dropped onto one end of the divan, where Chauncey was seated. Hooking a long leg over the sofa's padded arm, Sharif stared, unblinking, at Temple as she eagerly busied herself setting up the chess pieces for another game.

She and Chauncey were laughing companionably as they debated who was the better player. Her heavily lashed emerald eyes were shining with pleasure, and her pale cheeks were flushed with color. She wore a vivid green chiffon evening gown that was a favorite of Sharif's. The color was extraordinarily becoming to her green eyes and fair skin and golden hair. He had once—in a weak moment of fiery lovemaking—made the foolish comment that she looked so beautiful in this particular dress, she should never wear anything else.

Now, staring at her as she sat there squirming about and clapping her hands whenever she made a clever move and smiling radiantly at his best friend, Sharif wished he had told her he disliked the dress. Wished he had forbidden her ever to wear it again.

A muscle bunched in Sharif's tanned jaw when Temple crossed her arms over her waist, clasped her elbows with her hands, and leaned forward to study the chess board. The innocent gesture caused her low-cut bodice to fall away and further reveal the already generously exposed swell of her pale, full breasts.

Sharif hated the damned dress.

He hated *her*.

He was up off the sofa again and going back outside.

"What's the matter with old Cold Eyes?" Chauncey said when he'd gone.

"I have no earthly idea," Temple replied. She advanced her knight, then pulled it back. "Furthermore, I don't particularly care."

Both laughed.

They were laughing again when Sharif came back into the tent moments later and announced in a flat, low voice, "It's after midnight. I'm rather tired."

"Well, don't let us keep you up," said Chauncey, smiling wickedly and winking at Temple. "Off to bed with you."

Neither Temple nor Chauncey saw the quick flash of jealousy that leapt into the Sheik's dark eyes as he turned away.

Temple didn't realize that it angered Sharif every time he caught her laughing and talking with Chauncey. She didn't suspect that her growing friendship with the big outgoing Texan bothered the dark, inscrutable man who revealed no feelings other than the white hot passion that blazed between them in the darkness of the night.

And Temple loved having Chauncey around. Not only was he great fun, but he had all kinds of interesting news and gossip from Europe and the States. She was totally at ease with the amiable Texan, felt as if she had known him always. She laughed uproariously at his jokes, of which he had an endless supply, giggled girlishly when he teased her, and spontaneously threw her arms around his neck in greeting when he'd been away from camp all day.

She truly enjoyed his company. And he was a veritable wellspring of information about the paradoxical Sharif. Chauncey delighted in entertaining her with stories of their wild days together at Oxford and wilder nights in London's poshest clubs.

Still, Chauncey told her just so much and no more. Temple strongly suspected that he knew a great deal more about Sharif than he revealed. Many of her questions drew answers that were ambiguous or vague, and then Chauncey would pointedly change the subject.

She had asked him—on more than one occasion— why an Arab sheik's son would be sent away to England for his education. Why not France? Each time she'd asked, Chauncey had shrugged it off with a "Why not England?" After all, he told her, Sharif already spoke fluent French; he'd wanted to learn the English language and customs. Wanted to get a well-rounded education.

When she pleaded with him to tell her why Sharif had kidnapped her, why he had brought her to his desert village, Chauncey would look at her with big blue eyes that conveyed a deep desire to be totally honest with her. But he would say only, "Temple, honey, all I can tell you is I know Sharif better than anybody, so I can promise you that he would *never* harm you. You need not be afraid of him."

"How can you be so sure?"

"I'm sure," he would reply, and then add almost as an afterthought, "Physically, I mean." And his face would redden.

Temple understood completely. Left unsaid was that she might be hurt in far more profound and lasting ways. She knew it was true. Emotionally she would suffer from her strange love-hate relationship with the handsome Arab Sheik.

There were, though, many things Chauncey could tell her, and Temple never tired of hearing about the man she knew only as Sheik Sharif Aziz Hamid.

When Sharif was present, Temple had a great deal of trouble keeping her eyes off him. Chauncey noticed that she worked very hard not to look at Sharif. But she couldn't keep from it.

At first he had supposed it was because Sharif made her extremely nervous. That was it. She was—with good reason—tense around him and therefore was constantly on guard, glancing at Sharif often to ascertain his shifting moods.

He had been mistaken. She was not afraid of Sharif. She was in love with him. How foolish he had been to suppose otherwise. Women didn't stay around Sharif very long without falling in love. Sharif had been holding Temple prisoner in his desert village for more than a month. It was naive to suppose that she stayed—slept—in any tent other than Sharif's.

In any bed other than Sharif's.

Chauncey hoped he was wrong, for Temple's sake.

He knew his good friend too well. To the handsome Englishman who lived as an Arab, women came too easily and therefore had no value. Christian Telford had been lover to some of Europe's most desirable women. All of them—many of whom were titled noblewomen—had fallen deeply in love with him. None of the affairs had lasted. A restless, easily bored man, Christian's hot passion quickly turned cold upon possession. With easy acquisition came quick disenchantment. The excitement of the chase faded swiftly with ownership.

Did Christian already own the beautiful Temple as he owned any woman he touched? Would she, like all the others, soon be discarded and forgotten? Was it already too late for her?

One afternoon two weeks into his planned month-long visit, Chauncey found himself studying Temple carefully. Sharif was gone from the village, and Chauncey and Temple were down at the water's edge, seated on a thick, colorful rug, playing two-handed poker.

Temple looked like a carefree young girl as she sat there cross-legged, her bare feet peeking out from under the skirts of her cool summer dress. Her glorious golden hair was pinned haphazardly atop her head, and a few rebellious strands had fallen down around her cheeks and the nape of her neck.

Her bottom lip was sucked behind her top teeth as

she fanned her cards carefully, holding them close to her chest, taking great care to keep him from seeing what she held. She had mastered the poker face but could not keep her brilliant emerald eyes from lighting when she drew a good hand.

Looking at her now, Chauncey found it almost impossible to believe that she was the celebrated heiress, Temple DuPlessis Longworth, one of the world's most beautiful women and one of the richest as well. It didn't seem possible. She was so down-to-earth, so lovable, although just as spirited and intelligent and daring as the penny press made her out to be. But she was much more. She was sweet and creative and sensitive. And she had a wicked sense of humor and a dislike of pretense that matched his own.

Chauncey stared at her, enchanted. It was all too easy to picture the beautiful Temple at home in the big adobe hacienda on his southwest Texas ranch. He could see her out on the range, astride one of his tough mustangs, her blond hair flying around her laughing face. He could see her, elegantly gowned and sparkling with diamonds, seated at the head of his long dining table, graciously entertaining moneyed cattlemen and bankers and politicians.

And if he did not check himself carefully, he could picture her upstairs in the hacienda's master suite, wearing a satin negligee with her long golden hair brushed out around her slender shoulders.

Chauncey mentally shook his head to clear it.

It was, he realized, time for him to leave Sharif's desert village. He could not stay on for another two weeks and not fall in love with the beautiful Temple Longworth. And he knew, regretfully, that there was absolutely no chance she might ever care for him. How could she when she was probably head over heels in love with Sharif?

He had to know.

"Know what I think, Temple, my girl?" he said casually, tossing in his losing cards and stretching lazily.

"Tell me, O wise one."

Chauncey waited until her eyes lifted to meet his. "I believe you've fallen in love with old Cold Eyes."

Caught off guard, Temple stared at him for a long moment. Then she laughed nervously and said, "That is the most outrageous thing I've ever heard in my life." She clicked her tongue against the roof of her mouth and added, "Have you forgotten this . . . this . . . desert pirate kidnapped me?"

"Have you?"

An extended pause.

"No. Loser deals. Shuffle," she said finally with an impatient toss of her head. "And stop looking at me like that. For your information, I am of sound mind and have never had any difficulty keeping my wits about me. I am here totally against my will, and there's nothing I want more than to leave this horrible place and Sheik Sharif Aziz Hamid. Furthermore, let me assure you that if ever I were to fall in love—which I have no intention of doing—it most certainly would *not* be with the lawless Arab chieftain who kidnapped me and brought me here to this desolate back-of-beyond hellhole! And if it's all the same with you, I'd like to change the subject. Deal!"

Chauncey simply nodded. He had his answer.

Temple was in love with Sharif.

"It's getting awfully warm out here," Temple said, folding her cards and tossing them on the rug. "Could we finish this game some other time?"

"Sure, honey. Sure."

33

The bloated Turkish sultan reclined on a great couch of silver satin shantung as the late afternoon sun spilled in through the tall sea-facing windows. On his round head was a fez of maroon silk, its black tassel hanging over his left ear. His robes were of matching maroon silk, heavily gilded with gold trim.

Mustafa dipped his short fat fingers into a silver bowl of scented water. But the sticky residue of the candied dates he'd greedily consumed still clung to his fingertips.

"You . . ." He pointed to Samira, a beautiful young slave who had been brought into the large chamber a half hour ago.

A mere child of fifteen, Samira had been stolen from her family's small home place four miles outside the village of Hofuf. Bands of the sultan's men combed the country-side constantly, searching for the fairest in the land, looking for new blood. Hunting for the very special female who could make their jaded master forget the blond American whom he had never seen but wanted desperately.

Because she was Sheik Sharif Aziz Hamid's woman.

This young lovely Arab girl now standing before the

emir had been spotted filling earthen jugs at a desert well with her two brothers. A natural beauty, she was a sweet, shy, modest virgin. The Turkish abductors had watched the girl from a safe distance for more than a week before they'd moved in on her. An untouched jewel, she was destined to become one of the sultan's favorites. Surely she could divert him, please him, sate him for a few tempestuous weeks.

On a day when Samira's father and mother had gone into the village, leaving the girl alone with her two muscular but unarmed brothers, the Turkish raiders had swooped down on the unsuspecting trio. The boys had been shot dead and the girl snatched up and spirited away.

Once at the palace, Samira had been taken straight to the Nubian eunuchs, who had bathed her, washed her long dark hair, removed all the hair from her slender body, outfitted her in see-through harem pants of vivid magenta and a matching satin vest, draped her wrists and ankles with gold bracelets, and then taken her to meet her new master.

Left alone in the room with the obese sultan, the terrified young girl had stood there for at least half an hour while he'd lain sprawled on the silver satin sofa, gobbling his candied dates and leering at her lasciviously without saying a word.

Then, plucking the last date from the silver platter and stuffing it into his mouth, he'd pointed to her and called out, "You . . ."

Samira flinched at the sound of his voice.

"Come here," he ordered, and the frightened child obeyed.

Trembling, trying very hard not to cry, she crossed the marble-floored room to him. When she stood directly beside the silver couch, the fat ruler looked up at her and, grinning wickedly, said, "What is your name, my pretty child?"

"Samira," she said softly, avoiding his beady black eyes.

"Samira," he ordered promptly, "kneel down here beside the couch so I may see you better." The girl sank to her knees, keeping her eyes downcast. "What is it?" he asked, needling her. "Don't you like your new home? Don't you like your new master?" Samira said nothing. He laughed at her obvious discomfort, then commanded her to raise her head and look at him.

When her fear-filled eyes met his, he told her, "Do not fret so. You and I are going to spend many a long afternoon together, Samira. There is nothing I enjoy more than training a new love slave." He chuckled heartily then and confided, "There are those who find my sexual tastes unconventional, even perverted. But you needn't worry about any of that. Since you are an innocent, everything I teach you will seem entirely normal to you because you know no better. Isn't that wonderful? I can make of you anything I want."

Tears swam in Samira's large dark eyes, spilled over, and splashed down her cheeks.

"Ah, now, do not cry," soothed the sultan. "I am very good to my favorites, and I'm sure you will become one of my most favorites."

Abruptly he thrust his fat right hand up before her face and said, "My fingers are sticky from the dates. Lick them clean."

Repulsed, Samira, thinking fast, looked about, saw the silver bowl of scented water, and said, "Allow me to wash your fingers in the—"

"No!" he said petulantly. "You heard me. I want you to suck my fingers."

Samira had no choice. While the wicked ruler

moaned and sighed and squirmed about on his silver satin sofa, the young girl held his plump, beringed hand in both of her own and licked the sticky brown date residue from each stubby finger.

Mustafa's head tossed. The maroon fez's black tassel whipped about his fleshy face. His small black eyes gleamed with pleasure as the beautiful young girl licked his fingers. He watched, transfixed, as her pink tongue slipped between her parted lips, again and again, touched his tingling fingers, and swept upward in a licking motion that effectively cleaned away the sticky date particles.

That wet pink tongue on his short sausage fingers did the trick.

"Oooooh," he praised, "you're like a little kitty cat. *My* own little kitty cat, curling up close beside me, licking me clean."

Finally finished with the distasteful task, Samira raised her head and was about to move away. But Mustafa reached out swiftly, wrapped his licked-clean fingers around the back of her neck, and began to fumble inside the folds of soiled maroon robes.

"Wait, my little kitty cat," he said, and his black eyes became demonic. "I have something else for you to lick clean."

At that moment there was a loud rap on the door.

Samira seized the opportunity and jerked away as Mustafa looked up angrily. Alwan, his personal servant, flanked by his two bodyguards, entered the chamber.

"What is the meaning of this interruption!" Mustafa thundered.

"Excellency, forgive us," Alwan said apologetically, bowing in supplication. "It is your father, the Agha Hussain."

"My father? What about him? Can't you see I'm busy? I have no time for the old fool now."

"He is gone, Excellency. Your father is dead."

Mustafa's scowl of annoyance turned immediately to a smile of pure joy. "Dead? The Agha Hussain is dead?"

"Yes, master. His servant found him a few minutes ago. He tried to wake him but couldn't. The palace physician was quickly summoned, but it was no use. The old sultan was dead."

"Allah kareen!" said Mustafa, and fell back on the silver satin sofa, immersing himself in the pleasure of knowing he was, at long last, the most powerful Turk in all Arabia. *"Allah kareen!* God is generous."

Temple was surprised at dinner that night when Chauncey abruptly announced he was leaving.

"I'll be packed tonight," he said. "That way I can get an early start in the morning."

"No! You're leaving already? Why?" Temple asked. "You were going to stay another two weeks. You told me so yourself."

Chauncey smiled at her, then turned to the Sheik. "Tell her, Sharif. Tell her I'm a wanderer and it's time I get back on the road."

"Chauncey never stays in one place long," Sharif said to Temple. Then, to his old friend, "Still plan on heading west toward Makkah?"

"Yes, I'll get a steamer there and head up the Red Sea to Egypt."

"I wish you wouldn't go," said Temple.

"I have to," Chauncey said, and he meant it.

"Then I shall get up early to say good-bye," she told him.

"I was counting on that," Chauncey said, smiling as he reached out and affectionately patted her hand.

After she'd said good night and left the two men, Temple lay awake in the Sheik's bed. She could hear the drone of their masculine voices as Chauncey and Sharif continued to talk in the tent's main room. She caught an occasional word here and there, hearing enough to know that Sharif planned to ride out at dawn with Chauncey on the first leg of his journey. Which meant Sharif wouldn't be getting back to the village until after sunset.

So Temple began to make her own plans.

Since this afternoon, when Chauncey had teased her with, "I believe you've fallen in love with old Cold Eyes," she had thought of little else. It was, she had finally admitted to herself, true. She did love Sharif. She was in love with him.

Dear God, she had actually fallen in love for the first time in her life, and it was with an Arabian outlaw.

And because she was in love with the Sheik, she had to escape him.

She loved him, but for her there could never be any happiness. She was nothing to him, despite the fact that he'd held her in his arms and made love to her through the black desert nights. Sharif did not love her.

He had never even mentioned his beloved Emerald City. He had no intention of taking her there. And even if he did, what kind of life would she have? If she were very fortunate, she might be one of his favorites—until he tired of her and banished her from his bed.

Then what?

She would languish away in his harem, praying he would send for her, her heart breaking.

No. No, she couldn't stand that. She wouldn't let it happen. She would leave him. Escape. He trusted her now. He wouldn't be expecting it this time. When he rode west tomorrow with Chauncey, she would ride east with Tariz and find a way to elude the little servant.

Lying there in the great lonely bed, Temple made up her mind.

Why the Sheik had kidnapped her in the first place, she could only surmise. Had he seen her somewhere in London and desired her? What else could it be?

He was rich. He wanted no ransom.

He had brought her to this desert oasis to do just exactly what he had done: wait for her to fall into his bed so that he could make love to her until the day came when she no longer excited him.

Well, she would beat him to the punch. He would not get the opportunity to tire of her and cast her aside. This would be the last night she spent in his desert, in his village, in his bed, and in his arms.

34

It was long past midnight when Sharif came to
bed.

A full high moon shone over the Arabian deserts, its
brilliance permeating the thickness of the white silk tent.
Though no lamp burned in the spacious bedchamber,
Temple could see the Sheik clearly. Unbuttoning his
white shirt, he glanced inquiringly at her.

Having made up her mind to leave, Temple felt it
would be hypocritical to make love with him again. She
pretended to sleep. She watched from lowered lashes as
Sharif, assuming she was fast asleep, kept silent. He did
not want to disturb her. Quietly, languidly, he
undressed. Temple knew it was unwise to continue looking at him. But she never fully closed her eyes.

Watching helplessly, she realized—not for the first
time—that the Sheik did everything with complete poise.
He was debonair even in taking off his clothes. It was
rather like watching a graceful ballet dancer perform as
he smoothly peeled the garments away from his beautiful body.

Each movement was easy, lithe, unhurried. Each article of clothing seemed to glide from his lean frame. Each portion of bared flesh shimmered like brown satin beneath which powerful muscles rippled in exquisite splendor.

When he had shed everything and stood naked beside the bed, his tall, tanned body was appealingly silvered by the invasive moonlight. Temple gazed at the perfect male body that had given her so much ecstasy and knew in that instant that she had to have him one last time.

Now she wished she hadn't feigned sleep.

She yearned for him to get into bed and take her in his arms.

The Sheik swept back the silken top sheet and got into bed. He stretched out on his back, folded his arms beneath his dark head, and did not so much glance at Temple. Her head already turned on the pillow, she saw that his eyes were open. She saw as well the beads of perspiration dotting his hairline and throat.

It was, she realized suddenly, very warm and close in the bedchamber. No cooling breeze rippled the tent walls. The dry air had changed little with the coming of night. The fierce, furnacelike heat of day lingered even at this late hour.

It was very still. Very quiet. Very hot.

Temple too was very still. Very quiet. Very hot.

Long, tense seconds passed.

Temple knew in her heart she should continue to lie there, still and quiet and hot. That was what she *should* do. But, if she did, it would mean this mysterious man she loved so much would never again make love to her.

A stabbing pain shot through her at the thought, and she knew she *had* to feel his arms around her one final time. Not knowing if he was in the mood for lovemaking or if he would coldly reject her advances, Temple began to inch closer to him. When her knee brushed his leg, she turned onto her side, leaned up, supported her weight on an elbow, and laid a tentative hand on his chest.

She heard his quick intake of air, saw his black eyes flash in the moonlight.

"Sharif," she whispered, "I can't sleep."

She stroked his muscular chest and at the same time dragged her toes up his long, hair-dusted leg, bending her knee and sliding it over his hips and across his flat belly.

He didn't move. He didn't speak. His arms stayed folded beneath his head. The male flesh beneath her bare thigh remained totally flaccid.

Temple bent her head, pressed a kiss to his chest, and whispered, "It's so hot tonight. Sooo hot. Unbearable." Her lips toyed with a flat brown nipple. "I wish the village were deserted. I wish we were the only two people here. Then we could go down to the water and cool off."

Sharif's arms came out from under his head. Temple raised up and looked at him hopefully. His hands cupped her face and he said, "There is a place where we can cool off." He rolled into a sitting position, brushed a quick kiss to her lips, and whispered, "Get dressed."

"How? I have no clothes."

He flashed one of his rare smiles and said, "I'll loan you a shirt."

Ten minutes later the two of them, both mounted atop Bandit, were racing across the moon-silvered sands toward that secret oasis known only to the Sheik.

Wearing nothing but one of Sharif's long-tailed white shirts, Temple sat across the saddle in front of him, her arms wrapped around his neck, her loose blond hair flying in her face and in his. Sharif, in a pair of riding breeches and nothing else, had Temple enclosed in his arms. But he wanted his hands on her as well. So he wrapped the reins around the saddle horn and controlled the fleet-footed stallion with the pressure of his knees.

The pair touched and kissed and grew more aroused by the minute as the galloping stallion thundered over the shifting white dunes. It was a beautiful night, though oven hot. The full white moon overhead turned the desolate deserts into a silvery wonderland.

At some point during all the kissing, Sharif unbuttoned Temple's borrowed shirt and pushed it apart. The wind caught the cotton fabric and the shirt ballooned out behind her back, leaving her pale body exposed to the flashing dark eyes of her lover.

"Take it off," Sharif prompted.

Laughing musically, Temple sat up and shrugged her slender shoulders while Sharif pushed the sleeves down her arms and off. She squealed and caught the shirt before it could fall to the ground. Clutching it with one hand, she leaned back in his supporting arm, naked in the moonlight.

On they rode—kissing eagerly, hotly, Sharif's hand caressing the soft warm flesh he had bared. Each kiss grew hotter, longer. Each touch became more insistent, more persuasive. Each caress made hearts beat faster, blood scorch through veins. Soon it became apparent that they couldn't wait until they reached the oasis.

After one particularly long, drugging kiss, Sharif lifted his dark head, looked into Temple's eyes, and said, "I want you."

"And I want you."

"Now."

Her heart pounding, her breath coming fast, Temple looked about, saw nothing in any direction but the endless silvered sands, glittering like millions of tiny diamonds in the desert moonlight.

"There isn't anyplace we can . . . ," she said breathlessly. "Except the sand."

"But there is," he told her. "Here. Atop Bandit."

Temple's green eyes widened. "You're not serious."

"I am," he said, and immediately spoke to the sprinting white stallion.

Bandit instantly slowed his ground-eating gallop to a comfortable walking pace. Knowing Sharif *was* serious and trusting his proficiency at accomplishing risky feats, Temple smiled and tied the borrowed white shirt to the saddle horn. Sharif put his hands to Temple's waist, scooted her up and forward in the saddle, and then helped her ease a leg up and around him.

When she sat facing him, he said, "Unbutton my breeches."

Her fingers were amazingly nimble on the buttons. In seconds the pants were open. She gave the trousers a tug. They parted in a wide wedge down his brown belly, and his awesome erection sprang free.

Trusting him to hold her securely, Temple lowered both hands and cupped him gently as if she were touching a priceless work of art. She looked at it lovingly, then raised her eyes to his.

"Should I lick my fingers to make you wet?" she asked.

"You tell me, *chérie*. Can you make me wet without it?"

"Yes," she told him quickly. "Oh, yes."

"I thought as much," he said, and slipped his hands down her to her hips. "Come to me, Temple," he urged.

Nodding, tingling from head to toe, she put her hands atop his shoulders as he lifted her in his strong arms until she was poised in position. Clinging tightly to his neck with one hand, she moved the other between them, wrapped gentle fingers around him, and guided the smooth, hot tip up inside. She moved her hand back to his shoulder, and her eyes held his as she sighed and boldly impaled herself upon him.

"Yesssss," he murmured, his lean fingers kneading the soft flesh of her bottom, his pulsing tumescence sliding easily into the silky wet heat of her. "*Naksedil,* make love with me. Make love to me. Do everything to me. Bring me, *chérie*. Make me come over and over again. Love me, Temple, love me."

His sensual words stirred her senses as did his masterful body. Challenged to take him to ever greater heights, longing to prove her sexual prowess, Temple told him brazenly, "I will, Sharif, you'll see." And she gave a slow, undulating roll of her hips as she promised, "I will make you feel as no other ever has. I will do things for you, to you, no other woman would dare. For tonight, my love, you are mine. Lose yourself in me, my Sheik. Immerse yourself in my burning love. Take it, darling. Take it all. It is yours and yours alone."

She thrust her hands into the raven hair at the sides of his head and pulled his mouth to hers. She kissed him skillfully, thrusting her tongue into his mouth and swirling it around as she moved her hips in a grinding, circular motion to match.

Forgetting everything, including where they were, the shameless lovers made hot, abandoned love as they rode the big white stallion across the moon-silvered sands. Neither was sure whether they found the stallion's rhythm or if he found theirs, but the three of them— man, woman, and horse—moved perfectly, erotically together, the bucking and thrusting of the lovers' bodies timed naturally to meet the rise and fall of the big beast's back as he strutted fluidly over the dunes.

When sensual pleasure escalated and the movements of the mounted lovers gradually speeded, the stallion picked up his pace, began to lope in long, easy strides. By the time the lovers were reaching their zenith and moving rapidly, frantically, in their quest for total rapture, the excited white stallion was galloping at such breakneck speed that Sharif had to cling to the saddle horn to keep them from falling off.

The racing stallion reached the final destination just as the lovers reached the ultimate ecstasy. While Bandit came to a sand-flinging stop on the smooth banks of the palm-fringed oasis pool, blowing and shaking his head about, his lungs expanding and deflating like a great bellows, the sweat-slippery pair on his back clung to each other, Temple crying out, Sharif groaning loudly, both shuddering violently in the throes of a phenomenal orgasm.

When the winded Bandit lowered his head and began to drink of the cool, clear water, Temple and Sharif sagged tiredly against each other, fighting for breath, willing their hearts to stop beating so rapidly.

Finally Temple raised her head from Sharif's shoulder, swept her tangled hair back off her face, and told him truthfully, "I haven't the energy left for swimming. I'm not sure I can even get off this horse."

The Sheik said, "Do not worry, *chérie*. You just took good care of me, and now I will take care of you."

He eased her up off him, scooted back out of the saddle, and gently deposited her in it. He slid off the horse's behind, quickly took off his breeches, tossed them aside, then came around. While she looked at him, puzzled, Sharif unbuckled his saddlebags and took out a fresh bar of soap. He handed the soap to her, then took his white shirt from the saddle horn and tied it loosely around his neck. He easily plucked Temple out of the saddle and carried her to the water's edge.

He jumped in, cradling her in his arms, and when

they'd cooled off and played for a while, he untied the now soaked white shirt, took the soap from her, and gave Temple a nice long relaxing bath.

It was heavenly.

She lay in his arms in the cool clear water while he patiently, thoroughly bathed every inch of her body, lathering her sensuously with the soap, then washing her gently with the soaking shirt.

When they came out of the water, they lay down on Sharif's breeches and let the hot desert air dry their bodies. They made love again on the soft green grass in the dappled moonlight filtering through the tall thick palms.

It was a slow, languid loving, and Temple purposely kept her eyes open throughout. She wanted to remember everything about this magical night with the Sheik. She wanted to recall—for the rest of her life—exactly how Sharif's handsome face above her own looked as he thrust repeatedly into her. She wanted to remember how his night black hair shimmered and his beautiful black eyes gleamed and his sensual mouth hardened with passion and his sculpted brown shoulders were silvered by the moonlight.

She felt as if she were in the midst of a beautiful, once-in-a-lifetime experience, half physical and half mystical. As though she were making love to a god.

And maybe she was.

35

Before sunrise, at that prescribed moment when a black thread can be distinguished from a white thread laid on the back of a hand and the faithful line up to say the morning prayer, Temple emerged from the Sheik's tent. She was dressed for a ride in the desert. She wore a white blouse, riding breeches, and tall leather boots. Her hair was pinned neatly atop her head, and tucked in her waistband was a pair of leather gloves.

A few yards away from the tent, two tall men—one dark, one blond—stood talking quietly. A large leather valise sat at the blond man's feet. Several yards beyond the two men, robed servants waited with saddled mounts.

Temple took a long breath, put a pleasant smile on her face, and walked directly toward Chauncey and Sharif.

"Well, there she is now," said Chauncey, and both men turned as she approached. When she reached them the blond Texan said, smiling broadly, "I was about to decide you'd slept in and I'd have to leave without—"

"You know better than that," Temple interrupted. "I

wouldn't dream of letting you get away without saying good-bye." Chauncey laughed, then, looking at her closely, teased, "I don't know, honey. Maybe you should have stayed in bed. You look a little peaked this morning."

Flushing, Temple glanced automatically at Sharif. To her utter surprise and amazement, she saw the hint of a conspiratorial smile touch his full lips. Her already aching heart squeezed painfully in her chest.

"Chauncey's right," Sharif said. "Why don't you skip your ride with Tariz this morning. Go back to the tent and get some rest."

"I'm not tired. Really," she said, her eyes holding his for a moment. "And you know how I love to ride."

Again that hint of a smile at her choice of words as he, like she, recalled the wild moonlight ride they'd taken together only hours ago, a ride like no other.

"Yes, I do," he said, his voice low, even, his black eyes burning through her.

"Well, why don't you just ride along with us," Chauncey suggested helpfully. "That way we could put off saying good-bye until—"

"No," Temple again interrupted. "I . . . I'd only slow you down." She looked at the travel stickers pasted to the sides of his valise—Red Star Line; Holland-America Line; Hotel Colón, Barcelona; Pension Isabella, Munich—and quickly changed the subject. "You're quite the globe-trotter, aren't you?"

"I get around," Chauncey confirmed. "From here it's up the Red Sea to Egypt, then on across the Mediterranean to Greece. Rome, Milan, and last, but not least, Monte Carlo." He winked at her. "Give the old roulette wheel a spin or two."

"Sounds like fun," she said.

"Yeah . . . I guess we can't put it off any longer. Time to say good-bye."

"Yes, I suppose so," Temple agreed, smiling warmly at him. "I can't tell you how much I've enjoyed your company."

"Same here, honey," Chauncey said, then reached out and swept her into his muscular arms. "God, I'm going to miss you," he said, hugging her tightly. He held her for a long moment, her face buried against his massive chest, one of his big hands patting her back affectionately. Then, abruptly, he released her, stepped back, and said, "Don't forget me now, you hear?"

"Never," Temple replied, and her gaze shifted from him to Sharif when she added softly, "I will *never* forget you."

Sharif's black eyes flickered, then he cautioned, "Make sure you get back this morning before it gets too hot." Temple nodded, said nothing.

The horses were brought forward, and Temple stepped back. Chauncey climbed into the saddle while a servant loaded his valise atop one of the packhorses. Sharif looped the reins over Prince's head, turned, and glanced about.

Everyone was busy, preparing to get under way. He motioned Temple closer. When she stood directly before him, he reached out, curled his fingers inside the tight waistband of her riding breeches, drew her to him, bent his dark head, and whispered, "Quick, *chérie*. Kiss me."

Then his lips were on hers, smooth and warm and possessive—but only for a moment. Then he raised his head, plucked at a button at the center of her blouse, and said, "I'll be back by sundown. Perhaps another moonlight ride tonight?"

Before she could reply he turned and swung agilely up into the saddle. Looking down at her, he saw the sadness she could not conceal in her expressive eyes, and he frowned. "What is it?"

Temple shook her head, fought back the threatening tears, forced herself to smile up at him. "Nothing," she said, impulsively laid a hand on his trousered thigh, and felt the muscles bunch and pull beneath her palm. Her throat so tight she could barely speak, she said, "I'm fine."

He nodded. "You're tired from last—"

"You coming, Sharif?" Chauncey shouted.

"On my way," Sharif called over his shoulder, laid his spread hand on Temple's, squeezed gently, then released it.

She stepped back. He neck-reined the big black about in a tight semicircle and cantered off to join Chauncey. At the head of the small caravan, they left the village as the sun began to rise. Temple watched them ride away. Chauncey turned in the saddle to wave.

Temple raised an arm high in the air and waved madly. She hoped the Sheik would turn and wave too so she could look one last time at his handsome face.

Sharif, look at me. Please! Oh, darling, please look at me. If you care even a little, then look at me, wave to me. I love you, Sharif, I love you. All I ask is that you look back and wave to me. My love, my love, look at me!

His dark head never turned. His hand never lifted. Sheik Sharif Aziz Hamid rode out of his desert camp that summer dawn without once looking back.

Temple stood there unmoving even after the caravan had ridden completely out of sight. Her hand pressed to her throbbing heart, her brimming eyes focused on the spot where last she'd seen Sharif, she was still there when Tariz came for her.

"Temple?" He spoke her name softly.

Startled out of her reverie, she blinked, spun about, and saw the smiling little servant leading their saddled mounts toward her. She forced herself to smile.

"Good morning, Tariz," she said as sunnily as possible. "I was waiting for you."

He nodded and grinned. "It is early," he said, his dark eyes twinkling. "You were up in time to see Mr. Wellshanse off, then?"

"Yes. Yes, I wanted to say good-bye to Chauncey." She patted Toz's sleek saffron-colored neck and said, "Give me a minute, Tariz. Let me dash back inside the tent and grab the robe Rhikia laid out for me."

"Ah, yes," he said, gesturing toward the tent. "Get the robe. The sun will be hot in a few minutes."

Temple went back into the tent. In the bedroom she pulled on the white robe in which she had hidden a canteen of water and some nonperishable foods. She picked up the kaffiyeh for her head but did not put it on.

There was no need to search for a weapon. The Sheik never kept anything other than his scimitar in the tent, and he had taken that with him. She had seen its jeweled hilt sticking from the waistband of his riding breeches.

She would just have to hope that she encountered no danger.

The cloth headdress over her arm, she crossed to the curtains, pulled back one side, and paused. Slowly she turned and looked at the big ebony bed in which she had spent some of the happiest moments of her life.

A violent shudder ran through her slender frame, and her eyes closed in agony. She swallowed with great difficulty, bit her lip, and swayed dizzily on her feet. She considered backing out of her plans.

She sighed heavily, and her eyes opened. She took a deep breath and shook her head. No, she wouldn't back out. Wouldn't change her plans. She had to go. She had to go now. She would *not* wait until the passion in the Sheik's black eyes turned to pity.

Temple rushed outside, purposely keeping her tear-filled eyes averted from Tariz. She climbed atop Toz, wheeled him about, and called over her shoulder, "Let's ride."

The sun was clearing the horizon when the pair rode out of the village. Temple kicked Toz into a gallop and forced herself not to look back.

Knowing it was important to behave as if everything were normal, Temple made herself carry on an amiable conversation with the ever-talkative Tariz.

When they were only a few miles from camp, Temple pulled up on Toz, dismounted, and told Tariz she felt like walking for a while. The smiling servant climbed down and fell into step beside her.

"Owwww!" Temple soon cried out and, pretending she had turned her ankle, yelped with pain. "My ankle! Oh, nooo," she moaned.

Frowning, the concerned Tariz immediately fell to his knees to examine her ankle. "We must take your boot off at once," he said.

Temple gave no reply. Silently asking his forgiveness, she reached inside her flowing robes, withdrew the water-filled canteen, and struck him on the head.

Tariz crumpled to the ground, out cold.

"I'm sorry, dear Tariz," she murmured, then bent and carefully spread the ends of his headdress over his face to shade it from the sun.

Then she whirled about, remounted hastily, and fled.

36

The sun, high and hot, poured down from a cloudless blue white sky. The dry air was filled with scalding heat. It was not yet noon, but already the heat was brutal, unbearable. A scorching wind came from out of the south, blowing from the vast arid wastelands of the Empty Quarter all across the Arabian peninsula.

Temple knew she must soon stop. She had listened well to the wise Tariz's warnings. It was suicide to travel the pitiless desert in the hottest part of the day. She wouldn't dare risk it. She had, on the many morning rides with Tariz, asked pertinent questions, learned the location of as many desert wells as possible, acquainted herself with the scarce shelters and various landmarks scattered along old trade routes.

If her calculations were correct, she should reach a small oasis containing a deep water well within the hour. She prayed she was right. Her eyes were burning from the lack of sleep and from the searing winds. Her head throbbed from the blistering heat, her back ached from being too long in the saddle, and her mouth was dust dry with thirst.

Squinting against the heat and the glare, she saw nothing but a great sea of golden sand stretching endlessly in every direction. Her heart kicked against her breast. How long, she wondered fearfully, would she survive if she didn't find the oasis? She had drained the last of the water from the aluminum canteen more than an hour ago and was now agonizingly thirsty.

She was also worried about Toz. The heavily lathered saffron stallion was wheezing and blowing, his great head sagging low as he trudged dutifully through the deep, scorching sands.

Scant moments later a small smile came to Temple's parched lips when she spotted—in the near distance—the distinct shape of tall, skinny palms rising black against the blue of the sky. The map she'd drawn in her mind had not let her down. Cool water and deep shade waited just ahead.

"See it, boy?" she said, patting the tired stallion's sweat-streaked neck. "Look, Toz, water. All you can drink. Just a few more steps now. A few more yards and then you can rest."

The stallion's ears pricked and his head rose. He scented the water and anxiously picked up his pace. Soon Temple felt the welcome shade on her hot, flushed face as Toz cantered under the sheltering palms.

The minute her booted feet touched the ground, Temple removed the bit from Toz's mouth. The big steed whinnied and trembled and nudged her out of the way as she struggled to slip out of her long robe.

"No!" she warned, stepping in front of him and out of the robe. "Wait your turn."

He whickered pitifully, nudged her shoulder, and lowered his head to the well as Temple fell to her knees. Slapping Toz's face away, she buried her own in the cool clear water, drinking thirstily. When she'd had her fill, she sat back on her heels, wiped her mouth, and before she could say, "It's all yours," the stallion's dusty muzzle was in the water and he was swilling loudly, greedily.

When both horse and rider had slaked their thirst, Temple unsaddled Toz and placed the saddle against the slender trunk of a palm. She folded her white robe into a pillow and placed it atop the saddle. She took off her boots and stretched out on her back, resting her head on the saddle. She nibbled on a fig but had no real appetite. She laughed and opened her palm when Toz, cropping grass beside her, stuck his muzzle against her wrist and sniffed. He ate the figs in one bite, then returned to the grass.

Temple sighed, closed her burning eyes, and told herself she must get some rest for the long night of travel ahead. But as tired as she was, sleep eluded her. It wasn't the fear of what lay ahead that kept her awake. It was the loss of what lay behind. The knowledge that she would never again see the only man she'd ever loved.

Her eyes opened and filled with a mist of tears.

It was over.

Nothing left but the memories. Memories of the early morning rides together in the matchless glory of the desert dawn. Memories of the last unforgettable ride together in the silver radiance of the moonlight.

A pain so intense it was physical pierced Temple's heart. She had been given a brief glimpse of the happiness that could never be hers. *He* was not hers. She would never see him again. Would never hear that beloved voice softly murmuring *chérie* as he held her in his strong arms in the hot darkness. Would never watch him light a cigarette and hold it in his long, tapered fingers while he gazed at her through the thick black lashes that curved down on his high olive cheekbones.

In the midst of reflecting sadly on how much she would miss the Sheik and his desert village, Temple realized that she hadn't missed her fashionable world of amusing parties, gossip, and mingling with nobility. Hadn't missed the constant round of balls, dinners, and theaters. Always another soiree, another club, another suitor.

How carelessly she had stepped on hearts without a twinge of pity or regret. How selfishly she had moved through the gilded days of her youth, thinking only of herself, searching endlessly for adventure and excitement, reaching continuously for the brass ring in an utterly hedonistic pursuit of personal pleasure. *Never* had she enriched another's life.

Temple began to smile wistfully even as the hot tears ran down her cheeks.

Now she knew what she had been searching for all those empty years. She had solved the mystery here in the hot Arabian deserts with the handsome Sheik. And if she never again felt as the Sheik had made her feel, if she never found another whom she could love half as much, it did not matter.

It did not matter that he had never loved her.

What did matter was that she loved him, and she was a better person for having loved him.

She had always thought there was something missing in her. That she was incapable of loving another human being more than she loved herself. She was relieved to know that she was wrong. She loved Sharif more. She loved him so much, she resolved she would never tell the authorities—or anyone else—what had happened.

With any luck she would reach Baghdad well before her scheduled date of arrival, and no one would ever be the wiser. No one need ever know that she had been abducted and had spent her entire desert tour as the Sheik's captive.

Resolute in her loyalty and happy she could protect the man she loved, Temple finally managed to drift off to sleep.

She awakened with a start at sunset. It took only moments to fill the canteen, saddle Toz, and depart. She rode through the darkness until the moon rose full and white to light her way. She sang to keep herself company, and when she grew hoarse and could no longer sing, she studied the brilliant stars above, picking out the various constellations.

With her head tilted back and her eyes on the heavens, it occurred to her that the same bright stars and full white moon on which she gazed shone down on the Sheik's peaceful desert village.

It made her feel a little less lonely.

Twenty-four hours into her journey Temple wondered how far she had gone. Tariz had once told her the bedouins could travel up to sixty miles a day on a camel. Surely she and Toz had gone that far.

Today seemed even hotter than yesterday, and Temple felt as if she had been in the saddle, riding across the pitiless Arabian wastelands, for an eternity. As if she were the only one left in the world and was doomed to ride these shifting dunes forever.

All morning the heat had been intense, but now, with the approach of noon, it was suffocating. Temple lifted a hand to blot away the moisture on her shiny forehead and realized she had been doing so every few minutes for the past hour. Sighing wearily, she swept the horizon with squinting eyes. She saw nothing through the shimmering haze except the wide expanse of sand rolling toward the north like lazy waves on a torpid brown sea. Her shoulders slumping, her brow perspiring, she turned her head, gazed at the repetitious landscape, and saw, far off to the south, a strange-looking dark line where the sky met the dunes.

For a long moment she stared intently, wondering if it was sand stirred up by a caravan that had just gone out of sight. Or one about to come into sight. She watched until she could no longer see anything and decided her eyes had been playing tricks on her.

On she rode.

She was dozing in the saddle when a sudden gust of wind, like a blast from an opened furnace door, slammed her in the face. Just then a loud peal of thunder boomed, shattering the stillness. Toz snorted and quivered, then lunged jerkily forward, clearly excited.

"What?" Temple asked the anxious horse. "What is it, Toz?"

Whinnying loudly, the stallion went into a gallop as Temple looked nervously over her shoulder. The strange streak she'd seen on the southern horizon was wider, blacker, moving swiftly northward.

Oh, God, no. The *schmaal!* The fast-moving Arabian sandstorm was headed straight at her!

Temple dug her heels into Toz's flanks as a bright flash of lightning streaked across the sky, followed by a deafening crack of thunder. The nervous mount, spurred on by fear, raced across the sands at a headlong gallop. Sensing the steed's anxiety, Temple leaned low over his neck and spoke to him in soothing tones while she patted his withers.

The storm was rapidly moving closer.

The sky was turning pewter. Hot gusts of wind became more frequent, whipping up the sands in spiraling, eddying circles. Blinded by the stinging sands and struggling to remain mounted against a wind so forceful that even the eighteen-hundred-pound Toz was reeling, Temple tried to yank her billowing white robe closer around her. She spat out a mouthful of sand and labored to pull the folds of her kaffiyeh higher over her nose.

Into the spinning whirlwinds the stallion raced, and in no time Temple lost her bearings. She no longer knew in which direction Toz galloped, could no longer distinguish sky from land. Day turned to night as whirling clouds of gritty dust obliterated everything and the roar of the storm intensified. Temple could see nothing in the blackness, could hear nothing above the howling winds, but she could feel the mighty stallion trembling beneath her gripping knees, knew that he was as terrified as she.

The wind-driven sands were stinging her face like tiny needles, and her gloves and the long leather reins were wet with mud. Ever-strengthening gusts of wind were threatening to tear her from the saddle, and if that happened, she would be lost. So she kept her knees tight against the stallion's ribs and clung tenaciously to the reins, praying Toz would not stumble and unseat her.

Eyes shut tight against the blowing sands, Temple felt the rains begin. She opened her eyes and looked out as the cloudburst came in sheets of blinding rain. She hung her head and hunched her shoulders forward. The wind drove the rain mixed with sand into her face and pummeled her body.

It was over almost before it began, leaving her soaked to the skin and Toz's big body caked with sand.

With the passing of the rain, the wind abated slightly, and Temple spotted, through the still swirling sands, the outline of a structure. She yanked on the reins, turning the stallion about, changing direction.

In moments Toz reached the shelter, which was nothing more than the crumbling masonry walls of a small hut built beside a dry well.

Temple leapt from the saddle and led Toz inside the partial protection of roofless walls as the winds again picked up and the sand swirled wildly around them. Drenched from the rains and splattered with mud, Temple fell to her knees and sat flat down, pressing herself close against the jagged-topped wall. She turned her face in and was about to pull her robe up over her head when, to her surprise and amazement, the big, mud-caked stallion knelt down on his front legs, then stretched out close beside her. He leaned over her and pressed his great head against the wall directly above her own, as if attempting to shelter her from the stinging wind and sand.

"Oh, Toz," she murmured, grateful, "you're such a good boy."

He whinnied, and Temple took off her kaffiyeh, reached up, drew his head down, and tied the wet headdress around his muzzle. Then she pulled her dirty wet robe up over her head, closed her eyes, and pressed her cheek against the wall.

Shielded by Toz's big body, she settled in and rode out the fierce sandstorm. The roar of the storm was deafening, and Temple felt as if she would surely go mad if the high, howling winds didn't soon stop. Grains of sand crunched between her teeth and caused her tightly closed eyes to burn and tear and her sensitive skin to itch and prickle.

Miserable, she told herself over and over that she must remain calm. The storm couldn't last forever. They were safe in this crumbling shelter, if terribly uncomfortable. Soon the winds would calm and the sands would still and everything would be all right.

The storm raged on for hours.

Night had fallen when the violent tempest weakened and finally passed.

Toz rose first. Then Temple got to her feet. She pulled off the mud-caked robe and tugged the headdress from Toz's muzzle, and the two of them ventured out.

Temple turned about slowly in a complete circle. "Damnation!" she muttered.

She was lost.

The sky was black. No stars or moon for rough navigation.

She had never before passed by these tumbledown walls, had never heard about this dried-up well. The terrible storm had swept away any lingering traces of roads and routes. There was no gentle gulf breeze Tariz had spoken of blowing out of the east to guide her. No sand dunes piled and lined north to south. All caravan trails would be obliterated. The desert floor looked exactly the same in every direction.

Temple didn't know where she was. Didn't know in which direction Toz had carried her in the storm. She did not know in which direction she should ride.

She was hopelessly lost.

If she mistakenly rode west, she might wind up right back at the Sheik's village. If she wandered too far south, she would end up in the deadly Rub al Khali and perish. If she rode too far north, a roaming band of Turks might seize her.

She must ride east toward Baghdad. But where was east?

She had no compass. No map. She could wait until morning and follow the sun, but they were out of water. She couldn't risk riding in the full heat of the day in search of a well.

Temple took a deep breath, wet her fingertip, and stuck it in the air. There was the slightest hint of a breeze. She mounted the big stallion and rode away. Late in the night they came upon a wadi newly filled by the rain. They drank and rested there for a couple of hours, then pressed on.

Temple, dozing atop the stallion, was awakened by the blinding rays of the rising sun. The first thing she saw was a band of robed men riding fast, coming straight toward her. Sure it was the Sheik already after her, she wheeled Toz about and kicked him into a gallop. Lying low over his neck, she urged him to go faster.

Her tired, winded mount was overtaken easily, and Temple looked up, expecting to see the angry, handsome face of Sharif. But it was not Sharif and his men. Temple realized with horror that she had fallen into the hands of the Sheik's hereditary enemy.

The hated Turks.

37

The chief gatekeeper swung open the heavy steel gates to admit the mounted men. The riders thundered up the palm-lined concourse to the domed-and-turreted pale yellow palace on the cliffs. A strong garrison of Mustafa's soldiers waited inside the palace, and the sultan, seated on an imposing gold-and-crimson throne, was attended by several palace guards.

An hour earlier the advance rider had charged through the palace doors. Word had passed quickly through the cool corridors. The sultan had been enjoying a small repast to tide him over until dinnertime.

Gnawing gluttonously on a roasted leg of lamb, grease dripping down his double chins, he dipped his short fingers into a huge bowl of rice pilaf, carried it to his mouth, spilling several clumpy grains on the way.

Before him on dishes of solid gold was an assortment of his favorites delicacies. Goat cheese wrapped in grape leaves. Onions stuffed with minced lamb and hot peppers. Chunks of boiled lamb swimming in a sea of greasy gravy. Sugared carrots and black beans and roasted potatoes. Black olives and dates and figs and apricots and grapes.

And to top off the light midafternoon meal, the sweetmeat known throughout the world as Turkish Delight, a tasty treat consisting of the pulp of white grapes, semolina flour, honey, rosewater, and apricot kernels.

The famished sultan was biting into a stuffed onion when his personal servant, Alwan, rushed in, all excited. Chewing the big mouthful of onion and lamb, Mustafa glared at him as the servant approached.

Bowing and salaaming, Alwan said anxiously, "Forgive me, Excellency, for disturbing you, but I bring good tidings."

Then, rushing his words, Alwan announced that Mustafa's desert brigade was now, as he spoke, approaching the palace with Sheik Sharif Aziz Hamid's beautiful American captive.

The sultan spit out a half-chewed onion, reached up and grabbed the front of Alwan's robe, jerked his face down close, and said, "Why wasn't I told?"

"Excellency, I am telling you now. The outrider has just arrived. The brigade will be bringing this woman through the palace gates within the hour."

"Help me up," said the sultan.

"Yes, master," said Alwan, signaling a couple of guards forward.

While the muscular palace guards eased the rotund ruler up and out of his massive chair, Alwan took a damask napkin from the table and wiped grease and food particles from Mustafa's fleshy cheeks and chins.

"Would His Excellency desire a bath before meeting the American?" Alwan asked as he scraped a glob of rice off the sultan's badly stained peacock blue satin robe.

"Bath? I need no bath," said Mustafa. "But fetch up one of my finest gold-trimmed robes." He instructed his manservant to bring the fresh robe straightaway to the *hunkar,* adding, "I must look my best to meet this woman who is soon to become my most prized plaything."

Dirty, exhausted, badly weakened, but still struggling, Temple was forced inside a huge, high-ceilinged chamber by a pair of palace guards. A long red carpet rolled out on the gleaming white marble floor led to the far wall of the royal reception room. There on a raised dais, seated on an enormous high-backed throne of gold and scarlet, waited Mustafa Ibn Agha Hussain, the Turkish sultan, trained from boyhood for despotism and self-indulgence.

Temple was half dragged, half pushed down that long red carpet until she stood directly below the sultan.

"Unhand her," said Mustafa.

The palace guards released her and stepped back. Temple didn't hesitate. She spun about and ran for the nearest exit. The guards were on her before she could reach the door, and the sound of the sultan's evil laughter rang in her ears as she was hauled back before him.

His beady black eyes twinkling with joy, Mustafa ordered, "Bring her here to me."

The guards swiftly obeyed. Temple, with her arms pinned behind her, was forced up the marble steps to the dais, then pushed down onto her knees directly before the throne and the obese man seated upon it. The smiling sultan reached out to touch her cheek. She jerked her head away. He chuckled merrily.

"Ah, the American has spirit," he said. He captured

her chin, roughly turned her face back to his. "I like a spirited woman."

"You go to hell!" she spat, her eyes flashing with fury.

Again he chuckled. "I am sorry, my fair one, I do not understand your language." His hand gripping her chin, a fat thumb seeking entrance into Temple's tightly closed lips, he shouted to his minions, "Get my interpreter in here! And have Alwan bring a basin of rose water."

Mustafa managed to get the tip of his thumb between her lips, and Temple, sickened, opened her teeth and bit him viciously. He yelped in surprise and pain, snatched his hand away, and sucked on his injured digit.

The door burst open and Alwan, carrying a gold basin filled with cool rose water, was followed by Jamal, the sultan's interpreter. They marched hurriedly to the dais, where their master was already firing instructions at them.

"Jamal, you be still until I order you to speak! Alwan, wash her face so that I may see her beauty."

Alwan knelt beside Temple and bathed her face in the cool rose water while Mustafa, leaning forward eagerly on the gold-and-scarlet throne, watched closely. When her face was free of the dirt and grime and perspiration, the sultan stared in openmouthed wonder, dazzled by her fair beauty.

"Ah, yes, yes," he murmured in delight, "I will make you my *odalisque*, my love slave."

Temple's angry, defiant glare pleased him. Smiling, he said to Jamal, "My *odalisque* must wonder how I, Mustafa Ibn Agha Hussain, came to know of her. Tell her, Jamal! Tell her I know who she is. Show her the intercepted message that was sent by that Arab dog to her American family."

While the smiling sultan sat there eagerly examining

the golden prize that had fallen into his fleshy hands, Jamal withdrew from his robes the crumpled velum message taken—weeks ago—from Naguib, the Sheik's messenger, while he was en route to Baghdad.

In accented English, Jamal read the message to her. Temple listened, eyes wide, lips parted, as she finally learned the reason for Sharif's mysterious abduction.

"May I . . . see it, please?" she asked.

Jamal looked at the sultan and translated. Mustafa nodded. The guards released her arms, and Jamal handed her the Sheik's ransom note. She stared at the crinkled velum paper, and her hands began to shake. She'd have known Sharif's distinct handwriting anywhere. There was no doubt in her mind that he was the author of this intercepted message.

In it he proclaimed that he, Sheik Sharif Aziz Hamid, was holding her somewhere in the Arabian deserts. She would not be harmed. The press, the public, need not know. She would be released in Baghdad on the exact date she was originally scheduled to arrive—but *only if the flow of DuPlessis munitions* to the Sheik's oppressive enemy, Mustafa Ibn Agha Hussain, and his murderous Turkish band was halted immediately.

Temple lowered the vellum communiqué.

Jamal took it from her and, following Mustafa's orders, translated, "The DuPlessis family never received this cable. They are still unaware you were abducted." He looked her straight in the eye and said, "And now, emphasizing the sultan's words, no one will ever know what has become of you."

Temple realized he was right. Her heart sank.

She tried to get up but was forced to remain on her knees before Mustafa. Her flesh crawled as the obese, magnificently robed sultan examined her leisurely with his beady black eyes. He grinned lasciviously and licked his loose, fleshy lips. He conversed excitedly with his servants, and although she understood not a word of Turkish, there was no misunderstanding the fat Turk's plans for her.

"You are a fortunate young woman," he told her, looking straight into her angry eyes and reaching out to pluck at a strand of long, dirty blond hair. "If, once you are bathed and readied for me, your body is half as beautiful as your face, you will spend this night and many more in my bed." His tongue darted out and licked at his loose bottom lip in a decidedly lewd gesture. Then he said, "You and I will engage in carnal acts that the backward Arab has never even thought of!"

"I have no idea what you're saying, you disgusting pig," Temple replied brazenly. "I can only hope you understand that I am sickened by the sight of you!" Emerald eyes blazing, she turned to the interpreter and ordered, "Tell him, Jamal!"

Jamal didn't dare repeat what she had said. To Mustafa he said, "She said she is quite weary and would like to rest now."

"Yes, yes," said the sultan. "Let her rest for a while, then prepare her for the visit to my bedchamber."

His fat fingers still gripping a lock of Temple's tangled hair, he puckered his lips and leaned forward to kiss her. Her hand as swift as a striking serpent, she struck him fully in the face, landing a loud blow that echoed throughout the royal reception room.

Guards and servants alike winced in shock and apprehension. All tensed, expecting their ruthless despot to retaliate swiftly, cruelly. No one present would have been surprised if Mustafa had choked her to death there where she knelt.

His black eyes wide with astonishment, his bejeweled hand rubbing his stinging jaw, Mustafa Ibn Agha Hussain frowned angrily.

But only for a second.

Then he began to smile. His fleshy lips turned up in a smile of supreme pleasure. Soon he began to laugh. His jowls jiggling, his domed belly shaking and rippling beneath the crimson robe, the jolly sultan laughed merrily, uproariously.

When he'd calmed a bit he looked at Temple in frank admiration and told her, "Ah, my fragrant flower, my American spitfire, what happiness lies ahead for us! I have long dreamed of finding a woman with spirit and passion to match her great beauty. And here you are." His small pig eyes gleaming with desire, he predicted, "Do not worry, my impetuous jewel. Once you've lain with me, you will quickly forget that arrogant Arab swine, Sharif Aziz Hamid."

At the mention of Sharif's name, Temple bluffed boldly, "I will summon the Sheik here and he will kill you, you bloated barbaric beast!"

38

Temple was taken away.

The sprawling seaside kingdom was a baffling conglomeration of buildings of all shapes and sizes and on multiple levels. Temple tried, as she was led through a maze of shadowy hallways and sunny courtyards, to pay close attention in case she later got an opportunity to escape. But the sultan's pale yellow palace and the surrounding grounds were huge, a confusing labyrinth of shady arches and narrow passages and sparkling fountains and flower-filled courtyards and shadowy corridors and high fretted windows and domed tiled ceilings.

By the time she was ushered into a spacious, sunsplashed chamber filled with laughing, chattering women, Temple couldn't have retraced her steps if her life depended on it.

The guards who escorted her to the women's quarters left her there without a word and retreated immediately, closing and bolting the door behind them. Temple stood uncertainly on the marble threshold, her curious gaze sliding around the room while the women, falling silent, stared openly at her.

The chamber was spacious, airy, the sun coming in through barred and latticed windows, the lower sills of which were higher than the head of the tallest of men. At the room's center was a fountain fashioned entirely of fine crystal, clear water misting and splashing from it into a circular crystal pool at its base. The crystal fountain, caught in the rays of the sun spilling through the high latticed windows, glittered like millions of fine diamonds.

Carpets of gold silk covered the floor, and on the walls were elaborate hangings. Overhead the high, domed ceiling of bright blue was dotted with gleaming gold stars. Silk-covered sofas and hassocks and cushions scattered about were the resting places of dozens of young, beautiful women. Women who were clad in nothing but gauzy harem pants and gem-encrusted bolero vests.

Temple spotted an empty pink-and-gold divan at the far side of the room. She immediately started toward it, so tired she could hardly put one foot before the other. The silence passed. The harem women pointed and chattered and frowned. She was, Temple realized, an oddity here among these dark-haired, olive-skinned women. She read in their dark flashing eyes the surprise, the curiosity, the jealousy.

Ignoring them, she headed directly toward the pink-and-gold sofa, her only wish at the moment to lie down. To rest. She couldn't think clearly in this state of sheer exhaustion. She had to sleep, if only for a little while.

Temple sighed when finally she reached the divan. She sat down and was leaning forward to take off her hot, dusty riding boots when the sound of weeping caused her to slowly turn her head.

Not thirty feet away a woman sat on the gold silk carpet beside a big square ottoman. Her bare arms were folded atop the ottoman's soft cushion, and her face was buried as she wept.

Wearily Temple sat up and stared. Then she looked around. No one else gave notice to the unhappy young woman. None of the harem women came forward to comfort her or even to ask why she was weeping. Seized with a surge of compassion, Temple went over, sank to her knees beside the sobbing woman, and laid a gentle hand atop her dark hair.

The girl's head lifted and she looked at Temple with big dark puffy eyes that were red rimmed and swimming in tears. Temple was horrified. This was not a woman, but a child. She couldn't have been more than sixteen or seventeen. What was an innocent child doing in the evil emir's harem?

Temple spoke softly but could tell immediately that the young girl didn't understand English. Temple switched to French, the only foreign language she had studied in college. Immediately the young girl's sad eyes lighted a little and she nodded.

Quickly Temple untied the silken sash spanning the girl's narrow waist and lifted it to dry away her tears, all the while speaking French in soft, low tones. She put her arms around the shaking, sobbing girl, drew her close, and continued to soothe her.

When the girl had stopped crying and was calmer, she began to talk. To answer Temple's questions.

Her name was Samira, and she was fifteen years old. She clung to Temple as she related the horror of how her brothers had been murdered and she had been kidnapped by the sultan's Ottoman brigade.

Samira confided that she was now a *guzdeh*, a girl who had been noticed by but not yet bedded by the sultan. She had, she said, already been forced to spend miserable hours alone with the Turkish ruler while he leered at her, teased her unmercifully, and told her of all the frightening things he was going to do to her once she was in his bed.

Feeling extremely protective of the terrified young girl, Temple comforted Samira. "The fat Turk will *not* be allowed to bed or harm you, Samira," she promised, though how she could keep her promise was a mystery.

Consoled by Temple's presence and promise, Samira ceased her crying. With Temple's help she dragged her hassock closer to the pink-and-gold sofa. As Temple stretched out tiredly, Samira, seated on the floor nearby, told her with a child's guileless honesty that up until now she had had only one friend in the harem.

"The other women, they hate me," she said. "They are mean to me, all except one. A kind woman named Leyla. Leyla keeps the others from constantly tormenting me." She paused, looked down, and added sadly, "When she is able." She looked up and, with tears again welling in her red eyes, explained, "Leyla is in the infirmary. Again. The sultan is cruel to her. He beats her and he cut off part of her earlobes." She shuddered.

"Don't . . . worry, Samira," Temple said sleepily. "No one is . . . going . . . to . . . hurt you."

Unable to hold her eyes open a moment longer, Temple fell asleep. Samira, feeling safer than she'd felt since being brought to the palace, laid her head on her hassock, and she, too, was soon sleeping.

The patterned sunlight spilling through the high latticed windows had turned from the hot white of afternoon to the pale pink of evening when Temple was rudely shaken awake.

She was taken from the chamber by the chief black

eunuch while Samira, watching helplessly, knowing what was in store for her newly made friend, looked after them anxiously. Wishing she could save Temple from her terrible fate, knowing that she could not, Samira hugged her knees to her chest and bit her lip, shivering with fear.

Fighting him every step of the way, Temple was led to the bathing chamber, where she was stripped and carried, kicking and screaming, into the pool. The chief eunuch's intent was to bathe her personally, as ordered by his master. But Temple put up such a fierce battle that the pinched, slapped, bitten, and bewildered chief eunuch finally gave in and allowed her to wash herself and shampoo her own hair.

When she was clean, she was dressed in gauzy harem pants of vivid green and a vest of rich green velvet trimmed with glittering emeralds and shiny gold spangles. On her feet were gold slippers without heels, pointed and curved slightly at the toe and richly embroidered with gold and emeralds.

Her long blond hair was parted down the middle, brushed out loose over her bare shoulders, and held in place by a golden rope encrusted with emeralds that was wound around her forehead and temples, the long ends flowing down her back.

Her lips were painted a bright blood red with henna, her large emerald eyes accentuated with kohl shading. Rings of gold and emerald were slipped onto her slender fingers, and a coiled snake of gold mesh with emeralds for the eyes was wrapped around her bare upper arm.

Two palace guards appeared to escort Temple down a long corridor to the bedchamber of the sultan. Alwan was there, just outside the door, waiting to usher her inside. He leapt up from his chair when he saw her, and his eyes sparkled with delight. Nodding, murmuring happily to himself, the pleased majordomo circled her, staring, clasping his hands in approval, straightening an errant lock of golden hair, fussing with a fold of her gauzy harem pants.

Then, taking a deep breath, he stepped in front of her and swung open the heavy door into the sultan's bed-chamber.

Temple balked, refused to enter. The guards stepped up beside her, forced her forward. As soon as she glimpsed the robed ruler lolling indolently on some odd kind of tilted resting board, she looked away, refusing to meet his gaze. She didn't see the expression that came into his beady black eyes. His mouth gaping open, his breath coming fast, Mustafa ogled her and the hot blood immediately pounded through his fleshy body, causing an instant erection to spring up beneath his satin robe.

He gaped at her with greedy lust, eager to make her his *odalisque*, his love slave. Yet at the same time he gazed on her with adulation, as if she were a golden angel to be worshiped and idolized.

After what seemed an eternity to Temple, the half-reclining sultan motioned Alwan to his side.

"This beautiful woman is far too precious to be only an *odalisque*," he said, his eyes never leaving Temple. "I shall make her my first wife! My only wife! I will marry her and we will sire many fine sons and daughters! I will be the most envied man in the Middle East! In all the Ottoman empire! Start planning our wedding. Command all my far-spread subjects to be present for the festivities! Make it clear to those who are prosperous that they are to bring expensive gifts. Oh, it will be a joyous occasion. The happy sultan and sultana!"

"Yes, Excellency."

Mustafa grabbed Alwan's robe front and said, "I will

prove what a strong and disciplined ruler I am and how much this beautiful woman means to me. As tradition demands, I will not touch her until after we are married." He looked from Alwan to Temple, almost weakened, and then ordered anxiously, "Take my priceless beauty away before I change my mind about waiting until we are wed!"

Puzzled by her unexpected reprieve, Temple was returned to the harem. There the young Samira hurried to meet her, asking in French if she was all right. Had His Excellency hurt her the way he had hurt poor Leyla?

Assuring Samira that she was fine, only very tired, Temple returned to the pink-and-gold sofa to lie down. *"Je suis fatiguée."*

Samira nodded, asking, "It is all right if I stay here close to you?"

Temple smiled, touched the child's cheek, and said, "We are friends, Samira. Of course it is all right."

Leyla, the beautiful Circassian who had suffered at the sultan's fat hands, was returned to the harem from the clinic the next morning. After hugging her, Samira eagerly introduced her to her new friend, Temple. Leyla, too, spoke French, so the three of them were able to communicate.

From Leyla, Temple learned more of the evil man who held her fate in his hands. As Samira napped that hot afternoon, Leyla spoke frankly with Temple. She told of the horrors she lived through. She revealed some of the bruises, old and new, that covered her flesh. She showed Temple where her earlobes had been painfully clipped.

"He is," Leyla whispered, "the most depraved, selfish, cruel, rapacious man alive."

She glanced at the sweet, slumbering Samira and lowered her voice even more when she said, "I'm so afraid of what he may do to Samira. He is vile and he does unspeakable things. He fortifies himself with aphrodisiacs, and he has a secret chamber deep in the palace that is covered entirely with mirrors to stimulate passion."

"Oh, dear God," Temple murmured.

"One of his favorite games is to strip twenty or thirty of his women naked and make them pretend they are mares while he, also naked, trots among them, acting the part of a stallion for as long as his energy permits."

"The vile, perverted pig," said Temple, making a sour face.

"After food, sex is his main interest in life," Leyla continued. "Another of his favorite harem games is to have naked women skid down slides onto their waiting lord and master. Him."

"Let's kill him," were the next words out of Temple's mouth, her green eyes narrowed with hatred and disgust.

"How?" asked Leyla. "Do you really suppose he plays these dirty games without armed palace guards being present in the room?" She shook her head. "Believe me, you'll be murdered where you stand if you dare to make an attempt on his life."

"There are," Temple said thoughtfully, "some things worse than death."

39

Temple lay awake that night long after the others had gone to sleep. Her troubled thoughts turned naturally to the Sheik. She saw his handsome face in the darkness as if he were beside her. Aching for his gentle touch, yearning for the safety of his strong arms, she wondered if she would ever sleep with him again, ever hold him in her arms.

And then it came to her. She *would* see Sharif again. It defied all reason and proof, but she knew it was true: Sharif would come and save her.

The Sheik would come.

Sharif, she murmured soundlessly in the darkness, *please come. I'm so frightened, Sharif. Save me, darling. Come for me, my beloved Sheik.*

Temple fell asleep with his name on her lips.

She was awakened early the next morning and taken away while Leyla and Samira watched worriedly. Still groggy from sleep, Temple was again escorted to the royal reception room, where the obese emir sat upon his gold-and-scarlet throne.

Alwan was present, as was Jamal, the interpreter. A half dozen palace guards manned the exits. Temple was marched down the long red carpet until she stood directly below Mustafa.

He began speaking immediately, waving his hands about excitedly, looking at her, his beady black eyes gleaming.

She glared at him, shrugged, and tapped her foot impatiently. But her breath caught in her throat when Jamal told her what His Excellency was saying.

"You are to be his wife," Jamal explained. "The wedding will take place—"

"There will be no wedding!" Temple interrupted angrily. "Tell the sultan I would sooner die! I will *never* marry him!"

Jamal translated quickly.

Mustafa was unfazed by her refusal. He chuckled merrily, more aroused than ever. Finally here was the fiery female he had dreamed of all his life. Never before had he had a woman like this haughty foreign princess. Not a single one of the hundreds of beautiful women he had bought or stolen or recruited from childhood had shown such fearlessness, such spirit.

Grinning, he said affectionately, "Ah, you sting me so! Thy mother must have mated with a scorpion."

Glaring, Temple replied bitingly, "You repulse me so! Your mother must have mated with a swine."

Mustafa continued to smile. And through his interpreter he assured Temple that she would indeed become his bride and the mother of his sons. Many sons.

Temple was just as vehement, just as forceful. No matter what he did to her, no matter how badly he might punish her, she would *never* marry him!

The sultan finally tired of the quibbling. He attempted to snap his short fingers, failed, and irritably shouted commands that Temple could not understand. Then all was quiet, and Mustafa sat there on his throne, grinning down on her as if he knew some delicious secret.

Temple flinched when she heard the heavy doors behind her open. She saw the heads of the guards turn. She spun around. Young Samira was being ushered up the long red carpet. Temple felt her heart kick against her ribs. What did the evil bastard have in mind? Why was Samira being brought here?

Too soon she found out.

The terrified young girl was taken directly past Temple and up the steps to the throne. She was placed atop one of the sultan's fat, spread knees, and as the guards moved back a step, Mustafa wrapped a short arm around Samira, squeezed her narrow waist, and gave her bare shoulder a slobbery, sucking kiss.

A sob tore from Samira's lips and Temple gasped in horror when the emir then drew from the folds of his robe a diamond-hilted scimitar. The long curved blade gleamed in the morning sunlight. Temple's hand flew to her thudding heart when he placed the sharp blade directly against Samira's throat.

"You sick son of a bitch!" Temple shouted, and started up the steps.

She was stopped and held with her arms behind her back.

His tongue darting out to lick his heavy bottom lip, Mustafa carefully pricked the flawless olive flesh of Samira's smooth throat, just below her right ear, with the blade's sharp tip. Samira screamed. A drop of bright red blood beaded on her neck. Temple shrieked and strained furiously against the strong hands that held her, desperate to get to the terrified Samira.

"You evil bastard!" she shouted at the sadistic sultan, her heart racing, her eyes flashing with outrage. "Let her go this minute! Do you hear me? You let her go, damn you!" Frantically she looked to Jamal, to Alwan, and to the others. "Please!" she beseeched them. "Make him stop. Make him release her."

Calmly Jamal said, "His Excellency has instructed me to tell you that he is going to slit the girl's throat."

"Oh, God, no, no!" Temple screamed, turning her full attention back to the fat man holding the curved scimitar blade to the trembling Samira's throat.

"Please, no . . ." She began begging for Samira's life. Pleading with him, she told him she'd do anything he wanted if only he would release the girl right now, unharmed.

Jamal informed her that there was only one way she could save the girl.

"How?" Temple asked, her slender body shaking with fury and with fear.

"You will marry the sultan by week's end."

Temple swallowed hard, looked at the gloating Mustafa, looked at the weeping Samira. "And if I won't agree?"

"If you do not say yes in the next sixty seconds," Jamal told her calmly, "the girl's throat will be sliced from ear to ear."

Temple shuddered. The wicked bastard would indeed slit Samira's throat without blinking an eye.

"Tell him," she said, defeated, "to let Samira go. I will marry him."

Temple was, that very hour, separated from the rest of the harem. It was the first step toward the envied position of imperial wife. She was given an apartment and offered slaves of her own. She quickly chose Leyla and Samira to attend her. And when the two grateful women were safely inside the private apartment, Temple sent word to her husband-to-be that Leyla and Samira now belonged to her and he was not to send for them ever again.

When the message was delivered, the sultan clapped his beefy hands in glee. She didn't want him bedding her personal slaves. Already his fair-haired beauty was jealous!

Temple did everything in her now considerable power to keep the three of them—Leyla, Samira, and herself—safely ensconced inside the walls of the luxurious apartment, which boasted a huge private bath and splashing fountains and fragrant gardens and an aviary filled with exotic birds. The rooms were ornamented with panels of painted flowers and hung with beautiful brocades. Doors and cupboard shutters were inlaid with mother-of-pearl. Lush carpets covered the floors. Bedsteads of ivory inlaid with large pieces of coral supported brocaded mattresses and cushions.

For three days and nights she managed to keep them all out of harm's way. They were allowed to take their meals in the apartment, and have their baths there, and sleep there, monitored closely by two uniformed palace guards.

Each afternoon Temple was required to spend an hour in the company of her future husband, the sultan. But she made it clear that those meetings were not to take place in his bedchamber and that in addition to his interpreter there was always to be at least one female servant present.

The sultan agreed to these terms. And he took no offense when she slapped his chubby hands off her and threatened him as if he were the slave, she the master. Had any other woman behaved in such a high-handed manner, she would have been flogged, mutilated, or worse for her insolent disobedience.

Repulsed by the salacious man who kept attempting to lay his pudgy hands on her, Temple fended him off and endured. And as she cursed him and slapped away his roving hands, she silently told the foolish, smitten ruler that his hours on this earth were numbered.

The Sheik would come to deliver her from this fate.

But as the hours passed and her wedding day approached, Temple felt something tearing at her spirit. Her faith began to waver. Her hopes began to dim. It seemed, after all, that her destiny was to be the bride of the repulsive Turkish sultan.

She would rather be dead.

Temple didn't realize the reason she was beginning to feel so defeated was that the crafty emir had been having the pomegranate wine she drank with her meals liberally laced with laudanum. A little more was added at each meal, to each glass.

She couldn't understand why she was becoming so lethargic, why she no longer had the will to fight her fate. She was puzzled by her inability to care as much as she should. Her thoughts were growing increasingly muddled. She felt as if she were constantly in a thick fog.

Temple didn't know what was happening to her.

The wedding date arrived.

Just four short days after agreeing to marry Mustafa, Temple was awakened early from a drugged sleep and reminded that at noon she was to become the bride of His Excellency, the sultan.

Confused and incredibly thirsty, she was served a light breakfast of fresh fruit and a big golden goblet of pomegranate wine. Temple looked around curiously, asked where Leyla and Samira were. The servant who served her breakfast shook his head. He did not understand what she was saying. He urged her to drink up, then poured a second glass of wine.

Temple felt dizzy by the time a guard appeared to

take her from the apartment. In limited French he told her she was to spend the morning being prepared for the wedding to her Turkish prince.

"No," she objected, "my servants will prepare me for the ceremony. Leyla and Samira will . . . Where are they? Why aren't they here?"

The guard gave no reply. Over her protestations, he took her from the apartment and to a place she had never seen before, the Imperial Bath. Two tall, magnificently built Nubian eunuchs, wearing nothing but loincloths of white linen, awaited her there.

Knowing their intent, Temple struggled briefly, but her strength and her will soon gave out. What was the use? She was no match for the pair of black giants. To fight them would be futile and foolish.

The guard disappeared, and the eunuchs ushered Temple inside the imperial bath, which was as large as a spacious bedroom. Walls and supporting pillars of Egyptian alabaster were veined with gold, and overhead was a dome of amber-colored glass through which light gave added brilliance to the marble floor and gold fixtures.

Temple was undressed and led to the very center of the bath, where a pair of marble benches faced each other. Magically the water came on, rushing in from all sides from gold spigots and fountains. For the next half hour Temple stood and sat in the great misty shower of hot and cold water while the twin Nubians bathed her and shampooed her long golden hair.

When she was fresh and clean and her body patted dry with thirsty gold-trimmed towels, she was taken to another room directly in back of the bath. There the mauve-colored walls were scented with roses, and pink light poured in through the high, rose-tinted windows. Alabaster basins of white and gold were at each end and on one side of a long cushioned table that was so high off the floor there were steps for mounting it.

Temple was guided up the set of steps and helped onto the padded table, where she was placed on her back. While the bright sun streamed down through the rose-tinted windows and turned her pale flesh a soft pink hue, the eunuchs went about the lengthy task of removing the hair from her body. Dexterous hands spreading a paste depilatory on her long slender legs, her underarms, and her groin, the Nubians kept her on the cushioned table for more than an hour, spreading, rubbing, peeling, washing, and searching for any sign of wispy golden hair they might have overlooked.

When both were satisfied that her flesh was as smooth and hairless as a newborn babe's, Temple was led back into the bath and bathed once more. Afterward she was taken to yet another chamber, a rose-hued room where the floor was covered with a rich rose carpet and a long table at room's center was draped with towels. A low divan of shimmering rose silk rested against an alabaster wall. Temple was placed on the towel-draped table and those same four large hands that had bathed and removed the hair from her nude body began gently to rub rich perfumed oils into her pale porcelain skin.

She lay on her stomach while one eunuch, standing at the head of the table, worked on her slender arms, the other, at the table's foot, on her long legs. Then one eunuch moved around to the right side of the table, the other to the left. One turned his attention to her shoulders and back, the other to her bottom and thighs.

Then she was turned over.

She lay spread-eagle while one carefully massaged her shoulders and breasts, the other her belly and thighs. When finally they finished, there was not a single pinpoint of flesh on her naked, hairless body that had not been perfumed with oil. Next they painted her finger-nails and toenails with henna, stained her lips with scarlet rouge, and kohled her emerald eyes.

Wondering if this terrible nightmare were ever to end, Temple was taken to yet another room. There, finally, she was dressed for her wedding, beginning with sheer stockings and ending with a white satin gown being lowered over her head and fastened up the back.

Her long golden hair was brushed out, and she was covered with priceless diamonds. They spilled in shimmering rivers over her breasts, were stacked in flickering cairns across her brow, and ringed her fragile wrists and ankles and throat.

Her stockinged feet were slid into white satin slippers, a white veil was lowered over her unsmiling face, a bridal bouquet of ivory orchids was handed to her, and Temple's heart sank.

The time had come.

The Sheik had not.

40

All was ready.

The noontime ceremony was to take place on the sunny rooftop of the sultan's seaside palace. Lush white carpets had been spread. Shimmering white silk sheathed the palace's many ledges and parapets. Two matching chairs of silver cushioned with white brocade were placed side by side at the end of a long white silken aisle.

The huge cannons on the sea wall were manned and ready to fire a thundering salute to the Turkish prince and his beautiful foreign princess. Dazzling fireworks displays were to begin the minute darkness descended over the seaside empire.

The Turkish sultan's many slaves and servants were dressed in their finest. The harem women were comely in varied shades of pastel with jeweled veils covering their faces. The palace guards especially were resplendent in smartly tailored uniforms of green and gold, the long flowing ends of their golden turbans wrapped around their chins.

Invited guests dressed grandly in intricately patterned

robes of linen and silk and satin had been arriving hourly since the command for their presence had been issued. None came empty-handed. They bore lavish wedding gifts of precious jewels and priceless paintings and marble statuary and opulent wall hangings.

The obese sultan was dressed for the happy occasion all in white satin with white egret feathers adorning his robe's long, flowing sleeves. The garment was exquisite, but shortly before the ceremony was to begin, the gluttonous sultan, sweeping past one of the heavily laden feast tables, couldn't resist. He grabbed up a whole game hen and dribbled drops of grease down his rounded belly as he greedily devoured the roasted game. His personal servant, Alwan, appeared immediately with a dampened cloth to tidy up his slovenly master.

"Never mind that"—Mustafa waved him away—"soon enough I'll be out of this robe and into my bride." He chuckled loudly, amused by his own crude wit. Picking a sliver of the fowl out of his teeth, he waddled down the long white silk aisle toward the waiting silver chairs.

A clock of alabaster and gold ticked steadily toward her impending doom.

Temple was alone.

The two Nubian eunuchs who had painstakingly prepared her for the wedding had left her locked here in the plush white dressing chamber. She waited now for the heavy bolt to be thrown and the door to be yanked open, signaling the palace guards had come for her.

Seated on a long satin-covered bench, Temple clutched the bouquet of ivory orchids in stiff fingers and gazed sadly at the veiled woman in white she saw reflected in the mirrored walls. She couldn't believe this was actually happening. It could not be true.

But it was.

She, Temple DuPlessis Longworth, was to be the wife of a depraved Turkish sultan. She shuddered at the prospect of what lay in store for her before this long day ended.

Temple sighed and slowly bowed her head.

All hope was gone.

The bolt on the heavy door was loudly thrown. Temple didn't bother to lift her head. She didn't look up as the tall green-and-gold-uniformed guard entered the mirrored chamber and strode purposefully toward her. Her head remained bowed as the bright green of the guard's trousered legs stopped directly in front of her.

A low, commanding voice softly spoke her name.

"Temple."

Temple's head jerked up. She blinked through her covering veil, stared wide-eyed at the tall uniformed guard. His dark face was half covered by the ends of his gold turban. She could see nothing but his eyes.

She would have known those beautiful black eyes anywhere.

"Sharif!" she murmured soundlessly, stunned, wondering if the sight of him was but an illusion to further torture her. "Sharif," she murmured again as the orchid bouquet fell forgotten to the white carpet.

"Yes, sweetheart," he said, pushing the gold turban from his face and falling to his knees before her.

Temple anxiously swept back her veil. "How did you know? How did you find me here?"

"I heard your call, Temple."

"Call?" She gazed at him, disbelieving, her fingers lifting to touch the dear, dark face.

The Sheik put his hand to his heart. "In here."

"Oh, Sharif," she said, tears filling her eyes. "I did call for you, I did. I'm so sorry I—"

"It is I who am sorry. For everything."

"Sharif, you must go! You must leave me. Hurry, before they find you here." She laid a hand on his chest, felt his heart beating steadily beneath her fingertips. "He will kill you, he will—"

"Shhh, *chérie,*" he said, rising to his feet and bringing her up with him. "I am not leaving you. I have come for you. I am taking you out of here."

"That's impossible," she said, shaking her head. "There's no way—"

"You must trust me, Temple," he interrupted. "Will you?"

"Yes, oh yes."

"I got into the palace and I will get us out."

Nodding, believing in him, certain he was capable of anything, she said anxiously, "Sharif, my friends . . . the two women who are to be my wedding attendants . . . they've suffered so . . . ."

He smiled at her. "Samira and Leyla await just outside the door. They will come with us." The Sheik touched her face tenderly then and said, "To get out of the palace alive we must also take the happy groom."

"Take the sultan?"

"Listen to me carefully, Temple. . . ." His voice was low, commanding. "I've only a few short minutes to explain exactly how this is to be done."

Guests and gifts continued to arrive in a steady stream.

A large, heavy golden chest appeared shortly before noon. It was whispered to be a gift from the wealthy bey of Algiers. Curiosity and speculation passed through the crowd when a uniformed palace guard, a big one-eyed giant of a man, carried the heavy chest atop his wide shoulder across the white-carpeted rooftop.

The sultan, more curious than anyone, motioned the guard forward. Mustafa ordered the strong-backed guard to place the heavy golden chest directly beside the matching silver chairs. The gigantic guard obeyed, then stepped back, stood there unobtrusively behind the chest, his hands folded behind his back. Envisioning stacks of shiny gold bars or hundreds of gold coins inside, the white-robed Mustafa leaned over and laid a fat hand on the chest's gold latch.

Just then his bride appeared on the sunny rooftop. A buzz of twittering excitement hummed through the wedding crowd, attracting Mustafa's attention. He looked up and immediately forgot about the golden chest and its contents. His beady eyes gleaming, his loose lips stretched into a wide smile of pleasure, he turned about, sat down heavily on the silver chair, and clasped his hands over his big satin-draped belly.

He watched, entranced, as the beautiful pale-haired woman he was about to wed swept gracefully down the long white aisle behind the two pretty slaves she had insisted attend her at the ceremony.

Mustafa looked past the veiled Leyla and Samira to the tall, exquisite creature garbed in white satin and dripping diamonds. His mouth gaped, and a string of saliva slipped down his chins onto his white satin robes. He felt his small penis stiffen and press against his big, overhanging belly. He could hardly wait to get this beautiful blond goddess into his bedchamber and avail himself of her many charms.

Mustafa wiped his mouth on his egret-feathered sleeve and exhaled with triumph.

The lusty coupling would be made all the sweeter knowing that the fair-skinned foreigner had been stolen from that hated arrogant Arab swine, Sheik Sharif Aziz Hamid.

* * *

Temple's knees trembled as she walked the last few steps toward the Turkish sultan. She glanced at the tall uniformed guard standing directly behind the gold chest. Temple recognized Sarhan, the one-eyed giant she had once hired as her desert guide. The Arab who had delivered her to the Sheik. She'd never dreamed that the day would come when she would be glad to see him.

The procession reached the seated sultan. Leyla and Samira moved around behind the empty silver chair. The sultan struggled to his feet and put out his hand to Temple. She took it, squeezed his fat fingers, smiled flirtatiously at him through the white transparent veil, and puckered her lips in invitation to be kissed.

Instantly beside himself with excitement and forgetting entirely the thronged assembly watching, Mustafa grabbed her satin-clad shoulders to draw her face down to his. A split second before his wet gaping mouth could clamp over hers through the veil, the lid of the gold chest flew open, a green-and-gold-uniformed guard leapt out and laid the sharp blade of a jewel-hilted scimitar to the sultan's fleshy throat.

It happened so fast, the sultan's many guards and soldiers had no time to respond. A few seconds of stunned silence, then screams and gasps went up from the startled crowd and guns were raised and cocked by the palace guards.

But into Mustafa's ear, the Sheik, speaking perfect Turkish, coolly warned, "If you want to live, tell them to put away their weapons."

Terrified, Mustafa shouted for his guards not to shoot, to lay down their weapons. While guests gawked in openmouthed horror, Sharif, with the sharp blade pressed again the Turk's throat and a loaded Mauser in his other hand, dragged the terrified sultan down the white silk aisle. Sarhan, a large-caliber pistol in each hand, put the three women between himself and the Sheik and backed his way down the aisle.

A foolhardy palace guard who hadn't listened to his master's order took a shot at Sharif. The bullet whizzed past Sharif's ear and Mustafa screamed in terror, expecting to feel the slice of the blade on his throat. Sharif instantly fired on the guard, whose gun still smoked, killing him where he stood.

"That was for my mother!" the Sheik shouted to be heard above the nervous din. "The next will be for my father."

"Do not raise your weapons!" screamed the choking, struggling sultan. "Lay your arms down. Now!"

There was nothing the emir's horrified men could do. Dropping their weapons, they stood by helplessly while he was taken off the crowded rooftop, down through the palace, across the gardens, and finally out the sea gates.

There, from where they'd been hiding in the shrubbery, two more of the Sheik's men emerged. One lifted Temple into his arms, the other Samira, and both immediately began descending the rocky cliffs to the water's edge, where a high-powered motor launch was concealed in a camouflaged cay.

"Please," cried the sultan, stumbling on the rocks, "you are out the gates and safe now. Let me go. Release me!"

The Sheik spun him about so he could look him in the face. His eyes as cold as black ice, he said, "No, I will not let you go. I should have killed you years ago."

"Mercy," begged Mustafa. "Please . . . show a little mercy."

"The only mercy I will show is to kill you quickly," said the Sheik. "If I had the time, I would torture you slowly to death and allow all those who have suffered at your hands to watch."

"Money," blubbered the sultan, "I'll give you all my money and my—"

"Shut up! You dare to touch the woman I love . . ." The Sheik's hand tightened on the sultan's slippery white satin robe. "The price for that is death."

His dark face a mask of hatred, Sharif raised the scimitar. Weeping, wetting himself now, Mustafa turned his head away.

"Look at me, you cowardly bastard," ordered the Sheik. "Let my face be the last thing you see this side of eternal damnation."

His teeth bared like an animal's, the Sheik began to lower his arm. A sniper's bullet, fired from one of the silk-draped parapets high above, struck him in the back before he could plunge the blade into the sultan's heart. The scimitar slipped from Sharif's hand as his eyes closed and he crumpled to his knees.

Temple heard the shot, looked up, and saw Sharif falling. She screamed, struggled to free herself from the strong arms holding her, but was carried on down the cliffs by the loyal warrior, who had been given his orders by the Sheik and was determined to carry them out.

Sarhan was halfway down the cliffs when he heard the shot. He stopped in midstride, lowered Leyla to her feet, and, after ordering her to go on down, turned and went back for his fallen leader. Leyla, disobeying, followed Sarhan.

Sarhan reached his wounded master and swung Sharif easily into his massive arms. The nimble Leyla scooped up the jewel-hilted scimitar and went after the fat Turkish ruler. She pounced on Mustafa as he scrambled with surprising agility over the rocks in a desperate attempt to flee.

Shouting for Leyla to get back to the motor launch, Sarhan plunged down the cliffside, carrying the unconscious Sharif. Deaf to Sarhan's command, Leyla gripped the sobbing sultan by his robe front, threw him roughly to the ground, and straddled him.

Weeping, Mustafa began to plead for his life and to make wild promises. His kingdom would be hers if she spared him! It was her he wanted, only her. He loved her, worshiped her. Let him live and she would be immediately elevated to the exalted position of adored sultana, envied by all.

"Cowardly sniveling dog," Leyla said contemptuously, and up went the scimitar.

The point pricked the side of his fleshy throat and she gave the blade a strong, decisive jerk, severing the jugular. Hot blood spewed forth, and Mustafa's beady eyes widened with fear and pain.

"I hope you feel this, you evil bastard!"

And she whipped the blade sideways, slitting his fat throat from ear to ear. Then she spat in his dying face, shot to her feet, and fled down the rocky cliffs.

41

The deep silence of the desert was even more silent than usual.

Deathly silent.

The bedside lamp burned low in the darkness of the black desert night. The still, quiet bedroom and the still, quiet man in the room's bed were cast into deep shadow.

A circle of mellow light spilling from the single lamp lighted the blond head of the still, silent woman seated beside the bed. It softly illuminated, as well, a pair of pale slender hands enclosing a lean, bronzed hand.

And it revealed that the Starfire ruby on the third finger of that dark masculine hand had lost its brilliant red color.

The stone was black.

Dead black.

Temple had been at the Sheik's bedside for the past twenty-four hours. She had been there when the French surgeon had removed the bullet from the unconscious Sheik. She had been there when the Sheik had tossed and turned in feverish delirium. She had used her body to press him back to the mattress when he'd thrashed wildly about, incoherent and in pain.

She had bathed his clammy face with cool water, murmured to him as one would to a child, and promised—even though he could not hear her—that she would not leave him.

She would *never* leave him.

Temple had been there with tears streaming down her cheeks when the unconscious Sheik, agitated, unable to lie still, had mumbled and murmured in Arabic. *"Naksedil, Naksedil,"* he'd whispered frantically, over and over. Temple knew he was talking to her, but she didn't know what he was saying.

The Sheik's faithful servant, Tariz, had been there, too. The worried Tariz had stayed at his master's bedside continuously, just as Temple had.

He was there now, as still and silent as the desert night. Seated in the shadows on the far side of the bed, Tariz watched quietly over the deathly pallid Sheik.

And over the sad young woman who loved him.

Tariz knew how much Temple was suffering. Time after time through their long, shared vigil, she had wept brokenheartedly and told the lifeless Sheik she was sorry, so sorry. When she was not apologizing to the unresponsive Sheik, she was apologizing to Tariz.

She had, she admitted, been unforgivably thoughtless and foolish when she'd struck him on the head that fateful morning and fled alone into the deserts. She regretted the rash, unpardonable act more than she could say, and she only wished there was some way she could make it up to them both, to him and the Sheik.

Tariz watched her now, and his tender heart went out to her.

Distraught, feeling as if it were her fault the Sheik lay near death, Temple clung to his limp brown hand and silently begged him to open his beautiful eyes and look at her. To wake up. To speak to her.

To live.

She lowered her face, kissed his fingertips one by one, then laid her tear-streaked cheek against his muscular forearm. She closed her burning eyes, recalling unhappily how—once they were away from the sultan's seaside palace—she had begged the Sheik's men to keep going up the coast until they reached a city where Sharif could be treated at a hospital.

But they had refused.

A few miles up the sea they had turned the motor launch back into land. On shore a dozen of the Sheik's men had been waiting with fresh, speedy horses. Four had volunteered to take young Samira back to her parents and Leyla to the destination of her choice.

The rest of the party, including Temple and the wounded Sharif, had ridden straight up into the hills and back across the desert. Temple had argued that they were endangering the Sheik's life. He wouldn't live unless he was tended immediately—for God's sake, take him to a doctor!

But they would not listen.

Their leader had given them orders from which they were not to deviate. They were to ride home. All the way home. They were not to stop until they were back at his desert oasis.

No matter who was wounded or killed.

Temple sighed softly now, rubbed her hot cheek against Sharif's cool arm, and raised her head wearily. She looked again at the face of the enigmatic man she loved so much. Sadly she mused that this revered leader of men had trained his loyal warriors too well. They respected his judgment too much. They obeyed his commands without question. They did exactly what their chieftain ordered them to do.

That unquestioning obedience might cost the Sheik his life.

Temple shook her head sorrowfully. She studied the dark, beloved face and wondered how she could go on living if he died.

The thought was overwhelming, unbearable.

"I love him, Tariz," she said miserably, continuing to look only at Sharif, "and I have killed him."

"No, Temple," Tariz said in a low, soothing voice. "The Sheik will live. Sharif is very strong. He is not so easily killed."

She smiled wistfully. "Perhaps you are right. You desert Arabs are physically superior to us."

Tariz, too, smiled, and said, "Sharif is not an Arab."

Temple looked up, stunned. She blinked at Tariz in the shadowy light. "Not an Arab?"

Tariz sighed and shook his turbaned head. He rose, came around the foot of the big ebony bed, and smiled kindly at Temple. "Perhaps it is time you learn more about Sheik Sharif Aziz Hamid."

"Yes . . . please . . . tell me." She was staring at him, stunned, curious. "Tell me everything."

Nodding, the leathery-faced little servant drew up a straight-backed chair and sat beside Temple. Without preamble he began to speak, to tell the secrets of the past, and Temple learned of the Sheik's true heritage.

Tariz told her of that day so long ago when he and the old sheik had come upon the horrible scene in the northern desert. Temple's mouth dropped open in shock and then compassion as he spoke unsentimentally of the pain and degradation Sharif's mother had suffered at the hands of the bloodthirsty Turks.

Into Temple's mind flashed the vision of Sharif shouting, "That was for my mother!" when he had shot and killed one of Mustafa's palace guards.

"Sharif was born Christian Telford," said Tariz. "His biological parents were Sir Albert Telford, a titled nobleman, and his wife, Maureen. Lord and Lady DunRaven. Christian was their only son."

Wide-eyed, Temple looked from Tariz to Sharif and back again. "But he's so dark and . . . "

Tariz nodded. "His mother was a beautiful black Irish lass. The blood of the Moors flowed through her veins. Sharif took his coloring from her."

Tariz talked and talked, telling Temple how the old sheik had raised Sharif as if he were his own son. Explaining why Sharif had been sent to England for his education. It was his mother's dying wish.

"Does Sharif know?"

"Yes. He was told when he was five years old. The old sheik explained everything to him. And he told Sharif— when Sharif went away to the university—that if he did not wish to return to the desert and the Arab way of life, we would understand."

"But Sharif came back," Temple said softly. "He prefers this way of life to—"

Proudly, "Yes. He was born an Englishman, but his heart is that of an Arab."

The two continued to talk in low voices as the long dark night passed. Temple, full of questions, interested in anything having to do with the Sheik, listened and nodded and attempted to digest all she was learning of the man she loved.

Finally she said, "Why, Tariz? Why did Sharif find it necessary to abduct me? To bring me here?"

"You saw the intercepted message that was meant for your uncle, did you not?"

"Yes, Mustafa had it. But I still don't understand why Sharif—"

"He never meant to harm you." Tariz's narrow shoulders slumped minutely when he added, almost apologetically, "For more years than either you or Sharif have lived, DuPlessis Munitions has been supplying arms to the hated Turks."

"And yet Sharif . . ." Temple's words trailed away.

"Yes. He risked his life saving you."

"Oh, Sharif," she murmured, gazing lovingly at the dark man in the bed.

"Sharif tried," Tariz continued, "as did the old sheik before him, to reason with your family, to make them understand that death and destruction were being rained on the Arabs by the DuPlessis-armed Turks. Sharif doggedly endeavored—using every avenue available—to persuade the munitions company to stop providing the Turks with weapons and ammunition. They would not listen."

The servant rose abruptly from his chair, circled the bed, and went directly to the tall ebony chest. He picked up the spent shell casing that he had taken from the pocket of Sharif's bloodstained clothes. He came back and held out the brass casing to Temple.

"Take it," he said, "and look at the bottom."

Temple took the shell casing from Tariz's palm, turned it up, and looked at its end. She drew in a sharp breath when she saw the distinctive manufacturer's stamp.

Du-P

"That casing was in Sharif's hand the day we found him in the desert thirty-four years ago," said Tariz. "Agha Hussain's men killed Sharif's parents with bullets supplied by DuPlessis Munitions."

Shaking her head, picturing the nine-month-old Sharif with the shell casing gripped in his tiny fist as he sat beside his dying mother, Temple said almost inaudibly, "Oh, God, no."

As if she hadn't spoken, Tariz said, "The Ottoman Turks are vicious murderers who have killed many of our people. Their weapons are far superior to ours in number and precision. Every skirmish is a bloodbath, every battle a scourge."

Temple said nothing, merely stared at the damning shell casing in her hand.

"It is said that your uncle James DuPlessis is childless and that he dotes on you as if you were his own daughter. Is this not true?"

"Yes. Yes, it is."

"That is why Sharif abducted you. He sent the cable knowing that your uncle would do anything to insure your release. Even stop shipping arms to the Turks." Tariz exhaled wearily. "As we both know, the cable never reached DuPlessis."

"No," Temple said softly. "Mustafa's men intercepted the message. That's how the Turkish sultan came to know about me. How he learned that the Sheik was holding me."

"Yes," Tariz said simply. He waited then for Temple to say something more. She said nothing, just closed her eyes, overwhelmed by all she had learned.

Finally Tariz rose, patted her slender shoulder, and said, "I will be just outside the tent if you need me."

Temple opened her eyes and nodded. Tariz turned to go.

"Wait, Tariz," Temple said abruptly.

He stopped. "Can I get you something?"

She shook her head. "Exactly what does *Naksedil* mean?"

Tariz smiled at her. "'My beautiful one.'"

For a long time after Tariz had gone, Temple sat there cupping the spent shell casing in her palm.

Sharif moaned in his sleep, and she immediately forgot

about everything but him. She rose anxiously from her chair and laid the shell casing on the night table beneath the lamp. She sat down carefully on the bed, facing Sharif. She took his hand in hers again, leaned down, brushed kisses to his handsome face, and whispered to him that she didn't care what he had done, she loved him. Would always love him. Could he love her? Just a little?

Temple stayed there with the wounded Sheik through the long, silent night. Touching him. Kissing him. Murmuring words of love.

Near dawn, Sharif's dark lashes began to flutter on his high olive cheekbones. He was struggling to cast off the chains of unconsciousness. Finally, after several failed attempts, his eyes opened to see a tired, tearful Temple hovering above him.

"Oh, my love," she said with relief, "you're awake at last. Thank God."

"What did you call me?" he asked in a whisper.

She smiled, brushed a lock of limp black hair off his damp forehead. "My love. You are my love, Sharif, whether you want to be or not. I love you and I will go on loving you forever."

Surprisingly, a faint mist of tears filled the dark, beautiful eyes of the supine man and he said, "No, Temple. You cannot love me. I will not let you love me."

"I am not asking your permission. I am telling you that I love you."

"Have you forgotten? I abducted you."

"I've forgotten nothing. It doesn't matter."

"I've been cruel and heartless to you."

"So cruel and heartless that you risked your life to save me."

"Our cultures are—"

"Cultures?" Temple said, shaking her head, incredulous.

"You are American. I am an Arab."

"No, you are not. You are British, my darling Sharif. An English lord, nonetheless."

He frowned. "Yes, but I live as an Arab."

She smiled. "I'll get the doctor." She leaned down, pressed a kiss to his lips, and said, "Rest, my dear, and when you are better, I will persuade you to let me love you."

42

The Sheik stood beneath the tent's shade canopy with one foot raised on a hassock and his arms folded over his bent knee. His dark face was set in rigid lines, his eyes fixed on some far distant point on the northern horizon.

The hour had come.

She was to leave today.

This morning.

Sharif lowered his booted foot to the carpet, moved to the edge of the canopy, gripped a supporting pole, and swallowed hard. The dull ache in his upper back where a bullet had ripped through muscle and bone was nothing compared to the sharp steady ache in his heart.

A week had passed since his French physician had extracted the bullet from his back. Too bad, Sharif mused wistfully, Temple couldn't be so easily removed from his heart. Already the bullet wound was healing and he had regained much of his former strength.

But the injury to his heart would never heal.

Sharif drew a long, painful breath and took one of his Cartier cigarettes from the pocket of his white linen shirt. He lighted the aromatic cigarette, blew out the smoke, and told himself—for the thousandth time—that he was doing the right thing. He could not think of himself. It was Temple's welfare with which he must be concerned. It was her happiness that was important.

Last night he had attempted to make her understand that this was best. That she belonged in America with her family and friends. That there could be no future for the two of them. She was American and he was—no matter whose blood flowed in his veins—an Arab.

He was sending her away.

Sharif had agonized over the decision since he had regained consciousness and opened his eyes to see her beautiful face above his own. From that unforgettable moment there followed six sweet, golden days with him confined to the bed and her spending every moment at his side. Those days—and nights—had been the happiest of his entire life.

And the most torturous.

Always decisive, he had found himself hesitant, tentative, vacillating from one hour to the next. Just when he had made up his mind that he had to let her go, she would look up from the book she was reading to him, smile endearingly . . . and his resolve would weaken.

The woman was hard to resist.

In those precious tranquil days she had constantly amazed him, revealing sides to her many-faceted personality he had never seen before.

On those occasions when he could not totally conceal his suffering, she was the kind, compassionate nurse, bathing his feverish face and changing his soiled bandages and soothing him with soft words of comfort and caring.

When the pain temporarily passed and peace took its place and he felt blessed slumber overcoming him, she would look at him with undisguised love shining from her beautiful emerald eyes and say, "I'll be right here when you wake. I will never leave you."

There were those enjoyable, fun-filled times when the throbbing pain had subsided and he was feeling better and she would entertain him eagerly. Articulate and witty, she was full of amusing stories to share with him. She was a great mimic; she could do Tariz and Chauncey—and him—to a T. Enchanted, he egged her on and applauded and laughed until the tears rolled down his cheeks.

And then, as he quickly began to mend, there were those tender, tormenting moments when she would kick off her slippers, climb onto the bed, stretch out beside him, and press kisses to his face, his throat, his chest, whispering kittenishly of all the forbidden things she was going to do to him when he was fully fit again.

Finally, last night, on his first evening out of bed, he had told her.

"I'm sending you back, Temple," he'd said quietly. "Tomorrow."

She'd looked at him as if he had struck her but had said nothing.

He'd cleared his throat needlessly and continued, "A dozen of my men will escort you safely to the coast, where you will sail immediately to France. From France you will return to England for the voyage home to America." He'd tried to smile, found it impossible. A long, strained silence had passed between them. Then he'd said gently, "Temple, it wouldn't work for us. This desert is my home."

Her huge emerald eyes shining with tears, she'd said, "It could be my home as well."

Sharif had shaken his dark head. "There is," he'd said, "an old Arab saying: 'Trees transplanted seldom prosper.'"

Now, as he stood here in the rising sun staring out at the desert, Sharif felt all the breath leave his body.

Though not a sound had been made, he knew Temple had exited the tent, was standing close by. He was acutely conscious of her nearness. He could feel her presence as if she had lain a soft hand on his shoulder. He flicked away his cigarette and turned slowly.

Temple, dressed much the same as the day he had first brought her here, was not looking at him. Rhikia had followed her out of the tent, and Temple had turned to say good-bye to the stoic woman who rarely showed any emotion.

To Sharif's surprise, Rhikia's dark eyes were swimming in tears and her arms went around Temple's slender waist to hug her tightly.

"Good-bye, Rhikia," Temple said softly. "Thank you for taking such good care of me." Affectionately she squeezed the Arab woman's shoulders and said, "I know you can't understand my words, but I hope the tone conveys my meaning." She pulled back and smiled at the teary-eyed Rhikia.

Embarrassed by her inability to hide her feelings, Rhikia released Temple and hurried back inside the tent.

Then it was Tariz's turn to say good-bye. The wiry little man who was always grinning was grim faced this morning. He approached the white tent with his turbaned head bowed, his eyes far from merry.

Temple smiled warmly when she spotted him and stepped forward with her hand outstretched. He took it, then impulsively swept her into his arms and hugged her so tightly that her ribs hurt. Temple pressed her cheek to his and said, "I will miss you terribly, Tariz."

He replied, "My heart is like Arabia's dead southern waste." Choking then, he quickly released her, and Temple saw the bright tears before he could turn away.

She patted his shoulder and watched as he hurried away, wiping his eyes with the end of his turban.

She glanced at the mounted men amassing at the palm-fringed lagoon fifty yards below the tent. She saw a groom lead the saddled stallion Toz into view.

Temple squared her slender shoulders, drew a shallow breath, and crossed the carpeted shade canopy. She moved to the solemn Sheik, looked up at him as tears filled her emerald eyes, and said, "DuPlessis arms and ammunition will stop flowing to the Turks. This I promise you." She lowered her eyes. "I promise as well that you are going to miss me until your last day on earth."

She started to step away.

"Wait—" The Sheik spoke at last, reaching out to take her arm.

"No," Temple said, slipping free of his grasp. "Don't touch me." Keeping her eyes lowered, she said, "Don't look at me." She drew a shallow breath. "Don't watch me walk away."

Her parting words caused a painful wrench in his already aching heart. Sharif jammed his thumbs into his belt and watched, unblinking, as the beautiful golden-haired girl of his dreams walked away from him forever.

A deep, brooding sadness swamping him, he bit the inside of his jaw with sharp, punishing teeth. But he did not cry.

The Sheik never cried, was unfailingly cautious about revealing weakness or tenderness or sorrow. He had been well trained by the old sheik.

Temple held her head high and her back straight as she walked down the gentle incline to her waiting horse.

She knew he was watching her. She could feel his

eyes—those beautiful brooding night black eyes—following her every step of the way.

It was the longest walk of her life.

At last Temple reached the saddled Toz. The big saffron-colored stallion danced in place and whinnied his welcome. Shaking her head no to the offer of help from the groom, Temple took the reins from his hand and swiftly swung up into the saddle.

She immediately wheeled the big beast about and laid her boot heels to his shimmering flanks. Toz cantered away. Sharif's handpicked escort followed her.

The Sheik stayed where he was.

As he was.

He stood there beneath the shade canopy with his thumbs in his belt and watched her ride away. He watched as the others caught up with her. He watched as they put their mounts into comfortable loping gaits. He watched until the contingent was no more than small black dots on the horizon.

Than all at once he couldn't stand it.

His chest felt as if it might explode. A loud wail issued from his lips and he shouted for his stallion to be brought around. The smiling Tariz was beside him in a minute, leading the saddled black stallion Prince.

"Hurry," Tariz said, grinning broadly. "You must hurry!"

Then the little servant stood in the bright sun, clapping his hands happily as his master leapt astride the big prancing beast and raced across the burning sands.

His mount superior, his purpose momentous, the hard-riding Sheik overtook the detachment within minutes. Temple, hearing the approach of thundering hoofbeats, glanced over her shoulder, saw Sharif bearing down on them, and began to laugh with sheer delight.

She took off her cork sun helmet, tossed it to the ground, and shook out her long blond hair. Then she kicked Toz into a faster gait, shooting away from her mounted escort, ready to enjoy the chase that she knew the Sheik would win.

Galloping at breakneck speed, the determined Sheik quickly caught up with his mounted men. When he ranged alongside them, he lifted his right hand in the air. The ruby on his finger blazing blood red in the morning sunlight, he signaled them to stop and turn back.

Cheering the chieftain of whom they were so fond, the mounted men laughed and whistled and obediently turned back for camp.

The Sheik raced on with a wide grin on his face.

Her blond hair flying wildly about her head, a smile as big as Arabia on her glowing face, Temple urged the responsive Toz to go faster, faster, to outdistance the big black now in hot pursuit.

The chase continued for more than a mile. The valiant Toz gave it all he had. But he was no match for the big powerful demon black Prince.

Thank heaven!

Temple glanced over as Prince drew alongside the winded Toz. For a few yards more the stallions raced together stride for stride. Then the Sheik wrapped the reins around the saddle horn and controlled the speeding stallion with the pressure of his knees.

His strong brown hands reached for Temple. She eagerly threw her arms around Sharif's neck as he pulled her from Toz's back and sat her across the saddle before him.

Laughing and weeping simultaneously, Temple pressed kisses to Sharif's handsome brown face and teased, "What kept you, my lord?"

"Don't call me that, Temple," he said, drawing her close. "In my heart I am Sharif Aziz Hamid, the Arab."

"Well, kiss me, then, my desert Sheik, and tell me you'll make me your first and only wife."

"I will," he said, turning Prince back toward the oasis. "But you may be a widow when your family learns of the marriage."

43

The Emerald City Palace above the Blue Mediterranean

A Balmy Late Autumn Afternoon in 1898

A ruby was caught in the sun's golden light.

Tiny spangles inside the red stone reflected the six-rayed glow that gave the gem its name.

Starfire.

This Starfire had come from the fabled mines of Mogok, Burma, home of the world's finest rubies. The ruby was one of those prized gemstones so intensely red in color, it merited the descriptive term "pigeon blood."

Magical properties were attributed to the ruby, a coveted stone which was believed to bring peace and well-being to its wearer.

It was said that the ruby held magical powers and talismanic significance to its wearer. Legend had it that the rare pigeon blood ruby could warn its owner of imminent peril by turning dark or black.

And not returning to its normal color until the danger had passed.

The ruby captured in the glow of the warm Mediterranean sun was a bright brilliant red.

All rubies were valuable. But the rubies of the dark pigeon blood hue were among the rarest of all the world's finest gemstones. Especially those which were in excess of three carats. This Starfire ruby was in excess of six carats.

And it was but one of a rope of the brilliant Burma rubies.

The wearer of the magnificent rope of Burma rubies sat upon a huge white bed scattered with blood red rose petals. She was seated squarely at the bed's center, her back resting against the tall, bolstered headboard, which was stacked high with downy, satin-cased pillows.

The smiling woman didn't shift or fidget or twist about. She didn't so much as turn her head to the left or the right. She sat entirely motionless in the bed yet managed to look completely comfortable and relaxed.

A woman of incredible pale blond beauty, she was graceful, sophisticated, and totally sure of herself. Possessed of a body that was as splendid as her face, the tall, slender woman had smooth, porcelain skin and lustrous golden hair.

Her attire was the rope of rubies—a wedding present from her adoring bridegroom—encircling her throat.

Save for the rubies, she was gloriously naked.

So was the tall, dark man coming toward her.

Sharif had cast off the black silk robe he'd donned hastily a moment ago when the intrusive knock had come on the bedroom door.

The Starfire ruby on his finger flashing brightly in the shafts of late afternoon sunlight, the naked Sheik returned to the bed and to his bride.

Sharif handed the telegram to Temple, put a bare

brown knee on the satin-sheeted mattress, and got into bed with her while she eagerly ripped open the yellow envelope. He laid a bronzed hand on the arch of her hip and listened as she read the message aloud, her emerald eyes shining with happiness.

Her mother and father sent best wishes for the couple's happiness. Her uncle vowed that no more arms would be shipped to the Turks. Both uncle and parents requested an audience with the newlyweds either in America or Arabia, whichever suited.

"Darling, could we just go for one short visit?" Temple asked, lowering the telegram.

She looked hopefully into her husband's night black eyes as a strong autumn breeze swept in suddenly off the wide marble terrace overlooking the Mediterranean, charging the salt air with the fragrance of frangipani from an unseen garden, rustling the gauzy curtains of the enormous bedroom, and gently stroking bare, tingling flesh.

Sharif took the telegram from Temple and laid it aside. He put his arms around her, drew her close against him, and said, "I could never leave the desert for good, sweetheart, you know that." Temple laid a hand on his chest and nodded. He continued, "But to please you, I will agree to spending half our time in London and America."

Temple allowed her caressing hand to slide slowly down Sharif's chest to his drum-tight belly. She tilted her head back, looked into his burning black eyes, smiled, and said, "I'm not sure I'd be completely happy in America again." She gave his tanned jaw a quick kiss. "You've spoiled me, Arab."

The Sheik liked her answer.

He smiled with pleasure.

Then his strong arms tightened around her, he lowered his lips to hers, and murmured, "*Naksedil*—my beautiful one—I have not yet begun to spoil you."

The Sheik kissed his bride, gently pressed her onto her back amid the strewn rose petals, and agilely moved atop her.

And began to spoil her properly.

Let HarperMonogram Sweep You Away

BURNING LOVE by Nan Ryan
Winner of the *Romantic Times* Lifetime Achievement Award
While traveling across the Arabian desert, American socialite Temple Longworth is captured by a handsome sheik. Imprisoned in *El Siif*'s lush oasis, Temple struggles not to lose her heart to a man whose touch promises ecstasy.

A LITTLE PEACE AND QUIET by Modean Moon
Bestselling Author
A handsome stranger is drawn to a Victorian house—and the attractive woman who is restoring it. When an evil presence is unleashed, David and Anne risk falling under its spell unless they can join together to create a powerful love.

ALMOST A LADY by Barbara Ankrum
Lawman Luke Turner is caught in the middle of a Colorado snowstorm, handcuffed to beautiful pickpocket Maddy Barnes. While stranded in a hostile town, the unlikely couple discovers more trouble than they ever bargained for—and heavenly pleasures neither can deny.

DANCING MOON by Barbara Samuel
Fleeing from her cruel husband, Tess Fallon finds herself on the Santa Fe trail and at the mercy of Joaquin Morales. He brands her with his kiss, but they must conquer the threats of the past before embracing the paradise found in each other's arms.

And in case you missed last month's selections...

MIRANDA by Susan Wiggs
Over One Million Copies of Her Books in Print
In Regency London, Miranda Stonecypher is stricken with amnesia and doesn't believe that handsome Ian MacVane is her betrothed—especially after another suitor appears. Miranda's search for the truth leads to passion beyond her wildest dreams.

WISH LIST by Jeane Renick
RITA Award–Winning Author

Only $3.99

While on assignment in Nepal, writer Charlayne Pearce meets elusive and irresistibly sensual Jordan Kosterin. Jordan's bold gaze is an invitation to pleasure, but memories of his dead wife threaten their newfound love.

SILVER SPRINGS by Carolyn Lampman

Only $3.99

Independent Angel Brady feels she is capable of anything—even passing as her soon-to-be-married twin sister so that Alexis can run off with her lover. Unfortunately, the fiancé turns out to be the one man in the Wyoming Territory who can send Angel's pulse racing.

CALLIE'S HONOR by Kathleen Webb

Only $3.99

Callie Lambert is unprepared for the handsome stranger who shows up at her Oregon ranch determined to upset her well-ordered life. But her wariness is no match for Rafe Millar's determination to discover her secrets, and win her heart.

Harper Monogram